THE MYSTERIOUS BAD BOY

K.M. SCOTT

THE MYSTERIOUS BAD BOY

Liam Jackson personifies the old saying, "Still waters run deep." He keeps to himself, and he'd probably be a hermit living in a cave in the woods if it weren't for his large family.

As the son of Kane Jackson, he's a lot like his father.

Mia Shanoff lives in the spotlight. The newest star in the music business, she's so big the mere mention of her makes the media go wild. Her story is one everyone wants to know more about.

But you know what they say. Don't believe everything you hear.

Liam and Mia can't help but be explosive when they get together, but no matter what happens, he never forgets his job is to keep her safe. Every day, that gets harder and harder, but now that Liam loves Mia, nothing will get in his way of being the protector she needs.

Unfortunately, there are those behind the scenes who have different plans for the new couple, friends and enemies with their own agendas.

They're about to find out that once a man like Liam Jackson falls for a woman, he'll move heaven and earth to keep her safe.

2023 Copper Key Media LLC

Published in the United States

ISBN: 978-1-955335-40-9

The two full-length books included in this one-volume book are Flirtatious and Mysterious (NeXt #5 and #6).

CHAPTER ONE

M ia

HOW MANY TALKING HEADS ARE GOING TO GET IN ON giving their opinion about my life? Their unneeded and unsolicited opinion, as far as I'm concerned.

You'd think these people would have better things to do than dissect every misstep and bad relationship I've had in the past few years. I mean, there is an entire world out there revolving around all sorts of things like war and famine and a million other terrible realities, yet these clowns yammer on and on about Mia this and Mia that.

I stretch my legs out across the king size hotel bed with the divine blue comforter and sheets to die for and feel the tension dissipate as I mute the TV. These sheets are heavenly. White cotton like any other I've slept in, but oh my God are they comfortable. I'm guessing they have to be at least twelve hundred thread count. I need to find out who makes them so I can get a set for my own bed back at the house.

The house. Ugh. Where everyone, no doubt, is rushing to and fro while pulling their hair out by the roots as they fret needlessly about where I might be. For a moment, I close my eyes and picture everyone looking in horror at their hands full of hair. Just something else to stress out about. It would be amusing if it wasn't so ridiculous.

I can hear all their worrying from here. The queen of worry, my mother, is the worst. "She could be dead in a ditch on the side of the road," she wails like some fool, all the while wringing her hands.

I've never even seen a ditch, much less been in one, dead or alive.

"Maybe someone kidnapped her?" Chloe and Ivy suggest in unison like they often do when they're excited about something.

Why my makeup artists are always so melodramatic is beyond me. Nobody kidnapped me. They know that and still I'm betting they've already said those exact words, which of course, made everyone else freak out even more.

I take a deep breath and let it out slowly, allowing my shoulders to come back down from around my ears. Maybe they wouldn't be totally off the mark with their concern. I've had more than one stalker since I got big, but none of those guys were ever the kidnapper type. They're more the kind of people who yearn from afar, but if they ever did get close enough to touch me, they'd probably piss their pants.

My life coach Ainsley is probably attempting, with little luck, to calm everyone down with her Zen sayings none of them will listen to. I like when she does her quiet pep talks, but then again, I'm willing to pay attention and consider the ideas she's presenting.

My mother and my entourage aren't fans of the Zen stuff, though. They prefer to swirl around in madness and chaos, which is the reason I had to hire Ainsley as my life coach in the first place.

I glance over at the TV sitting in the dark cherry wood cabinet across the hotel room and see some gray-haired news guy still talking about my sudden disappearance, but now they have an image of my ex Jonny positioned next to the old guy's head. What on earth could they be saying about my ex-boyfriend?

Unmuting the TV, I heard gray hair explain who Jonny is. Only an old dude like you wouldn't know he's the lead singer of the band Punk Slut, man. Jesus. Get with the times already. If you don't know what the hell you're discussing, maybe you should stick to segments on shitty politics or the climate crisis you don't really give a shit about and leave the current stuff to cooler people.

"I'm here with Doctor Elizabeth Walters, a psychologist on staff at New York's Mercy Hospital whose research on the interpersonal and sexual dynamics of the stars focuses on exactly the kind of issues Mia's had with her romantic relationships," old news guy says in his oh-so-solemn tone.

Holy shit! Are they really going to dive into my relationship with Jonny because I've been out of the public's sight for forty-eight hours? Here's a hint, Doc. We're going to need more time than they've given you to hash out that mess. Jonny and I were a toxic trainwreck from our first kiss.

Do they really think I went back to him? Don't they

pay attention to the gossip that says he's with that chick who's the lead singer for Banshee? Guess which couple is fighting tonight, for sure.

"Doctor Walters, if a young woman like Mia were to go missing, as she has, what is the likelihood she'd fall back into old, destructive patterns and return to an ex-boyfriend, even one as notoriously abusive as Jonny Chambers was with Mia?"

Fuck, there's a lot to unpack there. I don't think the pretty lady with the perfectly coiffed brunette bob is going to be able to tackle all of that. She was hoping to use this time to pimp her new self-help book she just knows is exactly what women need in this crazy world.

As I suspected before she began talking, Doctor Walters struggles to say anything definitive. Probably because she's never spoken a single goddamned word to me nor I her. Nice of them to try to diagnose me from miles away.

Not satisfied to assume the worst about me back with my shitty ex-boyfriend, old news guy introduces his second guest, another renowned shrink from some big city hospital I don't catch before he asks him, "Doctor Chesterbrook, as a psychologist trained to see destructive patterns in patients when it comes to addiction, what can you tell me about all you know concerning Mia?"

Curious how they plan to connect my recent stint in rehab with wanting to disappear from the limelight for two damn days, I sit up and listen to the African American doctor with the giant glasses.

"Well, Mason, I have never been one of Mia's doctors, but I'm seeing patterns I don't like with this young woman's life. I just hope her friends and family are seeing them too and doing all they can to get her the help she needs."

Damn, Chesterbrook, the doctor with the name that sounds like every rehab I've ever heard of. You were going so well there when you actually admitted you've never been within three feet of me, so you don't know a damn thing about me, but then you fell back into what I suspect is your usual spiel about patterns and my needing help.

Two fucking days is all I wanted. Two days without anyone talking to me or telling me what I should do or what I shouldn't do. Two damn days of peace and quiet in a great hotel room with junk food nobody ever thinks I should eat and a bathtub where I can soak in a bubble bath until my fingertips and toes get all pruney.

Is that so much to ask?

As I glance across the room at the third doctor Mason Cooperman has added to his collection of quacks all eager to talk about my problems, I know the answer is yes. Forty-eight hours, the last two of which I've spent watching these fools, and the entire world acts like it's been set on fire.

Trust me, people. You'd want a couple days alone too if you were me.

I gather up all the wonderful hotel pillows and make a wall next to the headboard as I laugh at all their guesses about me, what I'm doing, and what could be wrong to make me run away like they suspect I have. The lady doctor with the perfect brown hair is absolutely sure I'm off somewhere having a horrible time with my ex but thinking I'm in love. Chesterbrook with the googly glasses is terribly concerned I've fallen off the wagon and I'm drinking again and possibly back to using coke, which troubles him even more.

Dude, you have no idea. Honestly, you are so off base I can't even find you on the map.

And the third doctor, whose name I don't know because I'm no longer interested in giving them names, thinks that his book, Why Good Women Love Bad Boys, contains the answer to all my problems. I can't focus much on what he's saying because his forehead is so big, it's distracting. Damn, man, we could show movies on that space.

Wow. If I didn't laugh right now, I'd cry at how clueless these assholes are.

My tour that lasted eight months took me to five of the seven continents and hundreds of cities around the world. I've broken up with one guy, sworn off men entirely, and tragically, I'm rumored to have turned to booze and drugs. The reason why they don't give a damn about, but my being lonely after performances that left me feeling like a wrung-out dishrag might be a good place for everyone to start. I'm tired and my body aches after all those shows, and I'm only nineteen years old, but damnit, these jackasses and everyone else in the world is absolutely sure I'm off doing something destructive.

No mention about how hard I push myself to give audiences the best show they could ever experience. No hint about what it's like to be a homeless singer, living out of suitcases and missing your bed night after night. Not a peep about what it's like to feel like you're living in a fishbowl and every damn supposed journalist has their nose pressed to the glass, dying to catch me doing something that will get them a big scoop. Not a word about the fact that I'm still getting my bearings in life and it's not the end of the world if I make a mistake or two.

Or ten.

No, that would be boring. Instead, they diagnose from afar and make claims they can't possibly back up because they don't know me. They know the public face I put on, but they don't know me. They see Mia, the superstar, not Mia the person.

For four years, I've tried to be everything the world wants me to be. Can't I take forty-eight hours to be just who I want to be for once?

Mason with the gray hair interrupts the female doctor to say my mother is about to come out to hold a press conference. Good to know she isn't letting a chance go by to make this an even bigger circus. I'd hate to think she could just sit tight for a couple days and let me be alone.

I watch as Andrea Shanoff stands in front of the bank of microphones looking entirely too upset for the circumstances. My mother's a beautiful woman with long dark hair that lays perfectly against her head like Cher's did when she was young back in the day. I wish my hair would do that, but with every time my stylists insist on doing something interesting with my look for the crowds who come to see me, the chance that my hair will ever simply hang normally again becomes less and less likely.

Today, she's gone for a light brown jacket over a tan blouse, a look meant to convey her utter despair over my being missing. It's all very earthy and grounded, making me think she took some cues from Ainsley when she was getting ready for this performance of hers. She's gone with less makeup than she usually prefers too. No fake lashes or heavy eyeliner to accent her dark brown eyes. She wants to let the world know that this whole thing has been so trying for her.

"Thank you for all your concern about Mia. I'm here today to make another plea for whoever has her to let her come home. My daughter is a beautiful person, inside and out. She loves to share her God-given gift of her beautiful voice, and I only ask that you release her so all of us can hear her sing again."

I hear the words come out with the right emotion attached to each syllable, but the whole thing sounds hollow to my ears. All I see is panic that her control over me is slipping away. She looked much like this right after I turned eighteen and went off with Jonny to his place in Miami. That press conference was one for the ages. She should have won an Oscar for all that crying and wringing of her hands that her baby was dead in a ditch somewhere.

It's always a ditch with the drama queens.

She likes to fall back on the tried-and-true ideas. I imagine she'll mention that at some point in this press conference too, but I turn off the TV before she gets the opportunity. Something about her fascination with me in a ditch on the side of the road unnerves me.

I'm my mother's meal ticket. Sure, she loves me, but what she loves more is the lifestyle she has because of my fame and success. At fifteen, I had my first number one song. That was followed by two more before the record company and my manager, my mother, decided that I needed to get my ass out on tour since that's where the big money is.

So tour I did.

I celebrated my sixteenth birthday alone in the back of my tour bus right outside of Tucson. Everyone else had fallen asleep after congratulating me on that night's show, and I sat with a cupcake that Michael, one of my bodyguards, had left me. Carrot cake with cream cheese frosting, my favorite. My version of a sweet sixteen party.

It's thanks to him that I have this hotel room to lounge around in for a couple days. Thank God there's someone I can rely on to understand I need to decompress sometimes.

My seventeenth birthday I celebrated on stage in Rio de Janeiro with thousands of my closest friends waving banners with my name on them while I sang my version of Happy Birthday. They loved it. All I wanted was someone to sing it to me.

That never happened that night. Instead, we all boarded a plane to Mexico City and by the time we landed, the day had ended, and I didn't even get a cupcake.

By the time I turned eighteen, I was the biggest star in the world. And the loneliest. I had an entourage around me at all times, especially once the crazy letters from stalkers began to come and my mother felt the need to hire more people.

But eighteen was different because then I was officially an adult. I could be who I wanted to be. I could do what I wanted to do. I could theoretically say no to doing what I didn't want to do because I was an adult.

So, when Jonny Chambers with all his tattoos and piercings came to meet me after one of my shows a few weeks after I turned eighteen, I went back to his hotel room with him and lost my virginity. In retrospect, he wasn't my best choice to lose my V card, but I can't change the past.

As a belated eighteenth birthday present, he took me away to his place in Miami and gave me the biggest party the world has ever seen. The tabloids are still writing about it to this day over a year later. It's the reason why all the talking heads and shrinks on TV are so sure I'm with him right now.

They never saw what happened behind the scenes with us. They think they know things because he was all into drinking and coke when I was with him, and I had bruises they were sure were from him hitting me.

That wasn't what happened, though. He never hit me. What he did was worse. He made me feel like I was just another girl in his harem, that I didn't mean anything to him and he could replace me as easily as he found me.

Since I broke up with him, everyone's talked about how I was abused, and I guess in a lot of ways I was. Jonny never physically abused me, but he did a number on my confidence, so that's a kind of abuse, I think.

That's all behind me now, though. I've got someone I care about in my life who cares about me enough to risk God only knows what my mother might do if she ever finds out Michael was the one who got me this room. He protects me from what really can hurt me, and that means more than I can ever tell him.

To hell with everyone but Michael. My mother, every damn person who thinks they know my life better than I do, and all these jackasses on TV who spend their days and nights talking endlessly about things they know nothing about.

Sliding off the bed, I walk toward the bathroom with

the oversized bathtub, the main reason I wanted to come to this hotel. It was a risk since it's the best hotel in the Tampa area, but once I saw the picture of the bathtubs in their suites, I knew this was the place I wanted to hide out and simply relax for a few days.

I turn on the hot water full blast and drop a lavender bubble bomb in to create the perfect luxurious bath experience. As I undress out of my favorite pink yoga pants and white T-shirt that says Superstar in silver across the chest, I catch a glimpse of myself in the enormous bathroom mirror. Two days of gorging on junk food hasn't done nearly as much damage as my personal trainer claimed it would.

For a moment, I pose and smile at the thought of what Mitchell would do if he saw how much I ate in the past forty-eight hours. The guy would have a total meltdown and order me to work out twice as hard for the next month.

"See? I knew a couple days being bad wouldn't do that much damage," I say with a laugh as I climb into the tub.

The water stings it's so hot, so I quickly turn on the cold water to balance things out so I don't give myself second degree burns from the waist down. I pull the cooler water back toward me, which eases the temperature a little, before leaning back against the edge of the tub and closing my eyes.

This is all I wanted when I ran away. Not to fall off the supposed wagon, unless you count candy, cookies, potato chips, and diet soda falling off the wagon. Not to hurt anyone. Just to relax in a tub full of bubbles that smell like flowers after eating too much food that's bad for me for a couple days.

Meanwhile, the entire world outside this hotel suite is spinning out of control worried about what I'm doing. That's their problem, not mine. Maybe they should try some of Ainsley's Zen shit. Maybe then they'd calm the hell down.

CHAPTER TWO

iam

THE LATE APRIL SUN FEELS GOOD ON MY SKIN, SO I push off heading inside to take a few more minutes out here on my balcony. Glancing back toward the glass doors, I see Wilder pacing back and forth through my living room. Every day it's something more stressful with him. If our parents only knew how much trouble he brought into his life simply by being Wilder.

Then again, I doubt my father would be able to see that if it was written on a billboard and he was forced to stand in front of it for hours. Something about my younger brother makes Kane Jackson believe in things that simply don't exist.

I try not to agree with Cade and Alex about Wilder, but he makes it hard. Damn hard sometimes.

Today's crisis involves someone he's been seeing. For as much trouble as he gets into, he always seems to find room in his life for romance. You'd think they'd see him and all the nonsense he brings with him coming from a mile away, but he flashes them that Wilder smile and they get a look at his tats and piercings, and before you can say "You should have run by now," he's got himself a brand-new love in his life.

He tried to talk to me about whatever this new one's doing last night, but I got the hell out of that conversation before it turned into an hour-long discussion of whether or not he should drop all the other ones. It seems this one thinks it should only be the two of them in this relationship. My younger brother has never defined exclusive exactly that way.

As all of this rambles through my brain, threatening to ruin a beautiful day I was hoping to have all to myself, I hear the sliding glass door open behind me and know I should have run like his new love interest. Crashing into my quiet enjoyment of this sunny morning, Wilder sits himself down on the chair across from me and shakes his head.

As if he's got such a tough life that I should feel bad for him.

"It looks like I'm going to have to stay a little while longer. Hope you're okay with that."

I let out a heavy sigh. I don't really have much of a choice. He's family. Yes, he's an asshole and yes, he's an imposition, but my mother pulled me aside last month and begged me to let my brother stay here for a while so she and my father could enjoy some peace and quiet together. Since I thought I'd be on a job somewhere already, I happily agreed.

And then that job fell through when the client's husband realized his wife was the one sending herself threatening notes just to get attention and she didn't need security guarding her against herself. That left me here with my least favorite houseguest in the world.

Who now has just announced he's going to have to stay here a little while longer. To other people, that might mean a day or so. To Wilder Jackson, that could mean months.

Or even longer.

I cringe at the idea of the two of us being permanent roommates. If only his new addition to the harem wasn't so insistent on being the only one in his life.

"Explain to me again why you can't go hang out with one of the multitude of people who've paraded through here in the past few weeks?"

Wilder gets a faraway look in his eyes, like I've asked him some deep question that makes him rethink everything he's ever thought about love. Or parades. You can never tell with him. He's a weird combination of a dreamer and a criminal, so his thoughts go off in tangents I don't even try to understand anymore.

"They're nothing to me," he says in a tone that sounds like he's making some grand pronouncement. "Chris is the one. I know it."

I know what I say next won't register with him the way it would with other people, but I say it anyway because someone has to inject some logic into our lives here. "Then break it off with all the others. This isn't rocket science, man. If this one's the one, then go balls to the wall with this relationship and forget the others."

And just like that, his grand pronouncement look like he's posing for a statue fades away and he sags back in the chair. "I know this is the one. I'm sure of it. I just don't know if I want to give up everything I have going with everyone else yet. You know how it is."

In truth, I don't. I can't fathom running my life the way he does. Or more correctly, the way he's been allowed to since he came into our family. Nothing ever seems permanent to Wilder, despite the fact that he claims he's found the perfect soulmate or the perfect job or even the perfect club to go to practically every week.

That's not who I am. He's all over the place, scattered with everything from his thoughts to his feelings. I'm the opposite. I like my life calm and stable. The last thing I need is unnecessary drama, something my younger brother seems to crave.

There's no point in discussing that with him, though. He thinks his life is perfectly grand. That he causes upheaval everywhere he goes doesn't seem to faze him in the least.

"What about your friends, those guys you hang out with? You can't stay with one of them?"

He dismisses that out of hand with a shake of his head. "They all have lives to lead and girlfriends who live with them now. It's like in the past year every single one of them has gotten tied down," he answers with a healthy dose of disgust for his friends' happily ever afters.

This Chris should definitely run. Now.

"You, on the other hand, are a single guy with two bedrooms, so I figured you'd like the company," he adds.

I guess I should be thankful Wilder has saved me from a life of peace and tranquility. If I could get him to stay still long enough, maybe he could pose for a statue in his honor.

A hundred things pop into my head that I want to say about what he figured I'd like, but I remember my mother and her big blue eyes looking up at me as she pleaded for some time alone with my father and without Wilder. So I simply shrug and stuff all those ideas into a place in the back of my mind for some other time.

"Well, I tend to keep to myself, but feel free to stay as long as you like," I say before closing my eyes.

If he walks back into the apartment right now, this morning won't be totally ruined.

Wilder slaps me on the arm, and my eyes fly open to see him standing next to me looking far too excited. "Great! You know, Liam, we're brothers, so we should hang out more. I know we're as different as night and day, but we've got more in common than you think."

I look up at him as not a single thing comes to me that we may have in common. We're brothers because our parents adopted him, so we don't even share blood, even though he oddly looks like me with his dark hair and blue eyes. Other than looking like we're related, I can't think of a single thing we like that's the same. Or anything that we dislike together either.

"Stay as long as you need to, Wilder. Mi casa es su casa."

"Terrific! I'm thirsty. You want anything to drink?" he asks.

I shake my head as one thing in common between us occurs to me. We both came into the same amount of money when we turned twenty-one. Wilder pissed away nearly every dime of his on partying, sex, and then restitution to pay back for his crime that got him sent to jail. I, on the other hand, have all that I got and more after some wise investments.

He slams the glass door harder than it needs to be

shut, and I shake my head again. We have nothing in common.

I get maybe another ten minutes of peace in the sun before my phone rings. Grabbing it off the table next to where I sit, I hold it in front of me as my eyes adjust to see my cell's screen. VIP Security. Maybe there's a job for me after all.

Before I can even say hello, a man's voice begins speaking. "Liam, this is Jonah Bradley, president of VIP Security. I know we haven't spoken many times in the past, but I wanted to be the one to call you with a new assignment because you're the perfect man for the job."

Sitting up, I try to remember any time Jonah Bradley and I have spoken in the past. Maybe once at the Christmas party VIP held two years ago? No, that was his assistant I was talking to near that punchbowl of eggnog that ended up nearly leveling him after someone dumped what must have been an entire bottle of rum into it.

"Hello, Mr. Bradley. I appreciate you thinking of me for this job you believe I'm perfect for. It's nice to be recognized for my hard work."

"Fantastic! You've heard of Mia, the young singer whose name is on everyone's lips? She needs a security chief, and you're the right man for the job."

He sounds like an Army recruiting ad, except working as Mia's head of security would be a hell of a lot worse than enlisting in the military. Last year, she ran away and ended up in rehab after her people finally wrangled her somewhere in south Florida. Then when she got out, she insisted she didn't need a new bodyguard, which meant I'd waited all that time while she dried out for nothing.

No way I wanted to be saddled with this assignment. Nope. No thanks.

"This is the classical pianist I was supposed to go protect who ended up in rehab?" I ask, wanting to make sure I've got the right crazy person in mind.

Jonah hesitates for a moment before answering, "Yeah, well, about that whole pianist thing...forget everything you thought you knew about her because today's a new day."

Now he sounds like someone recruiting people to join a cult.

"I appreciate being in consideration, but I think this time I'm going to have to pass, Mr. Bradley. We tried this last year. It didn't work. I think someone else would be more appropriate."

Still, he doesn't give up.

"Nonsense. You're the best man I have, Liam. You might not know that I actually pay attention to the company I run, but I do, and I've seen what clients say about you. You're professional and get the job done. No muss, no fuss. That's exactly the kind of attitude necessary for this assignment."

I replay all the news coverage I've seen in the past few days about Mia being missing and the shitshow surrounding it. No man in his right mind would want to step into that mess. That girl and her life are nothing but a hassle.

"It all seems pretty moot anyway, doesn't it?" I ask, knowing if he's calling me that something's changed with her situation. "She's been missing for forty-eight hours. Seems to me this is like closing the barn door after the horses have all left the barn."

"I'm happy you've been keeping up. That's good

news! As for Mia being missing, that's been mostly a show for the press. Andrea Shanoff, Mia's mother, never misses an opportunity to create a media spectacle. They found out her previous head of security got her a room at some hotel with the help of his sister a day ago. Andrea's just been milking the madness."

What part of that is supposed to make me want to take this job? First, her drug and alcohol binge landed her in rehab, and then she balked at getting a new bodyguard at all once she got out. At least now I know it had nothing to do specifically with me. Mia simply didn't want to exchange an indulgent babysitter for an actual security professional intent on taking care of business.

But being the guy who has to deal with replacing the one who got her the room sounds like a thankless job. She's probably way too close to him and is going to kick and scream if her people try to fire him.

On top of all of that, she sounds like a huge pain in the ass. I've got enough money that I don't have to work. I choose to because sitting around day after day gets boring. Also, I want to make my own way in the world, even if I do have a nest egg to fall back on. If it means I have to dip into my money instead of going to work for the world's biggest diva, I vote for raiding the piggy bank.

"I think I'll pass. I'm not great with out-of-control children."

"Liam, I really need you on this assignment," Bradley says in a very different voice from just a minute ago. Now he sounds almost desperate.

My morning relaxation ruined, I stand from the chaise lounge and head back inside. "I wish I could, but this just doesn't sound like the kind of job I want to take.

I'm sorry, Mr. Bradley, but Mia's just too much hassle. I hope you find someone. I do."

"I understand. Thanks for hearing me out, Liam."

As I stuff the phone back into my jeans pocket, I wonder if that's the last time I'll be hearing from VIP Security. If it is, so be it. Some hills you just have to die on.

～

HIDING OUT FROM HAVING TO SPEND ANY MORE TIME with Wilder, I try to find a spot down near the water where no one can see me. Since it's one of the usual Jackson-March family get-togethers, that's unlikely, but a guy can try.

I get approximately sixty seconds of alone time before Alex finds me. Slapping me on the back, he laughs as he hands me a beer. "Trying to be invisible, Liam? Who are you avoiding?"

When I shrug and roll my eyes, he answers for me. "Let me guess. That brother of yours. Dude, I heard your father talking at the restaurant the other day. Is he seriously living with you now? That sucks big time for you, I'm sure."

As much as I don't want to talk shit about Wilder, I need to vent to someone, and since Alex probably won't go telling anyone but Cade, I don't censor myself. "You have no fucking idea. The guy is ubiquitous. I swear there are clones of him in every room of my place. I know it's not very brotherly of me, but I think I might end up chucking him off the balcony if he doesn't find somewhere else to go and soon."

Alex sits down on the sand and raises his bottle to tap

it off the neck of mine. "To family. They drive you crazy, but what can you do?"

I take a gulp of beer and mumble, "Toss him off the fifth floor of my building."

"You know, I thought I heard my father say something about him bringing someone with him today, but I didn't see anyone new. Just the typical couples of Cade and Hailey and Cash and Savannah, along with our parents and Stefan and Shay. That leaves Grandma and the rest of us single guys in the family."

Again, I roll my eyes. "The current love of his life probably figured out it's time to run for the hills before it gets really serious. That's why he says he needs to stay at my place for a little longer. 'This is the one,' he says, but he doesn't want to give up all the others."

With a hearty laugh, Alex shakes his head. "Then this one's not the one."

"That's what I told him. He doesn't listen. Then again, has he ever?" I ask, knowing the answer without my cousin giving his opinion.

From the porch, my mother calls out, "Liam! Alex! Come up and join us. Wilder was just talking about how much fun he's having staying with you, honey."

Nudging his elbow into my side, Alex jokes, "Yeah, honey. Let's go talk to your mother about how much fun you're having living with Wilder."

As we reluctantly give up our hiding place, I say to Alex, "Fuckin A. I should have taken that job, except for the fact that it would have been exchanging one pain in the ass for another."

"Which one is that? You still waiting for that girl to get her shit in gear? Isn't she the one who's been missing for forty-eight hours? Have they found her yet?" he asks with genuine concern in his voice.

I shake my head as what Jonah Bradley told me about that whole missing stunt she pulled this week. While we walk up the stairs to the back porch of my grandmother's house, I explain, "Yeah, she's fine. Well, she's not harmed. The whole thing sounds like it was a publicity stunt to me."

Turning to look at me, Alex seems surprised. "Oh, yeah? So she was never really missing?"

Before I can answer, my mother asks, "Who was missing?"

I really didn't want to have this conversation today since I'm trying to forget Mia and her circus of madness. Waving away my mother's question, I say, "No one. So what's going on up here?"

Cassian and my father sit off to the side talking about something in hushed tones. That means they're either trying to discuss business, which isn't supposed to be allowed at these family events, or they're planning something for Olivia or my mother. Shay and Stefan sit on the other side of the porch talking with my grandmother, leaving the middle of the porch to my mother and Olivia since Cash and Cade and their girlfriends seem to have disappeared, along with Wilder.

"Your father and your uncle are breaking the rules again, aren't they?" my grandmother says loudly. "Cassian and Kane, if you aren't planning some surprise party for one of your wives, you better get over here and join the rest of us. This is supposed to be a party. No talking about the restaurant allowed."

As they look over with guilty expressions and reluctantly move their chairs to the middle of the porch, my mother presses me for a second time about the missing person I was talking to Alex about on our way up here. "So who was missing? Are they okay?"

I open my mouth to deflect attention to my missing cousins and their girlfriends, but just as I begin to say their names, the two happy couples walk out the back door to join us all. Hoping to take advantage of that, I smile and say, "Just these four. Long time, no see. Where have you guys been?"

Cade senses I'm trying to push attention onto them and gives me a knowing smile. "In the house getting something to drink. So who was missing?"

I level a glare at him and shake my head. "Payback's going to be a bitch, dude."

Cash decides to join in and ask the same question, and within a few seconds, everyone on the goddamned porch is asking about who's missing. Jesus, this family is like a dog with a bone once they get onto a topic.

Since it's obvious I'm going to have to answer their question if this party is ever going to even have a chance of getting better, I say, "Mia. The singer. Well, I thought she was a pianist, but that seems to have been some mistake. She was missing. Now she's not. Are all you amateur sleuths satisfied? Now how about we turn the conversation to something interesting, like if today's the day we find out one of the happy couples are getting married."

Unfortunately, nobody takes the bait. From the other side of the porch, my grandmother chuckles. "He's just like you, Kane. We're not going to fall for whatever subterfuge this is, Liam. Everyone knows you're working for that girl, so what's the scoop?"

So much for moving on. Once Alexandria March

decides we're talking about something, we're damn well talking about that and only that. Fucking terrific.

"I'm not working for her. That fell through months ago. She's crazy on wheels, so when they asked me again to take on being her security chief, I politely declined."

Cash slaps me on the shoulder and laughs. "That's not your circus and those aren't your monkeys? Sounds like you made the right move considering all I've been seeing on TV about her. That press conference with her mother made it sound like some terrorists had taken her. So she's okay?"

"She's fine, so we can all stop talking about it since it has nothing to do with me or any of us. Time for a new subject. How about the one where the happy couples tell us all when the big days are?" I suggest before taking another gulp of beer.

I'm going to need a whole lot more of that if this party doesn't stop being a discussion of Mia and her insanity. The only thing worse would be everyone asking how living with Wilder is going.

Since my mother can't leave well enough alone, she asks, "Why did you turn down that assignment? I thought you were a lock for that."

As much as I want to say every reason I have can be found in the hour after hour of news coverage of Mia and her disappearance over the past few days, I simply smile and answer, "It didn't feel right, Mom. I'm not the right kind of person for that job."

Everyone around us agrees, but my mother won't let the subject die. "I disagree, honey. You're exactly what that girl needs and desperately, I might add. I've watched all the news reports about her. She needs someone to set her on the right path, Liam."

Looking down into her blue eyes so full of earnest concern for someone she's never met, I can't help but think my mother's too kind for this world. "Mom, she's never going to change. Too many years of being allowed to run wild means she would never want to work with anyone like me. For God's sake, her last chief of security was the person who helped her run away. It's not my job to set someone on the right path."

I want to add that if I could do that, I'd try it with her other son, but I don't. If I think this topic is tiresome, that's nothing compared to the Wilder discussion. Most of the family thinks he's good for nothing, but my parents keep hoping against hope that he'll turn out to be that sweet, wonderful person they're so sure he is deep down inside. They don't deserve to have to defend him yet again from the truth everyone else in our family already knows all too well.

My mother takes my hand and tugs me off to the side as everyone moves on to something else to talk about, thankfully. "Honey, that girl needs stable people around her. You're the most stable person I know. Why do you think I asked you to let your brother stay with you? Yes, I wanted some time alone with your father, but I also hoped you might rub off on him."

"That's not how things work, Mom," I say quietly, hating how the hope never fades from her beautiful eyes. "Not with Wilder and not with this Mia girl. If they wanted to be like me, they would be already."

She doesn't say another word, but even as that hope remains, I see disappointment begin to cloud her expression. Whether it's for the client I turned down or my brother, I have no idea.

• • •

By the time I get back to my place a few hours later, the discussion of Mia and her crazy life is a distant memory after a day of good times with my family. Falling back onto my bed, I hear Wilder turn up the music out in the living room, a sure sign he's planning to continue the party here tonight.

My phone rings, and I see it's VIP Security. Maybe I was too hasty in thinking they'd never offer me another assignment again.

"Liam, it's Jonah Bradley. I can offer fifty percent more in pay and a bonus of ten grand to take the job."

"The Mia job? You still haven't found anyone to take that assignment?" I ask, stunned I can't stop this woman's name from invading my life once again.

"Yeah. Fifty percent more than your usual pay and a ten grand bonus the second you say yes. So will you do it?"

Instantly, the word no forms on my lips, but then all that stuff my mother said about Mia needing stable people around her comes back to me. Maybe I could help her.

"Fine. Fifty percent more and ten grand right now and I'll do it. But you better warn them. I'm not taking this job to be just another clown in the Mia circus. I take my job seriously, so I expect them to understand I'm there to handle security like a professional."

"Great! I'll be sure to tell her mother that. She's her manager, so she's the one you'll be dealing with, for the most part. She returned back home two days ago, so you'll need to meet with them at her home tomorrow to get things going. I'll have my assistant send you the details. Make it late morning. She likes to sleep in."

"The mother or the superstar?" I ask, not trying to temper my snideness.

"Both. Good luck, and remember I have the utmost faith in you."

I toss my phone beside me onto the bed and let out a heavy sigh as Wilder's music fills the room around me. Christ, I hope I haven't made a mistake. The last thing I need in my life is a diva like Mia.

What are the chances she's going to like having a by the book security chief?

CHAPTER THREE

ia

MY HEAD SPINS AT HOW MANIPULATIVE MY MOTHER can be. Why I ever agreed to make her my manager is beyond me. Isn't there some law against sixteen-year-old girls signing legal contracts or something?

Four hours of fighting with her has left me drained and utterly unable to remember a single good moment in my life. The relaxing couple of days I stole feel like a distant memory, something I heard about once from someone but never actually experienced.

"I'm not going to explain myself, Mother. I needed time away. I'm done here," I say before turning on my heel and heading toward my room.

In my home. On my estate. Perhaps she needs to be reminded of that.

Behind me, my mother says in a low voice, "And one more thing. Michael's been fired. I hired another chief of security, one who hopefully understands the basic tenets of his job and doesn't confuse himself with your BFF. He'll be here today."

Every inch of my body stills in complete shock. Michael fired? She wouldn't do that.

Slowly, I turn around to face her as everything in the living room fades away, leaving only the two of us standing in a sea of white rage that surrounds me. "Don't. He doesn't deserve to be fired, so whatever you did, undo it now, Mother, or I swear to God, you'll regret it."

My mother's usually placid expression, courtesy of Botox, twists into an angry scowl. "He's gone, Mia. You don't need more people around you giving into every silly whim you have. You need someone who's going to do his job. Period. If you want someone to be a friend, then find a friend, but Michael's gone."

My heart pounds like a jackhammer in my chest. My mother's done terrible things before, but never has she done anything like this. Firing Michael is something I can't forgive. She's gone too far this time.

"Rehire him, or I will never perform again," I say flatly, desperately trying to keep myself balanced as every emotion inside me threatens to explode all over her.

"No. It's done and that's that. The new man Jonah over at VIP recommended will be here in a few minutes, so make yourself presentable and try to remember that unlike you, the rest of the world is just trying to do their jobs."

That's it. I can't keep anything in check anymore, so I scream, "I will never perform another show if you don't bring him back!"

Casually, she shrugs and sits down to drink her morning energy shake. "You wouldn't do that. You love singing."

I march over to where she sits doling out her unjust punishments for people I care about and scream, "I used to love singing. Now I hate it!"

She opens her mouth to say something else that will set me off, but just then, I see my mother's assistant Candy walk in with a man who towers over her. He's got to be six and a half feet, and he's built like a brick wall. Worst of all, he doesn't smile or even look happy to be here.

This is my new chief of security? I don't fucking think so.

"Oh, no! You replaced Michael with him? Nope!"

My mother's expression turns to one of pure horror, likely because she thinks I offended some ridiculous code of conduct she believes everyone should follow. I'm not going to be polite if I don't agree with something, and I definitely don't agree with having that miserable giant guarding me.

Why doesn't anyone understand there has to be a relationship between two people who work together? Michael was someone who cared about me. This guy looks like the Marines just let him go because he crushed his entire platoon with his bare hands.

I storm out and head up to my bedroom where at least I can be left alone and think. There has to be some way to get Michael back and that guy the hell out of here. I'm the goddamn moneymaking machine here, not my mother. She can't do this. I'm not some underage little girl who needs her help anymore. I'm a grown adult who isn't taking this shit anymore from her or anyone else.

As I pace back and forth across my bedroom floor, I can't help but be curious about what she's saying down there. I open the door a crack and listen for her usual nonsense about how we run a professional company and all that garbage.

Nothing happens here without me. Why is it she's forgotten that?

I strain to hear her talking, but eventually a few words begin drifting up the stairs. "I'm sorry. She's not herself this morning. Mia really isn't like this. Really."

Then the gigantic guy speaks, and I can barely contain my rage.

"I'm sure. I'm Liam Jackson. Jonah Bradley convinced me that I'm the man for this job. To be honest, I'm not so sure."

What kind of attitude is that? Who hired this jackass?

But of course, my mother is more than happy to ease his worries. "Trust me, my daughter is a wonderful person. Honestly. Plus, if Jonah believes you're the right man for the job, then I believe it too, Liam. Would you like something to eat or maybe some juice?"

Now she's offering him breakfast? Oh, no. Not happening.

I march downstairs to find the two of them chatting like they're the best of friends. "Sorry to break up this little morning coffee klatsch thing you have going on, but if anyone is going to interview prospective employees, it's me."

Turning toward the oversized thing in front of me, I march right up to him and size him up, starting from his feet. He's taller than Michael, but that doesn't mean he's any good at his job. In fact, it might mean he's like a big, bumbling clown who can't move fast if danger approaches.

Still, I feel like it takes my eyes forever to travel up his long legs and those black dress pants. Nice chest in that mint green dress shirt, although that doesn't have to be a good thing. Clearly, this lug works out.

"What makes you qualified to protect the likes of someone at my level?" I ask.

As I wait for his answer, my gaze drifts over his arms and I can't help but wonder how big those biceps are. Does he live in the gym? That's not going to happen if he works for me. I'm not paying some guy to be a gym rat. Let him do that on his own time.

When I look up at his face, I see nothing but disgust in his expression, which pisses me off. This could be the best gig in the world for someone like him, and he looks like he wants to throw up.

Nice attitude there, bud.

But his eyes are the bluest shade of blue I've ever seen, and next to his dark brown, nearly black hair, they seem to sparkle. Nice. Then again, what the hell does it matter what a bodyguard's eyes look like? As long as they see anything that could hurt me, I don't care what color they are.

Even if they're literally the most gorgeous eyes I've ever seen.

I take one final glance at him in total, noticing he's got great shoulders, but I can't let myself get distracted by that. It's not hard to get shoulders like that. Michael had nice shoulders. Hell, I've seen hundreds of men who have shoulders that look like this guy's. It's nothing terribly special. Just comes from some working out. Nothing special about that.

He doesn't look like anyone who would listen to my music, which is a huge problem. Even worse, the way he stares down at me but says nothing to answer my very simple question irritates me. This guy wants to work for me but thinks he can look at me with disdain?

Oh, no, pal. No way.

"Mia, it's clear the man is qualified," my mother says as he and I continue our staring match.

I don't tear my gaze away as I hold up my hand to stop her. "No. I want him to tell me, not you. I'm the goddamned client here. I'm the one he'll be expected to protect, so I'm the one he needs to answer."

But still he says nothing.

Staring me down, he finally clears his throat after nearly a minute passes of us staring at one another and says in a deep voice, "I've worked for Senator Stanford, the head of Cititrust, and an actress you may know, Angela Manning."

Still refusing to break the stare, I say, "Not a single one of those people are anywhere as big as me."

He shrugs, and for the first time, I see a hint of a smile that does nothing but infuriate me more. "Senator Stanford was a pretty beefy guy. Even bigger than you."

I step back from him and turn to glare at my mother. "A funny guy? Exactly the one thing in a man you know I hate."

"Then I guess it's a good thing I'm not here for that," he says smugly.

I snap my attention back to him to see him grinning. Who the hell does this guy think he is?

"Mia, he's exactly who we need," my mother says in

her soft, social worker voice that never fails to enrage me. I hate when she attempts to handle me like this. "Give him a chance."

Now I swivel my head to look over at her and bark, "Who we need? Are you now famous and need a bodyguard? I'm struggling to think of a single manager anyone ever gave a damn about."

I'm not interested in hearing another word from either of these people, so I march back to my room and slam the door. I had a head of security I could trust. Michael cared about me. We were friends. We were more than friends. He wasn't only a bodyguard who was willing to go behind my mother's back and let me have the happiness I so desperately crave. He was someone who truly cared for me.

And now my mother has sent him away just like she sends everyone away.

I grab my phone off my dresser and call Michael. He'll know what to do. He always does. He'll have a plan that will make this all better. Then my mother will see that I don't need Mr. Big and Rude downstairs. I just need the one person I can trust to protect me like he always has since I was sixteen.

My heart sinks as I hear his phone ring and ring and then my call goes to voicemail. I listen to his gentle voice tell me to leave a message, reveling in the sound of a familiar, friendly soul who cares about me.

With tears welling in my eyes, I say, "Michael, it's Mia. I know my mother fired you, but I can undo that. Call me so we can figure out what to do next. I miss you."

Falling back onto the bed, I hold my phone to my chest and wait for him to call back. He never makes me wait more than a minute or two. That's one of the things I love about him. He always shows that I'm his number one priority, unlike everyone else around me.

One minute turns to two and then turns to five. I lift my phone in front of me to see if it rang and I didn't hear it, but there are no missed calls. Maybe he's stuck in traffic. Or in a tunnel. Or somewhere there's shitty reception. That happens a lot.

I think back to that one time he and I had to go to one of those home stores to get him a new shower curtain. I'd never been in one of them before that day, and I was so thrilled to find out that a simple blond wig and sunglasses made it possible for me to walk around like any other person looking for tools or shower curtains. When I tried to call my mother, though, I couldn't get a call out, and Michael explained that the metal construction of the building made it hard to use cell phones there.

That's probably why he hasn't called back yet. He always knew the answer to why things happened like they did. That's what I need. Not some giant, angry guy who thinks this job is some kind of demotion for him. I need a friend like Michael who cared and answered my questions, no matter how stupid they were because I've experienced so little in life.

After ten minutes, I try to call him again, but this time it goes directly to voicemail. His phone never does that. Why would it go directly to voicemail?

Mine only does that if I turn it off or I decline a call. Did he deliberately not answer my call? He has to know it's me. My name comes up right in the middle of his screen with that picture of me he took that time on the ride back from a show in Oklahoma City.

Why would he not want to talk to me?

TEN MINUTES LATER, AFTER CHARMING THE GUY AT THE front gate and the helpful assistance of an Uber driver, I stand outside of Michael's apartment feeling like I'm about to unravel. Michael has never not answered one of my calls. He knows how much I depend on him to keep me sane when my mother insists on constantly making my life a living hell.

So why didn't he answer?

A second after I knock, I hear noises inside his apartment. It sounds like there's more than one person in there. Maybe his sister came over to visit when she heard he got fired. After helping me, she's probably going to be pissed, but I'll tell her like I plan to tell Michael that I'm going to get him his job back. He doesn't have to worry about that. I won't let my mother get away with this latest stunt of hers.

The door opens, and finally, I see a friendly face. "Michael! Why didn't you answer my call? I tried like half a dozen times."

He leans against the doorframe and quickly buttons his jeans, like I caught him right after getting out of the shower. Except he doesn't look like he's clean at all. If anything, he looks pretty nasty right now, as if he's been drinking ever since he found out what my mother did.

"My phone's been on the fritz. You know how it is. I should have gotten a new one a while ago."

I push past him to walk into his place, wrinkling my nose at the stench that hits me not two steps in. "I needed to come over and tell you I won't let my mother get away with firing you. She had no right, and I told her that. So, you don't have to worry. You'll have your job back today. I promise."

"Mia…"

With a shake of my head, I stop him. He doesn't have to say a word. None of this is his fault. I was the one who asked him to get me that hotel room, and I was the one who asked him to help me sneak away. He doesn't deserve to pay for merely doing as I wanted.

"It's okay, Michael. I won't let her do it. She brought some big guy in to replace you this morning, but I've already put my foot down and told her no way am I letting that happen. Just give me a few hours and you'll be back at the house where you belong."

A noise that sounds like someone snickering comes from the bathroom, and Michael nervously glances in that direction as I try to understand the vibe I'm getting from this place. He hasn't been drinking away his sadness at losing his job. There are no empty beer bottles, and that's all Michael drinks.

And that smell isn't stale alcohol. It's weed and something else, but I can't seem to place it.

"Mia, you should go. I'm sure everyone's looking for you by now, so you should go," he says as he begins to guide me toward the front door.

Why is he giving me the bum's rush like this? We're friends. We sit together every night and talk about everything. Why does he want me to go so soon?

"I don't want to go yet. I miss you, Michael. I want you back as my security guy. I feel safe with you."

Again, a sound like someone's in the bathroom laughing hits my ears, and I see Michael's eyes get wide. He heard it too.

"What's going on here?" I ask as I look around at the

mess of his apartment. "Why does it feel like you haven't been sitting here all sad about losing your job protecting me?"

Then I smell that scent I couldn't place a minute ago and finally know what it is. Sex.

"Mia, just go and whatever happens, it's okay," Michael says sheepishly.

My emotions begin to unravel inside me. I thought he cared about me. I thought we were friends. God, I thought we were more than friends.

I thought Michael and I were soulmates.

But one day after my mother fired him, he's here getting high and sleeping with someone? Even worse, he doesn't want to admit it and simply wants me to leave, to get out of his hair so he can go back to banging this woman?

"It's not okay!" I say, my voice breaking out into a sob as I storm over to the bathroom door to fling it open.

A blonde with ratty hair in a pink tank top and a baby puke green thong looks at me like I'm the skank and giggles again. "Who the fuck is she?"

Almost as if he's irritated he has to introduce us, Michael grumbles, "Mia, this is Tracey. Tracey, Mia."

The skeevy girl tilts her head to the side and gives me a crooked smile. "Hey."

I feel the tears begin to burn the backs of my eyes and hate that this is how my body chooses to react to the news that the one person I thought truly cared for me doesn't give a damn about losing his job or being removed from my life. Michael wasn't my soulmate. He wasn't even someone who missed me enough not to hook up with this nasty girl with bad taste in clothes.

"Mia, it's not like we were…"

His sentence trails off as I march past him toward the front door. I know what he doesn't have the balls to say to my face. It's not like we were together.

He's right. We weren't. I never slept with him because after the mess of my life for the past year, I wanted to be sure someone cared for me before I took that step again. After Jonny, I thought I needed that, and I thought Michael understood.

I thought a lot of things that obviously weren't true.

God, I'm such a fool!

"Goodbye, Michael. Enjoy your life here with her," I say, choking back the tears.

So much for him being my soulmate. All those nights we spent talking meant nothing to him. All the things I shared with him were simply part of his job, obviously.

With one last look back at Michael, I see Tracey walk up behind him and wrap her arms around his waist like she wants to show me he's hers. She doesn't have to worry. I'm a fool, but I'm not stupid. She can have him.

He was never anything to me anyway. At least, he never thought he was. The problem is I did think he was someone special.

My tears make running down the steps away from his apartment next to impossible, and I stumble as I hurry toward the bottom floor of the building. Crashing into the wall next to the stairs, I steady myself and wipe my eyes.

God, I was so stupid! Jonny told me when we broke up that no one was ever going to love me. That I wasn't enough for anyone to deal with all the bullshit that comes with me.

Now I know he was right.

CHAPTER FOUR

iam

ANDREA SETS A MUG OF COFFEE DOWN ON THE TABLE in front of me as I sit back on the sofa, already regretting my choice to take this assignment after that little outburst of Mia's. Her mother, along with her assistant, wear uncomfortable expressions and talk in hushed tones over near the doorway before Andrea returns alone to sit across from me in what looks like a chair that should be in a museum instead of a living room.

She eases down onto the blood red upholstered seat and instantly appears even more uncomfortable than just a few moments ago. Not surprising, I guess, considering it looks to be some antique from hundreds of years ago. The dark wood ornate legs and arms remind me of something Santa Claus used to sit in at the mall when I'd go see him as a little boy.

Cradling a mug of coffee in her hands, she says, "You

know, this life can be very hard, especially for someone like Mia. She's had a lot to adjust to. The stardom and fame. That kind of thing. She's actually a wonderful person. I just want you to know that so you don't think she's always like she was before. Things have just been difficult recently."

I have no idea what to say to that since I doubt this woman wants my true opinion of her daughter, so I force a smile and nod. "I'm sure."

That's all it takes to get her talking, and I let her tell me how Mia wanted to sing since she was a little girl and how they did the pageant circuit and she was crowned Little Miss Tampa. Andrea practically beams pride as she talks, and I want to believe the person I met a short time ago isn't the petty tyrant she appears to be.

But it's going to take more than a stroll down memory lane to convince me of that.

"Everyone who saw her perform as a little girl in those pageants told me she had something rare. I knew it, but hearing them say it made me think we should try to see how far it could go. So she started entering talent contests. You know the local ones you see advertised online and on posters at the mall? They weren't anything big at first, but then when she was fourteen, she won a contest and the prize was studio time. It was like a dream come true for her…for all of us, and from there, she took off like a comet. By the time she was fifteen, she had a number one hit. But it's a hard thing to get used to being famous, and she's so young, so that makes it doubly hard."

I get the sense that she's going to continue singing her daughter's praises, and I'm not in the mood to listen to any more of that. After taking a sip of the weakest coffee I've ever tasted in my life, I lean forward to set the mug back down on the table and level my gaze on her.

"I'm sorry if this is out of line, but no one, no matter how big, has a right to speak to people like that."

Andrea doesn't miss a beat and immediately defends her daughter once more. Drawing her eyebrows in, she looks truly pained when she says, "She's my only child. Her father and I couldn't have any more. When she said she wanted to be a singer, I devoted everything in my power to make that happen. Her father couldn't handle that, so he walked away five years ago. It's only been Mia and me ever since."

As much as I want to sympathize with her, that isn't my job. I need her to understand that the reason Jonah Bradley thought I was the right man for this position is because I'm not someone who falls apart at a sob story.

Changing the subject, I say, "About her last security chief. She obviously had a relationship with him above and beyond what it was supposed to be."

I'm surprised when she shakes her head and waves that little bit of truth away. "Oh, that was nothing. She's had to spend a lot of time on the road in the past couple years. It gets lonely. Michael fell for her like everyone does. I don't blame him. Mia's a flirt, like most young girls, so people can't help but fall in love with her."

A flirt? I haven't seen that part of her yet, obviously. She talks like her daughter is Venus or some mythical creature with the power to enchant all who come into her presence. I can't imagine how anyone could stand being in the same room with her for more than a few minutes, much less sleep with her. Sure, she's beautiful, possibly more beautiful than any woman I've ever met before, but she's awful and thoughtless to the people who care the most about her.

And that's downright ugly.

"I think I better go see how Mia's doing. I'll be right back. Please, make yourself at home. When I get back, we'll get everything straightened out about where you'll sleep and all of that."

She walks out of the room, leaving me to wonder if I want to stay here long enough to have to sleep. Right now, I feel like calling Jonah and telling him there's no amount of money he can pay me and no bonus big enough to make me want to stick around and deal with Mia's bullshit.

While I try to think of any reason why I should live up to my word, Andrea runs back into the room frantically waving her arms. "She's not in her room. She's gone again! My car is here, so I don't know where she could be."

Without thinking, I shift into work mode. I stand up and gently take her by the shoulders to calm her down. "Where would she go? Think of where you see her running to."

Andrea shakes her head and begins to cry. "I don't know. God, I should have never let her storm out of here like that. I should have followed her immediately."

"Listen to me. She doesn't have that much of a lead on us, so think about where she would go to. There has to be a place she'd want to be. A favorite spot somewhere? She can't be that far."

That calms her down and she begins to nod like she understands we have to use common sense to get through this. "Michael's. She'd go find him. He has an apartment in Tampa."

"Okay. Let's go there."

SHE PULLS UP TO AN APARTMENT COMPLEX AT THE address she has for Mia's former head of security and one glance at the place horrifies her. "Why would he live in a place like this? He made good money working for my daughter. This place looks like somewhere drug addicts hang out when they can't find their usual terrible spot."

I look out the window at the rundown tan buildings in front of me and wonder something similar myself. Nobody who has any decent income would live in a place with junk cars strewn about, broken glass in windows, and screen doors hanging off their frames.

As much as I'd like to imagine what this Michael's deal is, we don't have time to solve that mystery. "What's the apartment number?"

"Two seventy-three."

I open the car door and start to move. "Then let's go visit apartment two seventy-three and see what Michael has to say."

By the time we reach the door to the apartment, I'm sure I've seen half a dozen health code violations, and that's not counting the empty syringes tossed along the dead flower beds that line the sidewalks. This place isn't the Ritz, for sure.

"God, I hope she's not in there," Andrea whispers as I rap my knuckles off the wood door.

The number three comes loose from the door and drops down so it looks like we're standing in front of apartment two seven E. Andrea and I glance over at one another, and I can't help but think that's an ominous sign.

Christ, I hope I don't have to rush the client to the hospital on my first day at this job. I was hoping to ease into the madness, not jump in headfirst.

The door opens to reveal a shirtless man in a pair of faded ripped jeans he didn't bother to zip up all the way. His dark hair is sticking up like someone's been running their hands through it, and by the odor of funk coming off him, he and whoever he's spending his time with in there have been smoking some stink weed and getting busy.

Trying not to breathe in, I ask, "Where's Mia?"

Beside me, Andrea says in a voice full of fear, "Michael, did she come here? Is she in there with you?"

A half-naked blond woman wearing only a too-small pink tank top and a green thong inches up behind Michael. Sliding her hands around his waist, she strokes up and down his body, her chipped red fingernails getting lost in his chest hair, and asks in a sleepy voice, "Who is it now, baby?"

He turns to look at her and then back at me. With a shrug, he answers, "She left. When she saw Tracey, she ran out."

I look away in disgust and start pushing Andrea down the hallway. "Let's go. We need to move fast."

"Where could she be?" she asks as I guide her toward the stairs.

"I don't know, but we'll be faster in a car than she is on foot, assuming she didn't get into a cab or an Uber."

By the time we reach the car, Andrea's winded, so I jump in behind the wheel. "Is there anywhere she likes to go when she's upset?" I ask as I pull away from the curb.

As she tries to catch her breath, she shakes her head.

"I don't know. I swear to God this child is going to kill me. I don't think I've ever run that fast in my life."

I take the turn out of Michael's apartment complex sharp, sending Andrea sliding across her seat and nearly crashing into me. "Think. Anywhere she'd feel better."

Pushing herself upright, she says, "When she was a little girl, whenever she got sad, she'd go outside and sit under a tree we had in the backyard. But that was years ago."

"Where's the house?" I ask as I take another hard turn, this time to the right.

"St. Augustine."

Not helpful. I doubt she's making her way back across the state to sit under some damn tree in someone else's yard. Maybe her comment isn't entirely useless, though.

"I'm going to look for a park. I'm thinking maybe Mia has a thing for nature when she gets unhappy."

"That might be a good idea!"

Five minutes later, I pull up to a park and scan the area. No sign of her.

As I jump out of the car, I order Andrea to take the right side of the grass. "We'll cover more ground if we split up. You go over there and check out that side of the park. I'll take this side over here."

She hurries away while I take off running in the opposite direction, my eyes scanning every inch of the grass and trees in front of me. Thankfully, even though it's a beautiful day out, very few people have chosen to come to this park today.

I consider yelling Mia's name, but that would likely make her bolt in the opposite direction. She and I didn't get off on the best foot this morning, so I doubt she's going to be thrilled to see me.

Tree after tree passes in front of my eyes, but no Mia. After ten minutes, I'm about to give up and see if Andrea had any more success than I did when I spy a figure beneath a tree at the back of the park near a fence. The young woman's dark brown hair hangs over her face, but I recognize the black and pink yoga pants Mia was wearing back at the house. She's huddled with her arms around her knees and looks nothing like the person who chewed off my head and her mother's not an hour ago.

I stop a few feet in front of her and quietly say her name so as not to frighten her. "Mia."

She doesn't look up, but when she speaks, the pain in her voice comes through loud and clear. "I thought he cared. He's gone for one day and it's like we were never anything but strangers."

"We should go. Someone's going to recognize you here if we don't."

That makes her lift her head, and I can't help but be struck at how genuinely sad she looks now. And how fragile compared to just a short while ago.

"I know what you're probably thinking. That it was just sex. Well, it wasn't. We never even slept together. It was deeper than that. Michael listened to me. He understood me. Or at least I thought he did."

Tears well in her eyes, but I don't stop myself from giving her my honest opinion of her friend. "Your buddy doesn't strike me as an understanding kind of guy."

She shoots me a nasty look. "Go away."

Taking a step closer to her, I try to imagine how it feels to be let down by that dirtbag when I'm one of the biggest stars in the world. But I can't do it. I don't know what she saw in that guy, but whatever it was, it didn't actually exist.

"Mia, I'm hired to protect you. You're not safe here."

Confusion fills her expression, and she shakes her head. "What do you care?"

Scanning the area for any potential danger, I force a smile. "I care because it's my job. Now let's go."

I'm not sure which part of that convinces her it's time to leave her spot under the tree, but she reluctantly stands up and I quickly step closer to her to shield her from anything that might be lurking nearby. She tilts her head back and glares up at me like she did back at the house.

"You're going to want to work on that caring you supposedly do. This feels more like you're a cop and I'm your prisoner."

As I look down into her dark eyes full of fury for me, I think to myself that I should have listened to my gut and walked away from this job last night. This is what I get for listening to my mother and her wishful thinking.

CHAPTER FIVE

$\mathcal{M}$ia

FOR A WEEK, I'VE HAD TO GET USED TO THIS NEW security guy. Liam. He's pleasant enough, I guess, if you have a thing for authoritarian rulers and the straight and narrow. Like don't step a toe out of line or you're in big trouble kind of straight and narrow. If that gets a girl going, then I imagine he's nothing short of a god to that type of person.

For me, he's just standoffish enough to make me miss Michael every so often, and then I remember what he looked like the last time I saw him standing in his apartment with that floozy hanging off him like some sloppy, hand-me-down, ugly coat. No smile or attempt to stop me so I might think he cared. No hug like he used to give me whenever he came back from a day away.

Nothing but what looked like irritation that I showed up to interrupt his fucking with little miss skank.

As I lay on my bed and stare up at the ceiling, I remember why I love being out on the road so much. Everything is new, every city is different, and you never have to focus on what happened before because something interesting is right around the corner. Here it's the same thing every day.

Deal with my mother.

Be practically ignored by the bodyguard I pay to protect me.

Hide out in my room and pretend like any of this is normal.

If only I hadn't told the crew to take a few days off. At least if they were here, I'd have someone to talk to.

I'm sure my mother has instructed the new guy to stay away from me. God forbid a man pay any attention to me. Unless, of course, he's in the audience far enough away to never touch me and has bought a ticket for the pleasure of getting a look at me.

Nothing like feeling as if you're only one step up from being in the tent on the edge of the circus where they keep the bearded lady and other freaks.

God, I'm so restless. At least when Michael was around, I had someone to laugh with and watch old TV shows with. Now, I'm alone until my entourage returns from their vacation.

That leaves me with my mother, her idiot assistant, and Liam to entertain me. Things don't look good for the immediate future, sadly.

I get up off the bed and wander over to the window to look out at the grounds. I could go swimming. No. There's nothing sadder than one person swimming, unless they're exercising, and I'm officially not doing that until my trainer forces me back into the gym.

Maybe a walk around the property. God, no. As if I haven't seen every square inch of this estate. Little of it is what I want it to look like anyway. My mother and the gardener make all those decisions. I merely get to pose in front of the meticulously trimmed topiaries or whatever beautiful flowers they choose this season whenever some media outlet wants an in-depth look into the private life of Mia.

It's all a façade, but whatever sells, I guess.

Wanderlust courses through my veins, but after bolting from under my mother's watchful eye twice in the past week, I doubt I'd have any success trying to sneak out again. Maybe if Michael was still around, but with General Liam on duty, forget it.

As my gaze roams over the colorful flower gardens and the perfectly manicured green grass, I wonder if it's possible to tunnel out. Those prisoners did it from Alcatraz, right? If they could dig through rock, I certainly could dig through some sandy Florida land that sits beneath the sod.

Except by the time I actually got anywhere good, it would be time to head out onto the road again, so all of my work would be for nothing. Kudos to you, Mia, for thinking outside the box, though. Just for that, you get to spend another boring day all alone.

Out of the corner of my eye, I see Liam walk out toward the gardens. From the back of the property, my head of security for the estate Javier walks toward him. I've always liked Javier. He's quiet but never fails to have a smile for me, unlike the new guy whose face looks like it might break if he tried to be nice and show me his pearly whites.

For a few seconds, I wonder what they're talking

about, but something about the way Liam's dressed takes over my thoughts. His black T-shirt only serves to make his biceps look bigger than when I first met him wearing a dress shirt. I wonder if he's been spending all his off time in the gym. He must. Nobody looks that built naturally. Unlike that first day, now he's in jeans, and as much as I want to see him as merely an officious bastard of my mother's, I can't deny he's good- looking.

Then I zero in on something just peeking out from under his sleeve. Is that a tattoo? It's black, so maybe it's only his shirt. I can't tell, but it looks like a tattoo. I wonder what he's got a tattoo of. I didn't think he had that level of cool in him.

Go figure.

Tall, silent, possibly tattooed, and hot. Like some kind of disapproving statue of a modern Adonis that roams around my home saying as few words as possible to me.

Is he like Michael? Does he just say things because that's what he's expected to do but doesn't care at all about my welfare? Because clearly that's what my former head of security truly felt about me.

My thoughts meander from Michael back to my new security chief, and I can't help but wonder about this guy. What's Liam's life like when he's not walking around looking disgruntled here?

I watch him stand perfectly straight as he and Javier talk, Liam towering over him by more than a few inches. How tall is the new guy? I guessed maybe six and a half feet tall that first day, but now I'm thinking he might be even taller than that.

Did he play basketball in high school? He seems like he'd be tall enough, and he is pretty built. It's not like he's one of those stick guys who are really tall but don't have an ounce of fat on them. I hate those guys. I've always imagined sleeping with one of them would be like having sex with a rake. Definitely not something I want to experience.

My mind drifts to a place where I wonder what sex with Liam would be like. Certainly not like banging a garden tool. There's a lot to hang on to with those muscular shoulders and arms. I stare out my window and try to make out what his abs look like under that black T-shirt. I bet he's got washboard abs. Michael had a nice body, but he didn't have great abs. I used to tease him about being flabby in the middle all the time. I don't imagine I'd ever get to say that to Liam.

Suddenly, I realize what I'm doing. Why the hell am I imagining the new guy's body under his clothes? I don't even like him. He's sullen and bossy, and to be honest, I'm not even sure he has the ability to smile. Maybe those are the muscles he should work out more often.

Mumbling to myself, I stare at him and say, "Yeah, maybe try a few lifts of the corners of your mouth, miserable bastard. You might not look so disgusted all the time."

I know why he looks that way. It's me. He doesn't approve of me or how I act or what I say. Well, fuck him. I don't need his approval. I get that from millions of people around the world. Who the hell cares what some bodyguard on loan from my mother's favorite place to get them thinks of me?

Javier laughs, and my attention is drawn to Liam's reaction to another person being happy. For the first time, I see him smile—a genuine smile with teeth that makes him look really sweet, not the forced kind he gives me whenever I walk into a room, like he knows he has to tolerate me and he's been told that includes being nice, but he never really gets his mouth turned up enough to look anything but irritated.

So Liam can smile and be happy. Just not around me.

Does he have a wife? Girlfriend? Maybe that's why he's been so cool to me. He has someone back home waiting for him.

Where is home? I thought I heard my mother say to her assistant that he's from the Tampa area. He probably lives in a nice little house with a pretty blond woman who has long legs and doesn't have to crane her neck to look up at him. They have a three-bedroom home with one bath and a half bath the previous owner put in, but they like the place and figure it will work until kids come.

Or does he have kids already?

I shake my head and push that thought away. No man with a beautiful wife and little kids would leave that behind to come work for me. The one day a week he has off when I'm not on the road wouldn't be enough to sustain a relationship, and the weeks and months away from those he loves, even for the amount he's getting paid, wouldn't be worth it.

I mean, for God's sake, it's not the fucking Depression. A guy like him could find work anywhere.

So no kids, but I bet he has a girlfriend or wife. No guy with a body like that and good looks stays single for long. My gaze travels up and down those faded jeans as he and Javier walk around the grounds.

Maybe he's a player. A different woman every night of the week.

That thought makes me chuckle. No way this guy is sleeping with a different woman every night. No way, no how. He's too much a follow the rules type. Those guys are never manwhores. Men like Liam are the steady kind of guys. They don't sleep around on someone if they care about them.

The way he is may sound boring to a lot of woman, but I can see how it would be really great to have a man like that. I've had the other kind, and that made me feel like shit, so maybe it could be nice to have a stable, steady man.

His girlfriend probably knows that, though. She likes how reliable he is and how secure he makes her feel. She's smart in that way. She likely is intelligent. Beautiful with a good head on her shoulders. I can see him going for someone like that. Not flashy. Just classically beautiful and sweet.

I look over toward the mirror on the far wall and see the last remnants of the purple dye job from a couple months ago peeking out from underneath the disheveled dark brown mess on top of my head that's the result of not bothering to do anything with my hair this morning. Definitely not classically beautiful. More like startlingly appealing to some men who like their women to look like a cross between Medusa and Lady Gaga.

Liam's girlfriend definitely looks forward to seeing him when he walks through the door. Why wouldn't she? I mean, he's got a great body, and I imagine if he actually likes a person, he could be quite pleasant to be around.

I watch him and Javier stop near that ridiculous plant my mother insisted we have in the garden last year. Big and flashy with bright pink floppy petals that remind me of elephant ears, it looks like a flower that requires constant attention or it will wither away and die. No wonder my mother loved it when the landscaper suggested it.

What does it feel like to have someone to look forward to seeing? I've never had that in my life. No one I've ever been with made me look forward to seeing them. They were simply always around, and then one day, they weren't.

Clearly, I've never loved anyone, and I doubt anyone's ever loved me because I don't think any of the guys I've been with could honestly say they looked forward to seeing me. Anticipation isn't really a thing when you're going full tilt, twenty-four seven in a relationship.

But that's lust. That's not love. I might not have much experience with love, well none actually, but I know what it's supposed to feel like. I sing about it in practically every song I perform.

Love is supposed to thrill you but comfort you. It's supposed to make you think the world doesn't suck, even while it still does way too damn often, because at the end of the day after all is said and done, you have someone who truly cares about your happiness to come home to.

That's what love is. Not hearts and flowers but the knowledge deep inside that whatever the world throws at you, no matter how bad it gets, you have someone covering your back and worrying if you're okay or not.

I bet that's what Liam's girlfriend feels all the time. It's the reason she fell in love with him. It certainly couldn't be because he's a scintillating conversationalist or someone who makes her laugh all the time. No, it's because whenever life gets her down, she only has to look behind her to see him watching and making sure no one ever hurts her.

He's good at that kind of thing. That's probably why he works as a bodyguard. He said he cares because it's his job, but I think he protects people because that's who he is. His girlfriend loves that about him. Everyone loves that about him. A big guy choosing not to be some jackass bully and pushing everyone around but protecting people instead, even when he can crush them like a bug? People love that.

I can see why, though. I mean, the world has way too many oversized asshole guys, so when you come upon someone like Liam, why wouldn't someone think he's pretty great?

Assuming they don't have to deal with his utter disdain every time he's in front of them.

Lost in my thoughts about his perfect life with the woman he loves, I don't see him looking up at me until he waves his hand. I focus on him and see no smile. Just a mixture of curiosity and disgust coming off him.

As always.

Sneering, I turn away, partly embarrassed that he caught me staring at him and partly annoyed at this perfect life he gets to return to when he doesn't have to be here barely tolerating me. His girlfriend probably greets him at the door like some submissive fifties housewife wearing pearls and a dress with her hair perfect.

Whatever. Not everyone can have that life. Some of us got stuck with something very different and don't get that lovey-dovey welcome every time we come through the door.

Not even from people who are supposed to be happy to see us.

Fuck, I need to get out of this house. I think I'm starting to go stir crazy.

Desperate to find anything to take my mind off my new bodyguard's perfect life, I head down to the kitchen to find something cool to drink. I might even go lay out near the pool. Doing that alone isn't pathetic like swimming all by yourself.

Thankfully, my mother and her assistant are nowhere to be found, so I can enjoy a glass of iced tea in peace and quiet. I take a big gulp and let it slide down my throat, loving how it cools everything on its way down. I swear if my mother comes storming in and launches into a lecture about how caffeine can be damaging to the vocal chords, I'm going to douse this entire room in my favorite drink and laugh as she stands there dripping from head to toe in the stuff.

After my second refreshing gulp, I hear voices and know my precious peace and quiet is soon ending. Unfortunately, I don't sneak away back up to my room fast enough to avoid hearing my mother and Liam having some discussion about security at the house here, and it doesn't take more than a few words to make me see red.

"I think the changes I've started to make to the security here at the estate will be a big improvement," he says with so much confidence that I want to charge out into the living room and ask the obvious question.

Why the hell do we have to change anything? What was wrong with the security the way it's always been here?

My mother, of course, loves the idea of changing the security. She probably has him devising plans to see if a large wall around the property or a moat would be a good idea. Anything to keep me in where she can have her always-watchful eye on me.

"I appreciate you taking the time to assess the situation and make improvements, Liam. I knew Jonah made a good choice the first time I saw you," she gushes.

Cool your jets, Mom. He's half your age and has a perfect life to go home to, unlike the nightmare we have here.

Her fawning all over him sets my teeth on edge, and it's not long before I march out to confront both of them. I find my mother reclining on the white tuxedo sofa like some woman in a painting waiting for someone to come by with a large palm and start fanning her. Liam's standing a few feet away smiling at her like anything happening right now could be considered amusing.

How nice that both Javier and my mother have been on the receiving end of his happy smiles today.

When the two of them see me, all smiles disappear. Nice.

"You know, those people are professionals," I say to him, not bothering to discuss this with my mother. It isn't her money who pays everyone here.

"What makes you think you should be telling them how to do their jobs? Will you be instructing me on how to sing next?" I snap.

Liam looks dumbfounded for a few seconds. When he finally speaks, I get the sense that he's not talking to me but to the room in general.

"Because we're all working toward the same goal," he says calmly, but that casual tone is forced. He likely wants to bark his opinion at me.

"Whatever I can do to help them I will, and they need

to do whatever they can do to help me," he continues explaining.

It all sounds very logical, but I hate it.

"What was wrong with what they were doing before?" I ask, silently adding to myself that Michael had no issues with anything the people here did when he was my chief of security.

Of course, my mother has to jump in and try to help Liam, her new favorite person around here. "Mia, he's only trying to make sure you're the safest you can be. That's what we all want."

By the time she gets to her second comment, I know it's not only to help him. She's trying to handle me. God, I hate being handled.

I throw her a look that tells her I'm not in the mood for what she's trying to do, but Liam answers my question. "Nothing a little tightening can't fix. There's nothing wrong with making good even better."

Now he's trying to handle me too. I have to give him credit. He's a quick learner. It only took him just over a week to figure out how to do that.

Except I'm not playing that game today.

I take a few steps closer to him and stop dead when he glares down at me. Flustered, I snap, "You're trying to make my home a fortress to keep me trapped. I won't let you do that."

Once again, my mother tries to soothe my ruffled feathers, but I'm done playing nice with her today too. Spinning around to face her, I yell, "I ran away because I felt trapped. Why can't you understand that? I'm like a prisoner in my own home, and now you think more security is a good idea? Did anyone ever think to ask me how I feel about that? About anything?"

My outburst shocks my mother into silence, but not Liam. Behind me, he says, "Regardless of why you did it, running away put you in danger. It's my job to protect you, so there will be no more running. If you want to go somewhere, I'll be with you from now on."

Every word out of his mouth sounds more and more oppressive, so by the time I spin back around to face him, I don't even try to stop myself from getting in his face. I'm a foot shorter than he is, so it's not exactly like I'm in his face, but the intention is the same and he understands immediately, if the surprised look in his eyes is any indication.

Pointing my finger up at him, I square my shoulders and say, "I am not a child. I do not need you with me whenever I want to go anywhere. I am not the President's daughter, and you are not my Secret Service detail. If I want to go somewhere and I don't want you hanging on me, I'll decide what's going to happen, not you. You can follow behind where no one can see you so I can live my life as I please. That's how it will be from now on, Liam. If you don't like that, then don't let the door hit you on your way out."

I don't know why, but once I finish laying down the law for him, I don't storm out like I should since I can feel the tears welling up inside me, threatening to spill out all over the place and make me look like some overwrought teenage girl. Instead, I stand there staring up at him, unable to move.

For his part, he doesn't flinch either. We're like two enemy soldiers on the field of battle, neither of us willing to back down. Of course, the field of battle is my living room in my house and on my estate, so if I wanted to, I could simply have him removed from the premises.

Why I don't do that is something I truly don't understand. Let him go back to his perfect life with his perfect girlfriend who loves him because he's big, strong, and protective. I should just send him packing.

But I don't.

Or more correctly, I can't. Actually, it's I won't because I don't want to. I have no valid reason for wanting him to stay, but as I stand here staring up at him and he stares down at me, I think I'd miss having him around. It makes no sense. He's only been here for a little over a week, and he hasn't been nice to me a day of the time he's spent in my house.

Still, he's the only person in my world who refuses to back down. That intrigues me. I might be a masochist, but I like this standoff thing we're doing. It makes me feel more alive than I've felt since I stopped touring six months ago. Nothing has ever felt as invigorating as performing in front of a crowd.

Nothing until this thing with him.

When he sighs and looks away, a sense of victory washes over me. That round went to me. But I hope Liam doesn't give in that easily from now on.

Keep challenging me, Mr. Big and Serious. I don't know why, but I like it.

Next time, maybe I'll be the one to give in first. Wouldn't that be a change?

CHAPTER SIX

iam

ALONE IN MY ROOM ON THE OPPOSITE SIDE OF THE house away from my client, I hear a noise that sounds like people laughing. Since no one seems to do much of that in this place, I dismiss it, sure it's the sound from someone's TV.

When the laughter gets louder and then the sounds of what I think might be people dropping heavy things on the floor drowns out the fun, I head to the hallway to check on what's happening without putting on more clothes than the black basketball shorts and old T-shirt I'm wearing. If someone's breaking into the house, there isn't time for pants and shoes.

I barely make it out of my room before I see a hoard of people coming toward me. Five women and a man all around my age come strolling down the hallway with enough bags and luggage like they plan to stay for the rest of their lives. That explains the sounds I heard.

"Hey, who's the new guy?" a tall blond with legs that look to be almost as long as mine asks.

The six of them stop and stare at me while I wonder if I've been dropped into some way off Broadway production of a bad play Mia's decided to put on at the house here. When I don't answer after a few seconds, they appear to lose interest in who I am and keep walking down the hallway with what looks to be everything they own.

I watch as each of them walks into a room, except for two women who may be sisters or may just look very similar because of their short black hair and bright red lipstick. None of them close their doors, and for the next few minutes as I look on in shock, they float in and out of the rooms, laughing and singing, with the one who asked about me doing some kind of dance as she moves from one doorway to the next.

Since I'm sure I'm awake and not having some terrible nightmare, I decide to leave the cast of whatever shitty production this is and take a walk outside. It would have been nice if Andrea had told me to expect a cavalcade of boisterous people tonight.

As the minutes go by, they get louder and louder until I can't hear myself think. Who the hell are these people? I know they're with Mia, but are they friends or people who work for her? I had assumed there would be a bigger staff to handle all her needs, but since they never appeared over the past couple weeks, I guess I just forgot about them.

Now I don't think I'll ever be able to forget or even

ignore them since they all seem to live at a decibel level akin to the sound of a jet taking off.

I stop at the pool and suddenly realize I can't hear them as much from here. Or maybe they've all been muzzled by security. That would be nice. Hell, that would be more than nice. It would be heavenly. I'd buy Javier and his guys a round of drinks for that.

But it only lasts for a few precious seconds before they start up again and sound like a pack of wild animals up there. Christ, how am I supposed to sleep with that racket right down the hall from me every night?

Taking a seat on the pool deck, I dangle my feet in the water and close my eyes as I cover my ears, desperate for a moment's peace. Now on top of a client who's two steps away from driving me nuts and her mother who's just a step behind her, there's this troupe of nonsense.

Unable to focus on anything, I hang my head and wish I could remember how much extra money I'm being paid for this assignment. The fact that I have to focus on that instead of the job is a clear indication this is not where I should be. I don't even need the goddamned money.

Why didn't I tell Jonah Bradley no instead of caving in after listening to my mother and her Pollyanna talk? I love the woman, but I swear to God in her world there are unicorns jumping over rainbows every day.

While I question nearly everything I've done since I said yes to this nightmare job, I hear someone say my name. Looking up, I see Mia standing next to me in jean shorts and a pink T-shirt. She says something, but between the noise and my hands over my ears, I can't hear her.

"Sorry, the circus came to town and set up shop in

my hallway. Any chance you can get that to stop for the night and every night after that?" I yell up to her.

She doesn't answer but gives me a smile that tells me she thinks I'm making a big deal out of nothing. When she turns around and walks away, I figure I'm going to be stuck with this madness for the rest of my time here, which may not be long since a security chief who hasn't gotten any sleep night after night isn't much use to anyone. A minute later, though, everything falls silent.

Mia returns shortly after and sits down next to me on the pool deck, dangling her feet in the water like I do. Smiling again, she says, "I figured you for someone who insists on being asleep by ten. Sorry the crew woke you up."

"Yeah," I say, leaning back on my palms as the landscaping lights nearby throw shadows across the water in front of me.

"Is that yeah you prefer to go to sleep early or yeah for something else?" she asks with a chuckle.

When I don't answer since I'm not really in the mood for talking after dealing with her crew, she quietly says, "You don't think much of my lifestyle, do you?"

Tired of holding my tongue at this house, I turn to look at her and shake my head. "To be honest, no. Who are all those people and why do they act like that when they come to someone's home?"

"Well, Chloe and Ivy, the two women who look alike, they're my makeup artists. Crystal is my hair stylist. She's the one with the look that could turn a man to stone. I'm guessing you've seen that look already, though."

I try to remember if any of the women stared me down like she wanted to turn me to stone, but I can't recall that. Maybe I was too busy being in shock that they all thought they should traipse down the hallway in the middle of the night like they're at Mardi Gras.

Mia continues, "Mitchell is my personal trainer. I guess he's easy to figure out since he's the only man. Fair warning, he's got a thing for guys with great bodies, so don't be surprised if he hits on you."

"Sorry to disappoint Mitchell, but I'm straight."

She shrugs like my announcement means nothing. "He won't care. He has a type, and as far as I can tell, you're it. To be honest, he must be distracted tonight because if he was paying attention and saw you standing up there in those shorts, I know he would have made a move on you."

Fucking terrific. Yet another infuriating distraction in this house of madness.

"Tiffany is my choreographer, and Ainsley is my life coach. Oh, and Ginger comes whenever I need new clothes. She's my personal shopper."

"I assume I've met Tiffany since there was at least one of the women dancing all the way down the hall," I say and then realize she just said one of those people was her life coach.

"What the hell is a life coach?" I ask, curious to know since I've heard people claim to need one more than a few times in the past.

"Ainsley helps me out with focusing on the positive."

I don't even try to hide how stupid I think that is. "Ainsley, the life coach who needs someone to clue her in that she should have manners enough to keep her voice down after midnight. Is she the one who sounds like she's birthing goats in her room right now? Because whatever that is, it's obnoxious. And why do you need hair and makeup people?"

My frustration seems to amuse Mia, and she smiles and shakes her head. "Men. They never understand the importance of hair and makeup. I need them so I don't look like some washed out hag on stage."

"Somehow I doubt you could ever look like a hag, but fair enough. Why do they live here, though? You've looked fine without them for weeks. On the road, I understand. Here? I don't get it."

"I'm surprised you have a problem with the Three Musketeers. I would have thought you'd look down your nose at Ainsley out of all of them."

Laughing at how easily she read me about that, I look up to see her life coach waving some item of clothing out her window. "I think she's trying some new moves your choreographer taught her. Either that or she thinks that's the way to get your attention. Whatever it is, I'm not seeing the use of a life coach."

Mia's expression turns serious, and she looks down at her feet in the water. "She's all that stood between me and losing it a while back. She makes me see my life has a lot of positive in it when I have a hard time finding it."

"You're a gorgeous woman with incredible talent and a voice millions of fans around the globe love, and you live on an estate that ninety percent of the people in this world can only dream of seeing, forget about owning. There. Now you can tell goat girl to go away and maybe I can get some sleep."

She turns to look at me with shock written all over her face for a long moment. I can't imagine why, although I doubt she's used to people talking to her like that. But it's not like anything I said wasn't true. She's all that and more. Why she needs some flaky woman to help her focus on the positive is beyond me.

"You…you can take one of the rooms in the east wing, if you want. That way you can get some sleep."

I can't help but be surprised at her offer. The east wing is where she and her mother have their rooms. For a second or two, I consider declining, but then a loud howl from one of her crew convinces me that if I don't, I might never get a moment of sleep again.

"Thank you. I appreciate that. I wouldn't be any good to you or anyone else if I'm always exhausted. I wouldn't want my protection of you to suffer because of that."

We sit silently looking at one another until suddenly she jumps up. "It's nothing. I'm still the same spoiled star you can't stand. This doesn't change that. Goodnight, Liam."

As I open my mouth to correct her, she hurries away before I can tell her I don't feel that about her, especially after she was so generous to give me a room away from her noisy crew. A twinge of guilt pinches at me that she truly believes I can't stand her.

I'm supposed to be her protector, the one person she can count on to keep her safe. What kind of bodyguard am I if she thinks I feel that way toward her?

CHAPTER SEVEN

$\mathcal{M}$ia

I RUSH INTO AINSLEY'S ROOM AND SLAM THE DOOR behind me, pressing my back to it to make sure no one can follow me in here. I need to talk to someone, and out of all the people in this house, Ainsley is the one I can trust the most.

She looks up from whatever yoga pose she's in that makes her look like some kind of deformed pretzel and her eyebrows shoot up into her forehead, the only sign that she's surprised to see me. I usually let the crew settle in before I begin demanding anything of them.

"Sure, come on in. I guess I should be happy I decided to wear clothes for my evening stretch. You do remember I prefer to do this in the buff, right?" she says in that crabby voice she uses on me when I've overstepped my bounds.

I want to explain to her that this is my house, so there

are no bounds, but I don't, preferring to keep her as an ally for what I have to say to her. "Sorry, but I've seen you naked dozens of times, Ains. Why aren't you doing your pretzel thing in the buff like always?"

She untwists herself while I wonder if Liam saw her naked and that's why my life coach is clothed for her nightly routine. Ainsley is a beautiful woman with a great body and beautiful long blond hair I would love to have, and unlike me, she isn't considered a spoiled pain in the ass.

Then again, her goat noises bothered him, so maybe he doesn't like her either.

"Earth to Mia. Come in, Mia."

Her voice tears me from my thoughts of whether or not Liam saw her naked, and I shake my head. "What?"

"I'm wondering why you're here. Is something wrong? Do you need help?" she asks.

"Liam couldn't sleep. He was wondering if you were birthing goats in here," I blurt out, not even sure why I'd tell her that.

The look she gives me tells me she isn't impressed with the new addition to my staff. "Liam. Hmmph. He looks like a Liam. Or a Henry. Something overbearing and bossy. Since when does what I do at bedtime concern anyone else?" she asks, returning to her cranky mood.

I quickly wave her question away. "Don't worry. I told him he could take one of the rooms on my side of the house, so he won't be bothering you."

Instead of making her happy, my comment seems to confuse her. At least that's the way it appears as she gives me a funny look like she doesn't understand a word I've said.

"Since when do you allow anyone to stay that close to you?"

Feeling exposed, like she can see right into my thoughts, I shrug and look away. "He's my personal bodyguard and head of my security team, so it's only right he's nearby. Right?"

"Right? Are you asking my permission to have the large, opinionated man who's got brooding down to a science close to you? If you are, I say no."

I can't help but smile. Ainsley always has a way of making me happy.

"Well, I'm not."

"Fine, but none of your other bodyguards have ever stayed on that side of the house. Speaking of that, where is Michael? Why isn't he here instead of Liam?"

The way she says Liam's name sounds like she already hates him. I don't think I'll bother to tell her the feeling is likely mutual.

"Michael's gone," I say, not wanting to explain anything more about him right now. "History. The past. Liam is my chief of security now, so that's that."

"Oookaaay."

The two of us stand in silence as I try to contain my emotions about Michael's leaving and my finding him with that girl. I don't want Ainsley to see me upset over it or she's going to want to talk about it, and the last thing I want to do is talk about that situation.

So I focus on the ugly pink color she chose to paint the walls in here instead, silently telling myself that while we're gone, the painters need to get in here and get rid of this color. Is it salmon? Chartreuse? No, that's green. Why couldn't she pick a nice delicate pink instead of this muddy shade of what used to be my favorite color?

"Is there something you want to talk about, Mia? You sounded okay on the phone the other day, but I'm assuming since you didn't tell me about Michael leaving and this new guy coming on board that you might want to talk."

Turning around, I force a smile and nod at her question. "You're the closest thing I have to a friend, Ainsley," I say in a low voice, suddenly ashamed at how few people I have in my life who I can talk to. "I need that now, so please, none of the life coach stuff when I tell you what's on my mind, okay?"

She gives me one of her sweet smiles I hope is genuine and takes a step toward me. Touching my hand, she says, "I am your friend, Mia. You can tell me anything. I won't tell a soul."

Unsure how to approach what I'm thinking about because I don't know what I'm feeling at this moment, I simply repeat the word Liam used and ask, "Do you think I'm gorgeous?"

"Yes. Why?" Ainsley asks, sitting down on her bed.

"Even with this purple mess still in my hair?" I ask, nervously tugging on the ends near my nape.

"Yes. Again, why?"

"Do you think someone like me could ever find love?" I ask, looking down into her light green eyes to see the truth in case she lies because she feels like she has to.

"Yes, and hoping the third time's a charm, why?"

"I just wanted to know. That's it."

Her eyes fill with sadness, and she asks, "Is this about Michael? Is that what this is all about?"

Suddenly, I can't stop the tears from coming. Burying my face in my hands, I let the misery I've felt since I saw him standing there with that girl in his apartment wash over me.

"I thought he cared about me. I thought that it didn't matter that we weren't sleeping together because he loved me. I thought we were soulmates, Ains. I really thought he cared about me. That he proved that someone could care about me and prove Jonny was full of it. I was so wrong. God, how could I have been so wrong?"

I feel Ainsley's arms envelop me, and I sink into her embrace. I've needed this from the second I realized Michael never cared like I thought he did.

"Oh, honey. He did. He cared about you. Whatever happened, he cared."

Shaking my head against her shoulder, I sob harder as I say, "No, he didn't. My mother fired him for getting me the hotel room, and he had a girl with him not two days later when I went to his place to talk to him. I thought after all that time we spent together after Jonny and I broke it off that he really cared about me. Not the me everyone else sees up on stage but the real me."

"I don't know why he did that, Mia. I just know he cared about you and he would have never let anyone hurt you."

"Then why was he with someone so soon? Days, Ains. Days. That's all it took to replace me. Days. It's been weeks and I'm still all alone," I ask as I lift my head off her shoulder and wipe the tears from my cheeks.

Ainsley gently takes me by the shoulders like she always does when she wants to make sure I'm listening to something she has to say. She looks straight into my eyes and shakes her head. "He wasn't good enough for you. He knew that, I bet. Don't give him another thought. You deserve the best this world can offer.

Michael wasn't that. He knew it. Now you know it too."

I take a deep breath in and let it out in a rush, wishing all my sadness could go with it. "What if I'm not the best? What if I'm just some spoiled little girl who got lucky because of her voice?"

My life coach shakes her head again, but now she looks angry. "And just who told you that little bit of nonsense?"

"Jonny was the one who said that to me. Remember?"

Ainsley screws her face into a tight grimace. She never did like Jonny.

"Your ex was a horse's ass. Period. Full stop. You know better than to believe that guy. I know you do."

I hang my head and sigh. "Yeah. I guess."

"I thought maybe it was the new person in your life. I was really starting to dislike your new head of security if it was," she says, still scowling.

With a shrug, I try to tell her Liam isn't why I'm questioning everything about myself. Not really. "No. He didn't say anything. He's not like that. Well, maybe he is, but that's not why I'm asking you these things," I say as I sit down on the bed next to her.

"Then why? You're a beautiful person, Mia. Inside and out. I know you don't let everyone see that all the time, but that doesn't change the fact that you are. What's got you thinking that you're some spoiled little girl?"

I try to think of a way to explain what I'm feeling without bringing Liam into it. I don't need my life coach hating the only person I truly have to depend on when I leave this house. He's not the reason I'm doubting I'm worthy of having the best or ever finding love either.

Well, not the entire reason.

Wiping my tears away again, I shake my head. "I've been so lucky, Ains. So lucky. I wanted to sing, and the world has taken to my songs like I never dreamed it would. All the hard work has been worth it, so don't think I'm doubting that. It's just that at the end of the day, I sleep alone in my bed, and it's been a long time since anyone even tried to be with me. The tabloids and social media are so sure I'm sleeping with half a dozen guys a week. If they only knew how it really was."

I stop before I say the one word that will get me crying again. I can't say it or I'll turn into a blubbering mess because it's true.

But before I can warn Ainsley not to say it either, she blurts it out. "How lonely it really is for someone like you?" she asks.

The tears come just as I knew they would, and this time I can't stop them. My body shudders as sobs wrack every inch of me because that single word is the truest expression of what my life is like.

Lonely.

I read in those rags they sell at the grocery stores that my mother insists on buying that I can have any man I want and I pick and choose who comes and goes from my bed. What a joke! My bed has me in it every night. That's it. Me and too many pillows because I went through that faze when I couldn't have enough of them on the bed.

But that's it. Mia and pillows. No hot men lining up to spend their nights with me. No picking and choosing. Just a single lonely woman wondering why if she's supposed to have her choice of everything in the world does she has nothing she wants.

Ainsley wraps her arms around my shoulders and squeezes me to her. "Oh, Mia, I'm sorry. I didn't mean to say the wrong thing. I know this life is hard for you. From the outside, you look like you have a picture-perfect life with everything you want. Those horrible social media people make up all those stories about you being a terrible person or sleeping around, and every time I see one of them, I want to scream, so I can only imagine how you feel. Don't let them get you down. You aren't anything like those people say, and anyone who's close to you can attest to that."

"I wish."

That's not true, and she knows full well it isn't. My mother can't attest to that. She says what she knows the world has to hear to love me so the money can keep rolling in, but she doesn't believe a word that comes out of her mouth.

Her assistant and that person they hired to pretend to be me on social media don't believe any what Ainsley just said. They're like everyone else. They do what they have to in order to keep the world loving me, but they don't feel that way.

Liam doesn't think that way either. I know it. Every time he talks to me, I hear the disdain in his voice. I can tell even before my crew showed up that he regrets taking this assignment, as if protecting me is a chore and not something he truly wants to do.

"Honey, what's brought all of this on? Is it because we've all been away these past few weeks? You should have called me. I could have talked you down from this ledge so you didn't have to feel this way."

I push my hair off my face and wipe my tear-soaked cheeks for a third time. "I don't know, Ains. I just feel like in the past couple weeks everything I do is wrong. I don't want to feel this way, you know?"

Her pale green eyes fill with sympathy. My life coach has helped me weather all sorts of bouts of insecurity like this, and one of the most important parts of that is showing me she cares. Ainsley has no idea how much it means to see that in her eyes right now.

"Mia, I know you don't want to feel that way. Who would? We all want to feel like we're an important part of the world for ourselves and not for what we can do for other people. You're no different. What did I tell you the first day I met you? Do you remember?"

I nod and feel my mouth turn up into a smile like it always does when I think of that day. Ainsley had been referred to me by my ex-business manager, but by the time she got back from a vacation to see her family out in Colorado, George was gone, replaced by my mother, who didn't think I needed anything like a life coach. She tried to turn her away at the front gates, but Ains insisted, telling her that she wanted to meet me because she was a huge fan and could help my career. An hour later, I felt like I'd met my best friend in the world when she said those words to me I'll never forget.

"Everyone wants to be loved, Mia. Just because you look like you're loved more than other people doesn't mean you don't have the right to want to be loved when you're not in the limelight."

Those words come out like they're a mantra, something tattooed on my brain so I never forget that I deserve love like everyone else in the world. She smiles and nods as each syllable comes out loud and clear, just as she told me to say them that day.

"Exactly. You have every right to want to be loved in the way that makes you happy. Don't ever forget that."

And just as quickly as the good feelings come, they leave again when my fear that it will never happen surges inside me. "But what if no matter how much I want it, the love never happens?"

With a gentle smile, she shakes her head. "Impossible. You want it badly enough, it can't help but happen. Anyway, you're going to find someone who loves you in all the right ways. I know it. I knew it the first time I talked to you. You have such a great energy that people can't help but fall in love with you. Trust me. The man who's right for you is out there. You'll meet him. I have no doubt at all."

"Thank you, Ains. I needed to hear that tonight."

"That's what I'm here for, honey. It's literally my job to help you see how wonderful you are. Talk about a sweet gig," she says with a giggle.

"Well, thank you. Oh, by the way, I hate this pink in this room. It makes me feel like I'm in the middle of that medicine commercial."

Ainsley looks around at the ugly pink walls and lets out a heavy sigh. "It does sort of look like Pepto Bismol but with a dash of something gray. Maybe when we're gone the guys can paint it a nice pink."

"Exactly what I thought." Standing from the bed, I smile down at her. "I'll let you get back to your evening stretches. Thanks for helping me to see things clearly."

"Anytime, Mia."

When I get back to my side of the house, I wonder which room Liam took. I couldn't tell Ainsley how I'm starting to feel about him, and not just because she likely wouldn't approve, even if she does think I'm worthy of the kind of love I want.

I couldn't tell her because I'm not sure what I'm feeling. All I know is that when I saw him sitting by the pool tonight in those shorts and ratty old T-shirt, he looked like a different person and offering him a room near me on this side of the house seemed like the most natural thing to do.

Even if I've never once before with anyone who works for me even thought that for a second.

With one last glance down the hallway before I walk into my bedroom, I guess he's in the room farthest away from mine. It's a good choice since it has a fireplace that the other bedrooms don't. I can see him liking that, even though we rarely get weather cold enough to need that kind of heat here in Tampa.

Or maybe he chose that room because that's the farthest he can get away from me without being on the other side of the house where all the noise is.

CHAPTER EIGHT

iam

WHEN I WAKE UP AT FIVE TO GET MY WORKOUT IN, I'M thankful to hear nothing but silence. Never before in my life have I been so grateful to hear not a single noise. I know it won't last for long, so I hurry and get dressed so I can at least get something accomplished before the circus wakes up.

Then again, if they're like Mia, they might stay in bed until noon. I can only hope that's the case.

An hour later, my day has started out better than I could have expected after the arrival of the entourage. Nobody interrupted me while I was in the gym, and as I stroll around the pool area considering a swim before I get down to work, I see not a single soul.

This might just be okay. Sure, they were loud and obnoxious last night, but that doesn't mean they act like wild animals all the time. Maybe I was too hasty in my impression of them.

I enjoy some laps in the pool and then a good, hot shower afterward, regretting how easily I jumped to conclusions with Mia's crew. Toweling off, I gaze out my window and remind myself not to think so negatively. It's a habit I got into living with Wilder recently, but I need to break it now. Just because he's who he's always been doesn't mean everyone else is simply because I judge them on first impressions.

As I wrap the towel around my waist, I mull over what I have planned for today. I need to move the rest of my things to this new room on this side of the house, and then I need to speak to Andrea about who handles the security on Mia's tours since she's scheduled to go on the road in less than a month. I would have liked more time to prepare, but her mother's kept putting me off, saying we could talk the next day.

Of course, the next day came and went over and over, and still we haven't discussed plans I need to know in order to effectively keep her daughter protected.

But first, I need coffee. Caffeine then work.

The scent of that delicious blend from Sumatra that everyone here loves beckons me down the stairs. I have to admit, while much of this job is less than wonderful, the extra benefits of what I get to enjoy for meals makes up for a lot of it, and that coffee Andrea raves about is the best I've ever had, now that I asked the cook to make me my own pot that doesn't resemble hot beige water.

I pour myself a mug and splash in some milk and sugar, happy I'm the only person awake at this hour. It's barely seven in the morning, and I'm loving every moment of silence. Even the cook seems to have decided to leave me alone today.

An enormous room, the kitchen somehow feels cozy. It's probably the tan and brown granite the designer chose for the backsplash. Even with all the stainless-steel appliances and white cabinets, this room is warm and welcoming. It may be my favorite room in the house after my own.

Just as I lift the cup to my lips to enjoy that first sip of coffee for the day, my heart sinks as the sounds from last night begin again. Shaking my head, I sit down at one of the two islands in the center of the kitchen and silently mourn the loss of peace at the estate.

With every second that passes, the racket grows louder and louder. Someone's playing some kind of music that sounds like it wants to be salsa but whoever's playing the instruments have no clue about that kind of music. Or maybe it's that another one of the crew begins to play music in their room that clashes with the first person's, creating nothing but an auditory horror.

It doesn't matter because the end result is the same assault on the silence and my ears.

Before I can finish my coffee, all six of them flood into the kitchen and begin to make breakfast for themselves. Each person talks over the others, and I'm sure no one is actually listening to anyone but themselves. They laugh, presumably at their own jokes since they can't hear anything else, and in a matter of minutes, I feel like I'm trapped in the world's busiest beehive, except this one involves pancakes and something the personal trainer brings out of the refrigerator that smells like feet.

None of them acknowledge my presence, which is

fine, but it's almost like they insist on pretending they're the only people in the house. Since Mia's not up yet, I have to wonder why none of them are worried they might wake her.

I consider asking, but I can't seem to get the words to form as I watch in dismay while they demolish the kitchen that had been clean before they arrived just a few minutes ago. One of the women, the one I think might be that ridiculous life coach who was making goat noises last night, gives me a sideways glance that may be a glare, but that's about all the acknowledgement they afford me as they buzz around like the most annoying bugs ever to exist.

When I stand up to set my dirty coffee mug on the counter, I have to push my way through the trainer and his stinky breakfast and one of the two hair stylists to get even near to the sink. The woman huffs her irritation that I've interrupted whatever the hell she's doing with an onion bagel and the jar of peanut butter she's dunking it into, but I ignore her and deposit my mug where Andrea told me we put the dirty dishes.

"You know, you could wash that," one of the women says behind me. "It's not like it's that hard."

Something snaps inside me, and I whip around to see five women and Mitchell staring at me with looks of disgust on each of their faces. So they're disgusted with me? Well, they have no idea how much I already can't stand them. Forget all that nonsense about jumping to conclusions. I was right with my first impression of all of them. They're rude, presumptuous, and whatever the fuck the woman next to the sink is doing with the damn peanut butter is downright gross.

"You know what's not that hard? Remembering that

the world doesn't revolve around you? Oh, and if you think I'm talking to someone other than you, you're wrong. You burst into the house last night like you own the place, waking everyone up with your bullshit, and guess what? None of it is funny or charming or whatever the hell you think you are. Nope. Just irritating. Some of us actually have jobs here that involve something other than focusing on our own needs, so why don't you get the hell out of the way so we can do them?"

I think the last time I had that many people staring at me with such anger was when Cash, Cade, Alex, Wilder, and I came home from jail, and we had to face all of our parents at once. At least they had some feeling of affection for me. These six look like they'd hog-tie me and roast me over a fire if any of them were strong enough to take me.

In the silence, their hatred for me comes through loud and clear, so I leave without having a single thing for breakfast, just another reason I can't stand any Mia's crew. On my way upstairs, Andrea catches me looking all happy, like any of what's happening around us is normal.

"Good morning, Liam. Did you have breakfast already?" she asks in a chipper voice.

"No," I grunt out, still fuming from all those people ruining yet another day in my life.

"I'm sure Cecelia would be happy to make you anything you want. I know you don't tend to eat like we do, but she's a fantastic cook. We love having her working here for us."

Something about the way she says that stops me cold, and I turn around and march back down the stairs to ask her about who all works here and why we all need to live here. The noise in the kitchen returns as each of those selfish people begins talking again, no doubt ignoring everyone else in the room once more.

I point toward where they babble on and on and shake my head. "What is this? How can people live like that? They show up last night making enough noise to wake the dead, and this morning they get up and it's the same decibel level of nonsense. How long will this continue?"

Andrea glances toward the kitchen and then smiles at me. "Oh, they're here until Mia goes out on tour. This is her routine when she's getting ready to go on the road. Everyone lives with her here and they spend every waking moment together getting in synch."

The way she explains it makes it seem perfectly normal that a circus has moved into Mia's house. Sure. Who doesn't have a hoard of obnoxious people storming in at midnight and then taking over?

Then I realize the worst part of this all. "They don't go until she does, and they'll be around all the time when she's out on tour?" I ask in dread as images of chaos fill my mind.

I'll never have another peaceful moment on this job. Fuck.

Nodding her head enthusiastically, Andrea answers, "Oh, yeah. They're Mia's people. She can't do a tour without them. She'd be lost."

I wish they'd get lost. Permanently.

"Okay. Thanks. It might be a good idea for you to inform me ahead of time of any people joining the household, Andrea. My job is to protect your daughter. It's ten times more difficult when I don't know the circumstances of who's living here."

Patting me on the shoulder, she smiles. "Next time. I didn't think of it this time because I'm used to them all. They're so full of life. I love how they make Mia feel."

Like the Mad Hatter?

I don't say that, but instead take advantage of having Andrea here to ask her about the security on the tour. She explains that it's hired out through her management company to local officials and contractors. Why she couldn't tell me that the first time I asked her about this and every time since I have no idea.

"Then I'm going to need a full list of every agency and contractor involved and ASAP. I need to coordinate with each group in every city on the tour."

I take a step to walk back upstairs, but Andrea's look of confusion stops me. "Is there something wrong?"

She shakes her head, but it's obvious she has some issue with what I've just requested. "No. It's just that we've never done it like that."

The noise in the kitchen suddenly grows loud enough again that my head starts pounding. "Never done what like that? I'm sure Michael as the head of her protective unit dealt with each group on the tour stops, didn't he?"

"No. I've always been the one who's handled things. The businesses we use are very professional and have never failed to keep Mia safe."

Is this woman serious?

"So what did Michael do when Mia went out on the road?" I ask in stunned amazement that one of the biggest stars in the world has had such lax protection.

Andrea shrugs. "He went with her, of course."

"To do what, exactly? See the sights? Take a vacation? What was he doing if he wasn't making sure everything was in place with the security for Mia?"

"He was always nearby. It's not like he left her alone or hung out at the hotel. I don't want you thinking that's how things were because they weren't. I'm just not sure why you need to coordinate with every place that provides security for the shows."

I lean down so I'm in Andrea's face and answer her. "So no crazy maniacs get close to your daughter. She's one of the most known people on the planet, Andrea. You don't think there are people who want to get to her? Consider yourself lucky that she didn't get hurt because of the way you people have been handling security up to this point. Christ, you should consider yourself lucky that someone didn't just pluck her up and take her prisoner. She's a superstar. People get obsessed with women like Mia. So get me that list and get it to me today so I can start to contact each of these people and make sure no one gets to your daughter who isn't cleared to be near her."

As I storm up the stairs, I can't decide if Mia's mother is simply negligent or actually someone who might want to see her daughter get hurt. Maybe not consciously, but damnit she has a funny way of showing she wants to protect her. She gets Jonah to convince me to take this job, supposedly because I'm perfect for it, and then she just thinks things are going to stay status quo when basically all her last head of security did was lounge around like one of Mia's friends on an extended sleepover.

I should have known this assignment would be a nightmare just by how much he was willing to pay me to take it. All the warning signs were there, but I ignored them because my mother convinced me of something that isn't remotely close to being true.

Thankfully, within an hour, Andrea emails me the list of each contractor and security personnel in the cities Mia's scheduled to perform in, but it only takes a few calls for me to realize I need more men working directly with me if this tour is going to be as safe and secure as I want it to be. The locals Andrea has always worked with are good, but they aren't good enough for one of the world's biggest stars.

I find Andrea in her office down on the first floor near the living room and have to marvel at the quiet that's come over the house. The entourage must have all gone out for the day. Thank God for small favors.

As I walk in to sit down so we can discuss how to get the men I need here as quickly as possible, she smiles and asks, "You got my email? I made sure to send it as soon as I got in here this morning."

"I did. That's what I'm here about. I need more men, so I'm going to contact Jonah at VIP today and get things moving so they can get up to speed before the tour starts. I don't want to work with anyone who isn't fully on board when things get going. I think four should do it."

Her smile quickly disappears, and she shakes her head as worry settles into her expression. "Oh, Mia isn't going to like that."

"Well, I'll explain it to her. She'll see I'm right," I say as I stand to leave, already tired after only half a day awake.

"You're going to have to do more than that. Only Mia can approve your request. I may handle things involving security, but I technically stepped over the line when I got rid of Michael. If you want more men, you need to get her to agree."

"Okay. I'll handle that now because I don't want any of us to be caught flat-footed when the tour begins," I say as I head out to find Mia.

After our talk last night, I don't anticipate any problems with my request. The woman gave me a room on her side of the house when she saw how noisy her crew was. This will be nothing compared to that.

I spy her out near the pool with the six of them and walk out there to get things moving on this project. All of them are sprawled out on chaise lounges in bikinis, all except Mitchell who somehow thought a white Speedo was a good choice for today. Stifling my need to chuckle at how idiotic he looks lying there, I stop beside Mia and look down at her.

It occurs to me that I've never seen her in a bathing suit in all the time I've lived and worked here. I had no idea she had such a great body. She never works out, so it must be natural.

At least that's what it looks like in her black string bikini.

"I need to speak to you for a few minutes. Nothing big, but it needs to be handled today," I say when she doesn't open her eyes to acknowledge my presence.

She looks up at me and waves her hand to dismiss me. "Later. We're busy."

Yet another time today I'm stunned. I look around at the group of them to see they're doing nothing but lying in the sun. She can do that anytime. Hell, as soon as she hears me out and gives me the green light for more guys, she can go back to doing nothing.

"No. Now."

Those two words get all eyes on me, and I find the six of her crew staring daggers at me. Mia sits up, almost as if she can't believe I said no, and shakes her head. "Are you deaf? I said we're busy."

I look down into her dark eyes flashing rage and shake my head at her. "And I said I need to talk to you. Now."

Grabbing her white cover up, she rips it off the back of the chaise lounge and storms away without a word, leaving me with the people who started my day off like shit glaring up at me like I'm some kind of fucking villain because I need to do my job. I follow her inside and find her fuming in the living room, pacing back and forth, her bare feet making a slapping sound with each angry step on the tile.

Before I can speak, Andrea walks into the room from her office and only takes a second to size up the situation. She probably feels the anger coming off both of us because as soon as she takes two steps toward us, she spins around and hurries back out. I stand there in amazement that everyone tolerates this nonsense from Mia. How the hell does anything get done around here?

"I heard what you said to my friends this morning. I should make you apologize," Mia snaps on one of her passes by me.

"For what? Informing them of the fact that they're the most self-centered people I've ever met? I won't apologize for telling the truth. Now what I wanted to talk to you about was security."

She stops in front of me and holds her hand up in front of my face. "I didn't finish what I wanted to say, so I'm not interested in what you have to say yet."

I tilt my head left and right, hoping to crack my neck and possibly ease the tension headache that's making me feel like the top of my skull is about to blow off. "Mia, I won't apologize to them, but if I upset you, then I'm sorry. Now I need to talk about security for your tour."

"Talk to my mother. She handles all of that. Now if you're done intruding on my meditation time, I'm going to go back and hope to find my center again."

Mia moves to walk around me, but I step in front of her, blocking her path. "Not yet. I need four more men to work directly with me while you're on tour. The locals your mother has aren't good enough. She says I need your okay, so as soon as you give it, we can be done."

Her face lights up in shock. "Four more? Four more men like you? No way!"

"You're damn lucky nothing's happened to you so far, Mia. The security situation your mother and those local people at each tour stop have going is lax, to say the least. I need men working directly for me to make sure you're safe."

Taking a step closer to me, she stops just before her cover up touches my arm and shakes her head. "No. I already feel like I'm trapped in this house. Four more of you and I'll feel like a prisoner of war. No way."

"I can't do my job without those four men. If you can't agree to this, then I'll have to resign. VIP will send someone to replace me by tomorrow, I'm sure. Your choice, Mia."

When I look down into her dark eyes, I see the idea of my leaving bothers her. She's probably worried that someone new would be even more of a hardass than I am.

"Two, but no more."

I shake my head, unwilling to bargain on this point. "Four or I go. Your choice."

She stares up at me with rage in her eyes, but there's

something else there I see now too. I can understand why so many men think she's one of the most beautiful women in the world. The way she can infuriate a person while at the same time looking so breakable like she needs him to protect her from the harshness of the world is very seductive.

That's nothing I can let in, though. Getting involved in any way with a client is always a mistake.

Still, I can't deny she has an effect on me.

CHAPTER NINE

$\mathcal{M}$ia

HE'S CLOSE ENOUGH THAT I FEEL THE HEAT COMING off his body. I've never felt that from anyone in my entire life. Is it because he's so much bigger than me, or was he working out before he came to talk to me out at the pool?

I glance down and notice he's wearing jeans, so he couldn't have been at the gym. Is he always this hot? Like literally hot?

Maybe if he didn't insist on wearing a dress shirt in eighty-degree weather. That would explain why he's so hot. I can't stop myself from inhaling, curious to know if he's sweating. It's weird, but this man intrigues me. One minute he has nothing but utter contempt for everything I am, yet the next minute he's here telling me he needs more people to make sure I'm safe.

"Tell me why you need four more of you. Michael

never needed anyone else. He thought the locals, as you call them, were fine."

Liam rolls his eyes and smiles in that way that tells me he's about to insult someone. I've only been around him for a few weeks, but I already know when he's about to lay some verbal smackdown on someone.

"Michael was a moron when it came to keeping you safe. I told your mother this and I'll tell you. You're damn lucky no one yanked you off the street and took you home to make you his personal Mia doll. With the security as careless as it's been in the past, I can't believe you're still here to go out on tour at all."

The way he says that, so intense and in that deep voice of his, frightens me. Taking a step back, I try not to be freaked out, but I can't stop myself. I feel vulnerable, something I hate.

"Really? It was that bad? Why would my mother do that?"

Liam frowns, making his very attractive face look even more serious than it usually does. "Because she's not a security specialist. For what it's worth, either was Michael. I am, though, and I'm telling you I can't stay as your head of security with such slipshod protection surrounding you."

Every word out of his mouth sounds more terrifying than the last, and I feel myself start to become overwhelmed by fear. I need to fight the urge to hide in my shell and never come out again, though. I've learned that from Ainsley.

"Liam, I can't live like I'm some caged animal. Even out on tour, I need to feel normal. I can't perform if I'm freaked out with people hovering over me like I'm always in danger."

"You won't have to be."

He says that with such certainty that I want to believe him. "You say that, but four more guards means exactly that. I'll be trapped."

Liam's face turns hard for a moment, and I brace for him to fight me more on this. He doesn't, though, pleasantly surprising me.

In a soft voice that might be even sexier than his usual deep voice, he says, "Mia, my one and only job is to protect you. That's it. That's all I'm trying to do."

I let out a heavy sigh and shake my head. "Why does it have to feel so oppressive?"

Still in that soft tone, he answers, "I don't want it to feel like that. I promise we'll be invisible. You'll probably forget we're even around."

I look up to see a kind expression on his face. "I doubt that."

"I'll do everything in my power to make sure you don't know we're around. I promise."

When I stare into his blue eyes, I secretly hope I won't forget he's around. I like knowing he's nearby. He drives me nuts and every person in my crew hates him, but I've grown to like Liam being in my life. I didn't know how much I needed to truly feel safe until he came along.

"I just don't want to feel like a prisoner, Liam. That's all."

"And I don't want to feel like your jailer."

Not able or even interested in fighting him on this anymore, I nod and let out a sigh of surrender. "As long as I don't have the four of them hanging around constantly."

"You won't."

"I mean, you being around is enough. Four more of you and I think I might go crazy," I say with a smile.

He understands I'm attempting to be nice and smiles back. "So you're okay with me being around? I can only imagine how much your entourage hates that."

"A lot, but you aren't working for them. You're working for me, and as long as you agree that I do what I want, when I want, we'll be fine."

Suddenly, all the softness and happiness in him fades away, leaving that hard man I met the first day he came here. The intensity in his gaze frightens me now as he looks down into my eyes like he's trying to make me understand something I refuse to.

But then he begins to speak, and I know he's still the man I've grown to enjoy having around me.

"Mia, I would lay down my life if it meant you were safe. If that's a problem, maybe you should tell me now so I can resign and VIP can provide you with another head of security. But if you want to be sure you're safe, then I need to do my job and that may mean you don't get to do what you want whenever you want."

For the second time in this conversation, he's mentioned resigning, and both times, my chest tightened at the mere words. I don't know why, but I hate the thought of him leaving and not being in my life anymore. I don't understand it since we barely know each other, but the pain in my chest tells me I want him to stay.

Even more, Michael never made me feel this safe, and never once did he say he'd die for me.

So I quietly relent and give Liam what he wants. "I can live with that. And the four more guys."

That makes him smile, and for a moment, I get lost in how sexy he looks when he gets what he wants. "I'll start working on that this afternoon so we're ready for when the tour kicks off next month."

"Thank you. For everything," I say, wishing I had more to discuss with him as he moves to walk away.

I can't think of anything, so he keeps moving toward the hallway, looking back at me as he says, "You're welcome, but there's no need to thank me. It's my job."

With every step, he gets farther away, and I wish I had any reason to stop him. I know it's stupid, but something about the way he said it's just his job hurt my feelings.

That's silly, though. It is his job to protect me. He was just stating the obvious.

Nothing would never work between the two of us anyway, so I need to stop thinking about how sexy he is when he smiles and how gorgeous his blue eyes are when he's trying to convince me to do something I don't want to do. He's not my type.

The Liams of the world are too serious for the Mias of the world. He's all rules and regulations, and I need to run free. Or at least I need to feel like I'm not being chained to the floor every second of the day. He spends his time worrying about security, and all I want to do is have fun and live my life.

No, we would never work out. Still, I can't deny I like him.

"What did Mr. Tight Ass want?"

I turn to see Ainsley standing next to me watching Liam walk away down the hall. "See anything you like there, Ains?"

Her cheeks instantly grow red, and she gives me a scowl. "Him? Are you kidding? His chi and my chi would not work together. The man has no yin in him. He insists on constantly conquering every situation he encounters. He's like yang overload."

Liam disappears out the door to the gardens as I get my last look at him and Ainsley's complaints about him filter through my brain. "He said he'd die for me. Michael never said that. No one has ever said that."

"He's a bodyguard, Mia. It's sort of in the job description. I'm sure they're paying him a king's ransom to keep you safe. I wouldn't put too much stock in him saying he'd die for you. That's just all that yang."

I smile and nod, knowing she's right. "Yeah, sure. I know. It did feel nice to hear, though. I mean, who wouldn't like to know there's someone who would lay down their life to protect you?"

"Mia, that guy doesn't have an ounce of the feminine in him. It's like he's a total Alpha. Just being around him takes all the happiness out of me. I don't know how you do it."

Shrugging, I smile, but not too big so she can see how much I like spending time around Liam. "I don't know. I think of him like a challenge."

Unimpressed, she makes a face that looks like she just ate something gross. "Sure, but does he ever not come into a room like he's Captain America? Maybe if he didn't give off the vibe that he hated everyone, including you, ninety percent of the time, I could see someone finding him sort of attractive."

"He doesn't hate you," I say before turning to head back outside to the pool. "Just your goat noises."

I chuckle when I hear her huff in disgust behind me. "They are not goat noises. You know, I think you and that guy spent too much time alone without me and the rest of the crew here to act as a buffer. He's already rubbing off on you. You never thought my evening stretches sounded like goat noises before he said that."

She's right, but I won't tell her that. I don't want her to hate Liam, especially now that I know I definitely don't hate him.

"I was only kidding, Ains. Let's go back outside and see if I can slough off all of his yang and make you happy."

Next to me, she grumbles, "That's going to take an old priest and a young priest, at the very least. Talk about yang overload. Someone should cut back on his energy drinks. I think he's got too much testosterone coursing through his system."

I wrap my arm around her shoulders and squeeze her to me. "I love you, Ains. You never fail to make me smile."

That makes her happy, so she gives up her complaining about the other person who always seems to have a way to make me smile. I won't tell her about that, though.

CHAPTER TEN

iam

MY EYES FLY OPEN AT THE SOUND OF SOMEONE yelping, or maybe that's the life coach with her goat birthing noises. I scrub the sleep from my face and look around. Where am I? Nothing looks familiar.

Oh, right. I switched rooms a couple nights ago. Nothing like waking up to the sound of some animal in agony to confuse a guy.

I slowly come to my senses and realize it's Mia's entourage making all the noise. Because of course it is. I yearn for the days before they arrived. I truly do.

As I grumble to myself about how selfish these people are, I look out the window and see the sun isn't even up yet. God, what time is it?

Grabbing my phone, I see 4:40 in big white numbers across the screen. Did I somehow sleep through an entire night of them partying, or has something else kept them up all night? It has to be that they haven't gone to bed yet because these are not the type of people to wake up early.

The noise continues, and I figure out it's not in the west wing. Did they decide to take over the entire house? How does Mia live like this? She didn't stay up all night before they got here.

I roll out of bed and grab a pair of gray sweatpants and a white T-shirt from the dresser that's on the opposite side of the room from where it used to be. Still sort of groggy, I don't bother putting shoes on, instead grabbing my slides. If these people want a professionally dressed me, then they shouldn't wake me up before five in the morning.

My head begins to throb with every step down toward the main living area where the six people I hate the most in the world have gathered to make a commotion for some reason. I see Andrea dressed in a white robe pacing back and forth across the living room and wonder if there's been bad news.

"What's going on?" I ask, still not fully awake and needing coffee, but curious.

Andrea stops her path across the room a few feet from where I stand and wrings her hands. I notice she looks genuinely worried too.

"Mia's stalker's back."

Stalker? How the fuck is it that the man in charge of protecting Mia hasn't heard about this goddamned stalker before this? I swear to God these people want to see her hurt.

Suddenly wide awake, I ask, "Back? What do you mean?"

I think if she gives me some nonsensical answer like

she does so often when she answers my questions that I'm going to blow a gasket this time. Thankfully, this morning, Andrea seems to be willing to tell all, which saves me from having to show yet again that I have no patience for these people.

"He's been silent for over a year. Everyone thought that he had just given up. Some of us, including the police, thought that maybe he died. I'd hoped he'd never return, but with her tour coming up, I guess we shouldn't be surprised," she says before she turns and resumes her pacing back toward the entrance to the hallway.

"Uh, did any of you even for a moment consider the idea of telling me about this stalker?" I ask, not even trying to hide my frustration at being kept in the dark about this.

Andrea shrugs as she turns around to come back toward me. "We didn't think it was worth mentioning. I mean, he's been gone for over a year. Stalkers usually don't disappear for that long without something bad happening to them, right?"

"Well, you should have told me anyway. How the hell am I supposed to keep Mia safe when I don't know all the dangers that may be lurking out there? I need you to tell me everything you know about this stalker. I'm serious, Andrea. Leave nothing out."

She stops in front of me again and sighs. "Okay. As I said, he's been gone for over a year. Every other time, he would start sending her letters just about a month before she went out on tour. The last time he didn't, so I thought we were in the clear. But a few hours ago, one of the letters arrived."

I hold up my hand to stop her before she goes any further. "How? It's the middle of the night. The post office certainly didn't deliver it after midnight, and I'm doubting Fed Ex or UPS did either. So how did it get here? Who found it and where?"

Andrea flails her arms in front of her face like she's trying to shoo away a bug and begins to cry. "I found it. It came in yesterday's mail, but I didn't get to look at everything that was delivered until late last night. I found it in the middle of the stack, the same white envelope with a heart drawn where the return address should be. I swear, Liam, my blood ran cold when I saw that because that's what the stalker always put on the envelopes before."

Okay, so it did come by mail. That's good. We can probably find out something from the post office if we have the envelope.

"What did you do with it?" I ask, certain she didn't call the police. If anything, Andrea would have called someone in the media first.

"I talked to her crew about it, and we agreed I should give it to Mia, like I always do. She has it up in her room. She won't come out. She's a nervous wreck. Every time before, the letters would start coming and she'd fall apart right before the tour. She's like that now too. She keeps saying, 'He's come back' over and over. We're all beside ourselves with worry."

"Okay. I'm going to go up to talk to Mia. You calm these people down. All this hysteria isn't going to do your daughter any good. If they keep this up, she's never going to be in any shape to go out on tour, so get them out of here if they can't relax."

Andrea's mouth drops open in shock. "What do you mean she won't be able to go out on tour? She has to. Three weeks from now, the first show is scheduled for the pavilion right here in Tampa. She can't miss the show that kicks off the tour."

"Then calm down her entourage. How can anyone expect her to perform with all this madness surrounding her?" I say as I start back up the stairs to go speak to Mia.

"This is always how they are, Liam. Mia's used to it."

Stopping on the staircase, I glare down at her and snap, "Then she's been used to being mistreated. Now stop those goddamned people from making all that noise and let me do my job!"

I storm away, already sick and tired of everyone excusing the behavior of the crew. How any of those people, especially her supposed life coach, help Mia accomplish anything is beyond me. They've brought nothing but chaos since they arrived, well, except for those moments out near the pool where they were all naval gazing about something or another when I interrupted them.

And why the hell would her mother give her a letter from a goddamned stalker before letting me examine it first? I swear that woman is as bad as Mia's ridiculous crew. They thrive on turmoil, but what good did she think would come from throwing her daughter into emotional upheaval?

Gently, I knock on Mia's door, and she barks, "Go away!"

"Mia, it's Liam. I need to talk to you."

I get nothing but silence in response, so I repeat myself and add, "I can help with this. I just need you to open the door and let me."

Still silence. I can understand her fear and even anger at having to deal with this right before she leaves the safety of her home for the road, but I can't do anything for her if she doesn't let me in.

Finally, after a few minutes of waiting, she opens the door only a crack and looks up at me. Her eyes are red, and it looks like she's been crying.

"You're still here. People usually get the hint when I go silent on them. Why didn't you leave?" she asks, clearly confused that someone finally either stood their ground or cared enough to bother to wait.

"Since your entourage woke me up in the middle of the night and I'm wide awake now, I figured I'd hang out. Can I come in?"

Mia steps back and opens the door wide for me to walk in, saying as I pass, "You wake up every day at five, Liam. It's not like my people woke you up that much earlier than you usually get up."

Surprised she knows my schedule, I smile as she shuts the door and walks over to flop down on the king size bed in the middle of the room. "Well, those fifteen minutes are precious."

She rolls her eyes and covers them with her arm. "I know what you're going to say, and you didn't have to bother coming up here to say it."

"What's that?" I ask as I glance around her room with its pale pink walls.

"That the police will find this guy and it will all be okay. Well, they won't and it won't, so if that's all you have to say, just go now and save us both the trouble."

"That's not what I came up here to say."

For a long moment, she doesn't respond, but then she lowers her arm and sits up to look at me. "Really? That's what Michael usually told me."

"And I told you Michael was a moron. You don't

have to be afraid. I won't let anyone harm you. I promise. I just need to see the letter."

Mia stares at me with a blank look for a few seconds and then asks, "Is that what you wear to bed? Who wears gray sweatpants to bed? By the way, don't let Mitchell see you in them or you're going to have your own personal stalker living less than a hundred yards away from you."

I don't try to stifle my laughter at what I think is her attempt at being cute. "I'll keep that in mind, and no, I don't wear these to bed. Now where's the letter?"

Pointing at the dresser on the other side of the room, she says, "Same as always. I guess there's something comforting in the fact that he never changes."

The first thing I notice is the envelope has no return address and a red heart outline drawn on the top left-hand corner instead, just as Andrea had described. What it does have is what every letter that's been through the post office must have—a barcode that will tell us where it was mailed from, hopefully, or at least what post office handled the letter.

Turning around, I look down at Mia and motion toward the bed. "Mind if I take a seat."

"Mi cama es tu cama."

As I sit down next to her, I ask, "Do you speak Spanish fluently?"

"No. I know the basics. In fact, I wouldn't be surprised if I screwed some of that up. I learned from the maid my mother brought in when I was thirteen. My tutors couldn't get me to learn anything in Spanish, and trust me, they tried, but Isobel had a natural ability to teach me. I can read it much better than I can speak it."

Interesting. I hadn't pegged Mia for someone who'd

take an interest in anything like speaking a foreign language.

"Okay. Here's the good news. See these little lines on the bottom of the envelope? That's a bar code. I'll be able to find out at least where this letter was before it came here, and hopefully, that will give us some clue."

"Really? Then why didn't the cops ever find that out all the other times I got a letter."

"No idea. Maybe they didn't get the envelope?" I ask, wondering why they wouldn't have been able to at least learn that detail.

Mia rolls her eyes again. "That would explain it. My mother probably threw it out and only handed them the letter itself. Speaking of which, it's the same as always. Again, some comfort in the status quo, I guess."

While I read over the actual letter, I mumble, "I guess."

Her stalker doesn't say much. The letter in its entirety is comprised of only two actual sentences. Your mine and always will be Mia. I will see you soon.

Not exactly Shakespeare.

"Well, I'm guessing your stalker is a male and young. The misspelled you're as your gives that away. Not that there aren't women who would misspell that, but my money is on a man. Not too old, though."

I glance over and see Mia smiling. "At least it's not some creepy old dude with a bald head and missing teeth."

Shaking my head, I chuckle. "I can't say if he's a toothless wonder or if he has summer teeth. I'm just saying it's a male."

She tilts her head to the side a little and looks at me with confusion in her eyes. "Summer teeth?"

"Yeah. Summer there and some are not. Summer teeth."

For the first time, possibly since I arrived at her home, I see her truly laugh, like she thinks my joke is genuinely funny. It's great to see her happy like this too. It makes her even more beautiful.

"You are too funny, Liam. Summer teeth. I like that. So amaze me and explain why you think this person is young, which by the way, I agree with but only because my fans tend to be under forty."

Remembering what I learned when I was guarding the senator last year and he had a stalker, I point to the misspelled your that begins this letter. "Older people aren't used to spellcheck as much as younger people, so they tend to spell better. Even when they're threatening people, they tend to spell things right." I stop and see her nodding before I add, "That and the demographics of the people who enjoy your music tend to be younger."

"So I have a young male stalker. Not really shocking, but I still hate it."

"This happens almost every time you're about to go out on tour?" I ask, wondering if Andrea knew more than she was telling me before.

"He didn't send anything last year, but all the times before that, yeah. And then I wait for another one that never comes and I spend all my time looking around corners assuming a stalker is waiting to grab me. It makes me hate who I am every time."

"Well, not this time."

"Really?" she asks in a tone of utter disbelief.

"Yeah. That's not how we're playing this game. I'm here this time, so no worrying about someone waiting for you because if he's around, I'll find him first."

Mia gets a sheepish look on her face and hangs her head. "You probably think I'm stupid right now. Just yesterday, I gave you a hard time about hiring more men. You probably feel pretty vindicated."

"This isn't a competition between us to see who's right. I'm here to keep you safe. That's all I care about."

Instantly, her entire demeanor changes, and she jumps up from the bed. "I don't want to talk about this. Go."

Confused, I stand to leave, not knowing what made her change from that happy and relaxed woman to this one that appears to be coming apart at the seams. As she stands in front of me looking like she's about to burst into tears, I try to think of something to say to make that happier version of her come back.

"Okay. I'll call the cops and report this. They're going to want to talk to you, but I'll be there with you, if you want."

Anger explodes out of her. "No! No cops! I told them the first two times he sent me a letter, and they did nothing. They don't care about stalkers until they hurt someone. I don't want to have to deal with them. Bring them in when he finally gets to me."

Before I can say a word to let her know I won't let anyone get to her, she collapses onto the bed and sobs into her hands. It's heartbreaking to stand here and watch her fall apart. I don't know if I should leave and tell one of her crew to come up here for her or if I should stay.

I sit down next to her, not sure if she'll begin yelling again or something worse, but all she does is cry. When she stops, we sit in silence for a long time. I don't know what to say. At this moment, I wish I was one of those men who knows how to cheer someone up, but I'm not funny or kind enough. I never have been.

Finally, she softly says, "I bet you're regretting taking this job, aren't you?"

As much as I have hated many things about this assignment, at this very moment, I don't hate it, so I answer truthfully, "No. No regret at all."

Maybe one. I wish I knew how to show others I care.

CHAPTER ELEVEN

$\mathcal{M}$ia

DRYING MY EYES, I LOOK OVER AT LIAM, SURPRISED he isn't regretting the fact that he said yes to working for me. "Really?"

"This is my job. It's who I am. It's what I'm good at. It's all I've ever been good at going back to when I was a kid. Protecting people. Back then, it was smaller kids being picked on by bigger kids who thought they could push others around. Now it's this. So I'd never regret this or any job where I can do what comes naturally to me."

"Even after the crew showed up?"

He hesitates for a moment and then shakes his head. "Even then."

"Your girlfriend or wife is a lucky woman."

Liam smiles and shakes his head again. "No wife or girlfriend."

Maybe Mitchell was right when he claimed last night Liam would be his by tour's end. "Are you gay?"

A slow smile lifts the corners of his very appealing mouth. "No. I just don't have anyone in my life right now."

"I see. You probably had a terrible relationship with your mother growing up and think all women are a hassle. I can definitely see you as one of those guys," I say, more than a little disappointed he's that type of man.

But he laughs at my characterization of him, which makes me smile. "Not at all. I love my mother. She's an incredible woman and one of my biggest fans. I have no deep-seated problems with women. Just haven't found anyone I want to be serious with, especially since I'm often away from home."

Happy to hear he isn't some troubled guy with mommy issues, I probe a little more about his life, curious about the man who didn't leave when I didn't open the door before and didn't leave when I fell apart a minute ago.

"I bet she's tall like you with legs that go on forever and dark hair with blue eyes that make her look exotic, right?" I wonder aloud, imagining a woman similar to him.

That's probably why he hasn't found the woman he wants to be with. He's looking for someone like his mother.

I secretly sneak a glance down at my legs and wonder if he'd consider them long. That's how they're usually described, but damn, if his mother is over six foot tall, her legs would be crazy long compared to mine.

Leaning off to the side, he takes his phone out of his sweatpants back pocket and brings up a picture of a tiny blond woman and a man who looks like the spitting image of him, just older. "The exact opposite, actually. Not tall. No dark hair. Obviously, I take after my father."

He hands me his phone, and I study the picture for a few moments. Nice couple. Very attractive. Liam comes by his good genes naturally. His father looks so much like Liam that I might get them confused from a distance. His mother looks sweet, like the kind of mom everyone would like but she's still really cool.

Turning to look at Liam, I say, "You really do. Did you get any of your mother's genes? She's beautiful, by the way. Really beautiful."

As he takes his phone back, he shakes his head and smiles. "Nothing physical, but I think I get my need to want to protect people from her. She loves to take care of everyone around her."

"Did you have a nice childhood? She's gorgeous and I'm sure all your friends had huge crushes on her at one point or another, but did she bake cookies and cut the crust off your peanut butter and jelly sandwiches?" I ask, imagining him as a little boy and the apple of his mother's eye.

Laughing, he answers, "She did, but don't go thinking everything was perfect because it wasn't."

"I don't believe for a second that those two people and you weren't perfect together. No way. They have perfect written all over their faces."

Before I say the same thing about him, I stop myself. "Do you have any brothers and sisters?"

Liam nods, but I notice he doesn't smile when he answers, "One sister. Annalea is older than me. And one brother. Wilder is one year younger."

Now I understand. Liam's the middle child. That's

why he doesn't think his childhood was perfect, even though he had a mom who baked cookies and cared enough to cut the crusts off his PB and J sandwiches.

"Ah, I get it. You're the middle child. It's the Jan Brady Syndrome. So which one was the bigger pain, the older sister or the younger brother?"

That brings a smile back to his face, and his eyebrows shoot up into his forehead to show his disbelief in my psychological diagnosis. "The Jan Brady Syndrome? What's that? I've never heard of anything like that."

Now it's my turn to look at him in disbelief. "The Brady Bunch? You know, the middle daughter was named Jan and she always felt left out. Marcia, Marcia, Marcia! Everything is always Marcia!"

By the look of complete confusion on his face, I see he has no idea about Jan Brady or her family's TV show from the seventies. What kind of person doesn't know about that?

"Well, now I know your childhood wasn't perfect because you've never seen the Brady Bunch. Dude, get some culture in your life."

With a chuckle, he says, "I'll see what I can do."

"So you didn't answer me. Which one caused you more grief, the older sister or younger brother?" I ask, pressing him for information even though I sense he doesn't want to talk about this subject.

He gives me an answer, though, so I have to give him credit for that.

"Younger brother. I'm curious. How did you know one of them gave me a hassle? Just a guess, or are you secretly a psychologist on the side?"

I point at his mouth and arch an eyebrow. "You

didn't smile when you started talking about your brother and sister. Just a little tell."

Liam nods, clearly surprised I didn't just guess. "I'm impressed. Where did you learn to pick up on people's tells?"

"You learn to figure people out when you're the one they all depend on."

Even as I say those words, I feel like a complete fraud. I never figured out Jonny or Michael, so my track record on being able to figure people out is pretty damn sad.

He falls quiet for a long moment before he asks, "So no baking or cutting off the crust on your sandwiches from Andrea?"

"God no!" I say, knowing I'm betraying how bad she was with that kind of thing.

"Sorry."

Suddenly, I feel like he's pitying me, and I hate that. "It's okay. This is my life. It's always been this way. The only difference is back then I wasn't famous."

When he doesn't answer, I quickly shift the attention back to his family. "The way you feel about your mother sounds so great. I'm jealous, if you want to know the truth."

He doesn't say anything but stands to leave, disappointing me. "Don't make the mistake of thinking my family's perfect. Trust me. I should take you to meet them all. Fifteen minutes with them and you'll be thankful you're an only child."

"All of them? I thought you only had one brother and sister. Who would I be meeting in addition to them?"

"My family isn't just my mother and father with my sister and brother. My father's brothers and their wives and my cousins are always around too. It's like one big family, the Jackson and March clan. Then there's my grandmother who keeps us in line too."

As I listen to him describe this big extended family of his that he calls a clan, I can't help but be jealous. They sound incredible. And nothing like I've ever experienced in my life.

"That sounds great. You should be thankful you have all those people who care about you just because you're family, Liam."

The sadness in my voice comes through loud and clear, and for a second or two, I think about making a joke to hide it. It's no use, though. He senses it, and I see in his expression that look like he's pitying me again that I hate.

"I guess, but sometimes when you're in the middle of a family that big, it can be a lot. Sometimes you just want to be alone."

Shaking my head, I say the only thing I know to be true in my life. "You don't want to be alone. Trust me. It's not all it's cracked up to be."

Liam nods, but he doesn't understand. No one with a family the size of his could know how it feels to be truly alone.

CHAPTER TWELVE

$\mathcal{M}$ia

AFTER A DAY FILLED WITH PEOPLE WHO ACTED LIKE they were all walking on eggshells around me, I want to hear more about Liam and his big family that drives him crazy. I want to hear stories and imagine what it's like to be surrounded by people who love you no matter what, not because they have to or because of what you can do for them.

Halfway to his room, I remember it's nearly eleven o'clock. Liam gets up at five every morning to workout. He's probably asleep already.

I should just go back to my room, but it's like I crave hearing more about what I've never experienced in my life. So I take a deep breath and knock on his door, hoping he doesn't answer it looking like he just fell asleep and I woke him up.

My heart races as I wait there in the hallway of my own house. It's silly, but I'm anxiously eager to listen to him tell me about that family of his.

When the door opens, I see him standing in front of me in just a pair of shorts with a towel in his hand drying his wet hair. My eyes fill with the sight of muscles and tattoos. Who knew my chief of security had such a great body and was all tatted up? He always wears jeans and dress shirts or T-shirts that cover them.

"I'm sorry. Am I interrupting?" I ask, my gaze roaming over his washboard abs, muscular chest, and incredible biceps that have never looked this good with shirts over them.

He's got great legs too. I had no idea he was so built. He just always seemed big until this moment.

"Give me a minute and I'll get dressed. Come on in," he says with a hint of embarrassment in his voice before backing up to let me walk into his bedroom.

Staring at a skull tattoo at the top of his chest, I say, "Please don't feel like you have to because of me. You're in your part of the house. You should be comfortable."

Seriously. Don't cover up all of this gorgeousness because of me. I'd much rather you stay this way, although I'm not sure I'm going to be able to focus much on anything else if you do.

"It will only take a minute. Make yourself comfortable. I'll be right back," he says before grabbing jeans and a blue T-shirt and disappearing into the bathroom.

I glance around his room and notice it's neat. Like pristine neat. Where are his shoes? Does he really keep all his clothes in the dresser and closet? Is he always this tidy? Is it because he's not in his own home, or is this how he is? It looks like nobody stays in this room. Even the bed is perfect, as if the maid just came in and made it.

When he returns a minute later, he's fully dressed but I notice his T-shirt shows a little of the tattoo at the top of his right arm I saw that day when I was staring at him from my bedroom window. God, he's good-looking standing there with his hair damp and me remembering what he looked like before he put on clothes.

How is this guy single?

Instead of sitting on the bed with me like he did in my room, he walks over to the chair near the window on the other side of the room and sits down. "So what did you want to talk about?"

I don't know why, but suddenly, it feels foolish to ask him to tell me more about his family now that I've had all these impure thoughts about his body. My mind races to come up with another excuse to be there in his bedroom this late at night, and all I can come up with is asking about the men he's hiring.

Not that I'm the least bit interested in them.

"Well, I was just wondering how it's going with finding four men you want to work with. Did the company you work for have people ready to go?" I ask, barely able to conceal my utter lack of curiosity about this topic.

For his part, Liam seems completely excited about the men and when they'll be arriving, and for the next five minutes, he talks about who they are, what their backgrounds are, why he chose them, and what seems like a million other details about these people I don't give one damn about.

Finally, he stops, but I'm focused on trying to remember what the tattoo on his lower stomach meant with its design that reminded me of some Celtic thing I saw at a store in Clearwater one time. I don't realize there are no words coming from him for a good half a minute, and when I do, I feel my face grow hot instantly.

"Oh, sorry. You were saying?"

Not my best attempt at covering up for not paying attention.

"It doesn't seem like you really want to hear about this."

I'm not sure, but I have a sense that I hear hurt somewhere beneath his words, so I quickly say, "No, no. I do. Why else would I have come here and bothered you?"

Liam smiles, and my stomach does a flippy thing at how sexy he looks right now. "I don't know. Is there any other reason you would come here to see me?"

Embarrassed, I look away and mutter, "You're very neat."

"I guess. I'm not sure I'd say very neat. Just neat."

Staring off at the curtains hiding the door out to the balcony, I ask, "Do you like your room?"

Suddenly, he doesn't seem to have much to say. "Yes."

Questions barely get answers and no detail at all, but he couldn't stop talking about all of the guys he's planning to bring onboard to work with him.

My gaze lands on the armoire that houses the TV, so I ask, "Is the TV okay?"

"Yeah."

God, why has he suddenly clammed up like he's being charged by the syllable? I've never felt this uncomfortable in my life! So much for being the owner of this house and his boss. You'd swear he's the one in charge and I work for him.

We sit silently, each second that ticks by more awkward than the last, until I turn to look at him and blurt out a thought about something I watched a few nights ago on one of the nature channels. "You know what some of my favorite shows are? Animal shows."

For a moment, he merely stares at me in what appears to be complete confusion before he finally says, "Really?"

That's all he says. Really.

So I keep going, almost as if I can't stop myself. "I saw one about a goose who had a dozen goslings. Do you know they look like geese after only a couple months? I thought they'd look like babies for longer."

He doesn't respond, so I bolt up from the bed to leave. Clearly, he doesn't want to talk to me tonight. It's okay. I shouldn't have come here anyway.

"I'm going to go."

Behind me as I take a step toward the door, he says, "I think I watched that the other night when I couldn't get to sleep."

Suddenly, a wave of relief washes over me. Spinning around, I see him smiling. "You did? I couldn't believe how quickly those baby geese grew up to look like full grown geese. I never knew that about them."

"I didn't peg you for an animal lover," he says, still smiling at me. "Why don't you have any here?"

With a nod, I sadly admit the reality I wish wasn't true. "I'm allergic. I would love to have a dog, but I can't."

"We had a cat when I was little. A Siamese my father

got for my mother before I was born," Liam says, finally giving me more than one-word answers.

Thrilled he's brought the conversation around to his family, I take a step back toward the bed and sit down. "That's so sweet. You have the greatest family, or at least it sounds like it."

Liam rolls his eyes and shakes his head. "It's not perfect. Trust me."

I want to hear all about his not perfect clan that sounds perfectly wonderful to me with its extended family and a grandmother who keeps them in line and a Siamese cat his father gave his mother. I imagine the kitten sitting in a box with a pretty pink bow tied around its neck like the perfect present.

"I bet it's more incredible than you realize," I say, trying to hide my desire to hear anything he'll tell me about them.

Unsure he's in the mood to talk much at all, I wait, hoping to hear even one story. Tilting his head back, he looks up toward the ceiling for a few seconds and then almost as if he knows how much this means to me, Liam begins to tell me about the time he and his cousins were all nearly teenagers and got in trouble at a summertime cookout at his grandmother's.

As silly as I know it is, I hang on every word and every gesture he makes as he tells the tale, laughing when he chuckles about how his parents were furious, along with his aunts and uncles, because all the boys had stolen beer and hidden it down near the water to sneak drinks from all day. By the time they sat down to eat dinner, every one of them were drunk off their asses, each from less than a full beer.

"Of course, as the oldest boy, my father assumed I should have stopped all of this from happening. I wasn't the ringleader—that was Cade and Alex, as usual. I was nearly thirteen, which put them at ten, but the two of them were always troublemakers."

"I hope I get to meet all of these people sometime. They sound like so much fun. I wish my family had stories like that. We don't have anything but my mother and me together doing the same thing we've done for nearly all my life."

And just like that, all the happiness the two of us had been enjoying evaporates with the truth of my life. I see the change in Liam as his eyes fill with sadness, or worse, pity for me. I'm sure my mother has told him the whole ugly story of how my father couldn't hack dealing with my work to become a singer and her efforts to do everything she could to make my dream come true. It's a pathetic story of a man needing to be the center of attention and unwilling to accept he couldn't be.

Then Liam says the two words that crush me more than anything else he could utter.

"I'm sorry."

I so desperately wanted to not be pitied tonight, but with just those words, that's all I am.

"Yeah, well, you don't have to be. I need to go. Goodnight."

He doesn't get a chance to say anything, and by the time I slam his bedroom door behind me, the tears are rolling down my cheeks. The tabloids and those ridiculous social media people should get a look at me now.

No man in my bed. No good times drunk or high.

Just me alone wishing I had a different life sometimes. Is that so much to ask? I don't want to give up all I have. I just want to smile and laugh for a few minutes without having to deal with the reality of who I am and what my life has been.

I guess it is too much to ask.

CHAPTER THIRTEEN

iam

THREE TIMES TODAY, I'VE WALKED INTO A ROOM IN this house and Mia has immediately walked out. I'm not sure what's wrong, but my gut tells me it has to do with last night. I thought we had reached a new understanding between the two of us after she came to my room clearly to hear stories about my family, but obviously, I was wrong.

Her crew, as she calls them, is more like an angry gang that glares at me whenever we have the misfortune of being in a room at the same time. Probably still upset I told them the truth about their behavior the other day. Too bad. Somebody needed to.

At least one benefit of setting them straight is they appear to have found some manners. Other than the nasty staring at me, of course. Or maybe Andrea finally made it clear that having their craziness around Mia all the time isn't good for her. I saw how rattled she looked when I said she might not be able to perform.

I haven't been around here long, but I've figured out that fear of her daughter's career ending is a true motivator for Andrea. At first, I thought she was the only good person here and Mia was the tyrant, but lately, I've been rethinking that opinion.

After a long morning meeting with Javier and his people regarding the changes we need to implement here at the estate now that I know there's a stalker in my client's life, I head toward the kitchen to grab some lunch. Two days ago, the cook Cecelia made me a hell of a grilled cheese sandwich and tomato soup, so today I'm looking forward to enjoying that again, assuming the hoard of people around here haven't devoured every last ounce of it already.

Hopefully, I'll get to eat by myself since I think I saw Mia's entire crew file across the lawn toward the practice studio on the other side of the estate with the star herself and her backup dancers who've begun to come here every day now. Too bad they can't all stay there permanently.

Cecelia smiles when I walk into the kitchen, waving at me as she walks out of the pantry. "Hungry, Liam?" she asks with more enthusiasm than I expect from anyone around here. It's almost as if she's happy to see me.

"I was hoping to have another of your grilled cheese sandwiches and some tomato soup from the other day," I answer as I stop near the enormous stainless steel refrigerator.

THE MYSTERIOUS BAD BOY

She walks over to me and tilts her head back to smile up at me. Short and very round, she's the nicest person here by a mile. "You're in luck! I saw how much you loved my soup and squirreled some of it away for you. Let me heat it up. It won't take long, and then you can have your grilled cheese and tomato soup lunch."

"Thank you, Cecelia."

Waving me away, she turns around to start working on my food. "Now go! Get out of my kitchen and let me do my magic. Go!"

I open the refrigerator to grab a drink, and my gaze lands on that green stuff that smells like feet sitting front and center on the middle shelf. With a grimace, I look past that to the jug of iced tea and reach into grab it. Whatever that stuff Mitchell drinks wafts up to my nostrils, and I swear my eyes begin to water at the stench.

The guy clearly knows how to take care of his body, but Christ, what the hell is that shit?

After pouring myself a glass of iced tea, I head out to sit at the dining room table. Nobody else comes into this room, so it's the perfect place to avoid any of the crew who might show up.

I hear a noise and look up from my phone expecting to see Cecelia with my lunch. But it isn't her. Instead, Ainsley stands in the doorway glaring at me for the fourth time today. Goat girl sure does hate me. Why, I have no idea.

Nor do I care.

"Sitting down for a nice lunch, Liam?"

Her tone says she's planning on saying something else after that, but I really don't want to hear it because then I'm going to want to reply. So I force a smile and nod before returning my attention to the news headlines on my phone.

"You have a pretty nice gig going on here. I hope you appreciate it."

Ah. So that's where we're going with this today. The life coach who does nothing, as far as I can tell, wants to know if I appreciate how great my job here is. It might be great if I didn't have to deal with her and the rest of Mia's crew.

I ignore her, even as every cell in my body screams at me to remind her how sweet a gig she has going on here. At least I have a purpose around this house. An actual job that involves tasks I have to complete.

She merely has to get her aura into the right zone or whatever the hell she does and fill Mia's head with positivity. How goddamned hard could that be living here? This house has every luxury a person could want, the estate is kept beautiful by a legion of gardeners and landscapers so it's like living in paradise, and her entire job here is to be a cheerleader.

But Ainsley doesn't take the hint and sits down at the table with me. I feel her angry stare practically boring a hole through my face. Somebody wants to have it out with me today, although I'm not sure why.

When I finally finish reading a story about how the Bucs are probably going to be looking at rebuilding their offensive line before next season, I calmly lift my gaze and see her still staring at me. Jesus, she is an angry person. Maybe she should go find some of that Zen she claims to know so much about.

"Is there something I can help you with?"

I want to add the nickname I call her—Goat Girl—but I figure I don't need to goad her into getting even angrier than she looks right now. I'm thinking at any moment, steam will come shooting out of her ears.

"You've been a big influence on Mia lately, and I'm not sure it's a positive one," she snaps, almost spitting the words at me.

Taking a deep breath, I let it out slowly, weighing how much I want to lay into my client's life coach today. I'd love to tell her exactly how little I think of her, but Mia is close to this person and the last thing I want to do is upset the delicate balance I'm trying to achieve with her.

"I think you're confused, Ainsley. I'm the chief of security here. I work for Mia. I'm neither positive nor negative. I simply do my job and that's it."

Her eyes narrow, and she points toward the grounds outside the window. "Javier is chief of security here, so I'm wondering why you need to live here at all if you're the person who's responsible for Mia's safety off the estate."

"I'm over Javier," I say in a sharp tone to match hers. "He works under me. Is there some problem with Mia's protection that you'd like me to look into? If not, we have nothing else to discuss since you're in charge of whatever you do, and I have an actual job here."

Ainsley's green eyes grow wide and full of anger. Fuck, I should have stopped myself at the question I asked her instead of continuing on to insulting her, but I'm tired of all of Mia's crew. I have a fucking job to do. Why can't these people understand that?

"What I do for Mia is none of your business, Liam.

All you need to know is I don't think you're a positive force for her, and I can't allow that to be."

She can't allow what to be? This woman and her positive force nonsense is grating on my last nerve right now.

"Aren't you in charge of making her see the positive, Ainsley? I would think that's your job to take care of. As I said before, I am neither positive nor negative. I'm simply the person in charge of her security. So why don't you go find your center or whatever the hell you do and leave me alone to eat my lunch before I have to go back to my actual job on this estate?"

By the time I finish speaking, my voice is loud enough that Cecelia pokes her head into the dining room to see what's going on. Turning to look over toward the doorway, I give her a smile that disappears the moment I return my focus to the life coach.

We stare each other down for a long moment before she closes her eyes and takes a deep breath in. I watch in confusion, hoping to God she isn't planning on staying here and meditating or whatever she does all during my lunch.

After she lets the air in her lungs out in a long exhale, she opens her eyes and smiles, but it's clearly forced. "You're right. I am in charge of helping Mia see the positives in her life. I care about Mia a great deal. She's my friend, and I'm concerned that how you see her is affecting her negatively."

Surprised by the sudden change in her demeanor, I rethink my desire to continue to fight with Ainsley and nod, still unsure what the hell her problem is but willing to at least listen now that she's not acting like she wants to attack me.

"I'm not sure what you mean. I see Mia as a client. She requires security, and that's what I'm here to provide. What I think of her or everything that surrounds her here doesn't figure into that."

As if someone turned on the nice switch on this woman, the life coach leans forward toward me and says in a low voice, "Mia is a good person. She's not spoiled or cruel, like the social media assholes say she is. She would give someone the shirt off her back if they needed it. But she's very susceptible to the people around her and how they feel about her. I sense you think she's not as terrific as she actually is."

"I don't think she isn't a good person. I'm not sure what's made you say all of this to me today, but I think Mia is a talented woman with gifts many people in this world would love to have."

Angry Ainsley returns, and she snaps, "But?"

I'm beginning to think this woman has multiple personality disorder and all her personalities are having a field day inside her today. All I want to do is eat a good lunch and return to work, but when I glance over toward the doorway and see no Cecelia with my sandwich and soup, I resign myself to the fact that I'm going to have to continue this conversation for the time being.

Even if it upsets Ainsley, which I suspect what's about to come out of my mouth next will.

"But you and the rest of her crew are a lot to deal with, which makes my job harder. Like with this stalker. Why the hell didn't any of you think to tell Andrea to give me that stalker's letter instead of handing it over to Mia? All of you are to blame for her unraveling because of that letter. She didn't have to be upset like that."

I stop for a moment, but I need to get the rest of my

ideas out, so I continue. "And you know what? I think all of you thrive on the chaos that happens here, and the reason you don't like me is that I want to create order for her. If I had gotten that letter instead of her, I would have investigated where it came from and who's behind it before I even mentioned it to her in the first place. That's my job, and you all make my job much harder, which hurts Mia, even if you don't want to admit it."

Ainsley opens her mouth to snap back at me but closes it like she's rethinking whatever she planned to say. With a frown, she shakes her head.

"We don't mean to do that, but you're right. You should have gotten that letter instead of Mia. I can promise you none of us would ever want to hurt her. We love Mia. We only want her to be happy, and what happened last night made her feel anything but happy."

Feeling the tension between us ease, I smile. "We're all on the same side here. I'm not trying to change Mia or anything that happens in this house. I just want to make sure that I can protect her the best I can, and the chaos that seems to happen all the time in this place makes that much harder."

Ainsley nods, although I'm not sure she agrees with me. That's okay. I don't need her to agree with me on anything. I just need her and the rest of the crew to stop the madness so I can do my job.

With skepticism filling her expression, the life coach says, "Mia told me you said you'd lay down your life for her. Is that normal in your business?"

"Yes."

She screws her expression into a look of disgust and says, "Michael never told her that."

As much as I want to unload about how bad my

predecessor was at his job, I restrain myself and simply say, "Michael wasn't good at his job."

With a smile, Ainsley says, "Michael was a tool who didn't appreciate how wonderful Mia is."

"That too."

Hoping this little conversation has ended, I look over toward the doorway and see Cecelia walking in with my lunch. Thank God. Another couple minutes of Ainsley and I'd have indigestion before I even got to enjoy a bite of my delicious meal.

She senses it's time for her to leave and stands up from the table. "Well, I'm glad we had this talk. I guess I'll go and let you enjoy your lunch."

I force a smile, even as I'm thrilled to see her leave. "Nice talk."

As Cecelia sets the plate with my grilled cheese sandwich and chips in front of me and then sets the bowl of tomato soup next to it, she pats me on the shoulder. "You enjoy your lunch, Liam."

This time, my smile is genuine. "Thank you. This smells incredible."

"By the way, don't tell anyone I said this, but I think you're just what Mia needs here. She doesn't need any more craziness. Keep up what you're doing. It's good for her."

"Thanks, Cecelia. I'm just doing my job."

She smiles and points at the sandwich waiting for me. "Well, don't stop. I put extra cheese on there special today. I thought after that little pre-lunch meeting you could use it. Enjoy."

Finally alone, I take that first bite and love how fantastic her grilled cheese sandwiches taste. She's right about needing something more after having to deal with Ainsley and whatever the hell she was trying to tell me.

After that, what I can use is a good stiff drink, but that will have to wait until later. I've got more work to take care of today finding out who Mia's stalker is and getting the extra men I need to make sure he never gets close enough to hurt her.

CHAPTER FOURTEEN

$\mathcal{M}$ia

AS MUCH AS LAST NIGHT ENDED UP GOING BADLY, I can't deny I like how I feel when I spend time with Liam. Somehow, even though he's my bodyguard, he makes me forget about stalkers and their stupid letters, my mother and her hysteria, and everything else surrounding me.

So tonight, I want to lose myself in a marathon of the greatest seventies TV show and educate him when it comes to The Brady Bunch. I still can't believe he's never heard of it. That perfect couple in the picture definitely have one flaw, for sure.

Not five seconds after I knock on his door, he opens it wearing a pair of gray sweatpants that look different than the others I've seen him in. These have front pockets, and I swear they act like a frame around his hips and crotch so all I want to do is look there.

Does he wear these things on purpose because he

wants to be a tease, or is Liam actually that straight and narrow guy who doesn't realize what he looks like in them?

Quickly, I lift my gaze to his face and smile, silently praying to God that my cheeks aren't turning as red as they feel. "It's not too late, is it? I wanted to help you become more cultured."

Liam shakes his head as a look of bewilderment settles into his chiseled features. "I'm not following. What do you mean?"

"Can I come in? It's sort of rude to keep someone standing out in the hallway like this, especially if it's the person who owns the house."

As if I reminded him of his manners, he quickly steps aside, opening the door all the way so I can walk into his room. "Sure. I'm sorry. I'm just not understanding what you meant by making me more cultured."

I notice the TV isn't on, and I wonder what he could have been doing in here. Maybe he meditates. He does seem like a very calm person. That's probably how he stays that way.

Or maybe he reads. I can definitely see Liam as a reader. He has a cerebral thing about him. He probably likes thrillers. Spy thrillers, I bet. I look around for any sign of a book, but I don't see one on his bed or on any of the other furniture.

"Were you busy doing something?" I ask as he walks past me to stand on the other side of the room over near the glass door to the balcony.

"Not really," Liam says with a shrug. "Is something wrong? Do you need my help with something?"

Always the job with this guy. No wonder he knows

nothing of great seventies sitcoms. That will change tonight.

I grab the remote off his bed and point it at the TV. "What's wrong is you know nothing of The Brady Bunch, which I think is a crime in at least ten states. I'm here to remedy that utter failure in your education."

My teasing makes him smile, and I can't help but notice how sexy he looks when he gives me a genuine smile. "And to think I was busy with math and science when I could have been binge-watching some old TV show."

Waving him over to where I sit on the edge of the bed, I say, "Some old TV show? Those subjects are nice, but the gap in your cultural education must be rectified. So that's what I'm here to do tonight."

"Aren't you too young for that show? Isn't it from the seventies?"

I look at him in shock. "Do people ask others if they're too young for the Mona Lisa? Let's get going. I think it's best to start at the beginning. We don't want you to not have the full experience."

"Oh, well, of course. I need the full experience," he says, clearly teasing me.

Undaunted, I roll my eyes. "Be sure to listen to the theme song for the show because that tells you a lot going in, okay?"

He sits down next to me on the bed and looks at me quizzically, raising a single dark eyebrow in skepticism at my claim about The Brady Bunch theme. "So the song at the beginning of the show is important? Aren't those usually just music without lyrics?"

I click through the various screens to get to episode one and nod. "I don't know, but it's important for The

Brady Bunch. The song tells you who these nine people are. Ready?"

"As much as I'll ever be," he says in a voice full of doubt and then mumbles under his breath, "Nine people. Wow."

The episode begins to play and with every important section of the theme song, I repeat the information. "So the lovely lady, she's the mother. The daughters are top to bottom Marcia, Jan, and Cindy. Cindy's the one with curls."

"Okay."

When it gets to the second verse of the song, I point at the screen and say, "So the father's last name is Brady, which makes sense since this is The Brady Bunch. His sons are from top to bottom Greg, Peter, and Bobby. A nice wholesome family."

Liam hums next to me like he's taking this all in.

The next verse begins about the lovely lady meeting the man, and I say, "So they meet, fall in love, and make one huge family that lives in the suburbs of LA."

He doesn't say anything at first, but when Alice appears in the center square, he quietly asks, "Who brought their mother to live with them? Should I assume much of the show is the hassle of having a mother-in-law around?"

God, he can be funny sometimes. I don't even think he realizes it either.

Laughing, I shake my head and freeze the picture of all nine characters in their boxes at the end of the show's intro. "That's Alice, the live-in housekeeper. She takes care of everything the kids need. There are six of them, after all."

With a smile, he nods and says, "Okay, that makes

sense. Both parents work, so they need a live-in housekeeper. I think I'm getting the basics here."

I hold up my hand and shake my head as I press play to begin the episode. "No, no. It's the late sixties, early seventies, and Mike Brady is an architect. Wait until you see the house they live in. They have money. So no working for Mrs. Brady."

"Okay. She doesn't work, but they need a housekeeper who lives there with them. I guess I get it."

His disapproval of the Brady household situation comes through loud and clear, but I don't bother trying to explain that what the mom does isn't really the focal point of the show. He'll get that as we watch the episodes.

I point the remote at the TV again to increase the volume and look over at him sitting next to me. "Ready? We're going to start from the beginning so you have a true understanding of this show."

With a smile, he says, "This feels like we should have popcorn or something."

"Maybe, but we'll get to that later. For now, you need to get this culture into your brain, Liam. Settle in and enjoy the greatest TV show of the seventies."

By the time the ending credits run on episode one, Liam is lying back on the bed with his hands behind his head like he's about to start doing crunches. The look on his face has changed from unsure to curious to disbelieving, but I remain undaunted in my quest to show him what he needs to know about The Brady Bunch.

He turns his head to look over at me and asks in a voice that tells me he's not yet seeing the true greatness of my favorite old show, "So you're telling me the parents felt bad and took their kids and the housekeeper on their honeymoon with them?"

"And the dog," I say with a giggle. "Don't forget the dog. They wouldn't leave Tiger behind."

"Of course. I guess if Alice can come along, why not bring the dog too?"

"See? Now you're getting it!" I squeal with excitement. "I'm going to grab us something to snack on and drinks. You start the next episode and I'll be back soon."

"Are we just going in order?"

I think about the episodes I like and shake my head. "No. I think we should jump to episode three. It's very cute. You enjoy, and I'll be back."

Before he can say another word, I rush out of the room, glancing back one last time to see him still lying back on the bed. Jesus, it should be illegal for a man who looks that good to wear those gray sweatpants. Seriously.

Ainsley and Mitchell are sitting in the living room and see me rush down the stairs toward the kitchen. Naturally, she follows me, curious to know what I'm up to since I must seem far more excited than usual.

As I grab a blue plastic bowl out of the cabinet for the popcorn, she comes up behind me and whispers, "What's the bowl for?"

I open and close cabinet door after cabinet door while I search for popcorn to pop. "Popcorn."

"If Mitch sees you eating that much popcorn, he's going to have you running until you drop!" she exclaims far too loudly.

Spinning around to face her, I put my finger to my lips. "Shhhh! I don't need that tonight, okay? I'm just finding some snacks while I watch some TV, so go back in the living room and keep him out of here."

"Want some company?"

I shake my head but don't explain I already have company. Ainsley doesn't like Liam, and I'm not in the mood to defend that I do right now.

"Clearly, we don't have any popcorn," I say as I close the final cabinet where food is stored. Then I remember the cook reorganized the kitchen a couple months ago and put everything like snacks in the pantry.

Ainsley follows me there as I search for what's become the elusive popcorn I can't seem to locate. "So what are you watching all alone up there?"

I look through shelf after shelf to find no popcorn. Damn! There is a bag of chips and a half-finished bag of pretzels I'm sure Mitchell would have a fit about if he saw them, though.

Oh, well. They'll have to do.

"Why won't you answer me? You're acting very weird tonight, Mia," Ainsley says behind me as I tear open the bag of chips and dump them into the bowl.

"Just in a hurry. That's all. We can talk tomorrow, okay?" I say, turning around to give her a smile I hope will make her happy.

Armed with my big bowl of chips and half a bag of pretzels, I head back to the refrigerator out in the kitchen. Do we even have soda in the house these days? Once Mitchell said no more ever again right before the last tour, I had the cook stop buying it, but I think that assistant of my mother's sneaks some in since I've seen her drinking glasses full of something that looks like cola.

I search but find nothing except iced tea. That's okay.

I like iced tea, and I'm betting Liam isn't a big soda drinker anyway. Now all I need are the glasses.

Setting the jug of iced tea, the bowl of chips, and the bag of pretzels on the countertop, I grab two glasses and tuck them under my arm. If I arrange this right, I should be able to carry all of this upstairs without dropping a thing.

"What do you need two glasses for? I thought you were watching TV alone in your room," Ainsley says, refusing to curb her curiosity.

"We'll talk tomorrow. Okay, Ains?"

I grab everything I need to have a fantastic Brady Bunch marathon with Liam and start heading back upstairs. Ainsley follows me, as she has with every step I've taken in the past five minutes and grabs me by the shoulder just as I hit the first stair.

"Are you and Liam hanging out together up in your room?"

This time her voice is full of all the judgment I'm not interested in dealing with tonight. Or any night, for that matter.

I don't lie to her when I shake my head and hurry up the stairs without saying another word. We aren't hanging out in my room. We're in his. It's a technical difference, but a difference, nonetheless.

By the time I reach his bedroom door, I'm just about to lose my hold on the iced tea jug and the bag of pretzels, so I slam my shoulder into the door hoping he'll get the hint and answer it. Then again, he might be so engrossed in episode three of The Brady Bunch that he may not get to me in time.

"Liam! Help!" I say just loud enough for only him to hear, hopefully.

Barely a second later, the door opens, and he rushes out to help me as the iced tea starts to fall to the floor. He catches it and the bag of pretzels as they slip from my hold too.

"I would have helped if I knew you were bringing up the entire kitchen," he says with a smile as I push past him into his room.

"Close the door. I think Ainsley might be following me," I say as I sit down on the bed and set the bowl of chips and the glasses on his nightstand.

"The life coach? Why? Does she want to watch lame TV too?"

I turn to look at him knowing my expression shows how hurt I am. "Lame? You didn't like that Cindy didn't want to choose between her mom and her new dad so the school set up a special dress rehearsal for the whole family to see?"

Liam stops dead in front of the bed and looks over at me. "Jeez, you really do like this show. Okay, not lame TV. Old. Old TV. That's fair, right? I mean, this show is like fifty years old."

"The classics never go out of style, Liam. That's another sign you need more culture in your life."

He walks around the bed and takes one of the glasses from me. "What's next? Are we going to head out to some museum? I'm thinking that's where we'd find some true classics, right?"

As he pours the iced tea, I roll my eyes at his suggestion. "Stop being such a Philistine and sit down. The next episode is coming up soon. By the way, I wanted to bring up popcorn, but we don't have any in this house. We don't have any soda either. So all we get are the second-tier snacks and drinks tonight. Sorry about that."

We settle in at the head of his bed, me next to the nightstand with the jug of iced tea and my glass and Liam beside me with the half-eaten bag of pretzels in his lap, his long legs stretched out in front of him. In between us, the big blue plastic bowl full of chips sits where both of us can reach it.

"So onto the next episode?" Liam asks as he takes a handful of chips.

I grab the remote and shake my head. "I think I want to go to one of my favorites. This one is focused on Tiger, so no saying anything negative because anyone who doesn't like a family's beloved pet would be a monster."

He chews for a few seconds and says, "Well, never let it be said that I'm a monster, so let's watch another one and see what Tiger's up to."

I can't help but smile at his change in attitude. "That's the spirit."

Liam can pretend like he doesn't enjoy this, but he's having a good time. I think it's possible he just doesn't know how to enjoy himself since he's Mr. Rules and Regulations, but I'm happy to give him help with that.

CHAPTER FIFTEEN

iam

THREE HOURS OF WATCHING BRADY BUNCH EPISODES and I have to admit this show doesn't suck as much as I thought it did for the first half hour or so. The episode about the dog was cute, but even better was seeing how teary-eyed Mia got when they finally found him at a neighbor's house. I suspect she's watched that show at least a few times in the past, but it still makes her get emotional when everyone gets their happily ever after.

She aims the remote toward the TV and turns to face me with a determined expression. "This one is about when the family goes to Hawaii. It's actually a three-parter, so get comfortable. I think you'll like it."

I want to ask why since nothing about this show seems on the surface to have anything I've ever mentioned liking, but I don't say a word. She wants to give me more culture, so more culture is what I'll get tonight.

The show follows the formula I've noticed it always follows, even after only watching a handful of episodes, and by the time the youngest Brady boy finds some relic rumored to be cursed, I know how it's going to end. Nobody's going to end up dead, for sure. This isn't that kind of show.

"Have you ever been to Hawaii?" I ask, turning to look at Mia while I wait for her to answer.

She shakes her head. "Not yet. I'd like to go, but I've never had a show there, and when I'm off, I'm usually too beat to do much traveling."

I nod my head and then she adds, "Plus, it seems like it's not the kind of place you'd want to do alone."

Mia waves off her comment and says, "You know, cursed tiki things and all of that."

She sounds sad all of a sudden, so I say, "You could go with your life coach. I bet she'd love a nice vacation like that."

"I guess. Maybe. It just doesn't feel like a girls' trip kind of place. Doesn't Hawaii always seem more like a romantic vacation to you?"

For a moment, I think about it and then shrug. "I can't say I've thought about it at all, but I guess so. The Bradys didn't think that way, though. Then again, that mother and father bring their kids and the housekeeper on their honeymoon, so I'm not sure they understand the idea of a vacation."

Mia elbows me in the side and gives me a look of utter disapproval. "They missed their family. You can understand that, can't you?"

"Not really. I'm not taking anyone on any honeymoon I go on. That's for sure."

Almost as if she forgets about the episode playing on the TV, she turns her body to face me and asks, "What's it like to have lots of family around you all the time? Is it as wonderful as it seems?"

My initial idea is to say hell, no, it's not wonderful at all, but suddenly I think I understand Mia's near obsession with this show. Like my stories about my family, it's something she wants but has never had.

Then it dawns on me why she keeps her entourage around her for weeks before her tour. She certainly doesn't need stylists and a personal trainer living here. The same goes for that life coach too. The only one who seems to actually do anything is the choreographer since she and Mia practice with the dancers every day now.

She wants them here so she can pretend like she has the family she's always wanted.

Maybe being part of a big family isn't perfect like she wants to believe it is, but now that I think of it, it's never been so bad either. It certainly seems a whole lot better than what she has with her mother.

I smile and answer her question as truthfully as I can. "You know, it's not bad. It can be a pain in the ass having all those people thinking they have a say in your life and what you do with it, but it's pretty great to have them around when it feels like the rest of the world wants to see the worst in you."

She sighs and nods. "I had a feeling that's exactly how it is. You're so lucky, Liam. Never forget that."

A sense of sadness hangs off her words, and I consider telling her about all the times my family got on my last nerve about something. I don't, though. Mia's built up the idea of a big loving family so much in her mind that I doubt she'd believe me anyway.

We don't say anything after that, and when the episode in Hawaii ends, I feel her head fall against my right shoulder. Turning my head, I see her fast asleep with a tiny smile on her lips and the remote still in her hand.

I move to gently slide it from her hold, but she mumbles something about Alice and the hula dance. Since I don't want to wake her, I carefully lean back against the headboard and settle in to watch parts two and three of the Bradys in Hawaii.

Mia lightly snores against my shoulder as I wonder if they brought the dog on this trip. Probably.

Nearly an hour later, she wakes up with a start and stares at me wide-eyed. "Did I fall asleep?"

Nodding, I point toward the TV and smile. "You missed their entire vacation. Do you want me to replay it for you?"

She wipes the sleep from her eyes and shakes her head. "No, it's okay. I've seen it a bunch of times. Did you like it?"

There's something so hopeful and sweet in the way she asks that, like she actually cares if I did enjoy watching the show while she slept, that I don't tell her the truth. "It had everything, right? Comedy, surfing, an ancient curse, and mystery. Who could ask for anything more?"

But she sees right through my answer and frowns. "You didn't like it."

When she hangs her head like my opinion on this show matters to her and I've crushed her with my teasing about it, I playfully nudge her shoulder to get her attention. She won't look up at me, so I nudge her again.

Still nothing.

"Hey, who cares what someone like me thinks? I've had to live with a family that size all my life. All that matters is you like it."

Finally, she nods and looks up at me. "I guess. I better go. Leave everything for the maid to clean up tomorrow."

"You don't have to go if you don't want to," I say, hating how things are ending with us for another night. "This is your house, after all. Technically, you could make me stay up all night watching The Brady Bunch."

She stands up, shaking her head. "No, I better go. Five o'clock comes early, I bet."

I quickly slide off the bed behind her and follow her to the door as a feeling that I don't want our time to end comes over me. "I liked it, Mia. I really did."

What I really liked was spending time with her, but I can't say that.

Her eyes light up, and she smiles up at me. "Well, then my work is done here."

We stand there for a moment saying nothing, and then before I know it, she stands on her tiptoes and kisses me. It lasts for only a second, but that's all it takes to make me feel like I've been hit by a bolt of lightning.

Before I can say a word, she hurries down the hall toward her room, leaving me staring at her as she runs away and wondering why the hell I keep letting her get so close to me. I know better.

Why the hell can't I seem to follow my own rules with her?

CHAPTER SIXTEEN

iam

THANKFULLY, JONAH MADE SURE THE GUYS I requested to add to Mia's security staff are available. The last thing I want to do is have to bring four guys I don't know up to speed with this madhouse.

By lunchtime, they all arrive, so I take them out around the grounds to introduce them to what we'll be doing. As usual, Jack Newsom barely lets me get a full sentence in before he starts talking.

"Hell of a job, if you can get it, I guess," he says with a chuckle that tells me he thinks I have some special in with the owner of VIP. Jack's not terribly subtle nine times out of ten, and this isn't the tenth time.

As the five of us pass by a topiary that's either some kind of dolphin or a mermaid, I roll my eyes and look back at the other men. "Nice to know good old Jack here never changes. As I was saying, it's Mia who we're guarding, not the myriad of other people who seem to mill about this estate twenty-four seven."

Turning around to face us, Jack walks backward with a shit-eating grin on his face and runs his hand through his light blond hair that makes him look like he should be at the beach instead of here with us. "And why would I ever change? Perfection is as nature intends it to be."

Barely twenty-five, he's got the confidence of a guy who's been on the job half his life. One of these days, he's going to learn some humility.

The one person in the group I'm closest to, Drew Larson, nudges my arm with his elbow. "These kids today. You'd swear they think they're God's gift to the world."

I can't help but laugh at his reference to a man just five years younger than him as a kid. Then again, Drew's always seemed like an old soul.

"Says the thirty-year-old," I joke to my friend.

"Thirty, but you try doing ten of those years with the family I had. You know what I'm talking about."

I do, and I nod my understanding. Drew's seen some shit and not only on the job. He watched his father get gunned down in his front yard when he was only seven, and then he saw his mother fall apart for the next five years. By the time he was twelve, he was in the foster care system, and I know from what Wilder's told me about his time in there that it's nowhere you want to be.

"Yeah, I guess you get to call Jack here a kid. You still look pretty young, though," I say with a laugh as he pats his very short black hair.

"Of course I do. I'm the twenty-first century Denzel, man. You can't beat that," Drew says with a wide grin.

"Well, Denzel 2.0, what do you think of this place?" Jack asks as he turns in a full circle to admire the grounds. "I think I might have died and gone to heaven. How is it you always get the sweet assignments, Liam?"

I don't bother answering him because he doesn't want to hear that maybe if he wasn't a clown so often that Jonah would like him more. Behind us, another new guy in the group Kip Jones stays quiet as he takes in the surroundings. Practically the polar opposite of Jack, everyone calls him Kip because he refuses to answer to his given name, Trevor. He says it's a dick name, so he won't even turn his head if you say it. Someone once joked that it sounded British like Kip, and from that day on, he's been Kip. Very much an American, he says little and I'm pretty sure he hates Jack, which hopefully won't cause any problems.

"Doing okay back there?" I ask him and turn to see him nod his head and smile.

"You know, I don't ordinarily agree with Jack up there, but I have to think you did something nice in a past life to get this assignment, Liam. I'm a little confused why we're all needed, though, if she has her own security in addition to you."

Just like Kip to cut to the chase. He says little, but when he does speak, it's to the point, unlike with Jack and his constant jokes and chatter.

The last guy I've brought on, Brett Marshall, nods as Kip voices his confusion about why Mia needs more protection. The largest of the four of them, he's the one you put up front to let everyone know there won't be any fucking around on a job.

"I'm with Kip. You've said she doesn't leave the estate much, except to go on tour. But she's already got a damn legion of people protecting her, so what are we for?"

Before I can answer, Jack laughs and says, "You mean, what are we four for."

Everyone groans at his attempt at a joke, and Drew levels his gaze on me with nothing less than disgust. "I trust you. You know that. I'm just wondering why you brought Bozo here onto the team."

As Jack begins to protest being called a clown, I explain, "Because I need people I can trust on this job. It's not that Mia doesn't have security everywhere she goes, but it's been pretty fucking lax in the past. I needed to know I have a crew I can depend on, and even though Jack here is a bit much with his humor, I can rely on him like I can rely on the rest of you."

Out of the corner of my eye, I see Jack nod. I have a feeling it isn't going to be long before I pull him aside and tell him to cut the damn funny business. I don't need dissension in the ranks while I'm dealing with everything else Mia dishes out.

"What aren't you telling us?" Drew asks directly.

I've avoided getting into the craziness of Mia's entourage, but I can't sidestep that and the issue of her stalker any longer. As I start walking toward the back of the property, I struggle to find a way to explain what this job is really like. Mia can be a wonderful person to be around, but when she's not, she's hell on wheels. And those people she keeps here are a royal pain in the ass, but I don't want to come right out and say that. On top of all of those things, the security Andrea keeps around all the time doesn't seem to care as much about the client as I'd like them to.

None of these things will make any of these guys happy they took this job because I specifically asked for them, so I try to soften the reality a little while still being truthful. It's a fine line, to be sure.

"Why don't you tell us about Mia? I mean, she's gorgeous and the entire world loves her, but what's she like?" Jack asks.

I take a deep breath and stop near a group of palm trees. "She's nice. She lives here with her mother and a bunch of people just arrived earlier this month. They're her crew, or that's what she likes to call them. Hairdressers, a fitness guy, a choreographer, someone who does her makeup, and a life coach. I haven't seen the personal shopper yet, but I'm sure she'll wander in at some point."

"Wander in?" Kip asks quietly. "Sounds like this isn't a very tight ship here, Liam. That's not your style at all."

All four of them look at me like that's exactly what each of them is thinking. "Yeah, I know, but it's been a challenge getting everyone here on the same page. People like us have different temperaments than artists and their friends, I guess. It's fine. The security at the front gate, which is the only way in unless you want to electrocute yourself, is good. Those guys are top notch. It's the others that her mother's kept around for a while who don't seem to be at our level. That's why I wanted you guys here with me."

Drew slaps me on the back, throwing his head back in laughter. "I bet you're going out of your mind here. Artists and their temperaments aren't really your style, man."

"Well, if any of them drive you crazy, the gym here is first-rate. I find that's the best place to take out my aggression."

I want to say the day after the crew arrived and that ridiculous goat noise woman who claims to be a life coach started with her nonsense, I spent extra time lifting that day. Either that or I was going to throw that woman in the pool. Repeatedly.

"Okay, so a bunch of artist types who don't follow the rules? Am I getting this straight?" Brett asks.

"Pretty much," I say, preferring not to go into it anymore. He and the others will realize just what I mean soon enough. "Andrea is Mia's mother. She's also her manager. You don't have to deal with her if there are any issues, though. Everything will go through me."

"Sounds pretty straightforward. Why do I get the feeling you've left the biggest thing for last?" Drew asks, knowing me all too well.

I take a deep breath in and let it out in a rush. "I have. She's got a stalker. I just found out about him myself a couple days ago. See? That's what I mean about things being lax. You'd think someone would have mentioned that right off when I came here as her head of security, but no. Nobody said a word until she got another letter."

"Just one?" Kip asks.

"As of now. He seems to send one every time she's about to go out on tour. Well, almost every time. He didn't do it last year. I haven't found any reason why that is. The letter went through the post office, so I checked with them, and they say it was mailed right in downtown Tampa. That's all I have so far, other than he misspells you're. I'm guessing a young guy, maybe local, but I don't know yet. Since Mia rarely leaves here, it's not a huge issue until she heads out on her tour. That's the main reason I wanted all of you on this job with me."

"You coordinate with the local people on security for her concerts, or are you in charge of finding enough people for that too?" Jack asks in a rare moment of seriousness.

"Her mother has always gone with locals, which I'd prefer not doing, but there's not enough time to change that for this tour," I answer, leaving out that I was brought on when the last head of security, that dickhead Michael, got fired just a little over a month before her tour starts.

All four men nod their understanding, no doubt agreeing with me that one person handling all the security details would be preferable. There's nothing I can do about it now, but having these men with me to cover as much ground as possible will hopefully be enough to keep Mia safe wherever we have to go.

"Okay, that's about it. Take the day to look around and get used to the place. We'll meet up again tomorrow when I hopefully have something more on that letter and where exactly it came from. I'll have your specific assignments then too. Until then, enjoy yourselves. Anybody have any questions?"

Jack, of course, steps forward with a big grin on his face. "Now when you say enjoy yourself, exactly what does that mean? Because I saw a pool on our little walking tour this morning, and I could do with a nice swim."

"Feel free to go anywhere you want, but if Mia and her people are there, come back later," I say with a chuckle, imagining how ugly it might get if we all descended on the pool while they were having their meditation time.

Behind me, I hear someone call my name, and I turn around to see Mia marching toward me in a red bikini and her white cover-up. I'd planned on introducing her to my crew later today, but now seems as good a time as any.

That cover-up of hers flies behind her she's walking so fast, and she starts talking before she even reaches me. "Liam, I've been trying to find you for half an hour. Where have you been?"

"Right here. These are the additional security detail I've brought on. Let me introduce you."

I don't even get the first name out before she snaps, "Later. I'm not really interested in meeting anyone right now. Maybe you should do that when I'm not running around this entire goddamned estate looking for you. I need you to talk to my mother about these guys anyway, so go find her now."

Mia turns on her heel to hurry away, that white cover-up trailing behind her again. I'm not sure why she needed to be so rude, but I don't appreciate being made a liar in front of my people after I told them not ten minutes ago she was nice.

Without looking at them, I say, "I have to go deal with her mother. Remember, if Mia or her people are where you want to be, go somewhere else."

By the time I reach Andrea's office, I'm fuming mad. I still have no idea what the hell her daughter wanted, and the fact that she chose to be so short with me in front of the men I have to work with pisses me off more with each passing moment.

I knock on the office door and walk in as I say, "Mia

said you needed to see me about the new guards? What's going on?"

Andrea gives me a blank stare and shrugs. "I have no idea. Jonah sent over all their pertinent details, and I've already got files on all of them. What else could I need? We're not going out of the country for the first leg of the tour, so I can't think of anything right now."

"Okay. Maybe we got our wires crossed. Sorry to bother you."

So what the hell was the wild goose chase about?

ALONE IN MY ROOM, I CAN HEAR THE NIGHTLY RACKET over on the other side of the house, but tonight, it's even louder than usual. It threatens to drown out the sound of the TV not even ten feet away from me. I wonder how the guys are handling it. I probably should have mentioned something about this when we spoke this afternoon.

Throwing my legs over the side of the bed, I head toward where their rooms are located and remember only Brett and Kip got lucky enough to be assigned a room on the first floor over in the west wing. Damn. Drew is going to want to kill me for this.

By the time I reach the top of the stairs, the noise from Mia's crew is so loud I can barely think straight. Music of all types blares from the rooms, and the two hair stylists keep running from one room to the next like some old school comedy.

Drew answers the door and shakes his head in disbelief. "Nice of you to give us a head's up about this," he yells in an attempt to be louder than his inconsiderate new neighbors.

I follow him into the bedroom and slam the door, happy to get some tiny bit of relief from the sounds filling the hallway. Jack reclines on his bed with his arms behind his head watching TV like he doesn't hear a thing. He waves to me and then goes back to whatever show he's so interested in.

"Let's go out on the balcony. It's a little better out there," Drew says.

We close the glass sliding door and I finally can hear myself think. Closing my eyes, I let the warm night air flow over me.

"Sorry I didn't tell you about them. It slipped my mind."

"I bet. Let me guess. You don't have a room over here."

I open my eyes and smile. "I complained and got a room on the other side of the house. These people are crazy. I get the whole artistic thing, but it's like they don't get that we have a job to do, and it starts way before they roll out of bed right before noon. I'm sorry you have to deal with this."

"So the client gave you a different room? She must like you," Drew says, wiggling his eyebrows.

"She tolerates me, I think. I'm far too straight and narrow for her."

"You know, Liam, I've known you for a long time. You and I have worked together more than a few times, and I'm not sure you're telling me the truth here."

Confused, I shake my head. "What do you mean?"

"Well, for someone you speak so highly of, she's not very nice to you. I mean, I get not really being interested in doing the whole meet and greet thing earlier, but she's more like a bitch than anything else, from what I saw by that little performance she gave us. You deserve more respect than that. Why are you so willing to take that from a client?"

I want to tell him that I think deep down Mia's a good person. That I've seen a side to her that he hasn't gotten to see yet. I don't, though, because I'd sound too pathetic.

So I do what I always do. Stay professional.

"You know how it is, Drew. We're here for the clients. Not the other way around. You've just gotten lucky with some great assignments. I admit I haven't had to deal with a lot of clients like this one, but I'm just looking at it as a challenge. She can be a diva all she wants. At the end of the day, as long as she's safe, I don't care how she acts toward me because I know I've done my job right. That's all that matters to me."

A slow smile lights up his dark brown eyes. "That's why you get jobs like this when the rest of us don't. You're the best, man. Jonah knows it. I appreciate you thinking of me for this job, though, Liam. We work well together."

"We do. We do our jobs and people stay safe. Fuck the rest of it, right?" I say with a laugh.

He nods, smiling as he says, "Exactly. Fuck the rest of it."

"I better get back to my room. One of us has to be awake for tomorrow."

As I step out into the hallway, Mia walks out of her life coach's room. I smile, like I always do when we run into one another, but she simply turns her head and walks away.

Glancing back at Drew, I chuckle. "Divas."

He nods and chuckles before closing his door to the

noise that seems to be quieting down, even just a little. Hopefully, he can get some sleep tonight, but I wouldn't count on it. I'm betting Ainsley is about to start her nightly routine of goat noises, so Drew will likely be up for a while.

CHAPTER SEVENTEEN

iam

I SILENTLY THANK GOD FOR SOME PEACE AND QUIET AS I climb the stairs to my room, thrilled to have nothing but the sound of my TV to lull me to sleep. Lost in thought about a movie I think I might want to watch, I don't hear Mia come up behind me until she speaks.

"What did you call me?" she snaps.

Turning around, I shrug. Barefoot and still in that red bikini that shows off her gorgeous body and her white cover-up, she stands with her hands on her hips looking particularly upset. She must have heard me say she was a diva. The truth hurts, I guess.

"If the shoe fits, I say wear it."

Anger flashes in her eyes. "What the hell does that mean?"

Unsure what she's referring to, I ask, "Are you saying

you've never heard the saying if the shoe fits before? I can't believe that. Everyone's heard that."

I know she hates when I play around like this, but she makes it so easy.

Throwing her hands up in frustration, she says, "I know what the saying means! I'm not an idiot. I want to know why you think it's okay to call me a diva."

As I open my door, prepared to end this conversation before it goes any further, I smile at her. "I'm sorry. I meant that about my friend's goat calling neighbor over there. Good night, Mia."

Happy to avoid an argument right before bed, I shut the door behind me and lean back against it. I'm not in the mood to spar with anyone tonight, least of all her.

But a few seconds later, I feel the door being shoved against me like someone's trying to push it open. I step away from it, and Mia comes flying through the doorway, nearly tripping over her feet as she tries to keep her balance.

Standing up straight, she barks, "I wasn't done talking, Liam. Now why did you think it was okay to call me a diva?"

Sure this is the most surreal thing that's ever happened to me, I look around my room, half-expecting a hidden camera catching all of this as some joke to be revealed. Does she realize what she just asked after barging into my room to ask it?

"I can't imagine why anyone would think it would be right to call someone who busts into another person's bedroom to berate them a diva. Go figure."

"I am not a diva!"

"Do you have another word you'd prefer to describe your behavior? And I'm not just talking about right now but before when I tried to introduce you to the new guys and you blew me and them off. You give me the word, Mia, and I'll use that one."

Her mouth drops open in shock, but I guess I shouldn't be surprised. I've rarely been this forceful with her in the past couple weeks since she was thoughtful enough to give me this room over on her side of the house.

A look of hurt fills her eyes for a second and then it disappears, replaced by more anger directed at me. "I never wanted four more guys. I didn't want any more, if anyone gave a damn to ask me."

Since she seems to have decided we're going to have this fight, I lie back on the bed and make myself comfortable. "Which I did, if you remember correctly."

"Don't act like you're doing me a favor by even talking to me. Stand up and be a man!"

Sometimes she's funny, and I don't think she even realizes it. Folding my arms behind my head, I lean back against the headboard and smile. "I can be a man lying down, you know."

That catches her off guard or confuses her. Mia stares at me, shaking her head, and finally asks, "Are you trying to be funny? Or was that something sexual and it came off stupid? Just wondering which it was so I can react appropriately."

"Go with funny because right now I couldn't be sexual if my life depended on it with the way you're acting."

I barely get the last word of my sentence out of my mouth and her eyes fly open wide full of fury. "Stop talking to me like you're my father! You are not the boss around here! I'll act the way I want and you, of all people, aren't going to stop me."

Pointing at the door, I say, "Then could you act whatever way you want outside of my room? I'm tired. It's been a long day."

Hurt fills her eyes, and she shakes her head as I watch her struggle to hold back tears. "Don't diminish my feelings just because you don't want to hear about them, Liam. I don't deserve to be called a diva, and I won't have that in my house."

"I'm sorry. I didn't mean to do that. Maybe we should just talk tomorrow."

My suggestion is met with silence, and she lowers her head to stare down at the floor. After nearly a minute, she quietly asks, "Why are you acting like this toward me? Is this how it's going to be now that you have people here you like?"

Her question and the sadness covering every word hit me squarely in the chest. I don't know why she's so unhappy, though.

"I don't dislike you, Mia. If you think that, you're wrong."

Probably heard that from her life coach. So much for coming to some meeting of the minds with Ainsley.

Still staring down at the floor, Mia refuses to look at me when she says, "Then why weren't you around like usual today? I had to go looking for you. You always get coffee early after spending time in the gym, and then you're around the house where I can find you. You weren't there. Why?"

Suddenly, I feel like I've misunderstood everything that happened today. Sitting up, I slide over to the edge of the bed and look up at her still focused on the floor.

"I had to handle things with the new guys, so I wasn't around like usual. That's why. I didn't know you needed me for anything."

"It just felt like you weren't here, and I didn't like that feeling."

"What did you need?"

Mia lets out a heavy sigh. "Nothing. I just feel better when you're around. That's it. I guess that sounds stupid, but I feel safer knowing you're nearby. When you weren't, I got anxious. It was nothing. Just forget it."

She moves toward the door, but I feel like I should stop her. We can't work together if she's not comfortable, so I need to make this right.

"You don't have to go, Mia. If you want to talk about something, we can talk. I'm not tired."

Hesitating, she looks up and gives me a tiny smile. "Are you sure?"

"Yeah. If you want to talk, we can talk."

"Do you want to talk?" she asks, and I'm surprised at how innocent she sounds.

"Sure."

Instantly, her smile disappears. "That's what people say when they're humoring you, Liam. I'm not stupid. I admit I don't get out into the world much, but there's this thing call TV here at the house. I've seen how people act when they're placating someone. I'll just go."

She moves too fast for me to stop her, so I hurry behind to follow her to her room. Just as I had before, she tries to avoid me now, but it takes very little to push the door open. Mia stands staring at me in surprise, which seems odd since she literally just did the same thing to me.

"I figured turnabout was fair play. I thought we were

having a conversation," I say as I close the door behind me.

"Go back to your room. I don't want to talk anymore," she says, turning her back on me.

"Well, now I do, so let's talk. I'm sorry I wasn't around when you needed me today. Would it be a good idea for me to let you know my schedule each day so you can know where I am?"

As soon as I finish speaking, I know that came out far shittier than I wanted it to. Mia heard what I said exactly as I worried and spins around to face me with tears in her eyes.

"Does it make you happy or bring you some kind of pleasure to make me feel stupid?"

Taking a step toward her, I shake my head. "That didn't sound like I wanted it to. I'm sorry."

"Stop saying you're sorry! You aren't sorry. You're handling me like everyone else does, and I hate it. You stopped doing that after the first few days when you set me straight on what your job is here, and I respected you for that. Why are you back to handling me like I'm some fool you have to tolerate?"

"I'm not. I swear. I just don't seem to have anything to say that makes you happy. Maybe it's all these people around. Or maybe you're right and I'm acting different. I don't mean to, Mia. I liked that we were finally getting along. The past couple times we talked and I told you about my family were fun, but then you avoided me all day yesterday, and since then, things have been bad again."

I watch as she collapses onto the bed and covers her face with her hands. I don't know why she's so upset, but I'm only making it worse.

Then she begins to cry and I feel like shit.

"This is all my fault. I'm sorry, Liam. You're trying to do your job to keep me safe, and I'm a total bitch. I don't mean to be. I don't."

Taking a seat next to her on the bed, I quietly say, "You aren't a total bitch. Maybe halfway."

Mia drops her hands from her face and stares at me. "That's you trying to be funny, right?"

"Yes. I'm not known for my sense of humor, just in case you're wondering."

"And I'm known for being a diva," she says sadly, covering her face again.

I know I shouldn't try to comfort her because it breaks all the rules I have for myself on a job, but it's almost like I can't stop myself from putting my arm around her to gently let her know everything will be all right. She melts into my embrace, resting her head against my shoulder.

"I'm sorry. I hate that I have to say that, but you deserve to hear it, Liam. I'm sorry. I shouldn't have been so rude to you in front of your guys today. You didn't do anything wrong. It's all me."

"No problem. They're used to people being rude. They're guys. We're rude all the time."

Mia lifts her head and sniffles as she wipes her eyes. "You're not. You're never rude, except when people deserve it. People being me."

Her dark eyes look all watery, like beautiful gems in a lake, and I shouldn't even notice that because she shouldn't be this close to me. But she is and I do notice, and something stirs inside me that definitely shouldn't be stirring.

"You're just being nice," I mumble, sure I should be

stopping what's going to happen if one of us doesn't move in the next few seconds.

She shakes her head, and then what should never happen between a bodyguard and a client happens. Her eyes slowly close, and even though I should back away and get the hell out of her room, I don't. I watch her brush her lips against mine, instantly closing my eyes to revel in the softness of them as she kisses me. It's sweet and sexy and absolutely shouldn't be happening.

Yet I don't stop and even kiss her back, loving how this feels while sirens and red flags go off in my head that I need to pull away right now. Or maybe a few seconds from now when it doesn't feel so good to kiss this woman.

But I don't pull away, and when she leans back, I feel the guilt rush through me. I'm her bodyguard. My job is to protect her, not make out with her. That's what the problem with that Michael asshole was. He didn't do his job because he got too close.

And now I've turned into him.

Mia slides her hand down over my chest, and my body reacts like it should because I care for her. I don't know how it happened. Maybe it was all that talking about my family. Or maybe it was the hours of The Brady Bunch we watched together. Hell, I don't know what it was, but all I know is I don't want this to end with a kiss and her hand moving toward my pants.

She leans in and kisses me again, and this time I don't stop myself. Burying my hand in her hair, I keep her mouth on mine as I slide my tongue in to tease the tip of hers. She moans softly, making my cock stiffen like it's made of steel. When her hand brushes over the front of my shorts, every cell in my body wants her so fucking badly I'm not sure I'll be able to think straight a few seconds from now.

Fuck. I need to leave this room before this mistake goes any further.

"Liam," she says in a dreamy voice. "I've wanted to kiss you for days. Was it the same for you?"

I want to answer her question with the words I know will make her happy, but I can't. This is wrong. Every rule I've lived by in my job says I have to stop this.

Pulling away, I force a smile and stand from the bed. "It's late. I better go. Have a good night, Mia."

By the time I reach my room, I have a sinking feeling I've messed up worse than I've ever done on a job before. How the hell am I going to be a professional around her when all I can think of is how incredible her lips felt on mine and how much I want her?

CHAPTER EIGHTEEN

ia

I watch my bedroom door close and my heart falls to the floor. Why did he bolt like that? Didn't he want to kiss me? Why wouldn't he? He's a man. I'm a woman. It's not like I was asking him to hand over some organ of his.

It was just a kiss. A good kiss, though. A really good kiss. I know he liked it. A woman can tell that kind of thing. The way he felt under his shorts tells me he was into it as much as I was.

For ten minutes, I stare at the door and wait for him to come back. Maybe he ran down to the kitchen to get us a drink. That would be very romantic and something I bet a guy like Liam would do. Or maybe he just needed to go change into something more comfortable. That's what they always say in the movies. "Let me go change into something more comfortable." That's the cue for the other person to have the green light.

He wants to give me the green light, right?

With each passing moment that the door doesn't open and I don't hear a knock, I begin to worry he's never coming back. But why wouldn't he? I was getting all the signals, wasn't I? He cared enough to be concerned about me and not just professionally. He told me those stories about his family. We had a good time hanging out.

At least I thought we did.

After twenty minutes, I know he's not coming back. Fighting back tears, I throw on a pair of black shorts and my favorite pink flip flops, grab my wallet, and run downstairs. My mother keeps her keys to her SUV in her office, so I sneak in and grab them out of her desk.

I can't stay in this house anymore tonight. I need to get away. I need to be somewhere I don't feel stupid or unwanted.

The moment I slide in behind the wheel of the car, I feel free. Maybe I'll drive to the beach. Or maybe I'll drive to someplace like New Orleans. Or Montana. I can go wherever I want. Why shouldn't I? I have money, wheels, and the desire to be away from everything in that house.

My freedom comes to a halting stop at the security gate. Sylvester, the older guard who works nights, smiles at me, so I flash him a toothy grin and say, "Hi, Sly! Just going out for some ice cream. Want me to bring you any back?"

For a second, he looks like he wants to let me through. He always has before. Before Liam, that is. It's clear he got to this nice old man who used to let me out whenever I wanted to leave when he sadly shakes his head and picks up the old school black phone in the guard shack.

"Just let me get clearance, miss. This will only take a second."

Clearance. This is my fucking life. I have to get permission from the man who just ran out of my bedroom when I kissed him. Anyone who thinks the life of a successful artist is all fun and games needs to see me as a cautionary example.

I rev the engine while I consider just driving right through this gate. My mother has insurance. I have insurance on the estate. Why not?

As I fantasize about gunning it and just blowing through this gate, probably scaring poor Sylvester to death, someone knocks on the driver's side window. I turn to see Liam staring at me with a look of horror on his face.

I could still bust through this gate. I want to.

Pressing the button to lower the window, I stare straight ahead as the glass disappears. He doesn't say anything at first, but I still don't turn to look at him. Check out the profile, buddy. Like it? Well, too bad. You could have had that and everything else, but you ran. Your loss.

"Planning on going somewhere, Mia?"

God, I hate the sound of his voice right now!

Still staring straight ahead at the gate blocking my path to freedom, I answer, "I don't have to tell you or anyone else in this world where I'm going or what I'm doing. I'm of age, so get this man to open this gate or I'm going to drive right through it and probably frighten poor old Sly to death. You want that on your conscience?"

In a much softer, less taunting tone, Liam says, "I wouldn't want that, no. But you know I can't let you go anywhere without protection. If you want to go out, I'll go with you."

Tears well in my eyes at his offer. He can spend time with me as my bodyguard, but as Liam, he disappears. No thanks.

Turning to look at him, I snap, "No. Not you. One of your other guys. They're here for a reason, so let's put them to work. What's the name of the one with the blond hair who smiles a lot? I liked the look of him today. Get him to come with me. Maybe I'll have a good time for once."

Hurt fills his eyes, but his voice when he answers me says he's angry. Why, I have no idea. Does he think Mr. Blond and Happy is going to want to kiss me?

"No," he answers in a clipped tone. "If you're going, it will be me who accompanies you."

"Whatever. One jailer is as good as the next, I guess."

He gets in and leans out the passenger side window to give Sylvester a smile. "It's okay. Thanks!"

As I watch the gate open, I mumble, "Thanks for making sure I can make this woman's life even worse than it was."

Liam asks where we're going, but I ignore him. If all he can be is my bodyguard, then there's no need for us to be friendly. I can be civil and ignore his presence as well as I do anyone else's.

I tear down the streets on my way to 275. Then I'll decide what to do after that. New Orleans does sound like fun. I've never been there, except for concerts, and then it's always been in and out, leaving no time to have any fun.

"Are you going to clue me in on where we're going, or do I get to sit here in surprise when we finally arrive somewhere?" Liam asks, but again, I ignore him.

Since I so rarely drive, I make a wrong turn and then another one, and fifteen minutes later, I'm sitting in downtown Tampa unsure how the hell to get to where I want to be. Frustrated and pretty sure Liam is having a good time watching me get more and more annoyed by the second, I pull over in front of some business with blue and green neon lights.

"This is where you wanted to come to? A check cashing place? Have a check you need cashing at eleven o'clock at night?" he asks with a chuckle, infuriating me even more.

"I just wanted to get out of that house. Away from everything. Away from you. And here I am, parked in front of some place I don't want to be at, just like I felt when I was at the house. Even worse, you're here to laugh at me."

Tired of feeling bad, I let my head fall onto the steering wheel. My forehead hits it so hard the horn blows, but even that can't stop me from crying. My tears come, the sounds of my sobbing filling the car.

I can't do what I want. I can't go where I want.

Worst of all, I can't have who I want.

I can have him follow me around like some overseer ready to pounce at a moment's notice to stop me from doing things I want to do, but that's it. He's too tired to kiss me, but he's not too tired to hover over me on this joyride to nowhere.

His silence tells me he was laughing at me, and it hurts more than anything else tonight. Or maybe it's just the last straw, but I fling the car door open and jump out, leaving it running. I'm unsure where I should go or what I should do, but I know one thing more than anything else at this moment.

I don't want to be what he laughs at anymore tonight.

The blue and green neon light in the window of the check cashing place distracts me, and I trip over the curb. I catch myself just before I hit the ground, my adrenaline coursing through me at the first taste of real freedom in weeks. I look down the street and wonder for the briefest moment where it will take me, but I don't care.

Anywhere is fine.

"Mia, get back here!" he yells, but I'm off running down the sidewalk in my flip flops.

Not exactly the best shoes for running, but I didn't exactly plan to be sprinting tonight. I turn around and see the car's headlights off. Of course, he turned the car off before chasing after me. That's so Liam. Always so worried about safety. My mother has insurance, dude. If someone takes her SUV while you're trying to catch me and take me back to that gorgeous prison of mine, she can just get another one.

"Mia! Stop!" he barks, but I'm half a block ahead of him and freer than I've ever felt in my life.

The warm spring night air rushes by me, cooling my already red-hot cheeks, flustered from running from a dead start. I'll have to remember to tell Mitchell how far I ran. He's always after me to do more cardio, but after hours of practice with Tiffany every day, I'm in no mood to get on that treadmill he so loves or any of the other machines in the gym he worships like gleaming metal gods.

Weaving between the smattering of people walking

on the sidewalk with me, I see a woman with blond hair point, but I'm gone as fast as I was there. A couple quickly steps out of the way as I barrel toward them, and as I pass, I hear the woman say my name.

I feel Liam behind me before I even hear his feet hitting the pavement. Is he wearing his shoes? Of course, he is. He's in his work clothes because this is work for him.

Who runs in shoes like those? Hell, even my flip flops are better for running than his work shoes. That's what you get for insisting on coming with me, baby. Keep up or I might slip away and then what will you tell my other jailers?

"Mia, stop this! I'm not going to tackle you to get you to come back to the car."

With a glance behind me, I see he's only a few feet away. In a second or two, he'll be able to reach out and grab me. I turn my head and a second later, I feel the hardness of his arm wrap around my body, pulling me against his chest.

"Stop this, Mia," he says in my ear.

I shake my head and try to push him away, but he won't budge. He's like a giant crushing me against him.

"Let go of me! If you don't let go, I'll scream. Those people know who I am."

"Then they'll call the cops, and they'll find out I'm your bodyguard who is doing the job he's been hired for. Now stop trying to get away and come back to the car with me."

Thrashing my head left and right, I try to escape, but he tightens his hold on me even more. "You're going to crush me. Let me go! I won't run."

He doesn't loosen his hold and laughs. "Yes, you will. I learned that the hard way."

I know what he's referring to, and it isn't this moment right now. Whatever. He doesn't know or doesn't care how I feel, so he can go fuck himself.

"Let me go, Liam. You can't keep me trapped like this."

For the first time, I turn my head and focus on his expression as he stares down at me. Why does it seem like there's hurt in his eyes? What the hell could he be hurting about? I didn't do anything to him.

"I'm not trying to trap you, and I'm not trying to be your jailer, Mia."

His face is so close, and as much as I hate myself for even thinking of kissing him, that's all I want to do. "Well, you're both."

"Promise me you won't run."

"You mean like you did after you kissed me? That kind of running, Liam?"

I feel his hold loosen, finally, but I don't run. I need to hear him say something to me about what I just asked him.

But he doesn't speak. He merely hangs his head and sighs. Was kissing me so much of a burden that it requires a sigh like he's just had the weight of the world set on his shoulders?

He takes a step back from me and shakes his head. "I didn't run after you kissed me. It should have never happened, so I left before even more happened."

"Why? Why shouldn't it have happened? Don't you like me, Liam?"

I hate that my voice sounds like I'm some sad, pathetic thing. Why do I want to cry when I get frustrated? I want to be tough and strong like other people are when they're angry, but it's always the water works with me every time.

Liam simply looks sad, like he doesn't know what to say or how to make me stop asking him questions he doesn't want to answer. "It's not like that, Mia."

The tears welling in my eyes make it hard to see him, so he looks like some watery giant standing in front of me when I ask, "Then what is it like? Tell me because I need to know. Please."

He sighs again, another sign all of this is a burden to him, but finally, he lifts his head and I see that sweetness I saw right before I kissed him tonight. "I'm your bodyguard, Mia. It's not right for me to be involved with you. That's what I mean."

I crave the feel of his skin on mine after he says that, like if I don't touch him he might disappear from in front of me, so I reach out and wrap my fingers around his pinky finger. "Why can't you protect me if you're with me? I don't understand."

His gaze moves to where my skin touches his and he winces. "Things get muddled, Mia. That's never good."

Stepping toward him, I look up into his eyes and wish my tears didn't make it so hard to see them because they're the most beautiful shade of blue I've ever seen in my life. Cool and almost icy, they somehow convey so much emotion that I can't help but stare at them whenever he's nearby.

"Would you protect me any less if you and I were together? Explain to me how caring about me makes your job harder."

Liam shakes his head. "It's not like that. It's that there

needs to be a clear line between the client and me so I can do my job."

I take another step toward him, and holding his pinky, I curl our arms up between us. "What if I don't want that line between us?"

"Don't make this harder than it has to be, okay? You don't want me. You think you do because I'm always there and I protect you."

Every word that comes out of his mouth hurts, and I push away from him, releasing my hold on his pinky. "I'm not a child, Liam! Don't tell me what I want and what I don't want. I know what I want! Is it so bad for a woman to want a man who protects her? Why do you make it sound like I'm foolish for wanting that?"

"That's not what I meant."

"Then what did you mean? Tell me!"

"You only think you want me, Mia. If you met other men or got out of that house more often, you wouldn't think twice about me. I'd be that invisible thing that watches over you, not a man you want to kiss."

"Why? Because I'm Mia, so of course, I couldn't want someone like you? You think I'm that shallow, don't you? Or you think I'm some pathetic thing that never gets out of her gilded cage, so she can't know what she wants."

Liam shakes his head sadly, like he's disappointed he can't make me understand why I shouldn't want a man like him. "That's not it. I'm fucking this up, and I'm sorry for that. I didn't mean that you're shallow or pathetic. I just meant—"

Cutting him off, I hold my hand up to stop him. "I know what you meant. I'm not stupid either, Liam."

I need to get the hell away from him before I begin

crying like a baby because I'm tired of him feeling sorry for me. Poor, pathetic little Mia. She has everything anyone could want, but she's not bright enough to understand she can't have the man she wants.

My feet move before the rest of my body understands it's time to run again, and I jump off the curb to dash into the street. Cars screech to a stop and horns blare, but I dodge getting hit. Liam follows me, of course. It's his job.

I don't care.

Then as if everything stops and falls silent, I hear him call my name and when I turn around, I see him collapse onto the pavement. Did a car hit him?

Frantic, I run back and find him on the ground with blood on his upper right arm. Clutching his elbow, he struggles to stand up but pushes me behind him. "Call 9-1-1. I've been shot."

I fumble with my phone to get it out of my pocket and call the cops. "Help! My bodyguard has been shot."

The dispatcher asks me questions I don't have the answers to, so I look around for a street sign. I tell her our location and she says someone's on their way.

As I hold on to him, he backs us up off the road. "Liam, they said someone's on their way. Are you hurt badly?"

He makes it to the sidewalk and behind a parked car, but then he collapses to the ground again. I stare down in horror as the wound on his right arm gushes blood, but I don't know what to do.

Dropping to the sidewalk, I kneel next to him and watch his eyes slowly close. "No! Liam, open your eyes! Open your eyes. The ambulance is coming right now. Please, Liam, open your beautiful blue eyes and say something to me."

But he doesn't move.

I stroke his forehead and gently press a kiss to it as tears roll down my cheeks. "Please say something to me, Liam. Tell me you hate me for driving down to this part of town and forcing you to run after me. Tell me what to do. Tell me you'll be okay. Tell me what I need to do because if you don't, I don't know what's going to happen."

Tell me what to do so you don't die.

CHAPTER NINETEEN

iam

SLOWLY, I OPEN MY EYES AND SEE NOTHING BUT white. Definitely not my bedroom. I try to place where I might be, but nothing makes sense. What is that sound? It's a constant beeping, but I can't figure out where it's coming from.

My phone? No. Maybe my alarm? No, I'd never choose to wake up to that noise.

I look left and right, but I see no one in this room with me. Did I change my bedroom to all white? No, that doesn't sound like anything I'd do. I hate all white rooms. They feel so sterile, so much like hospital rooms.

Then I remember I would be in my room at Mia's house. No, that doesn't make sense either because that room isn't all white. What color is that room? Tan? Beige?

Whatever color it is, I'm not there.

The memory of Mia running into traffic flashes through my brain, and panic rushes through me. Did she get hit by a car? Is she okay?

I sit up to get out of bed, and instantly, pain stabs down my entire right side. Fuck! What the hell is that? Turning to look at my arm, I see it wrapped in bandages and wires all around me.

Awake after feeling like someone sunk a knife into my skin, I finally understand where I am. That explains the wires and the beeping.

But why am I in a hospital?

"Please remain still, Mr. Jackson. You've suffered a gunshot wound to your arm, so we need you to keep still so you don't tear any of the stitches. The doctor will be in momentarily," a woman's voice says, and I turn my head to see a tall nurse with the palest skin I've ever encountered smiling down at me.

"Where is Mia?" I ask, desperate to know she didn't get shot too.

Jesus, if the bastard who got me got her too, I'll never forgive myself.

"Mia?" the nurse asks like she's doesn't understand the question.

Nodding, I answer, "Yeah. Singer. Superstar. She should have been with me when I was brought here."

God, I hope she was. The memory of her running away floods my mind, and all I can think of is Mia off on her own up to who knows what. Or worse, hurt by the son of a bitch who shot me and pulled over on some road bleeding to death.

The nurse's eyes open wide, and she smiles. "Oh, the young woman who rode in with you on the ambulance. Yes, she's here. She's been here the whole time. I'm sure she'll be thrilled to hear that you're finally awake."

"So she's okay?" I ask, suddenly fearful she needed to be in the ambulance like I did.

The nurse nods as I notice her nametag that reads Theresa. "She's okay, even if she is a little impatient. I'm going to assume she was just frightened that you might not make it."

I notice a hint of unhappiness filling the woman's voice as she says that first sentence. Knowing Mia, she had some kind of temper tantrum when she couldn't force them to make me better on her schedule instead of theirs.

"If I'm not mistaken, you have an entire waiting room full of people very eager to see you. As soon as the doctor comes in and takes a look at you, we can bring some of them in."

My mind fills with the image of my family out there scared to death I might not make it. Not my father, of course, since he's always of the belief that we Jacksons are indestructible, but I know my mother and she's let herself worry that the last time we talked at my grandmother's house that day when she convinced me to take the job with Mia was, in fact, the very last time she'd ever hear my voice.

Abbi Jackson is nothing if not an overreacting mother when it comes to me.

"Okay, thanks. I'm sure they're just frightened. It's not every day that you hear someone you know got shot," I say, preemptively hoping to excuse whatever madness my family has brought to the hospital while I've been in here.

Just as those words leave my lips, I hear Mia

arguing with someone right outside in the hallway. "I don't care what the rules are. I need to see him. He's the person in charge of my security. Where he goes, I go, and vice versa, so please move so I can get in there to see him."

I glance up at the nurse as she turns to leave the room. "I'm sure she's just scared. If you send her in, I can calm her down and probably make things better for all involved," I say sheepishly.

For a moment, Theresa doesn't seem too inclined to give in and break whatever rule there is that says I can't have visitors before the doctor sees me, but as Mia continues to berate someone out in the hallway, actually threatening the poor soul if they don't let her in, the nurse with the pale skin gives in.

"Just as long as she doesn't upset you."

With a smile, I shake my head. "She's just someone you have to get used to. Once you know who she really is, Mia's a lot easier to deal with. I promise she won't upset me."

As the nurse leaves, I think I hear her grumble under her breath something about Mia upsetting everyone else on the entire floor for the past two hours. That sounds like her.

A few seconds later, the woman herself rushes into the room and stops dead at the foot of my bed. Staring at me with horror in her eyes, she shakes her head before starting to cry.

"They wouldn't let me in until right now. What kind of place is this? A person gets shot protecting someone, and then they don't let the person you were protecting in to see you? I didn't know if you were dead or what might have happened, Liam. These people are monsters! I hate them for letting me think all those horrible things all alone out there."

"I don't think they meant to scare you. They had to focus on making sure the bullet didn't do any huge damage. At least that's what I assume all these wires and machines are about."

The horror in her eyes transfers to the rest of her expression when she looks up and sees what's commonplace in a hospital room all around me. "Oh, my God! Did you have to be on life support? What are all these machines doing here? Oh, Liam, it's bad, isn't it? You got shot because of me, and now you're going to be laid up for God only knows how long."

I hold my good hand up to stop her before she completely unravels. Thank God I have experience with a mother who overreacts or dealing with Mia right now might be too much to handle.

"It's going to be fine. It's not like I'm actually on anything to help me breathe or anything like that. These machines are standard in most hospitals. It doesn't mean I'm dying or anything."

Mia stares at the wall behind me for a long moment before returning her attention to me. "You're really going to be okay? You're not just lying to me to shut me up?"

With a smile, I shake my head. "Well…"

Hurt replaces fear in her expression, so I quickly add, "I'm not lying, but you have to be nicer to everyone here, Mia. They're just doing their jobs. They have rules about visitors, especially when someone's not conscious yet. That's why they didn't let you in to see me before. Take it easy on them. They're fixing me up, so I'll be fine. Don't you worry."

"Do you promise?"

For the first time since she barged into my hospital room, I see real sadness in her eyes. I don't want her to feel that way, so I quickly smile as broadly as I can and hope she sees I'm going to be okay.

"I promise. You aren't going to get rid of me that easily."

And in a flash, whatever happiness she felt when I said I promise disappears. Tears well in her eyes, and then she covers her face with her hands and sobs, "This is all my fault. You would have never been there to get shot if it wasn't for me trying to leave the estate without any bodyguards. I'm so sorry, Liam. I wasn't trying to get rid of you. That's not what I wanted at all."

"It's okay, Mia. This isn't your fault, so don't think that way. Whatever happened, I'm going to be fine."

Just as I hope I'm convincing her, the doctor comes in and looks at Mia still crying at the foot of my bed. "He's going to be fine, miss."

Mia drops her hands and sniffles as she stares up at him with genuine hope in her eyes. "He is? Really?"

"Really," the man says as I try to figure out if he's old looking with dyed dark brown hair or just someone who's spent too much time out in the sun and has the deep wrinkles in his face to prove it.

"Okay," she says, wiping tears from her cheeks. "Because he's very important to me. I need him to be one hundred percent, or I can't do what I need to do, which will mean a lot of people will be unhappy."

He seems confused by her explanation for a few seconds, but then a look of appreciation comes over him and he nods like he finally understands what she's talking about. "You're Mia, the singer! My wife loves your music. We played one of your songs for our dance at our wedding reception."

The center of his attention, she beams her happiness at being recognized. "I'm so happy to hear that. So you see, I need Liam to be able to go out on tour, and if he can't go, I can't go, so I need him to go or thousands upon thousands of fans are going to be disappointed every night when I have to cancel my tour."

My doctor turns to look over at me, but I have nothing to add. Mia seems to believe she can't go out on tour without me, so I'm just going to have to be well enough to do my job so she can do hers.

"So Mr. Jackson, you seem very important to this young woman. I've taken a look at your injury, and it wasn't too bad. You bled a lot, which probably made it look worse than it was, but I was able to sew you up with no problem. The bullet exited out the back of your arm, so you have stitches on both sides, but that's it."

I push myself up so I'm sitting instead of lying down and smile at the good news. "Great! See, Mia? No problem."

"But I do want your right arm in a sling so you have the least amount of movement possible for at least three weeks. Other than that, you can resume whatever your duties are."

Quickly, Mia explains, "Liam is my bodyguard. He's essential to my being able to perform, so just hearing you say he's going to be okay is the best news ever!"

"Well, he's going to be fine, so let the show go on."

The nurse who left just before the doctor showed up pokes her head into the room and asks, "Can Mr. Jackson see his family? They're out here very worried about him."

No doubt my mother has pestered every person at the nurses' station since the minute she walked into the building. It's my broken wrist in third grade all over again.

"If the patient is up for it, I'm fine with him having visitors. I'm going to get the process moving to get you released, but until then, you'll be in a holding pattern for a little while, so enjoy the visit from your family."

"Thanks, Doc."

CHAPTER TWENTY

iam

WHEN HE AND THE NURSE LEAVE, MIA RUSHES OVER to the right side of my bed. "Does this mean I get to meet the people in that picture you showed me?"

"I think so. I'm guessing at the very least my mother and father are out there, although the nurse mentioned something about the waiting room being full of my family, so some of the cousins and aunts and uncles might have come too. My mother probably made my injury sound way more serious than it actually was."

Gently pressing her palm to my chest, Mia shakes her head. "It was very serious, Liam. You got shot. Somebody put a bullet into your body. I don't care what that doctor said about it looking worse than it actually was. It was terrible. I thought you were going to die right there on the street. I don't ever want to feel that way again."

For the first time since I met her all those weeks ago, she sounds like she was genuinely concerned about me. Now as I look at her, it's hard to see the petulant client and the overwrought woman I chased into the street last night.

I cover her hand with mine and sigh, knowing I shouldn't be touching her like this, not even to show my kindness and gratitude for getting the ambulance to take care of me. Mia is the woman I protect. We're not supposed to be anything more.

The problem is it's clear to me that we both know we are something more than merely client and bodyguard.

With a gentle smile, she says, "I'm just so happy you're going to be okay."

Before I can respond, my mother, father, and Wilder come walking into the room, and I immediately see my mother's a mess. Her eyes are red like she's been crying, and her cheeks are all flushed.

"Liam! Honey, the nurse just told us you're going to be okay. I was so worried. When we got the call that you'd been shot, I felt like I was going to pass out right there in the kitchen," my mother says breathlessly.

She never disappoints when it comes to being emotional about her children.

"I'm fine, Mom. Honestly."

Hoping to direct the attention away from my injury, I smile and say, "Everyone, this is Mia. The woman I work for."

The way the words come out sound odd, like I'm trying to hide something, but none of them were a lie. I do work to protect her. That I don't want to share with anyone, including Mia, how I feel about her isn't a lie.

Well, maybe a sin of omission.

My family members all look over at Mia in unison as if they rehearsed the move, and I see my father raise a single eyebrow before looking back at me. I know what he's thinking. It's written all over his face.

What's written all over my mother's face is utter adoration. "Oh, it's so nice to meet you!" she gushes. "I've seen your picture a million times, but you're so much more beautiful in person."

"The same with me, Mrs. Jackson. When Liam showed me the picture of you and your husband, I thought you were so pretty, but in person, you're just stunning. I guess that teaches us not to believe what the media shows us," Mia says sweetly, instantly charming my mother with her compliment.

Patting under her eyes, she says, "Oh, thank you. That's so nice of you. I was worried I looked terrible after crying so much. I was so scared when we found out Liam had been shot."

As they enjoy their mutual admiration society, my father asks, "So do you know who shot you?"

Typical Kane Jackson. He noticed how beautiful Mia was and where her hand was on my chest, and then he immediately moved to wanting to know the details of the crime.

I shake my head, wishing I did know who the son of a bitch was who thought it was okay to take a shot at me. Assuming it was me he was aiming at, of course. I can't be sure of that yet, but I'll find out who did this to me. That's a given.

"No idea. We were downtown and there was some traffic, so I didn't notice anyone odd and certainly no one aiming a gun at me."

My father frowns and lets out a heavy sigh. "I hope the police find this person quickly."

Interrupting all this seriousness, Wilder walks around the side of my bed and sits down in the chair to my left. "So does this mean you'll be coming back to your place sooner than you expected?"

I look over at him and roll my eyes. "No."

Mia adds, "I need Liam to be my head of security for my upcoming tour, so he's going to be working for me for a while."

Her information clearly makes Wilder's day, if his grin is any indication. "Good to know."

Leave it to my brother to use a visit to see me after getting shot as a way to figure out how much longer he'll get to have my condo all to himself. Not that I think he's ever alone there. Something tells me he's living it up at my place, probably having parties every night of the week.

My parents shoot him a look of disapproval before turning their attention back to me. "I'm so happy your job is going well," my mother says and then adds, "other than getting shot, that is."

I can never tell if my mother is just subtly funny or off the wall bizarre when she says things like that. My father turns to look at her like he's sure it's the second option, but he's so used to her being like this that he simply shakes his head.

"What your mother means is it's clear you and Mia have cultivated a good working relationship. Most employers don't sit by the bedside of someone who works for them."

"Yes, that's exactly what I meant," my mother says, blushing.

It's all very strange and makes me wish Mia had moved her hand before they walked in, but still she keeps it resting on my chest. I'm sure my family thinks we're involved romantically, which isn't true.

At least not yet. Not really.

I glance over at her to see she has no idea anyone is paying attention to where she's touching me. Letting my gaze drop to her hand on my chest, I smile when I lift my eyes to look at her.

Finally, she understands what I'm trying hard to say without saying any words. Yanking her hand back into her body, she stands up quickly, clearly uncomfortable.

"I'm going to go talk to whoever is in charge to see why you haven't been discharged yet. I think I need to talk to the people who send the bill too since I don't want you to have to pay for this. It was very nice to meet all of you."

"Mia, I have insurance, so you don't have to worry," I say, but it's no use.

She shakes her head, frowning back at me. "No, you were shot doing something for me. I'll take care of it."

The four of us watch her hurry out of the room, and when she's gone, my mother says, "What's it like to have a superstar be a fan of yours?"

And there it is. At least I didn't have to wait long before one of them said something.

"It's not like that," I say, utterly unconvincingly. Even I don't believe what I'm saying.

"You may not think so, but she does," my mother says with a knowing smile as she looks over at my father nodding his agreement. "I'm not the only one who saw how much that girl cares for you, honey."

"I think you definitely have a fan, Liam," my father says with a twinkle in his eye.

"Seriously, guys, it's not like that. She's just upset because she saw me get shot. It's nothing more. Don't make a big deal out of this. Please?"

Wilder taps on my left forearm, and I turn to see him wearing a shit-eating grin. "If Grandma was here, you know what she'd be saying? You're protesting too much."

I shake my head and roll my eyes. "Nice butchering Shakespeare there, man. And I'm not protesting, so all of you stop it. I have to work with this woman. Don't make it weird."

"Nobody's making it weird, honey. We're just telling you what's obvious to everyone," my mother says sweetly.

"Well, stop mentioning it. Maybe we can focus on the fact that I got shot. How about that?"

As soon as the words leave my mouth, I know I said the wrong thing. My mother's face contorts into an expression of pure sadness, and it looks like at any second, she's going to start crying.

My father throws me a dirty look, just to reinforce my knowledge that I screwed up, so I quickly say, "But I'm going to be fine. Just some stitches. Nothing else. I mean, they wouldn't let me out of the hospital if I was in bad shape, would they?"

A muted happiness returns to my mother's face, so at least that's something. Of course, she's never more thrilled than when she thinks I've met The One. That's how she refers to every woman I've gotten into a relationship with for the past five years. The One. They never are that one single soul who I want to spend the rest of my life with, but hope forever springs eternal in Abbi Jackson's motherly mind.

"Will you be able to return to your job?" my father asks in his typical no-nonsense fashion.

I nod, happy to be talking about something other than Mia and how the two of us feel about one another. "Absolutely. She's got a tour coming up, and I need to be there to make sure at every city she stops in that there's the right kind of security. You should have seen what they used to do for her. The biggest new star in the music world and I swear they used to cross their fingers and hope everything would work out. She's lucky she didn't get kidnapped or worse with what her former head of security used to do."

"She's lucky to have you then," my father says with a smile I know means he wants to bust my ass about how I'm breaking my number one rule I've always followed in my business.

Never get close to the client.

A nurse thankfully ends any chance of that conversation occurring when she walks into the room with papers for me to sign. My family takes that as their cue to leave and come around to where Wilder has been sitting.

Leaning down, my mother presses a kiss to my cheek. "Please be careful, honey. I worry about you, and this only makes me more worried."

I smile up at her and see in her blue eyes she isn't exaggerating about her concern. "It's okay, Mom. I'll be fine."

"I love you, honey. Call more often so I can hear how things are going once you go out on the road with Mia, okay?"

My father nods, chiming in with his request for me to call home more than once in a while too. "Your mother's right. We want to hear all about it."

"I will. I promise."

After she gives me another kiss, my mother tousles my hair that's technically too short to mess up these days. "Good. Parents like to hear from their kids, even when they're grown men. Stay safe, honey. Okay? We love you, Liam."

My father simply smiles in that way that tells me he thinks he knows much more about what's going on with Mia and me than I'm admitting. "Have fun."

They turn to leave and Wilder taps me on the arm again. "Don't worry about your place. It's in tip-top shape. Just as you left it. But you won't need that once you and Mia get together, right? Because I'm thinking we might as well keep it in the family if you don't."

Typical Wilder.

I look over at the nurse trying not to smile at my brother's awkward attempt at making me promise he can have my apartment now and point toward the door. "Out! And keep my place in good shape for when I get back. Got it?"

My brother waves off my comments with a chuckle on his way out the door. "Yeah, yeah. I know what I saw, so just remember the whole keeping it in the family idea. And call your mother, Liam. You know how she worries."

The nurse points to where I need to sign on half a dozen forms. Feeling the need to explain all she's heard, I say, "That's just my family. You know how family can be."

"You seem to have a lot of people who care about

you, including that young woman out at the nurses' station. You're a lucky man, Mr. Jackson."

The look in her eyes tells me she thinks just like my family does. That Mia and I are involved. I guess there's no point in protesting. They're going to believe what they want to believe.

But I can't deny something's different between us now. I just don't know what to do about that.

CHAPTER TWENTY-ONE

ia

I SIT ON THE EDGE OF LIAM'S BED AS THE STAFF BRING in anything he could possibly want while he rests like the doctor at the hospital said he needs to if I want him to be able to accompany me on the tour. I made them buy every magazine a man could want from the bookstore, and Cecelia made sure to buy all of his favorite food after I insisted he make me a list so he can have whatever he wants as he gets better.

When the guys finish lugging in a mini fridge so he doesn't have to do anything to have a drink whenever he wants, we're left alone for the first time since those few precious moments we had together in the hospital. Damn that nurse who couldn't give us just a minute more.

"If you get hungry, Cecelia has strict instructions to make you whatever you ask for. All you have to do is tell her what you want. I gave her the list you wrote down, so she has everything you need. And if I have to hire a different chef to make something she can't make, then I'll do that."

Liam shakes his head, like he's embarrassed by all this attention he's getting. "You don't have to do all of this. I'm fine, Mia. Just a few stitches. You're like my mother. She's all worried too."

I smile at the comparison to that beautiful blond woman I got to meet a few hours ago. "I'm going to take that as a compliment. I knew your mother would be pretty after seeing that picture of yours, but it didn't do her justice, Liam. She's absolutely beautiful. And your father? I can tell where you get your looks from. They're so sweet too! Your mother told me about how you loved marshmallows in your sweet potatoes when you were a little boy, so I made sure the kitchen has all the sweet potatoes and marshmallows you could possibly want."

His expression turns sheepish, and I swear I see a hint of guilt in his eyes. "What? What's wrong?" I ask, suddenly fearful I've upset him.

"I haven't eaten that since I was ten, Mia. I don't even like sweet potatoes anymore."

"It's okay. I hear they're healthy, so I'll make sure Ainsley and Mitchell know we have them in the house. I just won't mention the marshmallows so I don't have to hear a lecture from him about how much empty calories one marshmallow has in it."

I feel myself beginning to unravel after hearing about my mistake with something he doesn't even like and hasn't eaten in over a decade. I only wanted to make sure he felt like he's at home as he's recuperating. That's all. He probably thinks I'm some stupid girl who just wants to buy everything in the world and bring it to my house because I'm feeling guilty that he got shot.

"Mia…"

He says my name in a low voice that sounds ominous. Like he's going to tell me he doesn't think he can go out on tour with me, or he doesn't want to after getting shot because of what I did.

My entire body tenses up as I wait to hear the next words that come out of his mouth. He remains silent for so long, though, that I can't stop myself from filling the empty space with a bunch of chatter that means next to nothing.

"So, no sweet potatoes and marshmallows. I hope you told your mom so she doesn't make them for Thanksgiving or anything. I'm sure you will so she doesn't waste her time making something you don't like. There's a ton of other stuff down there, though, so don't worry. You can have whatever your heart desires. I have to admit I was surprised the media were waiting outside the hospital when we left. Can you believe those vultures? Someone gets shot, and all they want to do is take pictures. I'm sorry about that. I should have gone out a side door or something so they didn't swarm all over you."

Liam leans forward and holds out his hand toward where I sit on the bed. "Mia, come here."

Afraid of the serious tone of his voice and the somber expression he's wearing right now, I slide up the bed until I'm right next to him. He takes my hand in his, and for a moment, everything inside me calms, but then I look into his eyes and see that seriousness in them.

"Mia, you don't have to feel bad about what happened. I think that's what all of this is about, isn't it?"

I shake my head, refusing to admit the truth, especially to him. "No, not at all. I just need you to be in the best shape possible for when the tour starts in a few days. As for those goddamned reporters and photographers, that's how I always feel, but you didn't deserve to have to fight your way to the car after being in the hospital."

His warm skin against mine makes me feel like my insides are melting, but I don't see anything like that in him at all. I thought when we were out on that street that he was trying to tell me he cared but he didn't think he should. Did I misunderstand?

"I'm going to be fine. Honestly. It wasn't that bad. I guess I'm just a big bleeder, like the doctor said. And the press was nothing."

The mere mention of him bleeding out on that sidewalk as I hovered over him praying for anyone to stop him from dying brings tears to my eyes, and I hang my head so he can't see them. If I'm wrong and he didn't want to tell me he cares about me, the last thing I want is for him to see I'm that affected by him getting shot.

"Hey, what's wrong?"

I shake my head again, but it's no use. The tears come streaming down my cheeks like I'm some pathetic little girl who can't control her emotions.

"Mia, look at me."

When I refuse to do as he wants, he slides his finger under my chin and gently lifts it so he can see my tears. "I was so scared you'd die there, Liam. I didn't know what to do. I felt helpless, and I hate feeling that. I control everything in my life as much as I can, as you well know, but I couldn't do a thing to stop you from bleeding from that bullet."

"I do know you like to control everything and everyone, so I imagine seeing me down for the count was a lot to handle. I'm fine, though. See?"

He flexes his bicep to show me his right arm works fine, and I smile. "So you can show off? That doesn't mean you're fine. You got shot, Liam."

My teasing him makes him laugh. "Okay, I wasn't trying to show off, but you don't have to worry. It's going to be okay."

I hang my head and whisper the ugly truth I've hated since I saw him fall to the ground last night. "You got shot because of me. I don't know how I'll ever forgive myself for that."

With a heavy sigh, he says in that way that sounds so reasonable when I want to be completely unreasonable, "You didn't shoot me, so this isn't your fault. And I don't want to hear anything about how you left the estate and if I wasn't there, I wouldn't have been shot."

Smiling, I lift my head to see him smiling too. "Well, since you've taken away my entire argument for feeling guilty, I guess I can leave you feeling utterly innocent of my crime. Thank you, Liam."

"Go get ready for your first dates. You don't have much time, and there's no way I want to be the one your entourage blames when you aren't on fire that first night. And you know they will."

I can hear Ainsley and the rest of them already saying he's a distraction I shouldn't give into now that the tour is so close to beginning. Not that I give a damn what they have to say about Liam now. He took a bullet for me, and no matter how much he wants to claim I'm not to blame for him getting shot, the hard facts are if I hadn't dragged him down to that part of town and I hadn't run down that sidewalk making him chase me, he never would have been in any position to be shot by anyone.

"Thank you for not hating me, Liam."

The words barely come out loud enough for anyone but me to hear them, but when he nods and winks at me, I know he heard me. I don't know what I'd do if he hated me. Not after last night.

"If I didn't hate you when I first got here, there's no way I could hate you now. You saved me last night. Don't sell yourself short, Mia. You called 9-1-1 and told them exactly where to go. A lot of people would have unraveled, but you kept your cool. Things might have turned out way differently if you weren't there."

I know what he's trying to do, and even though I won't argue with him about it, he's wrong. I set everything into motion for him to get hurt last night. Whatever I did to help doesn't make up for what I did that made it possible for someone to shoot him.

Joking, I stand up from the bed and look down at him as I say, "Well, this hero needs to get working. Let me know if you need anything, okay?"

"I will. Go rehearse so you're ready for this weekend."

For a moment, our eyes lock and I think I'd like nothing more than to kiss him right now. I wonder if he's thinking that too.

CHAPTER TWENTY-TWO

𝓜 ia

HAPPY AFTER THE TIME I SPENT WITH LIAM, I practically bounce down the stairs and meet my mother and her assistant when I hit the first floor. She looks particularly dour today, but she's probably just worried about what happened last night. I get that. She never handles when I go out on my own, but the fact that someone got hurt is likely making her ten times as stressed out.

"I want to talk to you about your security situation, Mia," she says, frowning.

As much as I understand her concern, I'm not in the mood to discuss this. My security situation, as she calls it, is the best it's ever been. That's because of one person. Liam. Now that I know he's going to be fine and right there with me when I go out on tour, I have nothing to worry about.

"Later," I say, pushing her off like I will every time she brings this up.

"No, now. With Liam laid up, we need to address your security. I think we should bring Michael back."

I stop, stunned by her suggestion. Spinning around, I try to make out if she's serious or not. "You want to bring Michael back? Why? I don't need anyone new, or in this case, old."

Setting her jaw like she always does when she insists on something, my mother takes a step toward me. "Liam is upstairs in his bed, which is perfectly natural since he's been shot. That said, he's not in any shape to protect you, and you need someone by your side when the first shows begin this weekend. We've got the media camped out on the street because they sense a story here. If ever you needed security, it's now. It's too late to get anyone else to replace Liam, so Michael's the logical answer to the problem."

My brain spins at the fact that she's serious about this. "There is no problem, first of all, so I don't need a solution. Liam is resting, as the doctor said he has to, but he'll be by my side when the tour starts. The first few dates are right here in Tampa, and all of his guys he's brought in to assist him can help him if he needs it, which he won't. It's just a few stitches in his upper arm. This isn't some injury he received on the battlefield. He'll be fine, so thanks but no thanks about Michael."

Still, she doesn't back down, even after I've told her no to replacing Liam. And why is she acting like having the media obsessed with me isn't exactly what she works to cultivate with every move she makes?

"Mia, I handle security for you, and I'm the one who brought Liam in, if you remember. Let me handle things.

It's only until he's back up on his feet. We don't really have a choice. Michael is the only one who can come with such short notice."

Everything she says confuses me. Shaking my head in disbelief, I struggle to understand why she's being like this.

"You were the one who fired Michael for helping me get that hotel room and sneaking me out. Now you think he's the only person in the world who can pick up whatever slack you're sure is going to happen now since Liam's been shot? Not the guys he trusts and handpicked to work with him to protect me because he wanted to shore up my security, which by the way was so lax that I probably was in more danger than anyone wants to talk about? No! Let Michael stay with his hoochie mama at his apartment. That's where he belongs."

Before she can try to give me another reason why I should take that poor excuse for a bodyguard back, I hurry over to Ainsley's room to talk out all these things I'm feeling about Liam. I know she isn't crazy about him, but that's good because she'll be happy to give me all the Devil's advocate arguments she can think of.

When she opens her door, I march right in, ready to talk about everything that's going on with Liam and me. Ainsley looks a little surprised but doesn't complain about my not asking to come in. Maybe she thinks after what I went through last night that she shouldn't give me a hard time.

"We need to talk," I announce as I flop down in the weird saggy chair with the blue cushions over near the window.

"Okay," she says warily. "What about?"

"I need you to be as tough on me as I need, but

remember that my feelings are a little all over the place today, okay?"

Ainsley sits down on her bed and crosses her legs under her. "Okay. I thought for a second there that you had some problem with me, but now I'm confused. What do I have to be tough on you about? Hey, shouldn't you be rehearsing with Tiffany and your dancers? The tour begins in only a few days."

"That's not what I need you to be tough on me about, but thanks. I'll get to her and them in a few minutes. First, though, I need you to give me all the reasons why I shouldn't care about Liam."

My life coach levels her harsh gaze directly on my face and grimaces. "You sure you want me to go there? Because there are about a million small reasons and one big reason I can give you for not falling for him."

I shrug, hopeful when she hears the truth that I'm already crazy about him that she won't pitch a fit. "Too late. I've already fallen."

"Then what the hell is this conversation for?" she asks in exasperation.

"To help me figure out what to do! Stop being so difficult. The man protected me last night after someone shot him. You act as if he's some scum off the street."

She lets out a heavy sigh full of irritation. "Fine. He did his job. Yay for him. That's no reason to fall head over heels in love with him."

My face heats up from a blush at her mention of love. "I didn't say I was head over heels in love with him. God, you are such a drama queen. I said I've fallen for him. Not in love. Let's just say in caring for him."

"Fall in care with someone? Okay, so now we're just making shit up? At least I know the rules of this conversation. So you care for him? Why? That seems like a good place to start. Tell me why you care for Mr. Rules and Regulations, who by the way hates your dear friend, yours truly."

"He doesn't hate you. He just hates how you sound like you're giving birth to goats when you do your evening stretches," I say, struggling to hold back my laughter.

But Ainsley doesn't find any of it funny.

"He's crazy uptight. Like if you stuck coal up his ass, you'd be able to pull out a diamond in a week."

I scrunch up my face at that visual. "I'm not sure if you're trying to make me dislike him or you with that description, Ains. Can we get back to talking about my caring for him? I need you to tell me why I shouldn't."

"Because he's your chief of security. That sounds like a good place to start. Isn't he breaking some kind of personal code of ethics people like him make a pledge to uphold when they take a job?" she asks in a tone that tells me she thinks he is.

"I don't know. Is that really a thing?" I ask, wondering if Liam could get into trouble for caring for me.

That isn't what I want. Nobody should be able to dictate who falls for who, especially if it means he might get in trouble with the owner of VIP over it.

"It should be," Ainsley says in a huff. "You still haven't answered my question. Why do you think you care for him?"

That's easier asked than answered. There are a hundred reasons why I care about Liam. He's good looking. I could tell Ainsley that, but since she thinks he's way too uptight, it probably wouldn't be an answer she'll agree with.

He's great at his job. That's a good reason, especially since his job revolves around protecting my life. Then again, she'll probably just say he's supposed to be good at his job.

He makes me smile. I like listening to him talk about his family and the nature shows he likes just as I do. I feel comfortable whenever I'm with him.

"Well? I think if you can't answer the question of why you care about him, then that's your answer why you shouldn't."

God, she is in rare, militant form today. Is this what everyone means when they say tough love?

Taking a deep breath in, I let it out slowly and tell her why I care for him. "Because when I'm around him, I'm happier than when I'm not around him."

Her eyes open wide, and I suspect she thinks that's the biggest load of shit she's ever heard. It's the truth, though. Even last night when I was trying to run away, simply having him with me made me feel better. I didn't really want him to leave me alone. I just didn't know how to handle all the emotions rushing through me after what happened between us.

And then as soon as I saw him bleeding from a bullet that may have been meant for me, I realized how much I'd miss him if he wasn't in my life.

My life coach's body looks like it deflates at my answer. "Well, I wasn't expecting something so deep. I thought you were going to mention his beautiful body or how he looks when he's working out in the gym. I'm impressed, Mia."

With a shrug, I smile. "Don't be. I like those things

too, so let's not get me set up for sainthood just yet. But other than abs that make my mouth water and how incredible he looks when he wears those gray sweatpants of his, I really like spending time with him."

I don't tell her the hundred other things I like about Liam, but even with what I've said, I know I'm in trouble. Ainsley knows it too. I see it in her expression as she tries to smile at me.

"You're not helping with arguments against him, Ains. Where did they go?"

Her cheeks blush a deep pink and she giggles. "With those gray sweatpants. Nothing I can say to you can beat gray sweatpants. Those are kryptonite to women. Why do you think guys wear them?"

We both laugh, but she's right. A hot man in gray sweatpants is truly the one thing that can make a woman forget everything she was thinking at that moment.

I stand up to leave, not any clearer on what I'm going to do about Liam. "Well, this wasn't helpful at all, but something tells me nothing was going to be anyway."

"I'm sorry. I'm really not a huge fan of his, but it's hard to have an argument against someone making you happy. What are you going to do? I mean, does he know how you feel? Have you said anything to him yet?"

Shaking my head, I admit the sad truth. "No, and I don't know how to do that. I thought last night when we were downtown that he was trying to say he cared for me, but now I'm not so sure. This whole getting shot thing has totally made things so much worse but a lot better too."

Ainsley looks at me in horror, so I quickly explain what I mean. "Not that I ever wanted him to get shot. It's not like that, so stop looking at me like I'm some kind of terrible person. It's just that it's given us a chance to just be nice to one another, which I really like. I don't mind sparring with him since even when he's fighting with me, I know he's only trying to help, but simply sitting next to him as he lies in bed is nice too."

I bury my face in my hands. "Oh, God, I don't know what I'm going to do."

She hurries over to me and takes me in her arms. "Don't worry so much. You have a lot on your plate right now. Take a deep breath, remember your priorities, and above all, don't freak out. Everything will work out for the best. It always does."

As I inhale and exhale, trying to calm myself like she claims I should, thoughts of my mother trying to push Liam out to bring Michael back flood my brain. I can't believe she thinks that's going to ever happen.

"You don't feel like you're relaxing, Mia."

I drop my hands from my face and explain why. "My mother wants to replace Liam with Michael until he's better. I told her no and put my foot down, but something tells me she's planning on doing it anyway. What the hell is she thinking? She's acting like Liam is bedridden or something. He just needs to rest for a day or so. God, my life is a mess, and I have to go out on tour in just a couple days."

My life coach pats my arm like she's afraid I'm going to completely unravel right there in her room if she doesn't pull her social worker thing on me. "Calm down. Seriously, I need you to relax. Whatever happens, you can handle it. I'll be right there beside you the entire time, so deep breaths. Do you want me to talk to Andrea? I can let her know this kind of stress isn't good for you right before a tour. That might make her back off a little."

The last thing I need is my best friend and my mother brawling over how much stress I have in my life, so I shake my head and smile. "No, but thanks. I hope she got the idea that I wasn't having any of that Michael coming back nonsense, but if she brings it up again, I'll have to handle it. As you always tell me, the key to being happy is to know when to ignore the bullshit. So I'll ignore it and her, if she keeps it up."

As I walk toward her door to leave, she chuckles. "I do say that. It just sounds a lot more strident coming from you. Maybe try smiling when you say it?"

Looking back at her, I paste a grin on my face. "Ignoring the bullshit is the key to being happy. Any better?"

"No, still pretty harsh."

"Oh, well."

Maybe harsh is what I have to be to get things the way I want when it comes to my mother.

CHAPTER TWENTY-THREE

$\mathcal{M}$ia

ALL OF US SIT AROUND IN MY DRESSING ROOM AS always to do our preshow ritual I've done since the first time I went out on tour. Back then, it was a tiny event that consisted of malls and galleries that held no more than a couple hundred people. Still, it was exciting in those days since I was only fifteen and couldn't do bars and clubs like other performers just starting out. But whether it's a mall show or one in front of an arena full of screaming fans, my entourage and I always sit together and share good vibes we want to carry us through that night's performance.

"Okay, everyone! Time to join hands," Ainsley announces to the entire group. "It's almost time for Mia to go out and see her fans, and we want to send her off with the best possible feeling we can."

One by one, each person I rely on to make me look

beautiful and toned and talented, along with my five dancers for the night, steps up into the center of the rather small dressing room at the Citrus County Pavilion. We all take the hand of the person next to us and close our eyes as I try to channel all the gratitude and happiness I have inside me.

"Thank you for all these incredible people who make my professional and personal life so much better than I ever dreamed possible. Let us have a great show and give my fans what they came here tonight to see."

As usual and our tradition, Mitchell chimes in with his lame joke, "Okay, break a leg! Well, not really because working out with a broken leg is complete crap and I don't want to have to deal with that."

By the time he finishes, everyone's eyes are open and we're all staring at my trainer in amused disbelief that he thinks any of that is funny. He's a terrific guy, but his sense of humor is shit.

"Thanks, Mitch. And thank you everyone! Let's have a great show tonight!"

Everyone cheers and throws their hands up in the air. This feels good, and I'm looking forward to the start of a fantastic tour with this show. We're all happy and rested, and I've got the best security man in the world protecting me.

What else could a girl like me ask for?

As everyone files out of the dressing room to leave me alone for the last few minutes before show time, I wonder where Liam has been for the past hour. I've seen each of his men milling around, but he's been absent.

Probably double and triple checking everything. He does like to be thorough. I like that about him.

A member of the stage crew opens the dressing room

door just enough to fit his lips into the space. "Sorry if I'm barging in on you, Mia, but fifteen minutes until show time."

He closes the door before I get a chance to thank him. Fifteen minutes. Like always, this is when I start to get nervous. I look down at my hand resting on my dressing table and it's trembling. I have nothing to be scared about. Liam and his men have taken care of security and made it tighter than it ever was.

For a few seconds, my mind races with the thought that the bullet that hit Liam wasn't meant for him but for me. Is it possible my stalker has taken things up a notch and turned to attempted murderer?

I shake my head in disbelief. No way. For all this time, he's only been a stalker and now suddenly, he's taken to trying to kill me? That doesn't make sense.

But if the shooter wasn't him, who was it? Of course, the police say they have nothing yet. It feels like every time something happens with me, that's all they have to tell me. "Nothing yet, Mia. We're working on finding all the clues we can and solving this, but it will take time."

Time my ass. I doubt they'll ever figure out who took that shot at Liam and me. Then again, maybe because it involved another person, the cops will actually try to solve this crime.

A knock on the dressing room door tears me out of my miserable thoughts about the police, and I hope to see Liam walking in to tell me he's checked everything and it's all as safe as can be. Then I'll get back to dealing with the preshow jitters that always plague me on first nights.

But when my mother walks through the door instead of him, I'm disappointed and don't bother pretending I'm not. "What do you want, Mother? I'm busy trying to get myself into the right mindset right now, so whatever you want to talk about, it can wait."

She forces a smile in response to my coldness and hurries over to where I sit. "I love that costume! I didn't realize you were returning to your red look for this show. You always look so great when you wear red on stage, Mia."

Her compliments make me smile, but I sense something frantic about her as she practically trips over her words. "Thanks, Mom. The girls and I talked it over and we decided red felt right for this tour. I want people to be wowed, and even though *Mine* has hit the top of the charts before the whole record releases, I feel like I have something to prove with this tour."

That's the most I've talked about my music and my songs to my mother in months. I didn't mean to confess all of that to her, especially since she rarely enjoys hearing about the artistic side of the business. She's all about the money side, and I have a feeling if it were up to her, she'd have me singing the same song over and over on a constant loop if it made money.

My talk about how this tour feels for me surprises her, but she nods like she understands, or at least like she wants me to think she understands. "Of course, the song is doing well. The entire record will too. Your millions and millions of fans love you, Mia. It's why this show tonight is packed, even though it's just a warm-up show to work out all the kinks."

"The audience doesn't think of this show that way," I say, reflexively wanting to defend my fans.

They don't view early dates on my tours like practice sessions, and they shouldn't. I would never want these fans tonight to think they got a lesser version of me or my performance simply because they showed up for the first date. These are my hometown fans, people who have watched me grow up from that little girl at the malls singing her heart out for a couple hundred people. They were there before the rest of the world. They deserve nothing but my best for being my fans the longest.

"Yes, yes," she says, not truly agreeing with me but placating me as she fixes the strap of my costume on my left shoulder.

God, I hate when she does that. I'm a grown woman, but as soon as I sense my mother placating me about anything, I turn into a pre-adolescent girl who wants to do nothing more than stomp her feet and have a temper tantrum.

"What did you come in for anyway?" I ask, tired of this dance the two of us do.

Suddenly, she looks guilty, like I caught her in the middle of doing something wrong. Looking away toward the sofa on the other side of the room, she says, "I just wanted to check that you were ready."

"This isn't my first rodeo, you know. I know I need to be ready, especially since Carl popped his head in a few minutes ago to say it was fifteen minutes until show time."

"Good, good. Well, I'll get out of your hair then. I just wanted to make sure you'll be ready when security comes to take you out to the stage," she says with her back toward me as she walks toward the door.

"I'll be ready. In fact, please send Liam in now so I can talk to him before I have to go out there."

My mother stops just as her hand lands on the doorknob, but she doesn't say anything for a long moment, further irritating me. Why does she have to be so dramatic about everything? All she needs to do is say okay and then walk out. Why act like this is some scene in a damn movie?

Slowly, she turns around and gives me the fakest smile I've ever seen on her face. Even faker than the ones she used to put on when I acted up and everyone thought she was to blame since I was underage.

The type of smile that means she's hiding something.

"About that."

"About what? Just send Liam in and stop making this whole thing a melodrama with you as the lead actress, okay? I need to get prepared to go out on stage in less than ten minutes."

"He's not here."

I've never been diagnosed with high blood pressure, but I swear at this moment I feel like the top of my head is about to blow off, spraying blood and brains all over this goddamned room. A headache instantly begins to throb at my temples, and my face feels like it's suddenly ten degrees hotter than the rest of my body.

When I stand up, I can barely keep myself from falling over. "What do you mean he's not here?"

"He wasn't ready to protect you for tonight's show. I knew it the second I saw him having one of his guys help him with that sling he has to wear. So tonight and tomorrow night, Michael will be your personal bodyguard and take you to the stage."

"What the hell did you do?" I say, feeling the tears start to well in my eyes as I struggle to keep my emotions in check. "The first night of the tour and you pull this shit?"

She moves into hyperplacate mode like she always

has when she's fucked up and I dare to tell her I won't stand for it. "Now don't get upset, Mia. It's only for a couple of shows. You should have seen him. He just can't do the job like I know he wants to, so I told him I'd have someone else do it so he could rest. Liam knows his men are right here for you. That's why he was perfectly fine with it."

I can't control my emotions anymore and scream, "Get out! Get out now! Leave me alone!"

My outburst startles her, and she quickly hurries out of the room like some guilty thing who knows if she doesn't get the hell out of my sight at this very moment that she risks me really blowing up on her. I collapse back down onto the chair and look around for some explanation how this could have happened after I explicitly told her I didn't want her to replace Liam with Michael.

Oh, God. Liam isn't here. I can't do this knowing he's miles away back at the house. How could he just let me come here without being by my side?

CHAPTER TWENTY-FOUR

$\mathcal{M}$ia

QUICKLY, I SCRAMBLE TO FIND MY CELL PHONE. I need to talk to him. I need to understand how he could let her do this. He knows how much I rely on him to be around me to feel safe.

He answers with his usual hello that sounds so casual that I want to scream. How can he be so calm at a moment like this? After all his lectures on how important my security should be to me and how it used to be practically Swiss cheese with all the holes in what Michael used to do for me, the first time I truly expected to have him in charge and he's back at the estate in bed watching some nature show?

"Liam, why aren't you here?" I ask, practically sobbing.

"Mia, what's wrong? Aren't you supposed to be going on in like three minutes?"

"Why aren't you here? My mother told me she replaced you. You're okay with that? Tonight, of all nights, you're okay with me being with lame security?"

"You don't have lame security," he says and then chuckles like any of this is fucking funny. "My guys are there, so trust me, there's nothing lame about your protection. Trust me."

I stand up to pace as the realization that my mother lied to him about everything concerning this show tonight. My legs feel like they're going to give out, but I can't sit down because I swear I'm going to explode at any moment.

"Your guys aren't handling my security tonight. My mother brought Michael back to replace you. She told me she wanted to do that the other day, but I flatly refused to agree to it. She knew I needed you here tonight, and still she went behind my back and brought Michael back. He's the one in charge, not your guys, Liam."

"What? That's impossible. Drew's supposed to be in charge, Mia. I made sure of that before they left here today. Your mother knew that too since I talked to her this afternoon. Why didn't she tell me she was planning to bring in someone new? He doesn't know any of the plans."

"He's not new! He's Michael, the one you told me was the shittiest bodyguard you'd ever heard of. He's the one in charge, and I swear to God I won't leave this room if she sends him down here to walk me to the stage. I won't."

My emotions are spiraling out of control so much that I don't think even Ainsley and her Zen stuff could calm me down now. My mother has done some terrible things in her time, but this is the worst. She knows I've been on edge since Liam got shot, and she turns around and brings Michael back after she fired him for being such a terrible security chief? What the hell is wrong with her?

"Listen to me, Mia. I want you to relax. This is all under control. I'll call Drew and find out what's going on. Give me a couple minutes and then I'll call you back. Don't worry. My guys wouldn't let me down and they won't let you down either."

When I don't say anything, he adds, "Trust me. I'll handle this and then you won't have to worry about any of it. You'll just be able to have a great show and thrill all those fans who are dying to see you, okay? I saw on the news that the line of people to get in is the biggest the Pavilion has ever had."

"Okay. Just fix this, Liam. I don't want to have him in charge. I don't feel safe without you."

"I will. I'll call you right back."

Slamming my phone down onto the table, I consider storming out to find my mother and firing her insubordinate ass for doing this on the biggest night I've had in so long. She knows how important these first shows are to me and everyone else in the crew. This is where we get the feel for how things are and what needs to be tweaked a little so everything runs smoothly when we're out on the road miles away from home. How could she pull this on me tonight?

A knock on the dressing room door startles me, and the next thing I know, there is Michael smiling at me like we're the best of friends and he didn't treat me like I never meant a thing to him the second my traitorous mother fired him just six weeks ago. His expression comes off as smug, like he always knew he'd get his job back and nothing he did to me would matter.

Well, he's wrong. Now he'll get to find out just how mistaken he was.

"Don't say a word because I don't want to hear a thing from you. Just turn around and walk out the way you came in. You are not my bodyguard anymore, so you don't belong in here. Whatever my mother told you was wrong, so leave."

Michael runs his hand through his dark hair and smiles. "Good to know some things don't change. I was wondering if you'd settled down since I left. I see you haven't."

"This isn't some happy reunion, Michael. This is me telling you to get the fuck out or I swear to God I'm going to scream at the top of my lungs until the cops haul your ass away from here," I snap, hating the very sight of this man.

My phone begins to vibrate across the table, so I quickly grab it and see it's Liam. The second I put the phone to my ear, I hear him say to me, "Mia, I just talked to Drew. I don't know what your mother is up to, but she's all but cut my guys out tonight. All they've been told is Michael is in charge, but when they've tried to brief him on the plans I set up, he walks away. I'm getting ready to leave right now. I'll be there as soon as I can."

Before I can say a word, the call ends. Furious at the man standing in front of me and my mother, I spin around to face Michael and shake my head. Whatever the two of them thought was going to happen tonight isn't, thanks to Liam.

"You and my mother screwed up, pal. You think you can just upend everything because she wants you back? Fuck you! I don't want you back, and my new chief of security is pissed that you've made a mess of his plans to protect me. So get the hell out and go tell my mother than I'm not leaving this dressing room until Liam gets here, so she better goddamned hope there isn't a lot of traffic or this fucking show won't happen at all."

My former bodyguard takes a step back and shakes his head. "Still doing the diva act, Mia? Fine. I'll tell her, but everyone's going to hate you for doing this just because you can't have your way."

"I'm doing this because I don't feel safe without the one person who makes me feel fucking safe, you asshole!" I scream. "Tell my mother that too!"

When he leaves, I sit down again, weak from too much yelling and knowing I've probably wrecked my voice for tonight. I can't decide if I want to cry or hit something. Or both.

My mother knows someone shot Liam not ten feet away from where I was standing, and she feels like bringing in some guy who made me feel like shit after she fired him is the logical next step she should take? I don't think I'm ever going to forgive her for this.

How can I?

I hear the crowd cheering for me to come out and entertain them like I'm supposed to. I want to. They have no idea how much I want to be out there singing my heart out for them on every goddamned song.

But I can't do it if I don't feel safe, and without Liam, I can't leave this room. I won't.

The door flies open, and my mother storms in like

she's got a bone to pick with me. She's as mistaken as her idiot new best friend if she thinks I'm going to just sit here and take her nonsense now.

"Michael says you won't come out. Is that true?" she asks in some kind of fake shocked voice.

"Your little errand boy moves quickly when he wants to. What did you promise you'd give him to get him to behave so well, Mother?" I ask, staring into her dark eyes to find the truth of her feelings.

"Don't be ridiculous. You're making a fool of yourself, Mia. Michael is doing us a favor, one he didn't have to agree to after I fired him and you made that scene at his apartment. Now let's get going because your adoring fans are waiting."

She turns toward the door as if her simply saying I have to go is all it takes. My feet feel like they're encased in cement, though. I'm not leaving this room without seeing Liam and knowing he's got everything under control.

"No. When Liam gets here, then I'll go because I'll know I'll be safe. So you and Michael go find yourselves someplace to bitch about me until then because I'm not budging from this room."

My mother's eyes open wide, and I know she isn't pretending to be shocked now. I've been stubborn on a great many points in the past with her, but I've never sounded like I do tonight.

"The press is going to cut you to shreds for this little stunt, Mia. Maybe you should think about that."

I open my mouth to say maybe I'll mention just who the architect of tonight's mess is, but she leaves before I can get a word out. Staring at the gray metal door as she slams it shut, I swear to myself that I'd fire her if she wasn't my mother.

Maybe I will fire her even though she is.

CHAPTER TWENTY-FIVE

iam

SYLVESTER MAY DO HIS JOB AT THE ESTATE FRONT GATE well, but as a driver in a dire situation, the guy sucks. A mile away from the Citrus County Pavilion and twenty minutes after Mia was supposed to start her show, he and I are stuck in a traffic jam that hasn't moved an inch in five minutes.

"Fuck! What's the goddamned hold up?" I grumble as I crane my neck to see why the hell we're all sitting here on a four-lane highway.

"I think these are all of Mia's fans," he says in guilty voice, as if he told all of these people to basically make the road a parking lot.

"Sorry, man. I'm just frustrated and worried what's going to happen if I don't get to this show in the next few minutes."

He gives me a tepid smile I hope means he's

accepted my apology, and I stick my head out the passenger side window in an attempt to figure out what the major malfunction is all around us. But he's right. It's Mia's fans all going to the show, so this bottleneck isn't going to get cleared anytime soon.

I have no choice. I have to get to her and clean up the mess her mother made with this Michael rehiring.

"Okay, Sylvester, I think this is where I get off. I'm sorry you're going to be trapped here for a while, but I'm hoofing it from here on out."

As I open the door, he gives me a shocked look like he can't believe what I just said and mumbles, "Okay. Are you planning on walking the mile to the pavilion?"

With a chuckle, I nod before stepping out of the car. "Something like that. Take care. I'll see you back at the house. Wish me luck!"

I slam the door shut and take off down the highway, weaving between cars as they slowly inch toward my destination. A few people holler at me, cheering me on as they watch me run past their cars like this is some kind of publicity stunt.

They have no idea. I have a feeling if I don't get to Mia and fix what her mother fucked up, watching me run through traffic is going to be the most fun many of these people have tonight.

It doesn't take me long to reach the pavilion, my right arm in a sling and all, but even though I work out every day, I'm winded after sprinting that mile. I'm more of a distance runner, if anything, but desperate times call for desperate measures.

The first person I see who I recognize is Kip, and I instantly know things are much worse than I imagined on my way here. His usually calm façade is nowhere to be found, replaced by a look of pure worry.

His eyes light up when he sees me, though. "Jesus Christ, Liam. You look like you ran all the way here, man. I thought you were supposed to stay in bed to rest for a couple days."

I take a deep breath in an attempt to get my heart back to some semblance of a normal beat and shake my head. "I'll rest when I'm dead. Right now, I've got other things to worry about. What the fuck is going on? I got a call from Mia saying her mother brought in the old head of security. Then Drew told me he cut you guys out. Where can I go to watch her from the side of the stage so I can make sure everything's okay?"

"She never went on. The crowd is ready to explode, and she's nowhere to be found. I heard her mother complaining that she refuses to perform. I'm telling you, Liam, somebody better get out on that stage and start singing or these people are going to freak."

The sound of thousands of people cheering for Mia all around me says Kip's right. "Let me see if I can do something about that. Gather up all our guys and meet me at the dressing room. Our plan we put in place when we did the walkthrough the other day is still the one that's in effect. Fuck that Michael guy. He must think we're goddamned rookies."

I don't usually let my crew see me react to anything with emotion, but this pisses me off. Andrea knew we had everything in order. What the hell was she thinking when she brought that guy back into the mix?

"Okay! Now you're talking! Let's just hope the crowd doesn't decide to storm the place before you get everything settled."

Nodding, I silently pray for the same thing as I turn to head back to the dressing room. Local officials and security line the passageway, but I hurry past them to get to the one person I know needs to see me.

The dressing room door is closed, and when I try the doorknob, I find it locked. Quickly, I knock a few times and say loud enough for anyone to hear, "Mia, it's Liam! Let me in!"

A second later, the door flies open, and I see Mia and her entire entourage and all her dancers staring at me. Mia runs to me and throws her arms around my body, clinging to me like I'm all that's keeping her safe right now.

"Liam! Everything is a disaster. I can't do this. My mother made everything a mess."

I look down at her sobbing against me and know things are much worse than I anticipated. I need to get her calm, but before I can do that, I need to get all these people out of this dressing room.

"Don't worry. We'll fix this and you'll be singing for all those people tonight."

I march in and immediately begin directing everyone out to where they belong. Pointing toward the door, I focus on the dancers first. "This show is about to start, so go take your places and be ready when Mia needs you."

The five women dutifully hurry out into the hallway, so I turn my attention to all the people who live at the house with us. "I need to speak to Mia, so everyone out. This chaos needs to end right now, so if you want to help her, find my security guys outside the door and they'll tell you where to safely position yourselves. That crowd is nearly at a fever pitch, and I don't want any of you getting hurt because you're in the wrong spot."

I expect to get some resistance from at least one or two of them, especially that life coach, but they all hurry out like the dancers did a few seconds ago, and finally, I'm alone with Mia. She still holds on to me like I'm a life raft, so I gently pry her arms from around my waist and smile down at her.

"Things are way more exciting than I expected them to be," I say with a chuckle. "You didn't tell me it would be pandemonium."

Her dark eyes stare up at me, and I can see beyond all the stage makeup that she's been crying. "My mother must have lost her mind. How could she do this to me on my first night of the tour?"

That's the question I want to have answered, but for now, I've got more important things to tackle. Taking Mia by the hand, I guide her over to the sofa and sit down next to her. I don't know anything about calming a performer before a big show, but I know this woman well enough to understand she needs to think of something good right now or she's never going to be able to walk out onto that stage.

"I left poor Sylvester out on the highway that looks like a parking lot because all of your fans are trying to get here. I guess it's a good thing for those people that things are running behind, huh?"

Mia hangs her head and sighs. "I bet you think I'm some spoiled rotten diva who's misbehaving, don't you?"

I shake my head and smile. "Nope. Not this time. This time, I'm putting all the blame on your mother. But we can't fix that right now. I need to get you out in front of all those people who can't wait to see you."

She looks up at me and smiles, and then her eyes get

big. "Did you have to run down the highway to get here? You did that for me?"

Nodding, I shrug, happy to minimize my mile long sprint at this moment. "It's my job. You told me you needed me, so here I am. That's what a bodyguard does for the person he's guarding."

"I can't believe you did that for me. Nobody's ever done anything like that for me when I asked them for help."

"Well, now I need you to do something for me, okay?"

Mia narrows her eyes, like she isn't sure what I could need at this moment. "What's that?"

Silent for a few moments, I let the noise of the crowd waiting for her fill the room. "Hear that? Those are the people who want nothing more than to see you perform, so I need you to forget all about your mother and her nonsense and go out there to give those people what only you can give them. Nobody else in the world is going to make them happier than you can just by singing your songs, Mia."

An expression of fear washes over her. "I don't know if I can, Liam. I feel so emotional right now. Even worse, I've been screaming at my mother for the past half hour, so I can only imagine what I'm going to sound like when I try to hit that first high note."

I take her hand in mine and give it a tiny squeeze. "You can because this is what you're great at. Everything else is bullshit we can deal with later. Right now, you need to go show that crowd what you can do. I know you can do this."

For a long moment, I'm not sure Mia believes she can do it, though, but she takes a deep breath in and smiles, nodding like she wants to try. "Okay. Thank you, Liam. I don't know what I'd do without you."

The fact that her mother wanted to see exactly what Mia would do without me tonight is what I plan to find out as soon as I locate Andrea. In the meantime, at least I've made the one person who needed to know she's safe feel like she can do this tonight.

She stands up and turns to look at me. "You'll be on the side of the stage, right? I don't think I can do this without knowing you're nearby so everything's safe."

I stand up and smile. "I'll be there, along with all of my men just where they're supposed to be."

Like she did when she saw me when I first arrived here, she throws her arms around my waist and presses her cheek to my chest. Her body trembles next to mine, and even though I know I shouldn't hug her back, it's like I can't stop myself. She's so frail right now that I can't let her think I'm not here for her in any way she needs.

The truth is that I like how she feels against me. Far too much, in fact. Alarms go off in my head as we stand there in each other's arms, but I ignore them by telling myself that it would be cruel to push her away at the very moment she needs to believe she has someone who cares about her.

That's a lie, though, and no matter how I try to convince myself I'm being some selfless guy to help her perform tonight, the truth is I care far too much about Mia to want to see her unhappy like she was earlier.

"Liam, I couldn't do this without you. I hope you know that," she says against me.

I don't respond, afraid anything I say will make her realize how much I know I shouldn't be standing here with her like this. Instead, I softly slide my hand up and down her back, as if that's any less a violation of all the rules I've always followed in my job. Her red satin dress feels so cool under my palm that I let myself get lost in the sensation for a moment, but thankfully, a knock on the dressing room door puts an end to my fantasizing.

Gently, I push her away and hold her by the shoulders as I look deep into her eyes. "Okay, I'm guessing that's one of my guys saying that if I don't get you out there that people will be coming after us with torches and pitchforks, so what do you say you go show them why they've waited this long?"

Mia takes another deep breath and lets it out in a rush as she nods her agreement. "Okay. Let's do this!"

When I take a step toward the door to leave before her, she stops me with a touch to my arm. I look back, and in a flash, she's up on her toes softly giving me a kiss I don't think I'll ever forget.

She pulls away, and with a sexy grin, she says, "Now I'm ready."

Jesus, I don't think I'm strong enough to not want this woman. Not when she does things like that and makes my legs weak.

I open the door and see my crew waiting for us. Kip and Jack know that's their cue to take their positions near the front of the stage while the rest of us escort Mia to the back of the stage.

The cheers of the crowd grow louder and louder until I'm not sure I can hear a thing anyone says to me as we make our way through the long passageway. Right before we reach the stairs that go up to the stage, I see Andrea. Mia reaches back right behind her to search for my hand, and I quickly grasp it to let her know nobody, not even her mother, can hurt her now that I'm there.

As we pass her, I mouth, "You and I will be talking about what happened when this is all over."

Andrea may not be able to hear me, but she understands what I'm saying and the angry look on my face as a warning that she better not pull any more bullshit tonight. I don't know what her plans were with Michael, but I intend on finding out. If she was innocently trying to help protect her daughter, then fine.

If she wasn't, then we're going to have to talk, and she's not going to like what I have to say.

With each step I climb behind Mia toward the stage, my heart races more and more. I've guarded important people before, but never in my life have I heard so many people yelling and cheering for anyone I'm protecting. My instinct makes me want to whisk her away from here so she can be safe and not have to hear all this deafening noise, but I have to fight that because I know this is where she belongs.

And if I didn't, the moment we reach the stage and she turns around to smile at me, I'd know then. Before my eyes, Mia blossoms into someone bigger than life. She's more beautiful and more desirable than she's ever been since the day I met her, and I know right then why millions of people adore her.

I can't hear a thing above the sound of the crowd, but I watch her as she mouths back to me, "Thank you."

A second later, she lets go of my hand and steps out onto that stage, and thousands of people go wild. For a few moments, I can't move I'm so mesmerized by this woman, but then the show starts, and I know I have to switch into work mode.

I search the sides of the stage to make sure everyone's in their assigned place and see my men have this handled. Michael lurks near the very back of the stage like some thief who can't wait to get away, but he's nothing now.

Mia opens her arms wide and makes a motion like she's hugging the entire audience before she says, "Thank you for waiting for me! I love you! Thank you!"

The crowd goes even wilder than before, and she sweetly giggles as she offers an explanation for why she's over thirty minutes late. "I'm sorry it took me so long to get here to you. At the last minute, my strap on my dress snapped, and I know you wouldn't want me to have a wardrobe malfunction right here in front of all of you."

Cheers and cries of "We love you, Mia" fill the air around us, and she blows them all kisses. "But now I'm here and ready to give you my best. Are you ready?"

I watch in awe as she makes them forget with a few simple words that they waited all that time for her, charming them before she even sings a single note. She really does belong out there with them. It's like I'm seeing a completely different person than I have all these weeks at the estate.

And I have to admit, I'm crazy about this Mia.

Then, when I don't think I can admire her more, she looks back at me and smiles before turning to face the audience. "I want to begin with a song that means the world to me, even more now because I can honestly say I know what it feels to be truly cared for. This is to the one person who makes me feel safer than I've ever known was possible."

I hear her begin to sing the first words of her hit song *Always There* and realize she's singing it about me. Out of the corner of my eye, I see Drew raise his eyebrows to let me know he knows too.

At that moment, I know one thing for sure. I'm in trouble because I'm crazy about this woman.

There's only one problem.

I'm not supposed to be. It breaks every rule a bodyguard follows. It breaks every rule I've lived my professional life by all these years and through all the jobs I've taken.

And I don't care.

CHAPTER TWENTY-SIX

$\mathcal{M}$ia

I FEEL LIKE I'M FLOATING ON CLOUD NINE BY THE time the night ends. When I settle in with the crew to celebrate a fantastic first night show, I can't help but feel Liam and his men belong right here down at the pool with us. They made it possible for me to perform and feel this incredible.

Well, Liam made it possible. Not that his guys didn't help, but if it wasn't for him rushing over to the pavilion to take care of the mess my mother made, I never would have been able to walk out onto that stage.

Ainsley hands me a glass of champagne and raises hers in the air. "To Mia! Congratulations, girl! Tonight was unbelievable. I don't think I've ever seen you perform like that. It was like you were a different person."

She's right. I felt different tonight. I felt loved and

protected like never before, and it came through loud and clear in every word I sang.

Everyone raises their glass to toast me and my performance, making me feel like the queen of the world. "To Mia!"

As they all begin to talk amongst themselves, Ainsley pulls me aside and whispers, "I have to know what happened when you and Liam were alone in your dressing room for all that time."

I roll my eyes at the less-than-subtle suggestion I see in her expression as she wiggles her eyebrows. "Not that."

Faking innocence, she shakes her head and opens her eyes wide like she can't believe I could think she was suggesting he and I had sex in the dressing room. "What? It might have happened. You never know. Since you were so happy, I was just wondering."

"I was happy because I knew I was safe when Liam showed up to take over security. Once I knew he was in charge again instead of Michael, I was able to relax and have the best show of my life."

"What was your mother thinking with bringing Michael back? Is she intentionally trying to sabotage you? I can't believe she did that even after you told her not to. Have you talked to her since the show?" Ainsley asks before taking a sip of champagne.

I shake my head and down my entire glass. "No, and I don't want to. I'm still so pissed at her that I don't know if I'll be able to keep my cool and not fire her for what she did tonight."

"Really?" my life coach asks in utter shock. "You wouldn't really fire Andrea, would you? I mean, she's not only your manager. She's your mother."

"Then she should act like either one of those goddamned things. She didn't do her job as my manager tonight, that's for damn sure. As for acting like my mother, well, she hasn't been good at that job for a long time."

I stop myself before I get too upset again. I can't think about my mother's antics tonight. I want to stay in this good mood for when I go to speak to Liam in a little while, and everything about my mother's behavior will only make me angry again.

Holding out my glass for Ainsley to refill, I force myself to smile and forget about all of the madness. "Tonight isn't for that. Tonight is to celebrate a great show, and that's what I'm doing. My mother will have to wait until tomorrow."

Wiggling her eyebrows again, Ainsley gives me a knowing smile. "So what are you planning to do to celebrate?"

I look around at the group of people who've been with me through thick and thin and then back at her. "This? You act like I have some secret plans to do something else, Ains. This is it. I'm going to finish this glass of champagne and then I'm going to take a hot bath full of bubbles. And if I don't fall asleep in the tub, I'm going to relax with a mud mask on my face because I swear to God my skin felt like it was blowing up with zits under all that makeup tonight. It's been a while since I had to wear that much."

"You looked gorgeous, just in case you're thinking you didn't."

Something about the way she says that makes me curious, so I ask, "Why would I think anything else?"

She shrugs, but since she's Ainsley, she can't help but

tell me what's on her mind. "I just thought maybe someone had said something negative about how you have to look for when you're on stage."

I know what she's saying, but she's wrong. Liam never said a word about how I looked. I'm not even sure he noticed.

"Well, you're wrong. Nobody said a thing about my makeup or the quantity I had to wear tonight."

Holding her hands up in front of her, she pretends to surrender on this point. "Okay, fine. I just wanted to make sure that you know you look beautiful no matter how much makeup you wear."

"Why do you always think the worst of him?" I ask, startling her with my very pointed question.

"I don't."

"Yes, you do. You never have a nice thing to say about him, and now you're accusing him of making me feel bad about wearing stage makeup when I never said a word about him even mentioning it. You know, I have thoughts of my own. I can decide that my face feels gross with all of that covering my skin all on my own."

I see I've hit a nerve when her expression shows how hurt she is by my words. "I wasn't trying to say that at all. I know you can make your own decisions. You might forget, but I'm a big fan of you doing that. I have been since the day you hired me. I'm just worried that he's got this wholesome thing in his mind about how women are and that's not you."

Instantly, I feel defensive. "Why? What has given you the impression that he's all about people being wholesome? I've never seen that in him. Liam is simply a good man. Why can't you just accept that and be happy that I like him?"

By the time I finish speaking, my voice is far too loud, and everyone turns to stare at me, ceasing their conversations to pay attention to ours. Ainsley throws them all a dirty look, and they resume talking, but I know they heard me say I like Liam.

So what? I like my bodyguard. I wish everyone would stop acting like it's the crime of the century or the most scandalous thing since Catherine the Great decided to hang out with horses.

I stand up from the pool deck to leave before I start to feel as unhappy as I did when I was dealing with my mother earlier. "I'm going to go take that bath. Enjoy the party," I say, looking down at Ainsley.

"Please don't go yet, Mia. I'm sorry. I think you misinterpreted what I said, and I want to fix that," she pleads.

But it's no use.

I didn't misunderstand what she said now or every other time we talked about Liam. She doesn't like him. I don't know why, and I don't care. She doesn't have to like him.

"It's fine. No harm, no foul. I just need to go relax."

Turning to look over at everyone enjoying themselves, I raise my glass in the air and smile at them. "To a great show with great friends! Enjoy, but remember we have to do it all over again tomorrow night!"

Ainsley reaches out to grab my hand to keep me from leaving, but I pull it away as soon as she touches me. I love her and she's my best friend, but I don't want to answer any questions tonight about why I care about Liam or why I feel better when he's around.

I just do, and that's enough for me.

. . .

I SINK DOWN INTO MY NEW STANDALONE TUB FILLED with hot water and lavender bubble bath, closing my eyes as relaxation comes over me. No more talking. No more thinking. No more anything but me and this tub and the bubbles that cover my body.

While I enjoy the silence, I wonder what Liam is doing right now. He's probably hanging out with his guys going over what needs to be tweaked for tomorrow night's show. All work and no play seems to be his mantra. He should change that. I can appreciate the work he does, but a little more play would be nice.

As I imagine them all seated around the table in his room with serious faces discussing how this guy should move his position to this place and that guy should adjust where he stands by so many feet, I can't help but sigh in relief that he came to my rescue when I needed him tonight. Michael never did that, but then again, I never knew he was doing such a shitty job protecting me that I had anything to worry about.

Nobody ever did anything like that for me before. I had no idea what I was missing.

And now that I know how good it feels, I sure as hell don't want to go back to not having that kind of feeling.

Lost in thought about Liam, I don't realize my hand has slid down my slick skin until my finger strokes between my legs for the first time. Mmmm…God, that feels good. I haven't been with any man in far too long, and although my hand and vibrators do the trick, they aren't usually as good as the real thing.

Now, though, as I close my eyes and imagine him between my legs lashing my pussy with his tongue, I can't help but notice this is much better than usual. Every inch of my body feels alive, like every nerve ending is wide awake and firing on all cylinders. It must be the subject matter of tonight's fantasy.

I can see him in my mind's eye without a shirt on, his hard, muscular body settled in between my thighs as he goes down on me better than any man ever has. I stuff my hand into his hair and run my fingers through it. Softer than I thought it would be, it feels like silk against my skin.

His thumbs hold me open so he can reach every delicious spot on me. Deep inside, the first tendrils of my orgasm begin to unravel, and with every inch the sensation travels, a feeling of utter ecstasy comes with it.

Finally, he sucks my clit gently into between his lips, and that's all it takes. Colors and shapes explode behind my eyes, and it's like every inch of my body is turned toward my pussy to watch it revel in how incredible this feels.

I smile at that fantasy, and a second later, my finger dips inside me as I come harder than I think I've ever done before in my life from masturbating. My legs shoot out until the soles of my feet slam against the wall of the tub, and I cry out in utter pleasure.

Exhausted, I slide down under the water until my whole body is submerged. Oh, God, I hope that fantasy comes true and he's as good as I dream he is. If he doesn't know how to do me better than my own hand, I think I might be depressed for a month.

A knocking noise rips me out of my thoughts of Liam going down on me, and I pop up above the surface of the water to listen to where it's coming from. Pushing my hair back off my face, I look around for any clue. It's not here in the bathroom. That's for sure.

I strain to hear it and realize a few seconds later it's someone knocking on my bedroom door. Probably Ainsley. She hates when we have disagreements, and I did leave her pretty abruptly. She probably wants to make sure we aren't really fighting.

"Come in!" I yell and then look down my body to assess the bubble situation. There's still enough for Ainsley to come talk to me.

As I slide my hands up over the top of my head to get a few stray hairs stuck near my eyes, I hear her come in. Now that I've calmed down and relaxed in the bath a little, I don't feel so much like going toe to toe with her about Liam. She'll come around to see how great he is. She just needs some time.

Ainsley doesn't say anything at first, so I look over toward the door to see why she's so silent. It's very much not like her to not start talking the second she walks into my room.

But when I turn my head, it isn't my life coach I see leaning against the doorframe but Liam! His arms are folded across his broad chest, and the white T-shirt he's wearing seems to strain against his biceps. I look up at his face to see him smiling, and for a second, I smile back.

Until I realize I barely had enough bubbles a few minutes ago. Now, I don't have enough to cover the major parts of my body, leaving much of me exposed.

"Liam, what are you doing here? I thought you were Ainsley!" I say as I scramble to cross my arms over my chest.

He doesn't look away, even as I splash around all

flustered that he's watching me naked in the tub. "I just wanted to come by and check on you after all that happened tonight."

Something about the lilt of his voice tells me he's enjoying how bothered his being here makes me. That and the fact that he hasn't stopping grinning since I first noticed him.

"I'm fine. Slightly unbubbled, but fine all the same."

Finally, his smile fades, and he asks, "Unbubbled?"

I drop my gaze to the bath quickly becoming merely water with almost no bubbles and then look up at him. "Unbubbled. As in, there were a lot more bubbles just a few minutes ago. Why don't you wait for me out in my room and we can talk as soon as I get dried off."

His smile returns, and I'm sure he can see right into my bathtub from the angle he's staring down at me. "It's okay. We can talk tomorrow. I just wanted to check on you."

For a moment, my embarrassment fades, and I feel nothing but happy that someone cared enough to see if I was okay after all that happened at the show tonight. I want to talk to him, so I say, "Please wait for me. I'll be right out. Just close the door and I swear it won't take long."

"Okay."

When the door clicks closed, I hurry to get out of the tub and grab one of my favorite white towels off the stand a few feet away. After a quick drying-off, I slip into my white robe that's made of the softest Egyptian cotton and rush toward the door.

Oh, God! I might look like a disaster. Ainsley was concerned about him saying something about my wearing a ton of makeup for the show, but now I don't have a stitch of anything on my face. I'm probably all blotchy from the heat of the bath too.

I take a look at myself in the mirror and see things aren't terrible. I wish I had some makeup on my eyes, though. They always look better with some dark eyeshadow to highlight the dark brown color of my eyes. Surprisingly, the rest of my face doesn't look too shabby, thankfully.

With a quick swipe of my tongue across my lips, I give them a little sheen and smile at my reflection. My heart's racing, and I feel like I might crumble to the floor I'm so nervous.

"Relax," I say to the me in the mirror. "You're great. This is fine."

I give myself one final smile and turn to walk toward the door. If I'm so great, though, why am I shaking like a leaf?

CHAPTER TWENTY-SEVEN

$\mathcal{M}$ia

I TAKE A DEEP BREATH AS I WALK TOWARD WHERE LIAM sits on the edge of my bed. He looks like he's ready to bolt at any second. Maybe I've been reading all the signals I thought were coming off him wrong? I was so sure he felt something for me.

"Okay, now I feel much better. A bath can do a girl a world of good."

He nods like he agrees, but I get the feeling he's not a bath guy. Maybe he would be if he had the right woman?

Sitting down next to him, I wonder where the smiling Liam who stood gawking at me in my bathroom a few minutes ago has gone. Now he seems uncomfortable, but that doesn't make any sense.

"So tonight was exciting, huh?" I say with a smile and hope he gives me on in return.

He glances over at me and nods. "Definitely more exciting than I had expected," he says quietly.

Then he looks away, like he can't stand to see the sight of me.

"Is there something wrong, Liam? You're acting strange."

I don't want to sound like his behavior is hurting me, but it comes through loud and clear. Is it that I don't have any makeup on, and my hair is still sopping wet? Is he disappointed by how I look now?

That can't be it. I looked pretty much like this when I was in the bathtub a few minutes ago.

He doesn't turn to look at me when he says, "Your robe."

"What about it?" I ask, wondering if this guy has some irrational hatred of Egyptian cotton or white robes.

I watch his expression as he winces like he's in pain before he points toward me, still not able to face me. "It's open."

Glancing down, I see my robe has come open right above my waist, so he has a clear view of my naked breasts. Horrified since he probably thinks I came out here looking like some cheap floozy hoping to get a little, I hurry to pull the parts of my robe together, covering myself up to my neck.

"Well, no surprise left with me, I guess," I say, trying desperately to make a joke of what feels like the most humiliating moment of my life. "You can look at me, Liam. Trust me. I'm so covered I look like I'm straight out of the Victorian Era over here."

When he finally turns to face me, he smiles and shakes his head. "You surprise me every day, Mia. I doubt that's going to change just because you flashed me."

I feel heat flood my cheeks at his words. Slapping his arm, I protest, "I did not flash you. Man, a girl doesn't tie her robe tight enough and a guy thinks she's flashing him. Trust me. If I flashed you, you would have gotten more than a little peek at my boobs."

This is not how I wanted this conversation to go. I had hoped we could talk a little so I could thank him again for coming to my rescue tonight, and then we could kiss. I didn't have the whole thing planned out, but it certainly didn't look like what's happening now when I imagined it.

When I see his face turn red, at least I know I'm not the only one feeling completely awkward here. Something about him being embarrassed too charms me, though. That's probably the uptight side of him. Not my favorite side, but if it's the part that blushes, I could get used to it.

"So now that we're both feeling weird, I wanted to thank you for what you did tonight, Liam. Nobody has ever bothered to worry about me like you do. I know it's your job, but still, nobody else has ever done your job like you do."

"I'm happy to do whatever it takes to make sure you're safe."

I watch his mouth as he says that and all I can think of is how much I want to kiss him right now. Well, that and how good he looks in that white T-shirt. Who knew a man could make a plain white shirt look so hot?

"I mean it when I say no one has ever taken care of me like you, Liam. I mean, my security."

My tiny slip makes his eyes get slightly wider for a

second, and I think maybe he's going to make a move. I stare into his blue eyes that never fail to amaze me with how gorgeous they are, but he doesn't budge.

"I'll find out what happened with your mother and make sure it doesn't happen again tomorrow night. I plan on telling her when we head to New Orleans that Michael isn't welcome to come along."

The mention of my former head of security makes me feel nothing but shame. I hang my head to avoid Liam's gaze, hating how I used to rely on Michael for so much when he cared nothing about my safety or happiness.

"What's wrong?" he asks, his voice full of the concern that I love hearing in him. "I need to tell your mother she can't pull that kind of thing again, Mia. She put you in danger, and I can't have that."

I look up at him and shake my head. "It's not that. Feel free to tell my mother whatever you need to. I'm just so embarrassed that I believed Michael cared about me or keeping me safe."

Liam's expression hardens, and his eyes narrow to almost angry slits. "How serious were you two?" he asks.

"We weren't. Did he claim we did something together? Because we didn't. We weren't like that. I thought he cared for me at least as a friend, but you saw the proof of how wrong I was about that when you went to his apartment looking for me."

He shakes his head as his expression softens. "He didn't say anything to me. We weren't exactly on speaking terms tonight."

"Then why do you think we were together?"

Liam doesn't answer, and suddenly I wonder if he believes I sleep with all of my bodyguards. I need him to know that isn't true at all. In fact, I've never slept with any of them.

Oh, God! I see it in his eyes. That's what he thinks!

"You think I just sleep with every guy who guards me?"

"No. I thought you slept with him, though. The way you were acting when you went to see him that day seemed like how someone would act if they were serious with someone."

I shake my head faster and faster as how Liam's acted all makes sense to me now. "No, Liam I've never slept with Michael or any of my bodyguards. That's not how it is. Is that why you've been so strange with me every time I show you I care for you?"

He abruptly stands up from the bed and shakes his head. I stare up at him in confusion and think to myself that we're like a couple of deranged bobblehead dolls.

"Why did you get up?"

"I should go," he says flatly, like all the emotion has left him suddenly.

"Why? What did I say wrong? I told you that Michael and I were never together. I've never been with anyone guarding me. Isn't that a good thing?"

Worry now seems etched into his beautiful features as he continues to shake his head like nothing I'm saying makes him happy. "It's not that, Mia."

I jump to my feet, needing to stop him if he moves to leave. "Then what is it? Because the way you're acting doesn't make any sense. You stand there in the doorway to my bathroom staring at me naked in the tub, but then you get weird when my robe comes open. You bring up Michael, and then when I tell you he was never anyone romantic to me, you grow cold, but I could have sworn you were upset at the thought that he and I were together. Why are you acting like this? I don't understand."

Still, he doesn't answer me. "I should go."

I grab his hand, feeling instantly better when I touch him. Even his fingers possess strength I don't think I could ever even dream of having. They're long and heavy in my palm, but I cling to them when he takes a step toward the door.

"Please don't go. Tell me what I did wrong, Liam. I've tried to show you I'm not that brat you thought I was or the diva you accused me of being. I thought I was doing everything right to make you see that I care about you, and I thought you cared about me. Was I wrong?"

He won't look at me now, turning away as he lets out a heavy sigh. "No, you weren't wrong. I've noticed it all. I see I misjudged you at first. I get why all those people come to see you. It's not just that you're an incredible singer. The person you were on stage tonight is the person I've seen so many times here at the house."

"Then why do you want to leave and why won't you face me if I'm so wonderful?"

I don't care that I sound desperate. I'm not, but I know he probably thinks I am. What I am is a woman who cares who wants to know if he cares about me in return.

Maybe I am desperate. All I know is I've never felt anything like I do when Liam's around me.

Finally, after what feels like an eternity, he turns around. In his eyes, I see all that emotion I had hoped he felt for me coloring those beautiful blue eyes of his. But his mouth is turned down in a frown that makes me think those emotions aren't the ones I had hoped to find in him.

"This can't happen. I'm to blame, so I take full responsibility for this. I shouldn't have stood in your doorway for so long watching you in the tub. I'm sorry about that."

God, I hate seeing him so unhappy!

I tighten my hold on his hand, sure he's about to leave before I can say another word. "You don't have to be sorry. I'm not. It's okay. You didn't do anything wrong."

He stares down into my eyes and says, "Yes, I did. I live by a code that's meant I kept a sharp line between me and my clients. Until you, I never had a problem respecting that line that kept me over here and everyone else over there. But I've stepped over that line, blurred it, and even tried to forget it existed because you make me want to do things I shouldn't."

"Why shouldn't you want to feel someone care about you? Why wouldn't you want to care about me?"

"Because it goes against everything I believe in."

"So you won't let yourself feel something you already know you feel for me?"

I wait for him to answer me, to tell me what I want to believe is true. That he does feel something for me like I do for him.

But he says nothing.

My father used to tell me that if you want things in life, you have to take a chance. He didn't seem to believe in that mantra when it came to my wanting to be a star, but I never forgot him telling me that when I was a little girl and my family was still something I had in my life.

I have to take a chance now. If it all goes bad, then at least I'll know that I took a chance at having the kind of man in my life that I've always sung about.

Someone strong who would stand against anyone who wanted to hurt me. A man who would brave the winds of a hurricane to protect me. I want that man, and since he's standing here in front of me, there's no time like the present.

So I stand up on my tiptoes to reach his mouth and kiss him with every ounce of desire coursing through me. My eyes closed, I don't know what he's doing as I move my lips against his. At first, he feels stiff, almost like a statue I'm trying to wake from its cold slumber, but slowly, his mouth softens and then he returns my kiss with one of his own as full of need and passion as mine and I'm suddenly soaring my heart is so full.

Liam's left arm wraps around my body, pulling me to him, and for the first time, I realize how much larger than me he is. I've always had to look up at him since I'm shorter, but pressed against me, his body is like that of a giant's.

Opening my eyes, I see his face close to mine filling my gaze. He leans back, breaking our kiss, and smiles as he lets out a heavy sigh.

"So much for that sharp line."

I lift my hand to his mouth and press my fingertip to the center of those delicious lips. "I didn't like that line anyway."

He gives me a big smile in return that makes this night the best night of my life. Then it fades, and I wonder if I'm going to need to kiss him again to calm all those unnecessary worries he has.

Ainsley is right. Liam really is Mr. Rules and Regulations.

"What's wrong? I swear to God, I will throw you

down on that bed and make you smile again," I say with a laugh.

"It's nothing, but what do you think about keeping this to ourselves? You may be used to the whole world knowing your every move, but I'm not."

He's got a point. To be honest, the last thing I want to have to deal with is the nosy press snooping around if they find out I'm with someone new. I've worked hard to make sure that the only time my name appears in the press is because of my talent.

Or when I run off and my mother makes it a media circus. But those days are behind me now that I'm with Liam.

I kiss him sweetly on the lips and smile. "Our secret. Just you and me."

CHAPTER TWENTY-EIGHT

iam

THE SECOND SHOW AT THE PAVILION WENT OFF without a hitch, and since that first night, Andrea has kept her distance from me, making herself practically invisible around the house and anywhere near Mia. I expected her to make an appearance today since we left for the first big show in New Orleans, but she wasn't to be found. I thought maybe she decided to hide out on one of the other tour busses, but neither the band nor the dancers saw her at all.

All night I've kept an eye out for her and Michael, just in case she wanted to try to pull something, even as I watched out for any of the more rabid fans of Mia's. In between that and making sure every one of my men and the local security were in their places, I've tried to sneak a few moments to watch her perform.

The arena falls almost silent and the lights dim until

only a single spotlight shines on her in the center of the stage. Behind her, the guy who plays keyboards sits at a grand piano playing a sad melody. When she begins singing, I feel like someone's stolen my breath away with how beautiful yet mournful the words are. She told me she writes all her songs, and as I listen to her sing about losing someone dear to her, I wonder who this one is about.

Whoever he is, he has no idea how lucky he is to have her write this song about him.

I pull myself away from watching her when it sounds like each word she's singing is filled with tears, turning around and seeing Drew staring at me. Instantly, my senses go on high alert. Is something wrong? Does he see something we need to handle?

Hurrying over to where he stands off left center stage, I grab him by the arm to get his attention. "What's going on? Is there something we need to deal with?"

A slow smile lights up his face. "I don't know. You tell me."

"What the hell does that mean? I need to know if there's anything we need to pay attention to, Drew. What's with the riddles?"

He tilts his head toward Mia out on stage and shrugs. "No riddles. I'm just wondering about what I was seeing a minute ago."

I still have no idea what the hell he's talking about, but if there's some danger I'm not seeing, he needs to let me know now and stop with this bullshit. "What? Was someone trying to get close to the stage? Those local guys have been good all night. What happened?"

Jesus, my heart is racing like someone's chasing me. I

need to calm down if I'm going to handle some problem he's about to point out to me.

Drew slugs me in the shoulder and laughs. "Not that, you jackass. I'm talking about you watching her like she's some angel sent from heaven. You got it bad, man. I can see it as clear as day."

So much for keeping this thing between us a secret.

"Damn. I thought I was being cool too. How obvious is it?" I ask, dreading the answer he's about to give me.

Grinning, he says, "Well, I guess if someone's blind they wouldn't know. It's not like any of the other guys have said anything, but if they've been watching you like I was, they have to know something's up."

I pinch the bridge of my nose, angry at myself for being so careless. "Okay, do me a favor. Don't say a word about this to anyone. If any of the guys say anything, I want you to blow it off like you think they're crazy. Or if you can't do that, just send them to me and I'll do it."

Drew and I are tight, but he isn't the kind of person to lie to others. I'm putting him in an awkward position with the rest of the crew. He shouldn't have to do that.

Before he can say anything, I shake my head and reverse what I just told him. "Forget that. I shouldn't be asking you to lie to people. That's a shitty thing to do to a friend. Sorry about that."

"It's cool. I don't need to tell other people your business. Hell, you didn't have to admit the truth to me, so let's just pretend I know nothing, and I'll funnel any questions your way. Word to the wise, though. Stop mooning over this woman in public or everyone on the goddamned planet is going to know what's going on between you two."

I grab his hand to shake it, thankful for his suggestion. "I'll definitely do that. And here I thought Mia was going to be the one who would blow our cover."

When she finds out I'm to blame for someone else knowing, she's never going to let me hear the end of it.

ALONE IN MY HOTEL ROOM, I WAIT FOR MIA TO finish her after-performance routine with her entourage. Now that Drew told me he knows about us, I have to let her know. The only problem is I don't know how to do that.

Pacing back and forth, I look out the window at the French Quarter below with every pass. It's been a bunch of years since I got to enjoy New Orleans. The last time I was here it was Cash, Alex, Cade, and me celebrating Alex's twenty-first birthday. That was a weekend to remember, except we partied so much I only vaguely recall arriving at the first bar on Bourbon Street and waking up on Sunday in the hotel room with the headache to beat all headaches.

When I walk back to the door, I hear three knocks, Mia's made-up code to let me know it's her. I open it up without looking out the peephole and immediately chastise myself for not following even that most basic of protocols.

This woman has me turned upside down.

She rushes into the room, and I slam the door behind her. When I turn around, I'm met with a look I hadn't expected. Instead of her brown hair, she has platinum blond hair about three inches shorter than what she usually has. She's also dressed in the tiniest black dress I've ever seen with four-inch heels dangling off the fingers on her right hand and a little red purse hanging off her left wrist.

"Do you like it? It's my disguise. I got it from Crystal. I want to go out into the French Quarter and have a good time tonight. What do you say?" she asks, practically bursting from excitement.

Still trying to get used to her new appearance, I smile. "Sounds good, but did you forget something?"

For a second she stops bouncing up and down in front of me and thinks about what she may have forgotten. "I don't think so. Wig for disguise. I've got money. Sexy bodyguard to protect me. Nope. I got it all covered."

I take a step toward her and lean down to kiss her. "You're not twenty-one, Mia. No one is going to let you into a bar without ID."

Although this would seem like an insurmountable challenge, she waves it off like it's nothing. "Ridiculous. You can walk around drinking right on the streets in this city. Do you honestly think anyone is checking people to make sure they're of age? Anyway, I have ID."

"That says you're nineteen."

Juggling the shoes and the purse, she whips out a small plastic card and holds it in front of her. "Wrong again. I have Ainsley's. She let me borrow it. So you have no more excuses. Let's go!"

Remembering the reason why my job guarding her happened later than it was supposed to, I quietly ask, "Do you think going to a bar is a good idea? I mean, since you're not that long out of rehab?"

Mia shakes her head and laughs. "Don't worry about that."

Hoping to put off having to worry about anything

dealing with heading out into public, I slide my good arm around her waist and pull her to me. "What do you say to postponing our tour of the French Quarter for a while?"

She smiles up at me as her eyebrows slowly raise into her forehead. "Oh? Do you have something you want us to do instead?"

Looking around at the private suite I've been given for tonight, I smile. "I just figured since your suite is filled with all those people, this could be a good time for us to finally be alone."

"Alone alone?" she asks in a surprised voice.

I nod. "Yes."

Suddenly, Mia narrows her eyes and gets a suspicious look on her face. "You know I'm all in on sleeping with you, Liam. I have been since that first night we kissed. You're the one who's been saying we should keep this on the down low and hasn't wanted to be alone alone because everyone's been around. So what's changed?"

Time to fess up. But first, I need her to know I've been all in on sleeping with her for all that time too.

"Well, before I tell you the reason, I want you to understand I wasn't trying to hold out on us being together for any reason but the one I said. I'm not really into public romances, so I was hoping one of these nights we'd finally be alone. Tonight's a perfect time for that since everyone's already drunk up in your suite."

She smiles up at me like she sees right through my attempt to soften the news I have to give her. "Okay. Good to know that you wanted to have sex and this waiting business wasn't because you didn't find me desirable."

Christ. This is going south fast.

I take her face in my hands and kiss her on the center of her beautiful mouth. "Of course I do. I'm just not used to being crazy about a woman who has an entourage around her at all times."

"Point taken," she says with a nod. "But there's another reason you're suddenly feeling that this night in the New Orleans Ritz Carlton is the perfect time for us to be together for the first time. So what is it?"

With a sigh, I hang my head and confess the truth. "Drew knows. He told me tonight. I wanted to keep our being together quiet, and I was the one who blew it."

"He saw you doing that moony-eyed thing you do when I'm on stage, didn't he?" she says with a giggle.

I look up and see she's not angry. Good. I'm still pissed at myself for being so transparent, but at least she's not.

"Yeah," I say, nodding as I admit my idiocy. "I had no idea I looked at you like that. I'm usually pretty stoic. At least that's what I've been told."

"Well, Drew seems like a guy who can keep a secret." In a flash, worry fills her eyes. "You did tell him to keep this to himself, didn't you?"

"Absolutely and he is. Drew's a good guy."

Mia shrugs and lifts herself up onto her toes to kiss me. "Then it's all good. You are going to have to practice looking at me like you don't give a damn, though, or everyone's going to know we're together by the end of the week."

"I'll see what I can do."

She trails her fingertips down the column of my neck and begins to unbutton my black shirt. "For what it's worth, I love seeing you look at me like that. I don't think anyone has ever actually looked like you do when you watch me sing."

"Moony-eyed?" I joke as she makes her way down my shirt.

Nodding, she looks up at me and gives me one of her beautiful smiles. "Yeah. I wish you didn't have to stop. It makes me feel better than I can even explain, Liam."

As she slides her hands under my shirt and down over my left shoulder, I shrug out of it as much as I can and lean down to kiss her. "How about I find something else that makes you feel that way?"

Her gaze roams over my half-naked body, and she says with a soft sigh, "Mmmm...I like the way you think."

Glancing over at my right arm, I smile as I start to slide the sling off my shoulder. "Just give me a second or two and I'll be good to go."

CHAPTER TWENTY-NINE

$\mathcal{M}$ia

I'VE BEEN DYING TO BE WITH LIAM SINCE THAT FIRST night we realized we didn't want to fight our attraction anymore. He wanted to take things easy and wait until we could spend some time alone, but if it had been up to me, I would have slept with him that night. His ability to control his desires impresses me, but at some point, control needs to go out the window.

So I'm rarely ever alone. That's my life. Any man who wants to be with me has to get used to that. Liam will. He's a great guy and smart. He'll figure out how to get around the entourage.

My heart thumps in my chest as anticipation tears through me. I love looking at Liam's body. At least the half of it I've seen naked before. And tonight's no exception. As my hands roam over his muscular chest and shoulders down to his thick biceps, all I can think about it how beautiful he is.

Then I suddenly realize I touched where the bullet entered his arm and quickly pull my hand back toward me. "I'm sorry. I didn't mean to just brush over your arm like that."

Smiling, he lifts his right arm and moves it around to prove to me he's fine. "No problem. That doctor was probably being extra careful because I feel one hundred percent. See?"

"Okay. I just wanted to be sure."

"Is that the way I look at you?" he asks with a chuckle, thankfully changing the subject. "No wonder Drew caught me. I guess I should be happy very few people pay attention to me because if they did, they'd all know."

My cheeks heat from a blush and I smile up at him. "Maybe."

I move my hands down his body to begin removing his belt and pants. "Now no more talking about the two of us and our moony eyes. I need to get you naked."

"What about you?" he asks with such a tone of innocence that I have to tear my focus away from my job getting him undressed to see if he's serious. I look up and see he's absolutely for real. Clearly, Liam isn't used to someone like me.

"Well, this dress I'm wearing offers easy access, but I've made it even easier by not wearing any underwear. You're welcome, by the way."

His blue eyes get wide in surprise, and I swear he looks downright sweet at this moment. "Really? I guess you had this all planned out. So we were never going out into the Quarter tonight?"

"Oh, yeah. I just figured we'd end up doing something like this in a dark alley way."

Again, surprise makes his eyes open wide. He opens his mouth to say something, but nothing comes out, so I stand on my toes and kiss him. "Now let me get these pants off you or we're never going to have any fun tonight."

Liam pushes my hands away from his body and hurriedly unbuttons his pants. A few seconds later, he shoves them down his legs and kicks them away across the room. "Problem solved."

He's still partially dressed in his black boxer briefs and black socks, so I point at both and shake my head. "There is no way I can have sex with a man who's wearing socks. Take them off."

For a second, he looks like he's going to protest, but then he bends down to slide them off his feet. Looking up at me with a wickedness in his eyes, he points at my dress. "Take it off. The first time we sleep together, I'm not doing it dark alley style."

I giggle, loving how cute he can be. "Deal."

By the time I slither out of my teeny-tiny black dress I had my personal shopper specially get for tonight, Liam is fully naked and staring at me with those moony-eyes I love. I doubt he loves my body as much as I love his as I stand there taking in every gorgeous inch of him. Damn, he's like a Greek god chiseled out of the finest marble and all for me.

When he doesn't make a move for a few seconds, a flash of insecurity takes over. My body isn't anywhere as perfect as his. No matter how many workouts and routines Mitchell and Tiffany put me through, I never get my body into the shape Liam's is in.

It's why all my costumes are made to hide the softness of my abs and highlight my best part. My legs. The designers do an incredible job, but at this moment, I can't hide behind sequins and a great dress.

"Better tell Mitchell I need more crunches, huh?" I mumble.

Liam shakes his head and steps toward me to cradle my face in his hands. Gazing down into my eyes, he smiles, and I feel like my entire body is melting.

"No. You're perfect just as you are. Don't change a single thing."

Oh. No one's ever said that or anything close to that to me.

"I just thought that since you're so built that you might have hoped I was."

Again, he shakes his head. "I don't want a woman who's the female version of me. I like this version of you instead."

I can't help but close my eyes. He feels too close, too much surrounding me at this moment. How is it he's single? He's gorgeous, sweet, caring, and protective. And right now, his long, hard cock is pressing against the space between my hipbones and driving me wild. Women must be climbing over one another to get to him, yet here he is with me.

"What's wrong, Mia?" he asks in a low voice.

Opening my eyes, I shake my head. "Nothing. Nothing at all." I don't know why, but I can't stop myself from asking how it's possible he's single. "How is it you don't have someone already?"

When he gives me one of those sexy smiles and subtly tilts his hips to press his body against mine, it's like someone's sucked all the air out of the room. I wait breathlessly for him to say something, and then he does, and it's the best thing in the world.

"I do. You."

He doesn't give me a chance to respond before he kisses me and once again takes my breath away. His mouth is soft but insistent, like he's a man who knows how to give a woman pleasure but also will take what he wants. It's a combination that turns me on more than I ever thought possible.

My hands slide over his soft skin as I silently worship how perfect his body is. I've never been with anyone like Liam, and it's all I can do to not stand here in the center of this hotel suite and admire every beautiful inch of him.

When he cups my breasts in his palms and presses his cock against my belly, I swear I get so hot I might come before we get past foreplay. Something about his strength and protective nature mixed with this body makes me more excited than I've ever been before with any man.

I break our kiss and smile up at him as my hands continue their exploration with his washboard abs. "You are perfect. I swear I could run my hands over your body all night long."

"The beauty of weights and working out, although genetics might contribute to it too."

All of this and humble too.

"I was feeling a little insecure there when I saw you with no clothes on. I mean, I knew you had a great body, but I guess just seeing it naked surprised me," I mumble, suddenly shy about what I truly want.

What I've wanted from the moment I realized I cared about him.

"Then I guess we're both feeling pretty stunned right

now because every fantasy I made up in my head about you pales in comparison to seeing you here with me right now."

Jesus. Even if this man is terrible in bed, I might just have to stay with him because he's so perfect in every other way.

But there's no way he's going to be anything less than phenomenal.

Reaching between our bodies, I wrap my fingers around his thick cock and stroke him up to the top. "I've fantasized about you and me together since the first time you kissed me. I can't wait to see if I was anywhere close with what I came up with."

Dipping his head, he whispers in my ear in the sexiest voice, "I'll do my best."

He lifts me by the waist and carries me over to the bed, placing me gently on the down comforter. It's soft against my skin, like a cloud cradling me ever so tenderly as he looms above me, staring down into my eyes with utter need.

Liam slides up my body, exciting nerve endings every inch of the way until his mouth reaches mine and he kisses me hard. I lift my legs and wrap them around his waist, rubbing my feet over his ass as I make my way up to his waist. God, even his ass is toned!

Pressing my heels into the small of his back, I urge him on, but he doesn't need any convincing. With one slow thrust, he fills me completely, yet again taking my breath away. Jesus, he's much bigger than I'm used to, so it's like I can't move without his permission.

I've never felt this way during sex. Usually, I'm the one who likes to set the pace, but with his hips pinning mine to the bed, I have no choice but to give in so Liam can decide how fast or how slowly we go.

I lazily slide my hands down over his back, reveling in the feel of his taut muscles with every time he thrusts his hips and sinks into me again. He's the personification of power and restraint both at once. I sense he wants to let himself go, but I'm so much smaller than he is, and he probably thinks I can't take it.

But I want to. I want all he has to give me. I want every delicious inch of him giving me all he has.

So I press my heels harder into the base of his spine and drag my nails across his broad shoulders. In his ear, I moan, "Don't hold back, Liam. I want all of you."

He stops for a few seconds and looks down at me, his eyes filled with need and desire. "I don't want to hurt you."

"You won't. You would never hurt me. I know that," I say, gently cupping his face.

As he covers my mouth in a kiss, he pushes into me hard, hitting a place inside that I never knew excited before this moment. His cock presses against that spot, sending me into overdrive just as he begins to fuck me in earnest.

I cling to him, riding every thrust and giving him all I have in me. We're savage and raw, and I feel like my emotions threaten to tear me apart at the seams. I don't have to worry about if he sees me fall to pieces like other men, though. This is Liam, the man who protects me, even when I don't want to be protected.

This is the man who looks at me with eyes full of love when I sing, not knowing that every word I sing now is about him.

When I feel that exquisite twinge that tells me I'm

about to come, I dig my nails into his back and moan, "Don't stop! This feels so fucking good!"

He rears back at my angry raking across his skin and plunges into me just as I begin to come. An explosion of color erupts behind my eyes, and then it's like I'm hundreds of feet in the air, soaring above everything that always worries and stresses me, safe in the arms of the man I know would never put me in harm's way.

I feel his body flood mine in warmth, and then he stills, holding himself so he doesn't put all his weight on me. I let out a heavy sigh, satisfied and happier than I've been in a long time.

"Hell of a first time," I say with a tiny giggle.

He nods and smiles as a dreamy look comes over him. "I'd say. I'm not usually surprised by people, but you surprised me."

"You said I surprise you every day. I really think you should have seen this coming, no pun intended."

With another nod, he admits the truth he told me just recently. "You do. I guess I just wasn't prepared for you to surprise me when we had sex."

I move out from underneath him and lie on my side, holding my head up with my hand. "Thought I'd be this tiny little thing in bed. After all the times I've stood toe to toe with you, you actually thought I'd be some dainty little thing when I have sex?"

Liam collapses to the bed and lies on his side, mirroring what I'm doing. Staring into my eyes, he smiles. "Your smallness confused me. I guess I wasn't expecting that much oomph."

The way he describes what I assume was all that scratching I did on his back makes me laugh. "Sorry about what I did with my nails. I bet your back looks like a wild animal got to you."

Wincing, he smiles. "I don't know. How's it look?" he asks before rolling over onto his other side.

Just as I suspected, his skin looks like something with very sharp nails came at him with an intent to shred him up. "Let's just say that if you decide to walk around not wearing a shirt within the next week or so, then someone's going to ask if you had a good time."

He rolls onto his back and shakes his head. "I guess it's T-shirts for me then because I'm not a fan of having to lie."

I look down at him lying there with the evidence of our great sex written all over his back and can't believe he's for real. "So let me get this straight. You're gorgeous, built like a Greek god, super sexy, great in bed, hung like a horse, and you don't like to lie? You must be too good to be true."

Liam gives me a sexy grin and says, "You missed great at my job."

"Which only makes you more unbelievable."

He pulls me over on top of him and kisses me, his tongue sliding against mine in a way that makes me want him for a second time. I don't care if he's too good to be true. Maybe a girl deserves that once in a while. After having too rotten to deal with and too shitty to stand, I'm happy to have someone like Liam.

Placing his hands on my hips, he sits me on his lap, and I feel his cock press hard against my ass. "We can discuss how wonderful I am later. For now, this Greek god with a cock like a horse wants to see you ride me cowgirl style."

I roll my eyes. "I should have never told you those things. They're already going to your head."

As he lifts his hips up off the bed, I get up on my knees to position myself so he can slide into my needy pussy. I slowly lower myself down onto him until he's fully inside me, filling me completely.

I look down at him smiling and say, "Then again, maybe since they're the truth, that's okay."

With his hands holding me, he begins to move me up and down on him, and I see it's Liam who'll be setting the pace for sex once more. For all those perfect parts of him, there's one I haven't mentioned yet.

He's strong enough to protect me, but Alpha enough to take control of me in bed. I love that and would love to tell him, but then he might think he can control me all the time.

I can't have that.

Better to keep how much I love the way he fucks me to myself until he realizes there are places a woman wants to be dominated and places she needs to control all on her own. For now, all I want to do is enjoy how good his cock feels and how incredible he looks lying there watching me ride him.

CHAPTER THIRTY

iam

HAND IN HAND, MIA AND I WALK DOWN BOURBON Street, getting lost in the crowds out on a Tuesday night in the French Quarter. Neon lights of blue, green, yellow, and red and old-fashioned streetlights erase the darkness of a moonless night, but as much as this area often has a carnival vibe to it, tonight it feels like the only place in the world I want to be.

I know that's because of the woman whose delicate hand I hold in mine. Mia points at a sign for a bar and tugs on my arm to move me toward it across the street, but she runs into a man standing in her way. For a moment, my body goes on red alert when he turns to look at her with pure drunken anger in his eyes and an expression that says he wants to hit someone for daring to walk into him.

Then he tilts his head back slightly and looks up at

me. I stare down at him with an unspoken warning in my eyes.

Don't say a word, buddy. This is not a woman you want to fuck with. Not tonight. Not any night.

It only takes him a second or two to figure out he'd be messing with the wrong couple, so he turns and walks away, making a space for us to continue moving toward that bar she wants to check out. She leads the way, and when we reach the sidewalk in front of the door, she turns around to smile at me.

"That guy was thinking he'd go all he-man on me. Then he got a look at you, and I think he might have pissed his pants. No wonder things go to your head. You didn't even have to say a word."

I sense admiration in her tone, and even though we're in public and we both agreed to keep the displays of affection to private, I lean down and press a tiny kiss next to her ear. "Sometimes size matters."

She laughs and her gaze slides down my body before she looks up at me again. "Size always matters, baby. The only people who say it doesn't are people who don't have it."

Nothing to disagree with there, so I point toward the door of the bar and smile. "Want to try this one?"

"Yeah."

"You know, I just realized with you in this blond wig, our first time really can't be considered our first since you're a different person," I joke.

Mia tugs at the bottom of her new blond hair and winks at me. "I do like how you think, Liam. Let's go in, have a drink, and then go back so you can have sex with the brunette me."

The man at the door doesn't give us a second glance,

just as she predicted, and as she passes him, she turns to give me a knowing look. I guess my follow-the-rules personality assumes everyone is like me.

Mia isn't, though. I've known that from the first day I met her. She is definitely not a woman who's about to let herself be restrained by rules.

When we reach the bar, I give her the only seat left and stand next to her, my nature needing to protect her as much as my desire to be near her wanting to touch her. Much larger than most people around us, I wave over the bartender, a guy with his dark hair in a man bun wearing an earring in his nose.

Leaning down, I say in her ear, "What do you want to drink?"

Without answering me, she leans over the bar and says to the bartender, "We'll have a pitcher of kamikazes."

The guy looks up at me and smiles like he's in on some joke between Mia and me before turning on his heel and walking away to make our drinks. Something tells me after a pitcher of kamikazes, this won't be the Mia I sleep with either.

"Didn't I tell you no one would care that I'm not old enough?" she asks. "You worry too much, Liam. I'm thinking after a couple drinks you'll chill out. Am I right?"

I smile, happy to correct her about who I am after a couple drinks. "Look at me. Does it look like two drinks would do anything to me? I'm thinking it would take two pitchers of kamikazes to make a dent, but tonight's not about me getting plastered. I can't do my job if I'm compromised."

The glee she's felt since we left the hotel instantly

drains from her face. "So you're here as my bodyguard?" she asks in a disappointed voice.

Quickly, I answer, happy to explain what I meant. "Not at all. That doesn't change the fact that if anyone gets too close to you or tries to lay a hand on you, they're going to find out what a world of hurt feels like when a guy my size hits them and doesn't hold back."

That makes her smile again. "Okay. So they'll get to find out what it feels like to get beaten up by my boyfriend."

"Exactly."

The bartender returns with our pitcher of drinks, and before I can reach into my pocket to get my wallet out, Mia hands him a hundred. "I'm going to need another pitcher when we get low, but the rest is yours."

That handsome tip makes him grin from ear to ear, and he happily agrees to check on us to make sure we don't run low on kamikazes. As I pat my unused wallet in my front pocket, Mia pours us both a drink and holds hers up in the air.

"To boyfriends and bodyguards!"

I smile and hold my drink up to join her, saying, "I think what you did right there makes me a bodyguard while we're here."

Her face twists into a confused expression, and she shakes her head. "What do you mean? Because I paid for our drinks?"

I shrug and take a sip of kamikaze. "Call me old-fashioned."

Mia laughs and tips her glass to her mouth to take a big gulp of her drink. "I will. Liam, you are old-fashioned. Can't a woman pay for a man's drinks?"

"Sure. I guess. I just prefer to pay when I go on dates."

Leaning in toward me, she pulls my head down so she can say in my ear, "Then don't think of this as a date. Think of this as an interlude between great sessions of sex."

When she sits back in her chair and takes another sip of kamikaze, I can't help but think she's the most incredibly sexy and infuriating woman I've ever met. One minute, she's driving me crazy in bed, and the next minute, she's buying my drink at a bar and poking fun at my being old-fashioned.

I'm not sure if I want to kiss her or drag her out of this bar to explain to her how I like being that old-fashioned gentleman my parents wanted me to be. Either way, I'd still be crazy about her.

Turning to face me, she smiles and says, "You know, about that whole rehab thing. You don't have to worry. I was never in rehab."

Now I'm confused. "That's what I was told was the reason why my job working with you started late."

"That's because that's what my mother told everyone. She paid the people at Sunnybrook Rehab to say I was there detoxing, but I've never used drugs in my life. I don't have a drinking problem either."

"So where were you if you weren't in rehab?"

Mia takes a deep breath in and holds it in her lungs for a long moment before letting it out slowly, almost as if she's afraid to tell me the truth. "I was at a place where they handle depression. My mother thinks the entire world will turn away from me if they find out I'm not one hundred percent perfect all the time. It's the reason she touts me as a classical pianist when I'm really more just someone who can play the piano pretty good if I practice a lot. She's sure if the world finds out I'm bipolar that I'll suddenly be an act no one would ever want to see."

She stops for a moment before adding, "Even though I take medication for it."

Her sadness makes me wince. After seeing her perform, I can't believe her fans would abandon her for anything.

"I'm sorry."

That gets me a smile I think is genuine. "For what? You didn't make me like this."

"Not for that. Just that you have to deal with worrying you'd lose your career if people found out the truth. Maybe you could go live on social media and let your fans hear you talk about it instead of having them hear about it through the media."

Mia shakes her head. "I don't go on social media anymore. I couldn't take the horrible things people would say when I'd post, so we hired someone who looks and sounds exactly like me to handle all of that. Some of the things they said were so cruel that I'd want to curl up into a ball and disappear. I guess to many people because I'm in the public eye, they think I don't have feelings, or I couldn't see what they wrote. But I did, and it hurt."

I hate seeing her so down, so I force a smile and say, "For what it's worth, I don't think you'd lose a single fan if they found out."

Mia raises her glass and lets out a heavy sigh. "For what it's worth, I don't either, but my mother has a different opinion about this. I'll fight her on most things, but I can't find it in me to risk that she's right and I'm wrong on this one."

As I watch her down her kamikaze, I can't help but

think about how Andrea has a huge effect on her daughter's life. She likes it that way too. No wonder she looked utterly stunned when I confronted her after the show that night she brought Michael back. She assumed things were going to be the way they'd always been — with everyone thinking Mia was the villain and she was the selfless hero in their story. She never thought anyone would dare to question her motives, least of all me.

But I know the truth now. I was so wrong about Mia in the beginning, but even more, I was wrong about her mother.

I DON'T KNOW HOW SHE DOES IT, BUT TWO PITCHERS of kamikazes later, of which I only had four drinks, Mia doesn't even seem slightly drunk. Afraid she might want to try for three pitchers, I suggest we hit another bar and step away from where she's sitting to encourage her to follow me.

Somehow, in those few seconds I'm not at her side, a fight breaks out right next to her between two guys who've had far too much to drink tonight. I step back to get in front of Mia to protect her, but I don't reach her in time. One of the guys gets pushed into her, and she falls to the floor, covered in the drunk's beer.

I spring into action, rushing over to pick her up before one or both of them fall on top of her. As I lift her into my arms, her blond wig slides off her head. Behind me, I hear someone say, "Hey, that's Mia," and then it's like the crowd suddenly can only focus on her and her alone out of the hundreds of people in the bar.

Hands shoot out from all directions to touch her, grabbing at her dress and her hair. She looks up at me with pure terror in her eyes, curling up into the fetal position in my arms. Never before have I seen her so frightened, and all I want to do is protect her.

I shoulder check half a dozen people as I push through the crowd toward the door. By the time I reach the street, she's sobbing in my arms with her face buried in my chest.

"It's okay. I've got you. Nobody's going to hurt you. I promise."

Her terrified voice muffled by my shirt, she says, "I want to go back to the hotel, Liam. Take me back there, please."

"Okay. Just hang on to me and I'll take care of everything."

She clings to my neck like a drowning woman, but she doesn't have to fear anything now. I won't let anyone hurt her.

With each step I take toward the hotel, regret fills me for letting my guard down. If only I didn't step away from her, none of this would have ever happened.

Out of the corner of my eye, I see blood on her bare shoulder. Someone scratched her skin when they were trying to get to her, and now she's bleeding. Anger mixes with regret, and it's all I can do to not march right back to that goddamned bar and beat the hell out of everyone I recognize.

"Are we almost there?" she asks in a tiny voice.

I come out of my haze of rage and see the sign for the hotel right in front of me. "We're almost there. Don't worry. I've got you, Mia."

The guy at concierge I thought had a pretentious way of speaking when we arrived sees me walk through the front door with her in my arms and rushes over to us. Whatever affectation he had earlier has disappeared when he frantically asks in a heavy southern accent, "What happened? What do you need, Mr. Jackson?"

"She's okay, but I need to get her up to her suite immediately," I say as I hurry to the bank of elevators across the lobby.

Mia lifts her head from my chest and smiles up at me. "Would you ask him to send up something to eat? My stomach feels weird, like it needs food in it right now."

Happy to hear her sounding better, I ask, "What do you want? Whatever it is, either he'll have them make it or I'll run and get it."

Tears fill her eyes. "I'd like a pizza."

The man from concierge presses the button to summon the elevator and hears her say she wants a pizza. "I will get one sent up to your suite immediately, miss."

"Can you send up some sweet tea too?" Mia asks with a smile.

"Of course, of course," he says, still flustered at having to deal with a major star being carried through his very posh lobby.

"Thank you so much. I really mean it. Thank you," she says as the elevator doors open, and we step in.

"It's our pleasure, miss. We only want your visit with us to be the very best it can be."

I force a smile for him as the doors close because he looks like he's about to have a breakdown. I guess it isn't every day that one of their guests has something happen to them and shows up in a man's arms.

We silently ride up in the elevator, but right before we reach her floor, Mia quietly says, "I overreacted back at that bar. I'm sorry, Liam. Those people just wanted to see me."

Staring straight ahead at the gold doors reflecting the image of her in my arms back at us, I growl at the memory of what those people tried to do. "They were like animals. That's not wanting to see someone. That's wanting a piece of someone."

"Are you mad at me, Liam? You're acting like you are," she says, her words full of hurt.

I don't look down at her, but out of the corner of my eye I see her staring up at me like she desperately needs me not to be angry. I'm not angry with her. I'm angry with me. I fucked up. I let those animals get close to her because I dropped my guard.

I'm saved from having to answer her when the elevator rings to announce we've reached her suite and the doors open. Her crew is having a good time, but everything stops dead when they see me walk out of the elevator with Mia in my arms.

"Oh, my God! Mia, what happened?" her life coach asks in a voice that sounds remarkably similar to the frantic one the concierge guy had downstairs.

She rushes over to greet us as I set Mia down on the gold print sofa in the lounge area of the suite. "You're bleeding. Let me get you a washcloth to wipe it up. What happened? You said you were going out for a little bit. I figured you meant you were staying in the hotel, though, like always. If I had known you were going somewhere with whatever attacked you, I would have chained you to the floor."

Mia looks up at me and rolls her eyes. "Ainsley gets a little freaked at the sight of blood. Sit down. You can have some of my pizza. It should be here soon."

"No, that's okay. I need to get back downstairs to talk to my guys."

She reaches out her hand to grab mine and keep me there, but I step back, needing to get out of this room full of all of these people gawking at her.

A look of hurt settles into her eyes. "What's wrong? Are you okay?"

I shrug, needing to get away from all of these people. Including Mia. "I'm fine. It looks like you're in good hands, so I'm going to go."

Before she can try to convince me to stay, I hurry over to the elevator, nearly running into one of the hotel's waiters coming out with Mia's pizza in his hands. Sidestepping him, I rush in as the doors close, quietly apologizing for nearly flattening him as he tried to make his delivery.

Regret fills me with every second that passes on my way down to my floor. I utterly failed in my job tonight. I can't forgive myself.

CHAPTER THIRTY-ONE

*M*ia

ALL THE PEOPLE BUZZING AROUND ME TO MAKE SURE I'm comfortable, happy, and fed only serve to make me wish Liam was still here. Why did he leave? He's angry, but I don't know why.

That's not true. I know him well enough to understand that tonight I broke one of his rules and now he's regretting going with me to that bar. I knew he was trying to keep us from going with all those reasons why we shouldn't even try to get into a bar, but I figured once we slept together everything changed.

Or is it that he's regretting that instead of what happened after we had sex?

God, I wish he was here. Everyone's attention seems fixed on me, and I feel like some freak at the circus. The blood on my shoulder was from a tiny scratch. Nothing big. I don't even think it was that much blood since I don't need a bandage or anything.

Liam's so overprotective. I love that about him, but he shouldn't be unhappy about what happened tonight.

Part of that is my fault. I overreacted when all those people started coming at me. I should be used to that. I've had people clamoring to get close to me for years. I had Liam there with me, the one person I trust more than any other in the entire world. If only I hadn't freaked out, everything would have been fine.

"So what happened?" Ainsley asks as Crystal sits down next to her to hear the story.

I wave away her question, not wanting to rehash my mistake. "Nothing happened. Liam and I were having a couple drinks at a bar, and it got crowded. Things got a little crazy, but he got me out of there before anyone could hurt me."

"Was it the stalker?" Crystal asks in a voice full of fear.

"No. It was just a bunch of people out having a good time that got a little out of hand. Really, it wasn't a big deal. I think the scratch on my shoulder happened when someone fell into me, and I caught my arm on a barstool. Seriously, you don't have to worry about me. Liam would never let anyone do anything to harm me."

Crystal lets out a heavy sigh, clearly relieved by what I'm saying, but Ainsley simply sits next to her shaking her head. I so don't need her ridiculous anger about the only man I can truly trust right now.

"What? Why are you sitting there giving me that look and shaking your head?" I snap, challenging her to give her opinion, even though I'm not in the mood for it.

I can see in her eyes she wants to tell me what's on

her mind, but she merely shrugs, keeping her ideas about Liam to herself for once. "Nothing. I'm just scared after seeing him bring you in and the blood on your shoulder. You know how I get whenever I see blood. A nurse I could never be."

"Well, you don't have to be worried or scared or anything. Liam took care of everything, including me. Nobody touched me. Nothing bad happened. It just got a little edgy for a few minutes there. If anything, it was my fault for telling him I wanted to go to a bar tonight. I should have known there would be people there who might want to meet me."

Ainsley listens to all I have to say and then leans forward toward me. "But how did they know it was you? You were wearing the blond wig."

Suddenly, I realize I don't have it on anymore. I feel the top of my head and know that wig is long gone somewhere in that bar. Looking at Crystal, I reach my hand out to take hers.

"I am so sorry. In the ruckus, it must have slipped off. I'll replace it. I promise. I'm sorry, Crystal."

"Oh, sweetie, it's okay," she says, genuinely happy only her wig got lost in the shuffle. "I have lots of wigs, and I even have a few exactly like the one you were wearing. You don't have to replace it, but if you want, you can get me a nice long one. I've been thinking that's the next one I want to add to my collection. A nice long, platinum blond wig. I saw one a few weeks ago and it was so great! Wait until you see it!"

Ainsley sits back and folds her arms across her chest. "Well, that's all well and good, but shouldn't Liam have made sure no one could touch you at all? Isn't that his entire job?"

My emotions nearly boil over at hearing her attack him like that, and I swing my feet off the sofa to stand up because I need to get the hell away from her right now. She stares up at me in shock that I don't answer either of her asinine questions before I march into my bedroom and order everyone to leave.

"Time to go, guys! I need to get some rest. Feel free to hang out in the outer room, if you want."

I hear someone walking behind me, so I spin around to see who it is. Ainsley stops dead and levels her gaze on me, like she expects that I'll answer either of her questions now before I go to sleep.

"Whatever you're trying to say about Liam, you need to back off. He did exactly what I wanted him to do tonight. I wanted to go to a bar, so he accompanied me and made sure I was safe. It's not his fault some assholes got into a bar brawl and knocked into me. So I don't want to hear your opinion, Ainsley. Good night!"

She stands in the doorway wide-eyed and surprised I've shut down any chance for us to talk about this issue right now. I might not even talk about it tomorrow or ever, for that matter. Her opinion about him means nothing to me. Ainsley needs to learn if you don't have anything nice to say, don't say anything at all.

Her mouth opens like she wants to rebut all I've told her, but I slam the door before she can utter a single syllable. If she wants to talk tomorrow, that's fine, but if all she has to offer is more negativity about the man I'm crazy about, she can keep that to herself.

I close my eyes and fall back onto the bed, exhausted but thrilled about tonight. Liam and I slept together, and it was incredible! Now I just need to convince him nothing that happened at the bar was his fault. Knowing him, that will be easier said than done.

Then a thought occurs to me. Maybe it would be easiest sung.

Scrambling across the bed to look for my journal and pen I keep with me whenever I travel, I begin to jot down some ideas for a song that will let him know how much he means to me and how much none of tonight could be blamed on him. For the first time in a long time, my mind works faster than my pen, so I have to hurry to keep up with my thoughts. They come faster than I can keep up, though, so I begin to sing them in the hopes that I'll remember each one better.

I sing and write, and it all comes out quicker than I ever thought a song could come. The music practically writes itself, a song meant to be sung by me alone with only a piano on stage. I imagine the lights dimmed and only a single spot on me as I share my feelings for Liam with the entire world, but only he'll know I'm singing about us. Everyone else will think it's just another love song written by Mia.

By the time I finish nearly two hours later, I couldn't sleep if I wanted to. I have to get this song recorded. I can't wait to be sure the track is down so I can listen to it and see where it needs little tweaks.

It has to happen tonight.

Grabbing my phone, I call my mother to get her onto the task of having the plane ready for me. She answers in a groggy voice like I've woken her up out of a sound sleep. I look over at the clock and see it's barely midnight.

"I need to fly to Miami right now. Get the pilot and

the plane ready. I'll leave as soon as I can get to the airport."

The response I get is silence from her end. Did she fall back to sleep, or is she simply in shock that I want to fly down to the recording studio I love the most to get this track down before dawn?

"Are you there? You heard what I said, right?" I ask, already irritated by her lack of enthusiasm.

She knows if I'm saying I want to go to Miami that I'm planning to record something. You'd think she'd be all for that. More songs to please the fans and bring more money in. She usually cares more about that than anything else.

"I heard you. I'm just not sure I understand. You want to fly to Miami tonight and do what?"

How is she not getting this? Inspiration has struck, and I'm sitting here trying to explain the basics of what I want to do tonight. Some manager she is.

"I want to fly to Miami to get into the studio. I have a song that needs to be recorded right now. So get that pilot and my plane ready. It will be me and Liam. Maybe more, if he wants to have more of his guys with him. I'm going to leave everyone else here to enjoy themselves since we don't have another stop on the tour for three days in Houston. I'll be back tomorrow, so I won't miss a date."

That seems to make it through the fog of her sleepiness, and she perks up. "Okay, the pilot will need an hour or so, I'm sure. You know what he says about filing flight plans and all of that. Maybe two hours. Do you want me to come with you like always?"

The thought of my mother there as I sing my feelings for Liam instantly tarnishes what this song means to me, and I shake my head in horror, even if I answer her like it's nothing big that she can't be there. "No, not this time. With everyone else staying here, I need you to keep an eye on things."

"Okay. I can do that. Now when I have to tell the pilot how many of you will be traveling, what do I say?"

"At least two, but maybe three or four," I say as I shimmy across the bed to begin getting ready to go.

"Got it. Okay, I'll call him now. Give him two hours, but if it's longer, I'll let you know. And when will you be coming back? He'll want to know so he can file a flight plan for that trip too."

My mother almost sounds like she's trying to make excuses for wanting to know my plans, something she never even attempts to apologize for. It's so totally her style to want to know the itinerary down to the minute. This attempt to respect my freedom feels like a change I will enjoy, if she keeps it up.

"I'd want to return tomorrow night. Liam will need to take his guys early to Houston to check everything out, so no later than tomorrow night by this time."

"Okay, Mia. I'm on it. I'm surprised you want to go into the recording studio so spur of the moment. You usually need time to gear up for a session. What changed?"

I hear her question and silently answer it for myself alone. Tonight changed me. Liam changed me. Having him in my life changed me.

Falling in love changed me.

But none of those answers are anything I want to share with her, so I casually answer, "Nothing much. Inspiration can hit at the strangest times, and I guess a suite at the Ritz-Carlton in New Orleans did the trick.

I'll talk to you when I get back. Thanks for keeping an eye on things while I'm gone."

"Good luck with the new song. I can't wait to hear it!"

Transportation to Miami handled, next up is telling Liam he needs to be ready to leave in less than two hours. Hopefully, his mood has improved by now.

CHAPTER THIRTY-TWO

iam

FOR OVER AN HOUR AND A HALF, I'VE PACED BACK AND forth across this hotel suite as my self-loathing has grown to fill every part of me. I should have never let Mia convince me to take her out to a bar tonight. What the fuck was I thinking?

I stop in front of the bed where only a few hours ago we lay naked in each other's arms and shake my head. Who am I kidding? She didn't have to convince me to do anything. I wanted to take her out because I knew it would make her happy.

That doesn't change the fact that I dropped the goddamned ball when it came to protecting her.

As I begin to pace again, thoughts of the two of us together in bed begin to crowd out my hatred for what I let happen tonight. I can't allow that. No matter how good it felt to be inside her, I don't deserve to enjoy those memories when the next thing that happened was a crowd of people nearly ripped her to shreds.

Someone knocking on my hotel room door tears me out of my thoughts, and I pad over to see who it is, hoping it won't be her. I can't face her tonight. Not after what happened.

I look through the peephole and see it's Mia smiling like she doesn't have a care in the world. Fuck. I thought she'd stay in her room until morning. I should have put one of the guys on each floor to make sure she didn't roam off.

Flinging open the door, I grab her by the arm and yank her into my room. Before I can slam the door shut, I snap, "What the hell are you doing just walking around the hotel all alone? You could get hurt, Mia."

She stares at me with a look of pure confusion and shakes her head. "I literally rode down one floor in the elevator from my room, got off in this hallway, and walked to this room. Since you guys and the rest of my entourage take up all the rooms on this floor, Liam, I think I'm safe to walk around on my own."

I slam the door and walk past her on the path I've paced for the past nearly two hours, avoiding meeting her gaze. "You take too many chances, you know that? I'm your head of security, and I can tell you when you do that, you don't make my job any easier."

"It's no big deal, Liam. Really. Why are you so upset?" she asks as I hear her walk up behind me.

Mia attempts to wrap her arms around my waist, but I turn out of her hold before she can and start my walk back across the room toward the door again. "It is a big deal. I need to know where you go at all times. I know you hate that, but it's the way it has to be. I thought you understood that."

"I do. You know I do. I haven't given you a hard time about how you protect me in weeks. Why are you so upset with me right now?"

Every word is filled with hurt, and I avoid meeting her gaze now because I can't see that in her eyes and know I put it there. "I'm not upset. I'm just trying to do my job the best I know how, Mia. I'm responsible for your safety. I can't forget that, even if I want to."

She doesn't say a word, and when I turn back to walk toward her, I can't avoid seeing how upset I'm making her. It's written all over her face, and just as I suspected, she's got tears in her eyes.

From me.

Finally, she asks in a tiny voice, "Why do you want to forget you're responsible for my safety? I thought that meant the world to you, Liam."

Christ, I should have just kept my mouth shut. I always get myself in trouble when I let myself talk too much. Now she thinks I don't care about being her bodyguard, a job that means more to me than she can ever imagine.

Facing her for the first time since she walked into my room, I try to find the right words so I don't make things worse. "That's not what I meant. Trust me. I don't want to forget anything when it comes to protecting you."

My answer makes her smile, but the corners of her lips barely rise. "Okay."

We stand there staring at one another like two strangers who don't know what to say next or two opposing armies that have little interest in continuing this battle. I don't want to fight with her. I'm too busy beating myself up to argue with the person I let down.

After nearly a minute, I ask, "So why are you roaming around the hotel after midnight? I figured you'd be sleeping by now after the night you had."

I don't go into detail about that, and I hope she thinks I'm referring to the show and not what happened afterward. Well, not the sex, which was great, but what happened after that.

Jesus. Now she's going to think I'm making some childish reference to our sleeping together. It would have been better if I didn't open the door at all.

"I need to fly out to Miami tonight to record a song. I know it's short notice, but when the muse comes, you don't ask her why she didn't wait for a more convenient time. So you need to get ready, and whoever else you want to join us needs to be ready in an hour. We'll leave right after one."

Her announcement stuns me. She wants to fly to Miami in the middle of the night to record a song? She can't wait until tomorrow?

"What do you mean? I need to take the guys to Houston ahead of the show there to make sure everything's set. I can't go to Miami tonight."

As I say those words, her expression falls, like she's just heard the worst news of her life. I want more than anything to spend every waking minute with her, and the sleeping minutes I'd love to spend with her in my arms together in bed. I just can't forgive myself for screwing up so badly at that bar tonight.

"I thought you'd want to be there since you're the one who's in charge of security, but if you need to go on ahead to Houston, then I guess I'll have to go with whoever you think you can trust. It's only a short overnight trip to Miami and back. I should be back within twenty-four hours," she says, trying to act like she isn't disappointed.

Damnit, I'm fucking everything up. I should just go with her. She's supposed to have her head of security with her when she goes anywhere like this.

I can't. Not tonight. My head is too full of guilt to be in the right place to protect her properly. She deserves better than I can offer right now.

"I'll get Kip and Brett to go with you. Then I can catch them up on any changes we make when we do the walk-through in Houston," I say flatly, hoping she can't see how much I'm blaming myself for before.

"Okay. Brett's the giant one who's even bigger than you? Is there a reason you're sending him?" she asks as she takes a step toward me and then stops.

She's close enough that I could stretch my arms out and pull her into me like I want to, but I don't move and instead answer, "It's always good to have someone his size around. Promise me you won't do anything but go to the recording studio and back to the airport while you're in Miami and then only go from the airport to the hotel here. And I need the number for the studio too."

With a smile, she nods her head and walks over to me, wrapping her arms around my waist like she wanted to do when she first got here. Looking up at me, she says, "I promise. No roaming around the countryside making things difficult for my bodyguards, and I'll text you the number the minute I get back to my room."

My entire body relaxes for the first time since I saw her get caught up in that fight at the bar hours ago. The simple feel of her against me makes me think I'm not the worst possible man in the world for her.

"Thank you. I'll let them know they need to get ready to go."

Neither of us makes a move so I can call Kip and Brett, though. Mia seems to want to hold on to me, and I can't think of any good reason to not let her.

"I'm fine, you know. Even that scratch on my shoulder that was bleeding before isn't. We didn't have any Band-Aids upstairs, but I didn't need one. So whatever you're thinking about that bar thing, don't. I wouldn't trade the time we got to spend drinking kamikazes for anything."

I look down into her sweet face and shake my head. "This is when you should be bitching me out for not doing my job. Don't let me off the hook so easily, Mia."

She slides her hands from around my waist and cradles my face. "You did your job, Liam. Nobody expects you to make sure nothing ever happens when I'm out of my house. You saw a problem begin to happen and you handled it, exactly what you're supposed to do. Stop beating yourself up because I got flustered over nothing."

"What happened to that woman who balled me out the first day I met her? I'm thinking she should make an appearance right about now," I say with a chuckle.

"Well, she met this guy who showed her she was being a royal pain in the ass, and now she tries not to be that because of him."

"Cute."

Standing on her tiptoes, she kisses me softly and whispers against my lips, "It's the truth."

"I think since you're going to be away for the day I'll

take the guys to Houston and get the walkthrough done tomorrow instead of the day after. That way we'll have one last day to do whatever we want before we head to the next show."

Mia turns her head to look over toward the bed and then turns back to face me, wiggling her eyebrows. "I've got an idea about how we should spend that time, so you and your guys handle your thing and I'll go record my song. I can't wait for you to hear it."

"Will you be singing it at the Houston show?" I ask, curious since I have no idea about how songs are written or how long they take to perfect for a live performance.

She thinks about it for a minute and nods. "Maybe. It only involves me singing and playing the piano, so theoretically, as long as I can get it down well enough for a show, I could do it then. Maybe the Kansas City show. But you'll hear it eventually. You can be sure of that."

I push her brown hair off her face and press a tiny kiss to her forehead. "Remember, you promised not to give the guys a hard time."

For that, I get a big smile. "They aren't you, but I'll go easy on them. Be ready when I get back. I'm already planning to spend hours in that bed over there with you."

"Thanks for the warning. I better hit the gym before you get back. I'm going to need to be in shape for our reunion," I say, secretly letting myself off the hook a little bit more with every time she makes me smile.

Mia's gaze drifts down my body and then back up to meet mine. "I'm not worried about you being in shape. From what I've seen, you're perfect. I, however, better take some vitamins for what I have planned. I'll see you tomorrow night by midnight."

She kisses me one more time and then pulls away

from my hold. I watch her leave and wish it was already tomorrow night and we were together in my bed.

Now to inform Kip and Brett that they're making an unscheduled detour tonight. I didn't tell Mia, but Brett's the only man I trust to take my place. I respect Drew more than anyone else in the business, but pound for pound, it's Brett I'll always call to replace me.

CHAPTER THIRTY-THREE

$\mathcal{M}$ia

MY RECORDING TIME AT MY FAVORITE STUDIO TURNED out better than I expected. Rarely have I ever gotten a song down in one take, but I swear it's like this song formed somewhere deep in my heart and knew it had to come out right now. At least it's done and now I can play around with it to perfect each note before I perform it the first time.

Poking my head into the control room, I smile at Larry and Craig sitting at their mixing board. Brothers, they're both big guys with long beards that make them look like they should be living in a cabin deep in the woods and not in a city like Miami. They started their business years before I was born, but they were the only people willing to give me studio time when I was first coming up. My mother always said they agreed because I was a cute kid.

Since that day they finally said yes, I try to record all my songs here at their studio. My record company always presses for me to go to bigger ones in LA or other places around the world, but I never agree.

"You were on fire in there," Craig says with a big smile. "I don't think I've ever heard you sound like that. You find Jesus or something?"

"Something," I say with a chuckle. "Thanks so much for coming in here in the middle of the night for me, guys. I owe you big."

The two of them look at one another and shake their heads. "You don't owe us anything, baby. We've been on the Mia train since it pulled out of the station right here in Magic City," Larry says, opening his arms to invite me in for one of those big bear hugs he loves to give.

I walk into the control room and hug each of them, so thankful for how much they've helped me. "This is going to be my next number one, guys. You watch."

"That's the attitude you need. Seriously, though, you seem different from how you usually are. What's going on with you?"

Knowing Brett and Kip are out in the hallway waiting to escort me back to the plane, I can't take a chance on telling the brothers about Liam and me. So I bend down and whisper to them, "I can't say much, but let's just say this. Love has a way of changing a girl."

The two of them light up at my news, but I quickly wave my hands to stop them from getting loud, just in case my bodyguards are listening. "But don't say anything, okay? It's really new, and I don't want anyone to know. Not yet, at least."

Always the one to put a fine point on things, Craig levels his gaze on me and says, "Then you better keep it from that manager of yours or the whole world is going to know chapter and verse about this new guy in three point five seconds."

"Isn't that the truth?" I say with a laugh. "You might be underestimating Andrea. I don't think it would take her that long."

"Well, enjoy yourself, baby," Larry says, grabbing my hand. "You deserve it. You've worked hard for a long time. Now you deserve some you time."

"Thanks, guys. I'll be back next week to see what I can do to get this just right. Until then, stay loose."

That's what they always say when I'm leaving. Stay loose. I guess it's some throwback to their hippie days. What it means to me is stay safe and be happy.

"Stay loose, baby!" they call after me as I walk out.

Brett stands guard just outside the door, so I breathe a sigh of relief that I didn't tell the brothers about Liam and me. Stony-faced, the enormous man stares down at me without a hint of a smile. He's definitely not like my favorite bodyguard.

"Time to go back to New Orleans," I say as I walk past him.

He doesn't respond, but the other guy Kip smiles as I make my way down the hallway toward the back door. I guess that's something, but I'm used to having someone to talk to around me. Liam always speaks. I've been thinking he didn't speak a lot, but now that I'm with these two, he's practically a chatterbox.

"Not a lot to say, huh?" I mumble as Kip opens the door for me.

I step outside into the hot south Florida early morning and look up at the blue sky without a cloud to be found. It's going to be a great day. Since it's barely seven a.m., I'm guessing we can make it back to the hotel by noon.

Then I remember I left my phone inside the studio. Spinning around, I point toward the door as my two bodyguards stare at me like they don't know what to do. "Forgot something. I'll be right back."

See, that's not like Liam either. He'd flat out ask me where I thought I was going. All this time, I thought he was pretty damn rude when he asked questions like that, but now that I hear nothing as I walk back into the building, I miss someone noticing what I'm up to.

On my way past the brothers' room, I explain, "I forgot my phone."

The two of them smile and nod, mostly because it's a very typical thing for me to do. I always seem to leave something behind.

I find it on the piano seat and hold it up for them to see through the window. "Got it! See you later!"

That gets me more nods and another smile from each of them. As I walk back toward the car, I stuff my phone into my purse and throw open the steel door to the gorgeous morning outside. I'm surprised not to see Liam's men, but I head toward the black SUV anyway. That's also not something my guy would do. I know he trusts these two implicitly, but is it standard procedure to just let a client roam around unprotected like this? He must have warned them about my tendency to want to go off on my own.

Then again, it is only a few yards to where the car is parked. I glance left and right to see no one around, so maybe I'm making a big deal out of nothing.

Liam really is wearing off on me. Next thing I know, I'll be quoting rules and regulations to everyone.

I reach out to open the backseat door, but the car's still locked. What's going on? Is this some strange bodyguard prank Brett and Kip are playing on me?

"Funny. You got me. Did Liam tell you to punk me?"

Silence.

I press my nose to the window and try to see in through the tinted glass. "Can you please open the door? You know, I'm not sure what you're doing, but Liam would never have me standing outside like this all alone."

Still, they say nothing. I try the door again, but it's still locked. What the fuck?

As I attempt to understand what the hell is happening, something hard hits me in the back of the head. I stumble forward into the car door, and then everything goes dark.

"Wake up, princess. You can't sleep all day."

I hear the voice telling me I need to wake up, but I don't understand. I struggle to open my eyes, and no matter how hard I try, I can't seem to get them to do as I want. It's like my brain isn't sending the right signal to get them to do the very thing they're being told to do.

"Open your eyes, Mia. Open your eyes!"

Now the voice, which I know is a male's, barks at me angrily. I want to tell him I'm trying my hardest, but I can't seem to speak either. What the hell is wrong with me? Did I catch some flu? Or tetanus? That's the thing that makes it impossible to close your mouth, isn't it?

No, that's lockjaw. Doesn't that come from tetanus, though?

I try to figure out the answer, finally deciding that the

opposite occurs, and you can't open your mouth with lockjaw. Not that it matters because I don't think the reason I can't get my damn mouth to work is because of that or tetanus.

"Jesus Christ, Mia! Open your fucking eyes!" the man yells again, this time directly in front of my face.

Wait a second. I know that voice. Who is screaming at me?

Finally, I manage to open my right eye enough to see the person in front of me, and instantly, I begin to shake my head. No way should he be standing in front of me yelling a single word in my face. What the fuck is Michael doing in my hotel room screaming at me to open my eyes?

"That's one. Do the second one and you'll get a treat," he says and then laughs.

I work to open my left eye, sure I've never used whatever muscle that is like this before in my entire life. It's like there's a five-pound weight attached to my eyelid, but I finally get both eyes open to see Michael sitting in a chair in front of me in a place that is definitely not my hotel room or any room I've ever been in before.

"Attagirl. Now which do you want, orange juice or apple juice?" he asks in a snide tone, like I'm some imbecile he's charged with making comfortable.

My mouth drops open, but at first, no sound comes out. Too bad because I want to tell him to fuck off in the worst way. I've got a splitting headache that's suddenly making the back of my head pound like a kick drum, and I feel sick to my stomach, as if I haven't had enough food in me for far too long.

"Use your words, Mia. You know I can't give you what you want if you don't use your words."

God, he sounds like some asshole stepparent who thinks that's the way you talk to a child. But I'm not a child, and he's definitely not any parent of mine, step or otherwise.

I try to wet my lips, but my tongue is like a giant cotton ball. It takes me a few seconds to get enough saliva, and finally, I can say something to this jackass. "Fuck off. Where the hell am I?"

He grins like any of this is funny, and I slowly turn my head left and right to look around. Is this where he works now? It looks like a factory with cement walls and floors.

Then I look down at my body and see my hands and legs tied to a chair that reminds me of the ones we used to have in our dining room when I was a little girl. I try to move my right hand, but it's securely tied to the arm of this old wooden chair.

"Don't try to move. You're tied there, so if you try too hard, you might fall over and hit your head. We wouldn't want you to hurt yourself," he says as he stares at me like he's enjoying this.

"Where am I?" I snap, getting angrier by the minute.

"Somewhere safe. Now which do you want, orange or apple juice?"

"Fuck off and I don't want anything from you! Where are the two guards who were with me? What did you do to them?"

Michael shrugs. "Their services weren't needed any more, so I relieved them of their duties. If they didn't bleed out, they're probably reporting back to your new head of security that they lost their client. I imagine he's going to be more than a little pissed since you and he are an item now."

The thought of Brett and Kip hurt makes my chest hurt. "What did you do to them, Michael?" I sob.

"I needed them out of the way, so I shot them. For what it's worth, I didn't aim for their heads or any major organs. I just needed them indisposed. Assuming someone found them and took them to the hospital, they'll be fine after some orthoscopic surgery. The knee is a tricky thing, Mia. You know that. Remember when you hyperextended yours a few years ago when you were rehearsing a new routine? We almost had to reschedule that tour because of that little mishap."

I hate the way he talks like he had anything to do with my business. He was the man in charge of keeping me safe for far too long, and he didn't even do that job well, but he sure as hell didn't have a say in whether that tour would be rescheduled or not.

"*We* didn't almost have to do anything. *I* had to make that decision. You never had any part in that." I practically spit out the words as I continue to attempt to get these ropes around my wrist loose.

"Don't bet on it, princess," he says, sneering like he knows so much more than I do about everything. "I've been in on everything that happened with you for years."

"What are you talking about? You're suffering from delusions of grandeur, Michael. You were the guy who oversaw my security, poorly, I now know, and you were the person I turned to because I thought you were my friend. Come to find out you were a piss-poor version of that too."

He jumps up out of his chair and lunges at me, sticking his face directly in front of mine as he presses his palms down on my shoulders. The weight makes my body instantly hurt all over and all I want to do is cry. I won't let him see me give in like that, though.

"I did everything exactly as you wanted me to. Everything, you bitch! You didn't want to feel like you were trapped in your own house, so I made sure you didn't feel that way. You didn't want to have to feel like your security took away from your precious, little life, so it never did. You were the reason you weren't safe, not anyone else!"

Turning away so I don't have to look at his ugly features anymore, I say, "I didn't know any better. You did. You're a grown man who is supposed to know how to protect a client."

Finally, he leans away from me, removing his hands from my shoulders, so I turn back to face him and add, "If more had to be done, then it should have been."

He smiles as he backs up toward his chair, but it's not a smile of sweetness or happiness. "Oh, you have the answers for everything."

I say nothing, unsure if his anger will escalate if I do. My mind races with questions about how long I've been here, if anyone knows I'm missing, and if anyone is looking for me.

Most of all, will Liam find me in time to save me from this madman?

"As for my being your friend, you knew I wanted more. You wanted it too, you little cock tease. I never knew how much until you showed up at my door that day and saw me with Tracey. Didn't like seeing me like that, did you? Poor little Mia missed her chance. You should have taken me up on my offers all those times."

His cruelty comes through loud and clear in every word, but I can't stop myself from setting him straight. "I never wanted you. That's not how I ever saw you. I thought you were my friend. So much for that, I guess."

Rage flashes in his eyes, and he barks, "I didn't want to be your fucking friend! I never wanted to be put into that box, and you knew that, you fucking tease!"

"What exactly do you think you're doing with this whole thing here? Are you planning on asking for a ransom for me? You'll never get away with this, Michael."

Instead of enraging him further, that makes him smile. "Oh, don't worry. I'm not alone in this, so I'll get away with anything I do. You can choose to behave yourself, or you can choose to get hurt. It's entirely up to you."

Never once in all the times I turned to this man for all those years did I think he could ever hurt me. Now I truly don't know for sure.

All I know is I've never needed Liam more. Where is he? Is he coming to take me out of this place?

"And if you're thinking where is your new head of security when you need him most, my partner has taken care of that. Settle in, sweetheart. You're here for the duration."

Michael walks away, leaving me sitting in that chair and more terrified than ever. His partner has taken care of Liam? What does he mean?

An ache settles into my chest at the thought that Liam's been hurt. Or worse, he's dead at the hands of Michael's partner, whoever he is.

CHAPTER THIRTY-FOUR

iam

I WAKE TO THE SOUND OF MY PHONE RINGING AND grab it off the nightstand to see it's right after eight in the morning. So much for sleeping in a little today. My eyes focus a little bit more so I can see it's Andrea calling.

Not the person I ever want to wake up to.

After scrubbing my face of the last vestiges of sleep, I answer the call. "What's up, Andrea?"

"Mia's been taken! Those two men you sent with her to protect her didn't do their job, and now she's God only knows where!"

She begins to cry hysterically while I sit upright in bed and immediately launch into work mode. My mind's racing with questions about where Mia could be, who could have done this, and where the hell Brett and Kip are in this whole thing.

"Tell me everything you know. I need to know every detail right now," I say as I swing my legs out of bed.

From the second my feet hit the floor, I'm running one hundred percent on adrenaline. The woman I've fallen in love with is missing and who knows where, and two of my men are unaccounted for. None of this is good. Every minute I waste waiting for Andrea to get her shit together and stop crying is a minute any of them may be hurt.

Or worse.

She continues to sob as she tries to tell me what she knows, but I can't understand a goddamned word of it. "Andrea, calm down. I need to be able to figure out how to go from here, but I can't find out where here is if you keep crying."

I listen to her slowly stop her wailing, and then she sniffles a few times before saying, "I got a call about ten minutes ago. It was someone saying they took Mia. They want a ransom for her."

So it's a kidnapping. That she waited ten minutes to tell me about. Okay, focus, Liam. That means they want something in exchange for Mia, so they're going to keep her alive.

At least until they get paid.

"How much do they want?" I ask as I yank my pants up my legs.

"What?"

"How much is the ransom?" I ask again while I button my pants and walk over to the closet to find a shirt.

"I don't know. I mean, I can't remember," Andrea says.

What the fuck does she mean she can't remember?

Ripping my grey dress shirt off the hanger, I try to find the patience to deal with this woman right now. "Okay, let's go over what happened, step-by-step. What did they say?"

"They said they have her and they want five million. That's it. That's how much they said they want. I guess in all of this I just forgot. They want five million dollars for her."

"Okay," I say as I let out a sigh, happy to be getting somewhere with her finally. "When do they want it by?"

"Today!" she squeals, like I should have known that answer without even asking the question. "They want it today or they're going to kill her. We have to get it to them immediately!"

"I agree, but they don't want to kill her, Andrea. Trust me. This is for money. Kidnappers rarely want to be murderers. They want money so they can go live the life they want to live. Being charged with a capital crime in the state of Florida is not what they got into this for, so they're going to keep her alive."

At least I hope so.

"Did they say where they want us to drop off the money? How is it to go down?" I ask as I finish putting my shoes on.

"No. They didn't say anything about that. Oh, God! Does that mean they're going to kill her because I didn't have the money to offer right then and there?" Andrea asks, sobbing again.

"No, no. Calm down. They said they'd call back, right? They want money, so they'll give us details about how to get them the money in the next call. Did they say anything else?"

"Yes. They said not to call the police or the FBI. I

wasn't going to, Liam, because they never do anything. I swear they want to wait until she gets hurt until they do something. Oh, my God! Is this her stalker? Has he graduated to kidnapper now?"

That already occurred to me, but I quickly dismissed that idea. Just as kidnappers rarely want to become murderers, stalkers rarely make the leap to kidnappers. It's an entirely different focus and unlikely one a stalker would want to get involved with.

"No, I don't think this is her stalker, so let's not get worried about that. We do have to contact the FBI, at least, though. This is a kidnapping, and as much as we might want to think we can handle things ourselves, the FBI knows how to deal with this better than anyone else in the world."

"Mia won't like that, Liam. She never wants to deal with the police or FBI. She doesn't think they ever want to help. That's why she leaves dealing with them to me, but I have to admit, I think she's right. I doubt they'll even take this seriously since she's only been gone for about eight hours."

I grab my suit jacket and head toward the door. "We're contacting the FBI, Andrea. Not to contact them will risk Mia's life, and we don't want that. I can be the one who deals with them. I've done it before, so it's no problem. As soon as I finish this call with you, I'll get in touch with them."

"No, no. I can't have you do that. They'll only end up wanting to talk to me because I'm her mother. I'll do it."

Confused, I say, "Mia's not a minor anymore, Andrea. You don't have to be the point person on this. I can do it. In fact, I should since two of my guys were with her and I need to find out where the hell they are."

"That's even more reason for me to handle the FBI. I'll take care of them, Liam. Just be ready when they get here because they'll need to know all the details about when Mia left. I don't know because I was sleeping. You deal with finding your men. God, I hope they aren't…"

She doesn't finish her sentence before she begins crying again. I don't need to hear the rest of what she was thinking. I've already said those exact words to myself.

God, I hope they aren't dead.

DREW ANSWERS HIS HOTEL ROOM DOOR IN A PAIR OF shorts and a T-shirt that says Auburn on it. I don't know why I notice that, but as he steps back to let me in, I ask, "Is that where you went to college?"

Confused, he shakes his head. "No. Why are you here early asking me about my shirt?"

"Mia's mother got a call from kidnappers a half hour ago. They have Mia and they want five million for her. I don't know where Brett and Kip are, but I've checked with the pilot, and they never came back to the plane."

"Jesus Christ, man. Where the hell did they go and why weren't you with them?"

I shake my head, hating myself right now. "Long story. Mia decided she needed to fly out to Miami to the recording studio and I felt like I should stay here to do the walk-through in Houston today. So I sent Brett and Kip to guard her. There's no way they'd let anyone take her if they had the ability to stop them."

My friend knows what I'm trying not to say out loud.

Holding his hand up, he says, "Stop right there. I know what you're thinking, but it's not a sure thing.

Kidnappers rarely like to kill people. They're in it for the money. Nothing else."

His attempt at making me think logically makes me chuckle. "Yeah, I just told Andrea that."

"So don't go thinking Brett and Kip are done for yet. You said you contacted the pilot, and he hasn't seen them. Did you contact the recording studio?"

I whip out my phone as I shake my head. "Fuck, why the hell am I not thinking clearly? That's why I came to you. My head is a fucking mess right now, Drew."

"Call there and see if you can find out anything. I'm going to get dressed and get the rest of the guys ready for when we head out."

Drew leaves me alone, and suddenly, I feel like nothing is going to be okay. I should have never assigned them the job of guarding her on this goddamned spur of the moment trip to Miami. That was my responsibility, but after fucking up things at that bar, I didn't think I should be the one to go with her.

Goddamnit! This is my fault.

The phone at the recording studio rings for what seems like five minutes before someone finally answers the call. Some guy named Larry tells me Mia left right before seven, more than an hour ago. He says she left with the two bodyguards she had with her, and he and his brother haven't heard anything since they walked out with her.

"I need you to check outside. Mia's missing, as are my two guys. There should be a rental car there. A black SUV," I say, my heart racing at the good news he's just told me.

They've only been gone for a short time. That's good. At least I hope it is.

"Okay. Hang on. I'll check."

Pacing back and forth across Drew's hotel room, I listen for any indication this Larry person found Brett and Kip, but I hear nothing. When he returns less than a minute later, he only has bad news.

"I checked, and the SUV is still here. The doors are locked, but I looked in and saw no one. I think I saw something red that looked like blood a couple yards away, though."

Fuck. Blood means someone's hurt.

"Okay, I need you to call the police. Tell them we've got the FBI on it here, but three people are missing down there and at least one is likely in need of medical attention. Have them call me at this number and coordinate with us here."

After I finish the call, I throw my phone across the room, furious that I let this happen to Mia and my guys. What kind of fucking chief of security am I if I can't keep the one person I'm supposed to keep safe from being taken right off the goddamned street?

Drew walks back in and picks up my phone where it landed after it hit the wall. "Chill out, man. You need to keep your head right now. You care about her and the guys, so keep things level, all right?"

Nodding, I stuff my phone into my pants pocket and let out a deep sigh. "I should have been there with her. I'll never forgive myself if all three of them don't come back safe and sound when this is all over."

"They will. Nothing's certain yet, so let's think positive. Have the FBI been called in?"

"Yeah, Andrea is handling that. I need to find Brett and Kip. I think we need to head down to Miami. Not that I don't think the cops can handle things, but I'd feel better if we were closer to the scene."

Drew grabs his jacket off the back of the chair next to the window. "I agree. When do we leave?"

As we walk out into the hallway heading toward Jack's room, I quickly try to find the best way to get there. It has to be by plane. We could drive, but that would take too long, and even if we have to wait a few hours to get a flight, flying will still take less time.

"You get ready and get Jack in on all of this. I'll get us a flight out as soon as I can this morning. Make sure you bring him up to speed on all that's happened."

I stop to reserve us three tickets, and Drew gives me a reassuring pat on the back. "Stay positive, man. Nothing's bad until we learn it's bad. Until then, it's all good. Don't forget that."

"Yeah, you're right. Thanks, Drew."

Left alone in that hotel hallway, I try to convince myself he's right, that we've heard nothing bad yet, so we shouldn't worry. But I can't stop myself from picturing Mia being held hostage in some terrible place with people who don't see her as anything but a way to get millions of dollars.

Even worse is the thought that two of my guys I brought onto this job could be lying hurt somewhere bleeding out or worse.

Fuck, I can't think like that! I need to get my shit in gear and be the man Mia and my guys need me to be right now. That means buying plane tickets and getting the fuck down to Miami to find them. Self-loathing can wait until after we save them from the assholes who thought it was a good idea to kidnap Mia.

CHAPTER THIRTY-FIVE

$\mathcal{M}$ia

MY WRISTS FEEL RAW AFTER ALL THESE HOURS OF trying to escape from these ropes. Fucking Michael! I swear to God if I get out of this alive, I'm going to make sure he pays for this.

I can't think that way. Not if I get out of this alive. No, Liam would never let this asshole kill me. No way. I don't know how, but he'll find a way to rescue me and make this shithead pay dearly for taking me.

Desperate to find some way out of here, I scan the room to see if there's anyone here other than Michael and me. I haven't seen anyone yet, but someone could be hiding out in another part of the building. I need to figure out a way to get out of these restraints. Even if I don't know where I am, if I could run, I know I could escape.

"Always fighting reality. You know, if you'd just go

with the flow, you wouldn't have ended up in this mess in the first place."

I see Michael walking toward me wearing that smug look he's had on his face nearly the whole time he's kept me here. Why does he think he's going to get away with this? He must be insane.

"It's not reality. This isn't reality," I say, trying to egg him on to explain what the hell all of this is about. "Kidnapping people isn't normal, you know."

Rolling his eyes, he shrugs like this is all in a day's work for him. "Famous people get kidnapped all the time. It doesn't make the news because they pay off the kidnappers and keep the whole thing hush-hush, but it happens a lot."

"People are going to miss me. I'm not sure how you think this is going to work. I've got hundreds of people on my staff between my entourage, my security, and my management team, not to mention everyone on my tour crew needing me to make it to Houston in just a couple days to perform. You don't think they've contacted the authorities to search for me?"

He shakes his head and grins. "No, I don't."

"Are you joking? My mother will be up one side of the police and down the other when she finds out I'm gone, and you can trust me, she already knows. I have no idea how long you've kept me here, but you can be damn sure the moment she found out, she made sure to call everyone up to the President himself to get me back."

There are few things about my mother that I truly appreciate, but her desire to make sure I'm safe and sound at all times is one of them. Most times, that trait of hers is nothing but oppressive, but at moments like this, I'm sure it's coming in handy.

When Michael doesn't respond, I know I've touched a nerve with my mention of my mother. "You may have convinced her that she should give you another chance to work for us, but you know her. Once she fires someone, she's done with them. I'm guessing you told her some sad story to make her hire you back, but Andrea Shanoff isn't someone you should rely on for tender feelings. I learned that years ago. I would have thought you'd understood that too after being around us for so long."

He laughs and walks behind me, sending chills down my spine when he wraps his hands around my throat. Leaning down, he whispers in my ear, "That mother of yours sure does have a way of being vindictive, doesn't she? She knew full well that I only got you that hotel room because you asked me to, and still she fired my ass. Andrea absolutely understands what it takes to be in the music business. She's got ice water in her veins. Odd that you didn't have any of that rub off on you."

I turn to look at him, hating how close his face is to mine. How could I have ever entertained the idea of Michael as anything to me even for a fleeting moment? His face is nothing but ugly to me now. The mouth I used to love to see smile appears merely like a nasty slit, and the dark eyes that I thought showed how much he cared whenever he looked at me are just empty as they stare at me in hatred.

For a moment, I want to cry at how wrong I was about him, but I harden myself to keep from falling apart. He needs to see the steely determination in my eyes. I'm not some wilting flower he has total control over. He may have my hands and feet bound to this damn chair, but he doesn't possess the power to stop me from thinking.

Michael seems to want to hear me talk, so he's going to get an earful.

"You think I don't have ice water in my veins. You have no idea who I am. I've fired people for practically nothing. I've risen to the heights I've reached in this business not only because I have talent but because I don't let anyone put me down. So whatever fantasy you have about Mia being a tender soul who wouldn't hurt a fly can just go fuck itself because that's never been who I am."

Michael throws his head back in laughter and comes around the chair to crouch down in front of me. I so wish I could wipe that arrogant ass smile right off his ugly face. Or better yet, I'd love to kick it off. If only I could get my hands and feet free of these ropes.

When he sets his palms on my knees, I stiffen, repulsed by the mere touch of his hands on my body. He enjoys how uncomfortable he's making me and lets out a low chuckle.

"So riddle me this, oh queen of ice water in her veins, how is it if you're such a cold-hearted bitch, why haven't you ever fired your mother from being your manager?" he asks in a mocking tone, all the while staring up at me with a knowing look I don't understand.

"Why would I fire my mother? She's a great manager," I say, wishing I didn't sound so half-hearted in my defense of my mother.

Our relationship is complicated, and I don't give a damn what this asshole thinks he knows about my mother and me. We've been through hard times that would have crushed other people. She was there for every rejection I got and every door that closed in our faces when I was first starting out. Yes, she drives me crazy, but she's my mother and I wouldn't be where I am today without her.

No matter how much I say I want to be in this business without her, I can't imagine singing another song or appearing on another stage without my mother as my manager. So whatever this jackass thinks he knows about Andrea and Mia Shanoff, he doesn't know squat.

"You complained to me every day I worked for you that she was anything but a good manager, nevermind great. It was nonstop. 'My mother makes my life a living hell. My mother won't let up.' Every day you bashed her, yet she's always employee number one in the Mia Enterprises world. Ask yourself why you practically despise her, but you won't fire her."

I shake my head, hating how he makes what I feel about my mother sound. "I don't hate her. You don't understand the relationship between mother and daughter. If you were a daughter, you'd know that no matter how much I complain, she's still my mother. She was the one person who stuck around when things weren't great, always believing that someday they would get better. Loyalty like that isn't the kind of thing someone forgets easily. We fight. I admit that. But she's my mother, and I love her."

Michael slowly slides his hands up my thighs as he asks, "Do you think she loves you?"

I twist my body in a desperate attempt to make him stop touching me. "Fuck you! I don't have to think about how to answer that. Of course, she loves me. She's my mother. She gave up everything so I could be where I am today. She shows her love every day, unlike other people who claimed to care but obviously didn't give a damn about me. And get your hands off me!"

He doesn't stop, though, and when he reaches the spot where my legs meet my body, I shake my head, not believing he'll do what I'm terrified he's about to do. Michael is a lot of things, but a rapist? I can't believe that.

"I cared, Mia. I cared and waited day after day for you to see I was the one who actually loved you more than anyone else, including Andrea. You never did, though, so at some point, I came to the realization that I needed to face the facts. You were fine with hanging out in my room and talking every night as you forced me to watch those stupid old TV shows you like. You loved having me at your beck and call, but you were never going to let me in like I wanted to. So I found a way to get some benefit from having to be around you after all."

I lower my head as tears fill my eyes. "I never led you on, Michael. Don't do this. You don't want to do this."

He digs his thumbs into the very tops of my legs and laughs, frightening me. "Do what? Fuck you? Right here? Don't be ridiculous! You aren't that good looking, and as you well know, I already have someone I can get it from whenever the hell I want. Jesus, Mia! You really are full of yourself."

"Stop it! You're hurting me," I sob, but it only makes him push into my flesh harder.

"Maybe you should have been nicer to me, Mia. Maybe you should have been the kind of woman who knew a good thing when she had it in front of her. But no, you're not that smart. Dumb bitch!"

Finally, Michael releases his hold on my legs, and I feel blood rush to the spots where his thumbs pressed down on my skin. I don't understand any of this he's doing. I didn't believe he was someone who would take a woman against her will, but then he acted like that's what was about to happen.

Now he's talking about how I wasn't nice to him and how stupid I am.

What is this about?

CHAPTER THIRTY-SIX

iam

DREW, JACK, AND I STAY IN MY HOTEL ROOM, THE two of them sitting on the bed while I pace back and forth waiting to get someone from the Miami police to talk to me. I've gotten transferred to three different divisions on this one call, and I'm about to lose my fucking cool.

"What's so goddamned hard about telling me where they are?" I snap as I pass the bed heading toward the window.

"Maybe they don't know?" Jack suggests.

I want to blow up and ask how the fuck they couldn't know that two men have been fucking attacked, with at least one of them shot in their city, but that's stupid. Miami's a big place, so maybe they don't know.

But somebody has to fucking know something.

"Try to keep your calm, man. We don't know

anything yet, so it all could be fine," Drew says in his attempt to be supportive.

I understand what he's trying to do. It's just that at this very moment, I want to beat the hell out of someone and I'm trying hard not to start a fight with either of the guys I know are worried just like I am.

Holding out of the phone toward them, I growl, "It's hard to stay calm when people keep putting you on fucking hold. I swear to God I'm going to explode on the next person who does."

Another two passes across the room and back and finally someone comes back onto the call. "Mr. Jackson, I'm Sandra Curry, chief of the fourteen precinct. I tracked down your men. They're at Jackson Memorial, ironically enough. One man, Brett Marshall, suffered a shot to his calf. The ER is handling him right now. The other man, a Trevor Jones, suffered a more severe injury with the gunshot shattering his kneecap. He's in surgery right now."

"Do you have any idea who did this? Because they were guarding a client and she's been kidnapped, I'm guessing by the same people who shot my men. Has the FBI coordinated with you there yet? She's been gone for over five hours."

My words are met with silence for so long that I pull the phone away from my ear to check if I somehow lost Chief Curry. I see the call is still live, so I say, "Is there something wrong?"

Still, she remains silent until she finally says, "Mr. Jackson, we have no information on any kidnapping or any involvement of the FBI in any kidnapping of a woman here in Miami this morning."

Panic swirls in my mind, almost immediately replaced

by pure anger. Andrea didn't call the cops or the FBI? Why? She doesn't think we can ride in on our white horses and find Mia all by our fucking selves, does she?

"Thank you, Chief Curry. The two men who were injured were guarding Mia, the singer. She was last seen at Hampton Roads Recording Studio this morning right around seven. We have no idea where she is or who took her or why. I'd been led to believe you and the FBI had been notified of her disappearance, but I see that isn't the case. I have to go handle this, but my men and I will be coming to Miami to hopefully find out who took her and see her home safe."

The chief says something about being sorry and offers her office's help in finding Mia, but I hear very little of it before I end the call and turn toward the door. As I storm past Drew and Jack, I bark, "Fucking Andrea never called the FBI or the cops. What the hell is wrong with this woman?"

I'm practically blind with rage as I run down the hallway to Andrea's room. Pounding my fist against her hotel room door, I yell, "Andrea, open this goddamned door so I can talk to you!"

She answers a few seconds later looking shocked I'm so angry. I push past her, barely able to focus I'm so furious right now. Inside her room, I see she's got what looks like an entire new wardrobe laid out on her bed, complete with sales tags still on the clothes.

"Did a little shopping this morning?" I snap, unsure what the hell I'm looking at.

"Well, yes," she says as she closes the door. "I've been waiting for the FBI and realized I didn't have anything to wear for when they meet with us, so I decided to get some new things. You don't understand how important it is when you appear on camera to look good. Men always look good because you get to wear a suit, but women have to choose an entire outfit."

I march over to her so we're face to face and shake my head, trying so damn hard not to lose my cool on this woman. "I know about you not contacting the FBI or the Miami police. I don't know what you're up to, Andrea, but your daughter's life is in danger and we can't be fucking around like this. Why didn't you call them?"

Sheepishly, she looks away to avoid my demanding gaze. "Mia wouldn't want that. I know I said I'd call like you told me to, but I know my daughter. She won't be happy when she finds out the police and the FBI got involved. We can handle this on our own. The kidnappers already told me where to bring the five million, and I'm in the process of waiting for the bank to send over the money right now. It's okay, Liam. Everything's going to be okay."

The top of my head feels like it's about to blow off, sending my brains all over this hotel room. My thoughts whirl from one terrible thing to another. It's going to be okay? How the hell does she figure that? Her daughter is missing, kidnapped by people who blew a hole in one of my guy's calf and a hole through another one of my guy's kneecap. What makes her think they won't hurt Mia once they get the money?

"I don't know what the hell you're thinking, but your daughter is in very real danger. I know I told you kidnappers don't usually turn to murderers, but that doesn't mean it never happens. The kidnappers clearly have guns. They shot two of my goddamned guys! One is going to be lucky if he ever walks right again, and although I'm not sure, it's highly unlikely he's going to able to work in my business ever again. Nothing is fucking okay, Andrea!"

Still she doesn't seem worried.

With a gentle pat to my forearm, she says with a smile, "Mia is going to be fine. You'd be surprised at how wonderful this is for PR. I've already contacted her agent, and she's getting the word out to the press right now. That's another reason why I needed new clothes."

Shaking my head in disbelief, I wonder if I'm losing my mind. "Are you honestly talking about how to capitalize on your daughter's kidnapping?"

Andrea nods and walks over toward the bed where all her new clothes lay to lift up a dark green dress. "In this business, you have to take advantage of anything you can, honey. The reviews for her Tampa concerts weren't fantastic, I'm sad to say. That one reviewer questioned whether Mia still has it. Can you believe that nonsense? Still has it? Screw her! Mia had that audience in the palm of her hand. Last night's show was one of the best she's ever put on, and there's no way I'm going to let some two-bit music writer from a Tampa newspaper drag down Mia's tour. Not if I have anything to say about it."

None of what she's saying makes sense. Maybe she's just compartmentalizing her fear over Mia having been kidnapped. Or maybe she's having some kind of psychotic break. I can't be sure.

All I know is every second I spend trying to figure out what the hell is wrong with her, the woman I love is in danger. She can fret about PR and reviewers' stupid comments about whether or not Mia still has it, but I need to find out what the fuck is going on and rescue her.

I turn to walk out of Andrea's room and say, "I've

already reported Mia missing to the Miami police, and I'm going to call the FBI right now to make sure they're coordinating with the authorities down there."

Her response is silence, but then right before I reach the door, she says, "They aren't going to take her disappearance seriously. They never do."

Furious, I spin around and point at her bed full of new clothes. "Maybe if you spent more time being worried about your daughter and less time trying to find the perfect promotional angle when she's in danger, they would."

Then it suddenly dawns on me, hitting me like a bolt of lightning out of the blue. Andrea isn't worried about Mia now because she knows far more than she's telling me.

"What's going on here, Andrea? I'm done playing fucking games with you! Tell me!" I yell, making her jump at the bellowing sound of my voice bouncing off the walls of her hotel room.

Her eyes wide in fear now, she shakes her head, refusing to say anything. I'm not leaving this room until she explains exactly what she knows. I swear to God if I need to shake it out of her, I will.

"I'm not playing around with you and this nonsense anymore," I threaten as I march over to her. "Tell me what's going on. Now!"

Once again, the boom of my voice makes her jump. Taking a step back away from me, she rolls her eyes and says in frustration, "Fine. She's not really in danger, okay?"

My mouth drops open in shock at what she's just told me. "What do you mean she's not in danger? My two guys who were guarding her were really in danger. Kip might never walk again if that bullet tore through God only knows what in his knee. Brett took a bullet to his calf. That's real fucking danger, Andrea, so tell me what you mean."

"He wasn't supposed to hurt them seriously. I'm sorry about your guy's knee. That wasn't supposed to happen. I told him if he had to use the gun, to make it that the bullet went through some fleshy part like the upper arm or the thigh."

"The thigh?" I say, thankful neither Brett nor Kip got hit there. "You mean where the femoral artery is? The artery that if you hit it, you fucking bleed to death before anyone can goddamned help you? What is wrong with you? No wonder your daughter thinks you're a monster. You are!"

Good God. The kidnapper holding Mia thinks shooting someone in the thigh is a harmless flesh wound because of this woman. If he does that, there's no chance I'll be able to save her.

"I promise we'll pay for any medical bills and rehab costs both of your guys have. They'll get the best care in the world. You don't have to worry about that. We'll make sure the one who got shot in the knee is up and walking and doing whatever job he wants for the rest of his life. I promise, Liam."

Unable to control my anger, I grab her by the shoulders and squeeze my fingertips into them, needing her to feel something about what she's done. "You put three people in danger for what? So Mia could be on the news as some sympathetic creature and reviewers would say nice things about her concerts? What the fuck is wrong with you?"

Unlike her daughter, Andrea doesn't buckle under

my interrogation of her and pushes against my chest to walk away from me. "I do what I have to so Mia can have all the success she deserves. Sometimes that means doing things that some people might not approve of, but you don't understand this business. If you aren't constantly in the spotlight, people forget about you. It's a savage world out there. I make sure everyone always has Mia's name on their lips. She doesn't know what I do, but if she did, she'd understand. She knows what this business is like. You better get used to it if you think you want to be with her too, or you'll get swept away like everyone else she's ever fallen for. Mark my words, Liam, you need to understand what it takes to be the man Mia's with, or you won't last for long."

So she knew about us? She knew Mia and I were together and still pulled this stunt?

Grabbing her by the arm, I spin Andrea around to face me. "You fucked with the wrong man this time. No wonder the authorities don't take what happens to Mia seriously. They must know it's always you pulling some PR stunt."

"I never call them, so it's not like they could possibly get in the way. They wouldn't do anything anyway, not until she's hurt, at least. Don't you watch the news?" she asks in a smug voice that tells me she doesn't understand the harm she's caused.

"I'm done listening to this madness. Tell me where she is so I can go get her. And you better pray to God that she's not hurt or I swear, Andrea, I'll make sure you pay every way I can."

She waves off my threat and my worry, smiling up at me. "She's fine. Michael would never hurt her. Trust me."

I stagger back, confused at hearing that name again.

"Michael? What is it with you two? First you bring him back to handle security, and now you're working with him to kidnap your daughter? What the fuck is going on with you and that guy?"

"That guy is the one who's helped me manage Mia for years, Liam."

My mind whirls with questions, and then one jumps out over all the rest. "Were you planning to have him kidnap her after the show in Tampa? Is that why you brought him back and tried to push my guys out that night?"

Andrea's eyes open wide, as if she's horrified that I could accuse her of such a thing. "Don't be ridiculous! He was there because I needed him to be."

"Why? Why the hell did some guy who was shit at his job of protecting Mia suddenly need to be her security head again? You were planning this the whole time."

"She was never going to be hurt. He would never hurt her, and neither would I. You don't understand. The world Mia and I live in is different than the outside world. That bad review of her Tampa show could start a domino effect with everyone asking if she's still got it. I needed to do something."

"You brought him back before that review, so what the fuck was going on?"

Andrea shakes her head. "I heard her rehearsals in the past few weeks. She hasn't been like she always was. I could tell she was too distracted, too focused on other things and not on this tour."

"Too happy? Why the hell did you have Jonah bring me onto this job in the first place if Michael was your righthand man in managing Mia?"

Andrea groans, like all of this questioning is a hassle for her. "I had to do something to show my daughter I was the one in charge. So Michael got a paid vacation for a few weeks, and Mia had to fall in line. You were the perfect man for the job."

"Until we started to care for one another."

"It was only a matter of time before the critics began writing their reviews saying she's lost it. She used to have fire in her soul before, but now those critics are hearing what I heard for weeks. That's what love does to a person. It makes them weak. Mia's career is built on her angst, so I had to make sure a plan was in place."

Her admission that she's had this kidnapping waiting in the wings for just the right time stuns me. "You had to make sure she went back to being unhappy. Christ, you are a monster. And here I thought you were the good one in that house."

Then I remember the stalker letter. "There's never been a stalker, has there? That was all you and Michael, wasn't it? All to whip up sympathy for Mia and keep her in the news. More angst and suffering."

Andrea arrogantly nods, like any of her behavior is something she should be proud of. "Yes, and that stunt did just what it was supposed to do. It kept everyone talking about her, and it helped keep her in the public eye so people would buy more of her music."

"Your daughter walked around in utter terror after every one of those letters. How could you do that to her? You have no idea what it feels like to think someone is lurking around every corner, stalking you and you have no way to stop them."

Again, she waves away my concern for Mia. "She

was never in any real danger. My daughter's a survivor. I knew she'd be able to take it."

And then one last mystery solves itself as I stand there in disbelief in front of her. "It was Michael who shot me, wasn't it?"

That makes Andrea uncomfortable, and she moves away from me toward the door as she stammers, "Tha- that was a mistake, and I am truly sorry about that. I never told him to shoot you or Mia. He was just supposed to follow you two that night."

"How? How did he follow us? We were in your car," I ask, stunned at what she's just admitted on top of everything else.

"All the vehicles at the estate are tracked. I had to do that once Mia got her license. If I didn't, then she might take off and I'd never be able to find her."

Taking a step back, I shake my head at how evil this woman is. "You fucking LoJacked your own car and never told Mia. Jesus Christ, Andrea."

"Stop acting like it isn't done all the time. It's perfectly normal, especially when you're dealing with someone like Mia."

"Someone like Mia? You talk about her like she's a pet who might get away or like she's a performer in a circus you have to keep in line. Your little friend Michael shot me and could have hit her that night with that bullet. Did that ever occur to you when you sent him out to follow us?"

"He got out of hand. I'm afraid he got a little jealous when he saw you with her. But you're obviously all right."

I point at my right arm and explode, "He fucking shot me! What makes you think that jealousy of his won't rear its ugly head and make him shoot her? Tell me where she is, Andrea. I need to get her away from him right now!"

She moves to run out of the room, but I grab her by the arm and yank her back, throwing her onto the bed and her new clothes. Staring up at me in utter terror, she sobs out the address where Mia's being held. It instantly imprints on my brain, and I run out of there to get Drew and Jack.

Just give me a little time, baby. I'm coming for you. I promise.

CHAPTER THIRTY-SEVEN

$\mathcal{M}$ia

SOMETHING'S HAPPENED. I DON'T KNOW WHAT, BUT something's changed with Michael. In the past hour, he's started acting strange, like all the cockiness he was giving me before has disappeared for some reason.

Instead of sitting in that chair across from me and smirking like he's the king of the world, now he's pacing back and forth in front of me and looking nervous. Worse, he's waving his gun around like he's expecting to have to use it on someone soon.

Using a much softer voice than before, I say to him as he walks over near a wall of boxes, "Michael, whatever happened here, this doesn't have to end badly. I don't know why you did this, but we're friends. We have been for years. I can help you put an end to whatever you're doing here so neither one of us gets hurt."

He merely shakes his head but says nothing to me. Worry looks like it's been etched deep into the lines in his face, especially around his mouth. Instead of smiling like before, now he frowns and mumbles something about people not being able to be trusted.

"I know how that can be," I say, seizing upon his aggravation with people in this world who say one thing and do another. "Sometimes you feel like you can't believe a thing people say, right? I feel that way too, Michael. It's okay."

Some part of that upsets him, and he whirls around with his gun in his hand and waves it angrily in front of my face. "It's not fucking okay! I did everything she ever wanted. Every fucking thing! It didn't matter how ugly it made me feel. I did it because she said that was the only way I'd get what I want. Well, this ain't what I ever wanted. That's for sure."

Confused, I try to think of something supportive to calm him down and make him see I'm not the enemy here. Whoever is screwing him over is. I don't know why he keeps saying she. Maybe he's getting me mixed up with whoever his partner is.

"I know you did, Michael. You were a good friend to me. You really were. I'm sorry you got fired for helping me run away to that hotel. That wasn't right. I never wanted you to lose your job over that."

He stops in front of me and stares down into my eyes, making me think I'm getting through to him. So I keep talking, hoping he'll untie these ropes and let me leave this place.

"I'm sorry about a lot of things. You deserved better than to be let go like that. I can talk to my mother when I see her, and we can figure out some way to fix this. You just have to let me go, Michael."

Shaking his head slowly, he finally says, "You have no idea about anyone around you. Do you realize that? You think I'm angry about getting fired. Andrea never fired me. If you weren't so stupid, you'd check the payroll when someone gets fired to make sure they don't keep getting paid. The only thing that happened was my job location was transferred from the estate to my apartment."

Now it's my turn to shake my head. What is he talking about?

"I don't understand. My mother fired you. She did that without even asking me, but she did it and brought in a new head of security. What are you saying? That you're still getting paid? For what?"

In a flash, he looks like the man who taunted me for hours earlier today. Smiling broadly, he laughs and sits down in that chair of his across from me. He holds the gun over his head and sighs heavily.

"No wonder she thought you were so easy to manipulate. You really are. You're so busy being lost in your life and your music that you don't pay attention to a damn thing. Andrea has kept paying me because she had things for me to do. Things only I could do because I'm the one who's been with her for all this time doing her dirty work."

A terrible thought races through my head. "Are you saying you and my mother are together?"

When I accused my mother of using Michael as an errand boy that night at the pavilion, I said that out of anger. Was I closer to the truth than I even understood? Have they been sleeping together?

"If you're asking if I'm fucking her, the answer is no. Not that I'd say no, necessarily, since I know she's got money, but that's not what Andrea and I are to one another. She's my boss. I work for her. I do what she tells me to do."

None of what he's saying makes sense. My mother fired Michael after I ran away to that hotel because he made the reservations for me. She blamed him for that stunt of mine, as she called it.

"I don't know what the hell you're talking about. You got fired for helping me run away. Are you claiming my mother knew the whole time where I was because you two were working together?"

Laughter explodes out of him, and he throws his head back. "Knew? Of course, she knew. I told her everything. I reported back to her whatever you told me. When you said you wanted to get away, I let her know. She was the one who suggested I reserve that room for you. What makes you think my sister could afford five hundred dollars a night on her credit card? I told you Aimee barely made rent most months."

I close my eyes as tears begin to sting the back of my eyes. My mother knew and still created that media circus with them analyzing and dissecting my entire life on TV while she held press conferences looking like the devastated mother of a missing woman?

"Why? Why would my mother do that?" I ask, not sure I want to know the answer.

"Because that's what she considers her job to be. She's your manager, so it's her job to keep your name in the public eye. She wants you to be on the front of every tabloid and the first story on every entertainment show around. That way the money never stops rolling in and her gravy train keeps on rolling down the tracks. You're the gift that keeps on giving, Mia. She realized that the first time you ran away back when you were sixteen. When she saw what the press did when she told them the news that you were missing, she saw what a goldmine your diva stunts could be. So she instructed me to tell her whenever you were planning anything so she could make the most of whatever shit you pulled."

When he finishes, I open my eyes as the tears stream down my face. "No. I don't believe any of this bullshit. My mother loves using the media as much as the next person, but she wouldn't stage manage me that way. She's my mother, for God's sake!"

My pathetic attempt to defend her makes him laugh even harder, but I sense a type of mania has taken him over, like he knows he's not going to get out of this the way he planned. I get the feeling he's going to hurt as many people as he can, whichever way he can.

All I can hope is he doesn't shoot me.

"You want stage managed, little Mia? Try this on for size. I told you she gave the orders, and I carried them out. If she said to mail a letter to you, I mailed a letter to you. If she said follow you, I followed you. If she said make Mia disappear for a few hours so she can alert the media and crank up the sympathy machine for poor little you, I made you disappear by taking too long on whatever we were up to. Sometimes it was a hotel. Other times, it's a factory like this one."

What does he mean mailing a letter to me? Then it all becomes crystal clear what he's saying. My mother hasn't simply used my behavior to our advantage with the media. She's created chaos and problems that I had nothing to do with to keep what he calls the sympathy machine for me running at full steam.

"You're the stalker? So I never really had a stalker? She's had you sending those letters to me for three years. Those letters terrified me. The two of you saw how scared I'd get every time I'd receive one, and still you kept sending them?"

Michael shrugs. "All part of my job. Andrea thought a stalker would help keep the public's focus on you when you were getting ready to go out on tour, so every time, she'd have me mail a letter. Just one and that was it. And it did the trick. Even this time with your new security guy right there. Made the entire house go into a tizzy, I think is how she described it."

The most horrifying thought of all fills my head as I watch him happily describe his dirty work for my mother. "So I've never been in any danger, but she knows you're holding me here, tied to a chair, with a gun pointed at me?"

Nodding, he says the words that break my heart. "She set this whole thing up."

"Why? The tour is going great. The audiences are loving my shows. What's behind doing this now?" I ask, wishing I could stop crying but the tears won't stop coming.

My questions seem to irritate him, like he's tired of explaining how evil he and my mother have been. "I'm not really sure what her motives are this time. She did say something about reviews of those Tampa shows being in the shitter, but I think it's also to make your new security chief look bad. At least that's why I'm doing this."

"Why do you two want Liam to look bad? What has he done to either of you?"

Before he can answer my questions, a noise like a door opening on the other side of the factory makes him jump up out of his chair. With his gun aimed to shoot, Michael looks back at me and shakes his head.

"Don't make a sound, or I swear to God, someone's going to get hurt."

As he disappears behind the wall of boxes, I know he's beyond reason now, so all I can do is pray that sound was Liam and his men coming to rescue me. But what if it's his partner?

No, his only partner is my mother. My own mother who cares only about the media circus she's created to ensure public sympathy keeps my record sales climbing higher and higher and she gets wealthier and wealthier.

Shaking my head, I try to stop myself from crying and start thinking clearly. If I call out for help and he shoots the person before they can reach me, then I don't know what he'll do in retaliation to me. But if I don't let whoever is here know where I am, he might get the jump on them and shoot them.

I have no choice. I have to hope whoever made that noise is here to help me and my calling out to them is what they need.

"Help! I'm back here! Behind the wall of boxes! He has a gun!" I yell as loudly as I can after hours without a sip of any liquid passing my lips.

No one responds, and I listen for any clue that someone has come to save me. Suddenly, a gunshot pierces the silence, and my heart skips a beat that it may have been Michael shooting Liam.

Then I hear his voice and it's like I can breathe again.

"Michael, you need to let her go! Do that and nobody has to get hurt. Don't and I'm going to make sure you get what you gave me on the street that night, except I won't just graze your right arm."

Oh, my God! Michael shot Liam? Did my mother order him to do that too?

"I'm not going to jail because that crazy bitch thought this was a good idea. No way, man! There's only one way out of this, but I'm not going out alone!" Michael yells in a panicked voice.

I swivel my head right and left to see where he is because he means he's going to take me down with him. Oh, God! Liam has to stop him!

"Don't hurt her," Liam yells, his voice closer this time. "I'm warning you. Don't hurt her."

A second later, a gunshot from behind the wall of boxes a few yards in front of me makes me jump in my seat. I wait to hear Liam's voice, to hear him say even a single word so I can know he's okay, but there's nothing.

"Liam!"

All I need to hear is his voice. "Say something! Say something so I know you're not hurt!" I cry.

Holding my breath, I wait to hear something for what feels like an eternity. My heart slams into my chest like a jackhammer, and all I can think about it how much I need him to be alive.

Please, God. Let Liam be safe. I love him, and he loves me. Don't take him away. Please.

"Liam! Liam! Please answer me!"

Still I hear nothing.

Frantically, I scan the part of the factory around me for some hint that he's still alive, and then I see the most beautiful sight in the world when he runs around that wall of boxes and spots me.

"I'm here, Mia. It's okay. I'm here."

He rushes over and crouches down in front of me to untie my ankles and then my hands as I silently thank God for letting him live. I fall into his arms, relieved but still terrified that this isn't the end of this nightmare.

"I got you, Mia. It's okay. I got you."

My sobs overwhelm me as everything that's happened replays in my mind. "I thought he shot you. I thought you were dead," I say, my tears making my words sound all disjointed.

"I'm okay. I came as soon as I could. You're safe now."

All I want to do is forget everything that Michael and my mother have done. But will I ever be truly able to do that?

Liam holds me to him, whispering in my ear, "I'm so sorry, Mia."

In his arms, I feel safe and protected, but I can't help but ask what happened with Michael. "Did you…?" I can't finish that sentence. I don't want to. It's too horrible to think my mother's stunt ended with someone losing their life.

"He's gone, baby. I didn't have a choice. It was him or me."

My mother's to blame for Michael's death, not him. Whatever it takes to make the world understand that, I'll do it because he doesn't deserve to pay for her crimes.

Leaning back, Liam looks up at me and gently wipes my tears from my cheeks with the pads of his thumbs. "I'm sorry it took me so long to get here."

I think I know why, but I have to ask. "Did she try to

stop you? My mother is behind all of this. She's behind the stalker and Michael kidnapping me. And I guess she was behind him shooting you too."

With a nod, he says, "I know. She admitted everything."

"I'm so sorry, Liam."

That gets me a big smile, and he asks, "What are you saying you're sorry about? You didn't do anything wrong."

Looking down into those beautiful blue eyes of his, I let out a heavy sigh, so happy to be with him again. "I'm sorry I didn't pay attention and I didn't listen to you when you said I needed to be more careful. If I hadn't fought you every step of the way, this may have never happened."

He cradles my face in his strong hands and smiles. "Your mother is to blame for all of this. Not you, Mia. So don't blame yourself. You trusted her, and she betrayed you. Nothing more than that."

I close my eyes and let that truth sink in. My own mother betrayed me. The woman I credited all these years with being at my side every step of the way on my rise to the top betrayed me.

And for what? I don't understand it. I would have never fired my own mother, no matter how much she got on my nerves.

Now I want nothing to do with her. I never want to see her again.

Liam eases me up out of the chair I've sat in for hours, holding me so I don't fall. I turn to look up at him so worried about me being able to take a step and know no matter what happens, this is the man I want by my side.

"I love you, Liam."

He leans down to kiss me, and breaking the very last rule he's held on to until now, says sweetly, "I love you too, Mia."

The coming days aren't going to be easy for either of us, but we have each other. And love.

CHAPTER THIRTY-EIGHT

iam

MIA CLUTCHES MY HAND TIGHTLY, WRAPPING HER fingers around mine as I pull the car up to the house. After what happened in Miami, we've had to deal with my being arrested for shooting Michael, the fallout from her mother being arrested for kidnapping her own daughter, and the postponement of a month of dates on the tour so Mia can recuperate from all that she's been through.

Two weeks into resting up, she heard me talking to my mother about my grandmother's birthday party out at her house and asked if she could come with me. So now, she's squeezing my fingers tighter than a vice and staring at the house while I let the car idle.

"We don't have to go in. Trust me. My grandmother will have more than enough family here to wish her happy birthday, and I completely understand if you're not ready to meet the rest of the Jackson and March clan. They can be a lot, and after what you've been through, nobody would blame you for bowing out of a get-together like this."

Her grip on my fingers loosens a little, and she turns to look back out the rear window. "No paparazzi. I guess even they feel bad for me."

"Everyone should feel sympathy for you, Mia. What your mother and Michael did was horrible."

With a tiny smile, she says, "It seems like a terrible waste of a day free of the media to not go inside for the party."

"Are you sure?"

With her typical sincerity, she nods. "I can't wait to meet your family, Liam. I guess I'm just feeling like I don't have one anymore. My father hasn't been around forever, and now my mother is gone too. It's a little scary."

"I get that. For what it's worth, my family has no problem taking in new people. We're sort of like a cult, except we don't do anything really terrifying. Just a lot of family get-togethers. So many parties. You have no idea what you're signing up for with these people."

She smiles at my attempt at being funny, so I lean over and kiss her softly on the lips. "Seriously. It's your call. Everyone will understand, and even if they didn't, it wouldn't matter because I would."

Her smile doesn't return when I lean back, and she lowers her gaze to look down at our hands. "Are you sure nobody blames me for what happened? You got arrested, Liam."

I slide my fingertip under her chin and gently lift her

head so she can see my face when I say, "Nobody blames you. It's okay."

"It's not okay. You lost your job. You love being a bodyguard, but now that you've been arrested, it's all gone. All because of my mother. And your friends got hurt and Kip may never get back to work again. None of it's okay," she says sadly.

"Nobody blames you. You didn't do this, Mia. Everyone here knows that. And as for my being a bodyguard, I'm still protecting the only person I ever want to guard for the rest of my life. But if it's too soon to be hanging out with a houseful of people, you say the word and we're out of here. We can go wherever you want."

Mia takes a deep breath in and lets it out slowly before turning to look at me. "Okay. I want to go in. I've heard so many stories about your family that I want to meet them all. I was just worried that they all think I've ruined your life."

I pull her to me to kiss away that crazy thought. "You didn't ruin my life. You're the woman I love. I did what I always hoped I would if someone I loved was in danger, and I'd do it again. Anyone who knows me isn't surprised that I did everything I could to protect you."

"You're going to want to temper that I'd do it again talk when you go in front of the judge next month, Liam. Judges aren't famous for being incurable romantics, honey."

"I will, but that's not the truth. I'm not sorry about what I did to protect you, Mia. I love you. You're the best thing in my life, so why shouldn't I have shot the man who was holding you hostage?"

She smiles and taps me on the tip of my nose. "I think

you might be the most stubborn person I've ever met. I love you, but you're stubborn, baby."

I can't believe my ears. Mia, the woman who fights me on everything from the moment we met, thinks I'm stubborn?

"I guess it takes a stubborn person to know one?" I ask with a chuckle.

Mia shrugs and turns to open her car door. "I'm headstrong. There's a difference."

As I get out and walk around to her side of the car, I can't help but laugh. "Exactly what would the difference be?"

She stands up, and I close the car door behind her while she walks away. "Headstrong is positive. Stubborn is just stubborn," she says with a giggle.

Turning back to look at me, she says, "I can't wait to see your mother again. She included the sweetest card with those flowers she and your father sent, so I want to thank her in person for saying such lovely things when I needed it most."

I take her hand in mine and bring it to my lips to press a kiss to her knuckles. "I love you. If this gets too much, just give the signal and we're out of here."

"Don't worry about me. I'm going to be okay. I love big families. Remember the Bradys?"

She's right. She will be okay. I plan to make sure of that.

MY FATHER PULLS ME ASIDE ON THE BACK PORCH OF my grandmother's house as Mia tells my mother, Shay, and Olivia about the time she met Elton John. They look like they're hanging on every word that comes out of her mouth, as if she's giving them the secret to a long life.

"She looks like she's doing all right. How about you?" my father asks in a low voice.

"I'm fine, Dad. My attorney thinks the D.A. down there isn't really interested in going through with this whole thing. I'm sticking with self-defense, so if it goes to trial, he thinks the jury will see things the way I do."

"You have enough money to cover things? I know you're going to tell me you don't need any, but your mother and I were talking and since we've taken care of Wilder's legal problems more than once, we think it's only right that we do the same for you."

The sincerity in his eyes that look so much like mine makes me smile. He wants me to know no matter how much he's done for my younger brother that he hasn't forgotten me.

But my father doesn't have to worry that I feel that way. Wilder is who he is, and I'm who I am. I don't blame my parents for wanting to help their kids in any way they can.

"I'm good, Dad. You and Mom don't have to worry. I have the money you guys gave me when I turned twenty-one, and Mia's got money. We're good."

His eyes open wide at my mention of Mia. "So it's a we're thing? Any plans I should know about?"

Turning to look behind us, I see my mother grab onto Mia's arm as she tells them all about how some singer invited her to co-write with him for his next record. "Well, I think Mia's going to be doing a song with some guy, but for the life of me, I can't remember his name. By the way Mom is reacting, I'm guessing he's a big deal."

My father elbows me and laughs. "Everything about

Mia is a big deal to your mother. She tells every person she comes in contact with that you and Mia are together. I'm thinking she's going to start approaching strangers to tell them soon."

"She is a big deal," I say as I watch her charm the women in my family now that my grandmother has joined the group.

"So about those plans? Anything you want to give me advance notice of?" my father says in a low voice.

I know what he's getting at, but Mia and I aren't ready to go there yet. Maybe someday, but for now, we're just taking things one day at a time.

With a shrug, I try to be as noncommittal as possible, even though I know whenever I talk about Mia and me looking casual flies right out the window. She's everything, my entire life, and I can't hide it. That's how it is when you're crazy in love with someone.

"Nothing yet, but if anything happens, I'll make sure to tell you and Mom first."

My father leans in next to my ear and whispers, "Tell me first. Your mother always gets the news in this family before me. For once, I'd like to be the one who knows before she does."

Shaking my head, I laugh at how funny my father can be. "Okay, Dad. If and when there's any big news about Mia and me, you're the first member of our family I'll tell."

Just then, Mia turns around to give me a smile and mouths, "They are so into this story!"

What they're into is her, and I can understand why. I've been crazy about her from almost the first day we met.

Well, maybe a couple days after that. Those first days, she just drove me crazy.

Next to me, my father says in a low voice, "You look happy, Liam."

I nod, unable to stop smiling as I watch the woman I love enchant my family just like she does her fans. And me every day.

Turning to face him, I shrug. "I am. I never thought I'd get to have what you and Mom and everyone else seemed to find, but somehow in all the madness in Mia's life, I found something incredible. Someone incredible, Dad."

My father smiles like he's just heard the best news of his life. He puts his arm around my shoulders, hugging me to him, and says in my ear, "You deserve it. I always wanted to see you this happy. It's been all your mother and I hoped for you."

He looks over toward where Mia and my mother are standing, the two of them smiling like they're the best of friends. "She fits in pretty well with this family, I'd say."

I smile at his observation. "It's all she's ever wanted in life—a big family. I warned her to be careful what she asked for. This family can get to be a lot sometimes, but she loves the idea of all of you guys."

"Just wait until the first time we all show up uninvited or it's your turn to host the holidays. Then she'll know the real truth of what a big family is like."

I turn to look at him, curious about his mention of the holidays. "So are you, Cassian, and Stefan handing off the baton to the next generation when it comes to Thanksgiving and Christmas? Have you told Cade, Cash, Alex, and Wilder yet?"

He shrugs, but I can tell he's thought about it.

"You're all grown up now. It's time for you boys to take over. I'm not sure how Stefan feels about that since you know he's the king of Christmas, but I wouldn't be surprised to hear Cassian say he's willing to see the baton be passed on. And when you all start having kids of your own, it'll be only right."

Startled by his mention of any of us having children already, I hold my hand up to stop him from going any further with that discussion. "Whoa, Dad. What makes you think we're having kids already? None of us are even married yet."

In his typical Kane Jackson fashion, he levels his gaze on me and frowns. "Your mother and I weren't married before we had your sister, Liam. People don't have to be married to have children."

The way he says that makes me sound like some out of touch, judgmental asshole, so I quickly answer, "I wasn't saying that. All I was saying is I don't think anyone's planning on having kids yet."

And a second later, across the porch I hear my mother squeal with utter joy. "Who's having kids? Oh, that would be the best news ever!"

From out of nowhere, everyone stares at me like they expect to hear some huge secret I've been hiding. Shaking my head, I try to calm my mother, aunts, and grandmother, but it's no use. They start talking about how they can't wait to have grandchildren and great-grandchildren like it's going to happen this afternoon.

Cade and Alex throw nasty glares in my direction, and Cash walks up to me looking like he wants to punch me in the face. "What exactly do you think you're doing? It's not bad enough they're always asking when we're all getting married? Now you throw having kids into the mix? What the hell were you thinking?"

Mia looks over at me helplessly as my mother and Olivia gush about how wonderful having kids is and I try to think of a way to put this genie back in the bottle. "Cash, don't look at me. I didn't mean that. My father was talking about passing the baton of the holidays to our generation and mentioned when we have kids. Nobody meant now."

"Man, just for that, I'm going to make sure every time we're all at one of these get-togethers that I ask when you and Mia are getting married. Brace yourself because your mother looks like she might go over the moon every time I bring it up."

Cade hears him threaten me and chimes in with his own promise to make my life miserable from today on. "And if he doesn't, I will. What did you say at the last family party? Payback's a bitch. You better believe it."

I look over toward Mia to see if she's angry with me too since I doubt she's thought about us having kids already, but she looks utterly content to listen to everyone talk about children and our big family growing. She gives me a tiny wave and beams a smile before turning back toward the people around her.

At least one member of the Jackson-March clan isn't pissed at me.

A few minutes later, she rushes over to me and excitedly says, "Your mother, aunts, and grandmother are taking me inside to watch some video of you in a school play. They say it was the cutest thing and I have to see it. Oh, Liam, please tell me you don't mind because by the way they've described it, it sounds wonderful!"

Beside me, my father says beneath his breath, "Sixth

grade end-of-year play where you were the coach of the baseball team, and you had that huge speech you gave your players."

Trying not to cringe at that memory, I force a smile and nod at her. "I don't mind. Just don't expect award winning acting."

Mia throws her arms around my neck and kisses me on the lips. "I bet it's going to be the cutest thing ever! Your grandmother mentioned she has pictures of you from when you were a little baby all the way up through high school too."

I should have expected this today, but now that the women of my family have decided to break out all the Liam memorabilia, all I can do is shrug. "Try to remember the early teenage years can be rough on a kid."

"You're so humble. I bet you were the most handsome thirteen-year-old around."

My cousins all break out into laughter behind me as my father snickers. Some family they are. Did I go laughing when Cade first brought Hailey around or when Cash brought Savannah here for the first time?

As Mia runs off, I turn around and throw them all dirty looks. "Can't a guy catch a break with you people? It's not bad enough she's about to sit through that terrible play?"

Cade slaps me on the back and laughs. "Dude, I wouldn't worry. She's clearly not going to be swayed by Grandma's school play video."

From across the porch, Hailey calls out to him, "Honey, we're all going inside to see the videos your grandmother has of all you guys. If you or Cash are looking for me or Savannah, just give us a yell, okay?"

Both my cousins' expressions fall, and now it's my turn to laugh. "Not so funny now, huh? Cade, remember you being a sad elf in that Christmas play in first grade? Grandma does. And Cash, I seem to recall you being a toothbrush in a third-grade school play for Dental Health Week. Good times, right?"

Now the only one laughing is Alex, but he shouldn't count himself safe yet. "Laugh now, man, but wait until you bring someone here for the first time. It won't be so funny then."

Still enjoying our misery, Alex shakes his head and smiles. "First off, unlike the rest of you, I didn't have any awkward years, so Grandma can show whatever she wants. But more importantly, I'm going to be single for as long as I can be, so you'll be waiting a long time for this guy to be bringing any woman here. I think I'm going to head in and take a look at these videos. I need a good laugh."

That makes all of us roll our eyes. "Dude, that's like the exact line the guy says in every movie right before he falls head over heels for some beautiful woman as she's rushing out of some office building and slams a glass door into him. He falls to the ground, and when he realizes what happened, he looks up at her and it's game over. He's in love," I say as he shakes his head while my other cousins agree with me.

"What happened to you, man?" Alex asks like he's disappointed in me. "Now you're as lost as these two," he says, pointing at his brother and best friend.

"It's inevitable," my father says with a chuckle. "You can try to fight it, Alex, but what's the point?"

A look of horror crosses my cousin's face. "The point is that I like being single."

He pushes past me and heads toward the steps down to the beach. "And I don't plan on that changing anytime soon!"

When he's gone, I turn to Cade and Cash and nod. "Oh, yeah. What's Grandma always say? Methinks he doth protest too much? Something tells me Alex isn't as single as he claims to be. It's only a matter of time, gentlemen. It's only a matter of time."

With a chuckle, Cash whips out a hundred and places it on the table. "I bet he's off the market within two months."

Cade pulls out his wallet and lays his hundred on the table between them. "I'll give it three. He's going to fight it, but he'll give in. What about you, Liam?"

I think about it for a moment while I fish my bet out of my pocket. Placing it on top of theirs, I hum to myself. "I think I'm going to take six months on this one. He's stubborn, and I know something about that. Six months and he falls like a ton of bricks."

My father laughs as he walks away to go inside the house. "I don't know how long it will take, but something tells me when Alex there falls, it's going to be hard, like Liam said."

Smiling, Cash taps the pile of money. "The countdown begins today. Whenever it happens, I think your father's right. Alex is primed to go down hard."

I look out toward the beach and see him sitting alone on the sand drinking a beer. It wasn't that long ago I thought I'd be single forever. Here's to hoping he finds someone as wonderful as I did.

CHAPTER THIRTY-NINE

Mia

WHILE LIAM FINISHES HIS CONVERSATION ON THE phone with Kip, I change out of the sundress I wore to his grandmother's house today and into the sexy lingerie I bought with Ainsley last weekend. Black and lacy, it's exactly what I wanted to surprise him in tonight.

After she found out all my mother and Michael had been up to, my life coach came around to seeing how wonderful Liam had been this whole time. When she told me about how she sat him down and told him he better not break my heart, I couldn't help but hug her for being a true friend.

Of course, when Liam heard her version of that conversation, he had to laugh. It seems she didn't tell the entire truth about that day in the dining room. Or maybe she just saw their talk differently. It's no big deal, though, now that my best friend and the man I love aren't mortal enemies anymore.

Twirling around in front of the mirror, I take a good look at myself in my new teddy and smile. Perfect for the man who has everything.

At least, that's the way he describes his life. I don't agree. Because of what happened with Michael, Liam can't be a bodyguard anymore. He claims he doesn't need the money and there's only one body he wants to guard now anyway, but I worry he's going to end up missing the job he loved so much.

As for my mother, well, she calls me dozens of times a day with hundreds of excuses for all she's done, but I'm not ready to forgive her yet. Eventually, I will, though. She's my mother. What choice do I have?

"Well, Kip is feeling much better. He says…"

In the mirror, I see Liam stop dead two steps into our bedroom, his mouth hanging open. I guess this black lacy number is as wonderful as I thought, after all.

Turning around to face him, I smile. "You were saying about Kip?"

Wide-eyed, Liam shakes his head. "Kip? Who's Kip? I don't know any Kip."

"Stop making jokes. How is he?" I ask, giggling at how cute my man can be.

Liam's mouth turns up in a big smile as he walks over to take me into his arms. "Kip's doing better. He said to tell you thank you for all you've done to make sure he's got the best doctors taking care of him. Now, what's this about and who do I thank for it tonight?"

I look up into those beautiful blue eyes staring down at me in utter appreciation and love how he still gets moony eyed over me. "This is a little surprise I bought especially for you, and you can thank me any way you like."

When he kisses me, I feel like I'm the luckiest girl in the world to have Liam as the man who loves me. To think I couldn't stand him in the beginning.

Well, for like a day. I'm not blind, and I'm not stupid either, contrary to some people's opinions. I know a great man when I see him standing in front of me, even if he was far more stubborn than I thought I could ever want.

He leans away and sighs. "I plan on thanking you all night."

"Then this teddy was money well spent. I told Ainsley you'd love it."

Liam rolls his eyes and jokes, "And she said then burn it?"

I give him a love tap on his chest and step around him to walk over to the bed. "Don't pick on poor Ainsley. She sees the error of her ways now and thinks you're great for me."

Behind me, he says, "The life coach finally comes around. The world can return to spinning on its axis once again."

Suddenly, a wonderful idea comes to me, and I spin around to face him. "Oh, my God! I just had the best thought! Your cousin who looks like the other one who's with Hailey? He would be perfect for Ainsley, don't you think?"

Liam stops and shakes his head, as if he needs to immediately remove that thought from his brain and shaking his head fast is the only way to do that. "Alex? No. Trust me. In fact, I can't imagine anyone who could be more wrong for him than Ainsley. Sweet Jesus, no."

His answer to my fantastic suggestion makes me

scrunch up my face. "First of all, some woman who smells like onions all the time and has warts all over her face from being cursed by an evil warlock would be more wrong for Alex, and second of all, he'd like her. She's beautiful, and he's got a real mellow thing going with him that she'd love. They'd be perfect together."

Horror fills Liam's expression with every word I mention about Ainsley being the woman for his cousin. "No, they wouldn't. Alex is mellow in a way that has nothing to do with Ainsley and her Zen business. He's more like the kind of cool that comes from having everything he could possibly want in the world, and that includes women, money, and anything else. That would not work for your friend. Trust me."

Baffled by his discounting my truly wonderful idea, I ask, "Why? Ainsley is very sweet, and she's proven herself to be a great friend."

He takes a step toward me and wraps his arm around my waist to pull me to him. Shaking his head again, he answers, "She's clingy as all hell, Mia. She didn't like me because I was intruding on her turf. I know you know that."

Disappointed, I nod. "I guess. She is beautiful, though. He'd like her. I just know he would. I want her to be happy like I am."

Liam gently pushes my hair off my face and kisses me sweetly. "I know, and that's why you're a great friend, but Alex isn't the man for her. My cousin enjoys his life with whatever women he chooses to date. She'd never want to be part of that harem. She could barely deal with not having you all to herself. Imagine how she'd be with a man."

Pouting, I sigh and accept he's right. "Okay. No more matchmaking for me, I guess."

He dips his head to nuzzle my neck just under my ear and whispers, "Now let's get back to this surprise you got for me. Any chance you're not going to be upset when I take it off?"

Sometimes he can be so cute.

I look up at him and smile. "That's the point of it, honey. Women wear these things expecting they won't stay on for long."

As he slides his hands up under the teddy to cup my ass, he smiles wickedly. "Good because I'm thinking it'll be off you in about five seconds."

My gaze rolls over his body still covered by clothes. As I begin to fiddle with the first button on his gray dress shirt, I say, "You know, that's some big talk from a man who's still fully dressed."

Opening up his arms out to his sides, he chuckles. "I'm all yours. Do what you want to me."

My fingers get stuck on the third button down. Grimacing, I look up at him and say, "What I want is to get this shirt off, but it's like these buttons are entirely against us making love tonight."

In a flash, he pulls the shirt up over his head and throws it onto the floor behind him. Grinning, he says, "Next problem?"

I slide my palms over his broad chest and down his chiseled abs until my hands come to rest on the top of his pants. "I do love a man who knows how to take care of business."

"Then I'm the man you want."

Tilting my head back as my fingers easily open the button on his pants, I take in the beauty of him. God, he's even more gorgeous than he looked the first time I saw him without a shirt.

"Is it possible you get more stunning every time I look at you?" I ask and then slowly pull down his zipper.

"Probably not," he says as he cradles my face in his strong hands. Liam presses a soft kiss to my lips and whispers, "I think that's what they call the haze of love."

I stare up into his gorgeous blue eyes that make me feel like I could get lost in them. "Maybe. Whatever it is, I love it almost as much as I love you."

"Even though I'm stubborn and as by the book as they come?" he asks with a sly grin as he slides his hands down to the bottom of my new lingerie.

Before I can answer that question, he slides my teddy up my body and says, "Arms up. It's time for this to retire for the night. It's done its job."

While I shimmy against the lacy fabric as he lifts it up over my head, I joke, "If I could use my arms, I'd check. As it is, I'll have to take your word on that, Mr. Jackson."

Liam tosses my brand-new black lace teddy on top of his shirt on the floor before guiding my hand to the front of his pants. "No need to take my word on it. Take his. He's ready to go."

I watch him strip out of his pants and underwear and ask, "Why do men always refer to their bits and pieces as he?"

When he finishes and he's standing naked in front of me, it feels like something has stolen my breath away. The man I adore is like a Greek god come to life, and he's all mine.

As I slide my hands over his chest, he answers in a way that sounds almost innocent, "I think it might be strange if we called them she. She's ready to go? Go where?"

He really is so cute sometimes.

Liam takes me by the hand and leads me over to the bed. When he sits down on the edge, it reminds me of that night we watched The Brady Bunch together and how I was crazy about him even then.

"Mia? Is something wrong?"

His question pulls me from my memories, and I shake my head. "No. I was just thinking about that first night when I came to your room, and we watched my favorite show. Were you wearing gray sweatpants that night?"

I gently push him down onto the bed as he shakes his head. "I don't remember. Why?"

"Because you look great in gray sweatpants."

He pulls me to him, kissing me hard like he wants me to know the time for talking is over, but then he smiles and says, "I thought women loved all guys in gray sweatpants."

As I straddle his hips, I shake my head. "Not all. It's female kryptonite, but gray sweatpants can only do so much. On you, of course, they're like your superpower."

With one slow thrust, he pushes into my body, filling me completely. Smiling up at me, he runs his tongue over his bottom lip, leaving it glistening wet.

"I like this superpower better," he says with a moan.

I roll my hips and sigh. "Mmmm...I agree. This one is the best."

We make love like it's the first time, like we can't get enough of one another. Liam is everything I've ever wished for in a man but never thought I'd get. He's sweet and sexy, tender yet gruff, and even his insistence on doing things by the rules charms me now.

But none of that matters when I'm in his arms and he gives me what every woman wants. True love, mind-blowing orgasms, and the security that whatever comes tomorrow, he'll be there to protect me.

His arms wrapped around me, he sighs after that first round of sex as we lie together in the bed we share in our house. It used to be my house, and I made sure to fill it with as many people as I could so I'd never be alone.

Now it's our home, and I have all I could ever want right here with him.

That's what the song I wrote that night in New Orleans is all about. I know when the world finally hears *Safe In Your Arms* for the first time that how I feel about Liam will come through loud and clear. It'll be my biggest hit yet too.

Even more importantly, I know when he finally hears it, he'll know it's my song to him.

My head on his chest, I think about our time at his grandmother's house today and sigh in utter contentment. "I loved being with your family today, Liam. Every one of them is now my new favorite person."

He presses a soft kiss to the top of my head, and when he speaks, the sound comes from deep inside him and makes his chest rumble beneath my cheek. "I'm happy you had fun. They loved you, just like I knew they would."

"You don't really hate having a big family, do you?" I ask, my voice trembling in anticipation of his answer.

Liam stays silent for a long moment but then

answers, "No, not really. They can be a lot sometimes, but I can't imagine my life without them."

"Do you think you might want to have a big family someday?" I whisper against his skin.

He doesn't take long to answer that question, thankfully. "Yeah, I think that would be great."

I lift my head off his chest and look at him, happy to see him smiling. "Me too."

It's only been a few months since we got together, and I have a tour to finish and a million other things to do, but all I can think about at this moment is how much I want to spend the rest of my life with him. Maybe it's crazy because I'm so young. Maybe we should date for longer.

I don't know. All I know is after spending time with his family today, I truly felt like I had finally found a home.

"You got quiet there, all of a sudden," he says. "Something on your mind?"

I could say the words right now and see what he thinks. Maybe it's not too soon. But then I look into those beautiful blue eyes of his and see how much my old-fashioned guy would want to be the one to say them, so I shake my head.

"Just thinking about the future. That's all."

Liam gently pulls me back down to rest against him and sighs. "I love you. We can deal with the future tomorrow. Tonight, let's just be Liam and Mia, two people crazy about each other."

He's right. Tomorrow is good enough for the future. Tonight is for us.

"I love you, Liam."

With his arms wrapped around me, I feel safe like

I've never felt before him. Now only one thing could make my life perfect.

I hope someday soon that big family of his will be my family too.

Be sure to look for the next book, The Sensuous Bad Boy, Alex March's story! And don't miss the Club X series, the original series of the March and Jackson family!

ABOUT THE AUTHOR

K.M. Scott writes contemporary romance stories of sexy, intense, and unforgettable love. A New York Times and USA Today bestselling author, she's been in love with romance since reading her first romance novel in junior high (she was a very curious girl!). Under her Gabrielle Bisset name, she writes paranormal and historical romance. She lives in Pennsylvania with a herd of animals and when she's not writing can be found reading or feeding her TV addiction.

Be sure to visit K.M.'s Facebook page at **https://www.facebook.com/kmscottauthor** for all the latest on her books, along with giveaways and other goodies! And to hear all the news on K.M. Scott books first, sign up for her newsletter today and be sure to visit her website at **http://www.kmscottbooks.com**

BOOKS BY K.M. SCOTT

Complete Club X Series Box Set

NeXt SERIES

Notorious (NeXt #1)

Infamous (NeXt #2)

Ravenous (NeXt #3)

Ambitious (NeXt #4)

Flirtatious (NeXt #5)

Mysterious (NeXt #6)

Sensuous (NeXt #7)

Desirous (NeXt #8)

CORRUPTED LOVE TRILOGY

If I Dream (Corrupted Love #1)

If You Fight (Corrupted Love #2)

If We Fall (Corrupted Love #3)

Corrupted Love Trilogy Box Set

ADDICTED TO YOU SERIES

Crave (Addicted To You #1)

Adore (Addicted To You #2)

Shatter (Addicted To You #3)

Claim (Addicted To You #4)

Addicted To You Series Box Set

PROJECT ARTEMIS SERIES

In The Darkness (Project Artemis #1)

After The Storm (Project Artemis #2)

K.M.'S BOOKS ARE IN AUDIOBOOK TOO!

BOOKS BY K.M. SCOTT WRITING AS GABRIELLE BISSET